# A SOLDIER'S REDEMPTION

## BY
## RACHEL LEE

### AND

# SECRET AGENT SHEIKH

## BY
## LINDA CONRAD

MILLS & BOON

A SOLDIER'S
REDEMPTION
by
RACHEL LEE

SECRET
AGENT REUNION
by
LINDA CONRAD

&

# A SOLDIER'S REDEMPTION

## BY
## RACHEL LEE

All the characters in this book have no existence outside the imagination of
the author, and have no relation whatsoever to anyone bearing the same name
or names. They are not even distantly inspired by any individual known or
unknown to the author, and all the incidents are pure invention.

First published in Great Britain 2011
by Mills & Boon, an imprint of Harlequin (UK) Limited,
Eton House, 18-24 Paradise Road, Richmond, Surrey TW9 1SR

© Susan Civil Brown 2010

ISBN: 978 0 263 88550 7

46-0911

Harlequin (UK) policy is to use papers that are natural, renewable and
recyclable products and made from wood grown in sustainable forests. The
logging and manufacturing processes conform to the legal environmental
regulations of the country of origin.

Printed and bound in Spain
by Blackprint CPI, Barcelona

**Rachel Lee** was hooked on writing by the age of twelve, and practiced her craft as she moved from place to place all over the United States. This *New York Times* bestselling author now resides in Florida and has the joy of writing full time.

Her bestselling Conard County series (see www.conardcounty.com) has won the hearts of readers worldwide, and it's no wonder, given her own approach to life and love. As she says, "Life is the biggest romantic adventure of all—and if you're open and aware, the most marvelous things are just waiting to be discovered."

For my dad, who taught me that a person is measured
by their dedication to honour, duty and loyalty.
You lived those values, Dad.  And they live on in me.

# Chapter 1

The knock on the door, as always, caused Corinne Farland's heart to skip a beat. Some lessons, once learned, could never be unlearned.

But after a year in Conard County, she found it a little easier to go to the front of the house. As always, she twitched the curtain aside at the front window by the door and looked out. She recognized Gage Dalton instantly, with his scarred face and his sheriff's uniform. Gage was her main protector these days.

She hurried to disengage the alarm system, then opened the door and smiled, an expression that sometimes still felt awkward on her face. "Hi, Gage."

He smiled back, a crooked expression as the burn scar on one side of his face caused one side of his mouth to hitch oddly. "Hi, Cory. Got a minute?"

"For you, always." She let him in and asked if he'd like some coffee.

"I'm coffeed out," he said, still smiling. "Too many cups of Velma's brew and my stomach starts reminding me I'm mortal." Velma was the dispatcher at the sheriff's office, a woman of indeterminate age who made coffee so strong few people could finish a single cup. The deputies, however, sucked it down by the pot.

She invited him into her small living room, and he perched on the edge of her battered recliner, his tan Stetson in his hands.

"How are things?" he asked.

"Okay." Not entirely true, maybe never true again, but the bleak desert of her heart and soul were not things she trotted out. Not for anyone.

"Emma mentioned something to me." Emma was his wife, the county librarian, a woman Cory admired and liked. "She said you were a bit tight financially."

Cory felt her cheeks heat. "That wasn't for distribution."

Gage smiled. "Husband-and-wife privilege. It doesn't go any further, okay?"

She tried to smile back and hoped she succeeded. Things were indeed tight. Her salary as a grocery-store clerk had been tight from the beginning, but now because times were hard, they'd asked everyone to take a cut in hours. Her cut had pushed her to the brink, where canned soup often became her only meal of the day.

Gage shook his head. "I'll never in a million years understand how they work this witness protection program."

Cory bit her lip. She didn't like to discuss that part, the part where her husband, a federal prosecutor, had become the target of a drug gang he was going after. The part where a man had burst into her house one night and killed him. The part where the feds had said that for her own protection she had to change her identity and move far away from everything and everyone she knew and loved.

"They do the best they can," she said finally.

"Not enough. It's not enough to buy you a house, give you a few bucks, get you a job and then leave you to manage. Not after what you've been through."

"There was some insurance." Almost gone now, though, and she was clinging to the remains in case of an emergency. She'd already had a few of those with this house they'd given her, and it had eaten into what little she had. "And they did do more for me than most." Like a minor plastic surgery to change her nose, which caused an amazing transformation to her face, and the high-tech alarm system that protected her day and night.

"Well," he said, "I'd like to make a suggestion."

"Yes?"

"A friend of a friend just arrived in town. He's looking for a place to stay awhile that's not a motel, but he's not ready to rent an apartment. Do you think you could consider taking a roomer? You don't have to feed him, just give him your extra bedroom."

She thought about that. There was a bedroom upstairs, untouched and unused. It had a single bed, a dresser and a chair, here when she had moved in. Her own bedroom was downstairs, so she wouldn't have this guy next door to her at all times.

But there were other things, darker fears. "Gage…"

"I know. It's hard to trust after where you've been. But I checked him out. Twenty years in the navy, all documented. Enough medals to paper a wall. You've met Nate Tate, haven't you?"

"Of course." She'd met the former sheriff. He might have retired, but apparently he still made it his job to know everyone in the county. She'd even had dinner with him and his wife a few times at their house. "Of course."

"Well, this guy is a friend of his son's. I don't know if you've met Seth Hardin."

She shook her head.

"Well, that's a story for another day. But Seth is a good sort, and he suggested this guy come here for a while to decompress."

"Decompress?" She didn't know if she liked the sound of that. "I don't know…"

"I'm not asking you to babysit." Gage smiled again. "This guy is quite capable of looking after himself. He just needs some time away. A change of scene. And he's not a talker. I doubt you'll know he's in the house most of the time."

"I'll think about it." But she had to admit, she trusted Gage, and she needed the money.

"How about I bring him inside and introduce you?"

Fear jammed into her throat. Every new person represented risk. Every single one. Hiding had become her raison d'être, and each time she had to meet someone new, the experience resurrected old fears.

"Let me get him," Gage said before she could argue. "He's in my car."

She wanted to scream for him not to do this, but she sat frozen, her fingers instinctively going to her side where the scar from the bullet still sometimes hurt. Where was her will? Her ability to say no? She seemed to have lost that on one dark night a year ago. Ever since, she had moved through her days like an automaton. Doing what was expected, pretending she cared. The truth was that the only thing she ever really felt anymore was fear. And grief. Sometimes fury.

She heard Gage limp back onto the porch, and with him

came a considerably heavier tread. She rose, an instinct these days, not out of courtesy, but out of a need to be able to flee if necessary.

First she saw Gage, but forgot him instantly as she looked at one of the biggest men she had ever seen. He must have been at least five inches over six feet, and even wrapped in a chambray shirt and jeans, he looked to be built out of concrete. Powerful. Strong. Overwhelming.

Scariest of all was the absolute lack of expression on his face. It was a hard face and appeared as if it would yield to nothing at all. His eyes were as black as chips of obsidian, and so was his short hair. She couldn't begin to guess a thing about him, not even his age.

Inside she quailed, helplessly, feeling like a mouse staring down a hawk.

But then he spoke, in a voice as deep as the rumble of thunder. "Ms. Farland. I'm Wade Kendrick." He didn't offer his hand.

The words sounded reluctant. As if he were no happier about putting her out than she was about taking this risk.

And his reluctance somehow eased her fear. "Hi," she said. "Have a seat."

He looked around as if deciding which chair might hold him. He finally took one end of the sofa. Cory sat on the Boston rocker, and Gage eased into the recliner again. The sheriff clearly suffered constant pain, but he never spoke of it.

"Okay," Gage said, since no one else seemed to be willing to talk. "Wade here needs a room indefinitely. Don't know how long, which is why he can't rent an apartment just yet. He's willing to pay monthly for a room. No food."

"I'll eat out," Wade said. "I don't want to get under-foot."

She appreciated that at the same time she wondered at it. He didn't look like a man who gave a damn about such things. "It's not...much of a room," she said hesitantly.

"I don't need much."

Nor did he volunteer much. Of course, she wasn't volunteering anything, either.

"I guess, if you think it's worth it," she finally said. "I've never done this before."

"Ma'am, it's worth it to have a place to lay my head."

She needed the money, and she trusted Gage. Battering down the fear that never entirely left her, not even in her dreams, she said, "Go take a look at the room. It's upstairs. There's a bath up there, too, and it'll be all yours because I have one down here."

The man rose and without another word headed up the stairs at the rear of the living room. Cory glanced at Gage, feeling her heart flutter a little. Panic? Fear? She couldn't tell anymore, since the only feelings she had left were bad ones.

"It'll be all right, Cory," Gage said kindly as they listened to the heavy footsteps overhead. "Sometimes we all need a bolt-hole. That's all he wants."

She could understand that. She was living her entire life in a bolt-hole now.

She stiffened as she heard boots start down the stairway. She didn't want to turn and look, afraid of the impact this huge stranger had on her. But she couldn't evade looking at him for long, because he came to stand in front of her.

"It's just what I need," he said. He pulled out his wallet and handed her six hundred-dollar bills, crisp from the bank. "I'll go get my stuff."

Then he walked out and Cory sat staring at the money in her hand. She was used to seeing money at work, but not holding so much and knowing it was her own. Her hand shook a little.

"That's too much," she almost whispered. It was as much as she made in a month.

Gage shook his head. "He offered it, Cory. It's what he thinks the room is worth."

A minute later, Wade returned carrying a large heavy duffel bag. And that was it. In a matter of less than half an hour, she had gained a roomer, a roomer who carried his entire life, it seemed, in a bag.

How apt was that?

After Gage left, she had to deal with the uneasiness of hearing someone above her head for the first time since she had lived here. She could tell what he was doing by the sounds the rumbled through the floor: unpacking and putting things in the battered dresser.

She needed to give him a key, she realized, and felt her heart lurch at the thought. Her safety not only lay behind a new identity, but also behind locks that were always fastened, and an alarm system the feds had installed. The idea of giving a stranger both a key and the alarm code very nearly caused her a panic attack.

But then she remembered how easily those men had gotten to her and her husband, and knew that no lock or alarm in the world would protect her if she opened her door at the wrong time.

*God,* she thought, *stop this, Cory!* The whole reason she was here in out-of-the-way Conard County, Wyoming, the whole reason she was working as a grocery clerk instead of a teacher, with all the public documents that would require, was so that she *didn't* have to look over her shoulder for the rest of her life.

Nothing about her life now in any way resembled her

life before. Not even her work. Not even her face. That was where her safety lay, not in locks and alarm systems.

She heard Wade come down the stairs. This time she made herself look at him. He hadn't changed, but she felt a shiver of fear anyway. This was still the man Gage had felt safe bringing into her life, and he might be big and appear ready to kill with his bare hands, but Gage trusted him. And she trusted Gage.

"I need to give you a key and show you the alarm code, Mr. Kendrick," she said. Her voice sounded weak, but at least it was steady.

He stood at the foot of the stairs, looking at her. "You comfortable with that?" he asked.

How had he guessed? Was her terror written all over her face? "I...you live here now. You need to be able to come and go when I work."

"No."

"No?" What kind of answer was that?

"I can manage."

She felt a bit stunned by his response. He could manage? He was paying what she considered to be an exorbitant rent to use that lousy bed and bath upstairs for a month, but he was willing to be locked out when she was gone? Had he read her fear so clearly? Or did she stink of it?

Probably the latter, she thought miserably. How would she know? She'd been afraid for so long.

"I'm going out to get sheets, towels, a few other things," he said after a moment. "Which direction should I head?"

Another thought struck her. "Do you have a car?"

"I can walk."

"I could walk, too," she said, feeling a smidgen of her old self spring to life. The resurrection was almost as painful as the death, but at least it was only a small thing, and thus a small pain she could endure. "But if you need a bunch of things, then you might need an extra arm."

"I'll manage."

"Yeah. You'll manage." Sighing, she stood up. "I'll drive you. I need some food anyway." And because of him she now had the money to buy it. Guilt, if nothing else, goaded her.

She went to get her purse. Before they stepped out, however, she insisted on giving him her spare key, and showing him the code for the alarm. If he thought it was odd there was such an advanced alarm system in such a ramshackle house, he didn't indicate it by word or look.

Instead he asked just one question. "Motion detectors?"

"Down here at night. I turn them on separately. Same code. Did you see the keypads upstairs in your bedroom?"

"Yes."

"Well, if you need to come down here at night, you can turn off the entire system from up there, too. To turn off the motion detectors, use the small keypad beside the big one. The rest of the system is on the big pad." She made herself look at him then. Another shiver passed through her as she realized this man could probably snap her in two if he wanted to. Once she had never had those kinds of thoughts. Now she had them all the time. "If you leave, for any reason, and I'm not here or awake, please turn on the entire system."

He nodded. Nothing in his face said he thought that was strange.

She explained the panic buttons, which would direct a call instantly to police, fire or ambulance. Their mere existence reminded her of all that had happened.

And none of it would have done her a damn bit of good fifteen months ago.

Then she set the alarm. It gave them only forty-five seconds to get out the front door and close it. It was long enough.

The U.S. Marshals had also given her a car along with the house. It wasn't a standout that might draw attention. In fact, it was practically a tank, four years old already, guzzling gas in a way that pained her conscience, but her protectors had insisted. The engine was new, as of a year ago, and was a full V-8 with more power than she would ever need.

Because if they came after her, they wouldn't give her a chance to get in a car and get away. She was sure of that. Someday soon, she promised herself, as soon as she could find a way, she would try to trade it in for a smaller but reliable car. She didn't need this steel cocoon.

If she could say nothing else for the Suburban, it gave Wade Kendrick plenty of room. She doubted he could even squeeze into the subcompact she hoped to have someday.

He didn't say another word until she dropped him off in front of the department store. Then it was just, "Thanks."

"When should I pick you up?"

He shrugged. "I won't take long. I'm not picky. Whenever is good for you."

Well, her needs were essentially meager, too. Not even with the extra money could she afford to be reckless. Cooking for one just depressed her, but she made herself buy something more nutritious, like vegetables, and salad fixings, and some chicken. She could shop for more after her next shift, but right now she was off for three days.

Three whole days, and now with a stranger in her house.

Evenings were long here in the summer, the sun not even hitting the horizon until after nine. But as it sank lower in the west, the dry air failed to hold the heat, and the early evening was starting to cool down by the time she emerged from the market with her two cotton bags of groceries. She drove back to the department store, and found Wade already outside on the curb. Apparently he'd bought more than one or two items, to judge by the number of bags, and she was glad she hadn't let him walk. She suspected that if she had, he'd have made several trips because of bulky pillows and blankets as well as sheets and towels.

And he probably wouldn't have said a thing about it. Gage had been seriously guilty of understatement when he said the guy didn't talk much.

She waited while he put his purchases in the back next to her groceries, then he climbed up front beside her.

"Thanks," he said again.

"You're welcome."

And not another sound from him. It was almost as if he were trying to be invisible in every way. Out of sight, out of hearing, out of mind.

If he'd been one of her students, she would have concluded that silence came from secrets, terrible secrets, because nothing about him indicated shyness. But he wasn't a student, he was a grown man, and maybe the same metrics didn't apply.

They reached the house and she pulled into the short driveway and parked. She never used the garage because it provided hiding places over which she had little control.

As soon as she put the car in Park, Wade climbed out. "I'll get your groceries, too," he said.

Part of her wanted to argue that she could manage, but she recognized it for what it was: a desire to exert some control, *any* control, over her life again. The man offered a simple courtesy, and maybe it was his way of expressing his gratitude for the ride. She knew better than to prevent people from offering such little acts of kindness, especially when they had just received one.

Ah, hell, she thought. She didn't ordinarily swear, but this day was beginning to make her want to. Needing to take someone into her sanctuary to pay the bills was bad enough. But finding that the teacher in her still existed, lived and breathed even though it was now forbidden to her, actually hurt.

She felt surprised that it still hurt. After the last year she had thought she was incapable of feeling any lack except the lack of her husband. God, she missed Jim with an ache that would probably never quit.

Head down, she climbed the front porch steps, going through her key ring for the house key. She had keys from the store, keys for the car, a key for the garage…so many keys for such a narrow life.

Just as she twisted the key, she heard the phone ring. It was probably work, she thought, needing her to come in to cover for someone who was sick. Eager for those hours, she left the door open behind her for Wade, punched in the alarm code as fast as she could, and ran for the cordless set in the living room.

She picked it up, punched the talk button, and said, "Hello?" Let it be more than a couple of hours. Make it a couple of days. God, she needed the hours.

A muffled voice said, "I know where you are." Then nothing but a dial tone.

The phone dropped from her hands and her knees gave way.

They'd found her.

# Chapter 2

"What's wrong?"

She looked up from the floor, at the huge man who had entered her life barely two hours ago. He stood in the doorway, his arms full of bags. She tried to breathe, but panic had locked her throat. Speech was impossible, and she couldn't answer that question anyway. Not to a stranger.

Finally she managed to gasp in some air. The instant she recovered her breath, even that little bit, tears started to run. And then she wanted to run. To get in her car and drive as far as she could on what little money she had left, which wouldn't be far at all in that damn Suburban.

And then she realized that if they'd found her, even stepping out her front door could cost her her life.

"Ma'am?"

The giant dropped the bags, and crossed the short

distance between them. He squatted beside her. "Put your head down. All the way down."

Somehow, with hands that seemed too gentle for someone she had already identified as threatening, he eased her down onto the floor, then lifted her legs onto the couch. Treating her for shock, she realized dimly as the wings of panic hammered at her.

"What happened?" he asked again.

The adrenaline had her panting. Who should she call? The Marshals? She knew what they'd do, and God help her, she didn't want to do that again.

"The sheriff. I need to talk to Gage."

At least he didn't question her again. Instead he reached for the phone she had dropped and pressed it into her hand.

"Need me to leave?" he asked. "I'll just go unload the car…"

He shouldn't hear this, but around his dark eyes she saw something like genuine concern. Something that said he'd do whatever was best for her, regardless of what it might be.

Her throat tightened. So few people in her life who would care if she lived or died anymore. Even the Marshals would probably just consider her a statistic on their chart of successes and failures.

"I…" She hesitated, knowing she wasn't supposed to share her true situation with anyone. Not anyone. But what did she have to say that he couldn't hear? She didn't have to mention anything about the witness protection program or her real identity because Gage already knew.

"It's okay," he said. "Just don't get up yet. I'll get the rest of the stuff from the car."

Amazing. He rose and went back to unloading as if she

hadn't just done the weirdest thing in the world: collapse and then demand to call the sheriff.

Amazing.

But she realized she didn't want her car left unattended and unlocked with bags in it. Bags in which someone could put something. And she didn't want her front door open indefinitely, or the alarm off. Her life had become consumed by such concerns.

Muttering a nasty word she almost never used, she brought up Gage's private cell phone on her auto dialer. He answered immediately.

"Cory Farland," she said, aware that her voice trembled.

"Cory? Did something happen?"

"Gage I…I got a phone call. All the guy said was, 'I know where you are.'"

Gage swore softly. "Okay," he said. "Okay. Most likely it was just a prank. You know how kids are when they have time on their hands. Stupid phone calls are the least of it."

"I know, but…"

"I know," he said. "Trust me, I know. I'm not going to ignore it, okay? Stay inside. Don't go out at all, and keep that alarm on. Do you have caller ID?"

"No, I can't afford it."

Another oath, muffled. "I'm going to remedy that as soon as possible. But Cory, try not to get too wound up. It's probably a prank."

Yeah. She knew kids. Probably a prank, like Prince Albert in the can. Yeah. A prank. "Okay."

Gage spoke again. "Think about it, Cory. If they'd really found you, why would they warn you?"

Good question. "You're right." She couldn't quite believe

it, but he was right. She drew another shaky breath, and felt her heart start to slow into a more normal rhythm.

"I'm not dismissing it, Cory," Gage said. "Don't misunderstand me. But I'm ninety-nine-point-nine percent certain it's some kind of prank."

"Of course." She said goodbye and disconnected, then lay staring at her ceiling. It was an old ceiling, and watermarks made strange patterns, some like faces she could almost identify. Like the face of the man who had killed Jim and almost killed her.

She heard the front door close, the lock turn, the sound of the alarm being turned on. The tone pierced what suddenly seemed like too much silence, too much emptiness.

She heard footsteps and turned her head to see Wade. Still impassive, he looked down at her. "How are you feeling?" he asked.

"I'm fine. I'm fine." Life's biggest lie, and it rose automatically to her lips.

"Your color is a bit better. Need help getting up?"

"I can do it, thanks." Yeah, she could do it. Get up, go to the kitchen, put her groceries away and resume the pretense of normalcy. Because there was no other option. All her options had been stolen over a year ago.

Sighing, she pulled her feet off the couch and rolled to her side to get up. A steadying hand was there to grip her elbow, surprising her. She looked into the rigid, unrevealing face of Wade Kendrick and wondered if he were some kind of instinctive caretaker.

She should have protested the touch. But all of a sudden, after a year of avoiding contact with other people, she needed it, even just that little bit of a steadying hand offered out of courtesy.

"Thanks," she said when she was on her feet. "I need to put groceries away."

One corner of his mouth hitched up just the tiniest bit. His version of a smile? "I think," he said slowly, "it might be best if you sit for a bit. I can put your groceries away, and you can supervise."

She should have argued. The independence thing had become of supreme importance to her since circumstances beyond her control had gutted her entire life. But she didn't feel like arguing at all. No, with her knees still feeling rubbery, and perishables like frozen food and milk in her two shopping bags, the task needed to be done soon, and she honestly wasn't sure she could manage it.

Adrenaline jolts had a high price when they wore off. So she led the way into the kitchen, her knees shaking, and sat at the chipped plastic-topped table while he emptied her two bags and then asked where each item went. He went about it with utter efficiency: economy of words and economy of movement both.

And she felt very awkward, unable to engage in conversation. She'd lost most of her conversational ability over the past year because she didn't have a past, at least not one she could talk about, and lying had never come easy. So she had become limited to the most useless of topics: the weather, work, a recent film. No depth or breadth of any kind.

And when faced by a man like this, one who seemed disinclined to talk, all she could do was sit in her chair and squirm.

"There," he said when the last item was put away. Then he faced her. "If you're okay now, I'll take my stuff upstairs."

She should have said thank-you and left it at that. That's what she *should* have done. But all of a sudden, maybe because of the phone call, being alone was the last thing she wanted. Solitude had been her fortress for a long time, so why she should want to breach the walls now, she couldn't understand. But she did anyway.

"If I make coffee," she said, "would you like some?"

One eyebrow seemed to lift, but she couldn't be quite sure. This was a man who seemed to have lost use of his face. Either that, or he had trained himself to reveal absolutely nothing. And the question about coffee seemed to give him pause. He treated it as if it needed real consideration.

"That would be nice," he finally said.

Only then did she realize she was almost holding her breath. Maybe she feared rejection of some kind. How could she possibly consider a *no* over a cup of coffee to be rejection? God, was she beginning to lose her mind?

It was, of course, entirely possible. In the past year she'd come perilously close to living in solitary confinement with only her memories.

"Okay." She tried a smile and it seemed to work, because he nodded.

"I'll just take my stuff up and be back down in a minute," he said.

She watched him walk out of the room and noticed his broad shoulders and narrow hips. The ease with which he moved in his body, like an athlete. Yes, she was definitely slipping a cog somewhere. She hadn't noticed a man that way in a long time, hadn't felt the sexual siren song of masculinity, except with Jim, and since Jim not at all.

She didn't need or want to feel it now.

Shaking her head, she rose and found that her strength seemed to have returned. Making the coffee was an easy, automatic task, one that kept her hands busy while her mind raced.

Surely Gage had been right. The killers wouldn't warn her they were coming. So it *must* have been kids pulling a prank. When she thought about it, her own reaction to the call disappointed her. There'd been a time when she would have reached the same conclusion as Gage without needing to consult anyone at all. A time when she hadn't been a frightened mouse who couldn't think things through for herself.

She needed to get that woman back if she was to survive, because much more of what she'd gone through the past year would kill her as surely as a bullet.

Piece by piece, she felt her personality disassembling. Piece by piece she was turning into a shadow of the woman she had once been. She might as well have lopped off parts of her own brain and personality.

How long would she let this continue? Because if it went on much longer, she'd be nothing but a robot, an empty husk of a human being. Somehow, somewhere inside her, she had to find purpose again. And a way to connect with the world.

As one of the Marshals had said when she argued she didn't want to do this, "How many people in this world would give just about anything to have a chance to start completely fresh?"

At the time the comment had seemed a little heartless, but as it echoed inside her head right now, she knew he'd had a point. She hadn't liked it then, didn't like it now, but there was a certain truth in it.

A fresh start. No real reason to fear. Not anymore. If they were going to find her, certainly they'd have done so long since.

Wade returned to the kitchen just as the drip coffeemaker finished its task. "How do you like it?" she asked.

"Black as night."

She carried the carafe to the table, along with two mugs and filled them, then set the pot on a pad in the center of the table. She always liked a touch of milk in hers, one of the things she hadn't had to give up in this transition. She could still eat the foods she preferred, drink her coffee with a little milk, and enjoy the same kinds of movies and books.

Maybe it was time to start thinking about what she hadn't lost, rather than all she had.

Brave words.

She sat across the table from Wade, trying not to look at him because she didn't want to make him feel like a bug under a microscope. But time and again her gaze tracked toward him, and each time she found him staring at her.

Finally she had to ask. "Is something wrong? You keep staring at me."

"You're a puzzle."

She blinked, surprised. "You don't even know me."

"Probably part of what makes you a puzzle," he said easily enough. His deep voice, which had earlier sounded like thunder, now struck her as black velvet, dark and rich.

"Only part?" she asked, even though she sensed she might be getting into dangerous territory here.

"Well, there is another part."

"Which is?"

He set his mug down. "It seems odd to find a woman so terrified in a place like this."

She gasped and drew back. His gaze never left her face, and he didn't wait for a denial or even any response at all.

"I know terror," he continued. "I've seen it, smelled it, tasted it. You reek of it."

She felt her jaw drop, but she couldn't think of one damn thing to say, because he was right. *Right.*

"Sorry," he said after a moment. "I suppose I have no business saying things like that."

Damn straight, she thought, wishing she'd never asked him if he wanted coffee. Wishing she'd never agreed to share a house with him. Those dark eyes of his saw too much. Way too much.

He'd stripped her bare. Anger rose in her and she glared at him. How dare he? But then, hadn't she all but asked for it?

He looked down at his mug, giving her a break from his stare, from his acute perception.

She thought about getting up and walking into her bedroom and locking the door. Hiding, always hiding. The thought stiffened her somehow, and instead of fleeing she held her ground. "Is it that obvious?"

He shook his head. "Probably not to anyone who hasn't been where I've been. Except for when you got that call, you put on a pretty good act."

"My entire *life* is an act," she heard herself snap.

He nodded, and when he looked at her again something in his gaze tugged at her, something that reached toward her and tried to pull her in. She looked quickly away. None of that. She didn't dare risk that.

"Look," he said finally, "I don't mean to upset you. I just want you to know…" He trailed off.

She waited, but when he didn't continue, she finally prodded him. "Want me to know what?"

"I'm not useless. Far from it. So if…if you need help, well, I'm here." Then he poured a little more coffee in his mug and rose, carrying the mug away with him.

She listened to him climb the creaky stairs and wondered what the hell had just happened.

Wade made up his bed with the skill of long years of practice in the navy. Perfectly square corners, the blanket tight enough to bounce a quarter off. His drawers were just as neat, everything was folded to fit a locker though, so the items didn't exactly match the drawers, but the stacks were square.

Old habits die hard, and six months of retirement hadn't killed any of them.

He sat on the wood chair in the corner of the room, and focused his mind like a searchlight on the present, because looking back got him nowhere, and the future seemed impossible to conceive.

That woman downstairs was as scared as any green combat troop he'd ever seen. As scared as the women and kids he'd seen in situations he didn't want to remember.

He hadn't expected to find that here. Hadn't bargained on the feelings it would resurrect. He'd come to this damn county in the middle of nowhere because Seth Hardin had promised he'd find peace and solitude, and that everything here was as far from his past as he could possibly get.

Right.

Apparently Seth hadn't known about this woman. Corinne Farland. Cory. Regardless, who the hell would have thought that he'd find this mess through the simple act of renting a room?

He leaned over and lifted the coffee mug from the top of the dresser, draining half of it in one gulp. Good coffee.

The back of his neck prickled a little as he thought about the situation, and he never ignored it when the back of his neck prickled. That sensation had saved his skin more than once, or someone else's skin.

But he couldn't figure out why the hell Gage Dalton had brought him to this particular woman. There must be other rooms for rent in this county. Surely.

Well, maybe not. The place didn't exactly look huge. So it *could* just have been coincidence. But he didn't believe much in coincidence. At some level, conscious or otherwise, Gage had thought of this woman, her terror and her room.

And there was a reason for that, a reason that made the skin on the back of his neck crawl. Cory's level of fear suggested a long-term, ongoing threat.

And here he was, smack in the middle of a place he thought he'd left behind. A place he *wanted* to leave behind.

He needed to normalize, to stop being a SEAL and start being a reasonably ordinary member of society again. He needed to stop sleeping with one eye always open, constantly ready for death to lunge out of any shadow or hole. He needed to let his reflexes slow again, at least to the point where someone wouldn't risk death simply by trying to wake him from sleep, or by moving too fast in the corner of his eye. That's what he needed, and that had just skittered out the door of his immediate future.

Because downstairs there was one hell of a scared woman, and she shouldn't feel that way. And a phone call, a simple phone call, had caused her to collapse.

From what he'd seen of Conard County and Conard City so far, he would have called the place bucolic.

Well, that was a hell of a reaction for a bucolic place.

It wasn't normal. It didn't fit.

Apparently he would have to keep sleeping with one eye open.

He could leave, of course, but that didn't even truly appear on his menu of options. He couldn't walk away from her terror.

Someone that terrified needed protecting.

For a change, he decided, he'd like to provide the protection, rather than the terror.

A bitter smile twisted his mouth. That, at least, would be a change. A much-needed change.

And wasn't that what he'd come here for?

The phone didn't ring again, thank God. Cory ate a small salad for dinner, then tried to settle in with the TV. She didn't think she could focus on one of the library books stacked on the small table beside the rocking chair, because her mind seemed to have turned into a flea, insisting on hopping from one thing to another, all totally unrelated. Even the sharpness of fear didn't seem able to get her full attention.

So it was easier to turn the TV on, for the noise, for the visual distraction, for the occasional moments in which she could actually tune into the program, whatever it was.

She noted that her roomer upstairs had grown quiet, utterly quiet. Probably sleeping, but with her senses on high alert, the inability to guess what he was about made her uneasy. Solitude was her friend, her fortress, her constant companion.

But she'd invited in an invader, and his silence was worse than the noise he'd made while settling in.

She flipped quickly to the weather station, but too late, because the image of a crime-scene team entering a home where a man lay dead, just a reenactment, was enough to set off a string of memories she tried never to visit.

Jim lying there, bleeding from multiple wounds. Trying to crawl to him despite the wound in her own side, gasping his name, knowing somehow as she crawled that he was lost to her forever.

She squeezed her eyes shut as if that could erase the images that sprang to mind. Gentle, determined Jim, a man with a huge smile, a huge heart and a belief in making the world a better place. A man who could talk to her with such kindness and understanding, then in a courtroom or deposition turn into a circling shark, coming in for the kill.

A gifted man. An admirable man.

The man she had loved with every cell of her being.

Their last dinner together. Jim had taken her to one of the best restaurants in Tampa to celebrate a positive pregnancy test that very morning. They'd laughed, coming up with silly names they would never in a million years give their child.

And shortly after midnight, everything that mattered in her life vanished. At least she didn't mourn the pregnancy as much as she might if she had had time to get accustomed to the idea. That little mark on the stick had scarcely been real to her yet when the gunshot ended it all.

But Jim…Jim had been everything. Jim and her students. The life they had barely begun to build together after only two years.

Now she drew a shaky breath, trying to steady herself, trying to prevent the gasping sobs she had managed to avoid for months now.

But awake, or asleep, she still heard the banging on the door. Banging that had sounded like the police. Jim had laughed drowsily as he climbed from bed to answer it.

"Somebody probably just tried to steal my car," he had said. His car was also a joke between them, a beater he'd gotten in law school. It was certainly not worthy of stealing, but the very expensive stereo he'd put in it was.

She had heard him open the door then…

Her mind balked. Her eyes snapped open. No, she couldn't do this to herself again. No way. It was done, the nightmares permanently engraved on her heart and mind, but that didn't mean she had to let them surface.

Sometimes she even scolded herself for it, because while

grief was natural, and the fear she felt equally so, every time she indulged herself in grief or fear, she knew she was giving that man even more power over her than he had already stolen from her.

And he had already stolen everything that mattered.

The phone rang, jarring her. This time she didn't jump for it, this time she didn't think it was work calling. Part of her wanted to let it ring unanswered, but she didn't even have an answering machine, and what if it was Gage?

Slowly, reluctantly, she reached for it, coiling as tight as a spring. So tight some of her nerves actually objected.

"Hello?"

"Cory, it's Gage. I just wanted you to know a few other women have reported similar calls, so it was probably just a prank, okay?"

Her breath escaped her lungs in a gasp of relief. "Thanks," she said. "Thanks."

"And I'm getting caller ID put on your service. The phone company says you should have it within a few days. And don't worry about the cost. The department will pay for it."

"Oh, Gage…" Words deserted her yet again. Of all the places on this earth the Marshals could have put her, she was grateful they had put her in a town with Gage Dalton.

"Hey," he said kindly. "We take care of our own around here. It's not a problem."

Before she could thank him again, he was gone.

"Is everything all right?"

Startled, she nearly cried out, and turned to see Wade Kendrick at the foot of the stairs. How had he come down so silently? Earlier his tread had been heavy. Or maybe she'd just been so distracted. She drew a few deep breaths, trying to steady her pulse.

"I'm sorry," he said quietly. "I didn't mean to startle you. I heard the phone ring, and after the way you reacted earlier…"

"Of course. Of course." She closed her eyes and consciously tried to relax, at least a bit. It didn't happen easily anymore, that whole relaxing thing. "Everything's okay. Gage…called." But what could she tell him about the call? Even a few words might be too much.

He waited, and it was clear to her that he wasn't satisfied. But he didn't ask, he just waited. And somehow his willingness to wait reassured her. She couldn't even understand it herself.

"I got a nasty phone call earlier," she said slowly.

He nodded. "I didn't think it was a funny one."

"No." Of course not. And now she was sounding like an idiot, she supposed. She gathered herself, trying to organize her words carefully. "Gage just wanted me to know that several other women received similar calls."

One of his eyebrows lifted. "Really."

"Probably just kids."

"Maybe."

His response didn't seem to make sense. "Maybe?"

"Well, that would depend, wouldn't it?"

"On what?"

"On what has you so scared, and who else received the calls."

"What in the world do you mean?"

He shrugged. "Life has made me suspicious."

"Oh." She bit her lower lip, realizing that nothing in her life had prepared her for dealing with a man like this. He seemed to come at things from a unique direction, unlike anything she was familiar with.

He started to turn away. "Well, as long as you're okay…"

He didn't ask a single question. She found that intriguing, given what little he had figured out about her in the short time since he moved in. Any other person would have been asking dozens of question, but this man just seemed to accept that she was afraid, she must have good reason for it and that it was none of his business.

In that moment she thought it possible that she might come to like him.

"Wade?"

He stopped and turned back to her. He didn't say a word, simply looked at her.

"I, uh…" How could she say that she didn't want to be alone? That she was tired of being locked in the prison of her own thoughts? That even though solitude had provided her only safety for a year now, she was sick of it, and sick of her own company. Tired enough of it all to feel an impulse toward risk. Just a small risk.

"Should I make coffee?" he asked.

He had understood, though how she couldn't imagine. She might have been about to ask him anything, tell him anything.

All she said was, "Thanks." Because there was nothing else she *could* say.

She switched the TV off so she could listen to his movements in the kitchen. Everything he needed was beside the drip coffeemaker, so he wouldn't have trouble finding it. And finally she could afford to have more than one cup each day. Imagine that, being reduced to one cup of coffee and a can of soup each day.

Sure, there were plenty of people in the world who had less, but her life had never before been restricted in such a way. She'd always been luckier than that. Always. Until recently.

Wade returned finally with two mugs, hers with exactly the right milkiness. The man missed nothing. Nothing.

He sat across from her on the easy chair, sipping his own coffee, watchful but silent. Maybe this wasn't going to work at all. How did you converse with a block of stone? But she needed something, anything, to break the cycle of her own thoughts.

Man, she didn't even know how to start a conversation anymore! Once it had come as naturally as breathing to her, but now, after a year of guarding every word that issued from her mouth, she had lost the ability it seemed.

Wade sipped his coffee again. He, at least, seemed comfortable with silence. After a couple of awkward minutes, however, he surprised her by speaking.

"Do you know Seth Hardin?"

She shook her head. "I know his father, but I've never met Seth."

"He's a great guy. I worked with him a lot over the years. He's the one who recommended I come here."

Positively voluble all of a sudden. "Why?"

He gave a small shrug. "He thought it would be peaceful for me."

At that a laugh escaped her, almost hysterical, and she broke it off sharply. "Sorry. Then you walk into this, a crazy widow who collapses over a prank phone call. Some peace."

His obsidian eyes regarded her steadily, but not judgmentally. "Fear like yours doesn't happen without a good reason."

It could have been a question, but clearly it was not. This man wouldn't push her in any way. Not even one so obvious and natural. She sought for a way to continue. "Gage said you were in the navy."

He nodded. "For more than half my life."

"Wow." She couldn't think of anything else to say.

"Yeah." Short, brief. After another moment he stirred. "You need to talk."

She tensed immediately. Was he trying to get her to explain? But then he spoke again, easing her concern.

"I'm not a talker." Another small shrug. "Never was. Making conversation is one of the many things I'm not good at."

"Me, either, anymore. I wasn't always that way."

He nodded. "Some things in life make it harder. I'm not sure I ever had the gift."

"Maybe it's not a gift," she said impulsively. "Maybe most of what we say is pointless, just background noise."

"Maybe. Or maybe it's how we start making connections. I stopped making them a long time ago."

"Why?"

He looked down into his mug, and she waited while he decided what he wanted to say, and probably what he didn't.

"Connections," he said finally, "can have a high price."

Man, didn't she *know* that. Maybe that was part of the reason she'd kept so much to herself over the past year, not simply because she was afraid of saying the wrong thing. Maybe it was because she feared caring ever again.

"I can understand that," she agreed, her lips feeling oddly numb. As if she were falling away again, from now into memory. But her memory had become a Pandora's box, and she struggled to cling to the moment. To now.

The phone rang again. She jumped and stared at it. Gage had already called. Work? Maybe. Maybe not.

Wade spoke. "Want me to answer it?"

A kind offer, but one that wouldn't help her deal with reality. She'd been protected almost into nonexistence, she realized. Protected and frightened. At some point she had to start living again, not just existing.

So she reached for the phone, even as her heart hammered and her hand shook. "Hello?"

"Cory!" A familiar woman's voice filled her ear. "It's Marsha." Marsha from work, a woman she occasionally spent a little time with because they had some similarities, some points of connection they could talk about. But they'd never really gotten to the point of random, friendly phone calls.

"Hi, Marsha. What's up?" Her heart slowed, her hand steadied.

"I got a phone call. I think Jack has found me!"

Cory drew a sharp breath. While she hadn't shared her story with Marsha, she'd learned a lot of Marsha's story over the past year. "What makes you think that?"

"The person said he knew where I was!"

"Oh. Marsha, I got one of those calls, too. Did you report it to the sheriff?"

"A phone call like that?" Marsha laughed, but there was an edge to it. "Why would he even listen to me?"

"Because I got one of those calls. And a few other women did, too."

Marsha fell silent. Then hopefully, "Others got the same call?"

"Gage thinks it was a prank. I reported it and so did some others."

In the silence on the line, Cory could hear Marsha start calming herself. She waited patiently until she could no longer hear Marsha's rapid breathing. Then she asked, "Do you want to come over?" She'd never asked that before, even though she'd gone to Marsha's a few times. Explaining expensive alarm systems could get…messy, and involve lying.

"No. No. I guess not. If Gage thinks it's a prank, and I'm not the only one to get a call, I must be okay."

"So it would seem."

"But I'm going to get a dog," Marsha said with sudden determination. "Tomorrow, I'm getting a dog. A big one that barks." Then she gave a tinny laugh.

"If it helps you to feel safer."

"It'll help. And if I'm this nervous after all this time, I guess I need the help. Want to do coffee in the morning?"

That meant going out, and Gage had told her not to. But that had been before he decided the calls were a prank. Cory hesitated, then said, "Let me call you about that in the morning."

"Okay. Maybe you can help me pick out a dog."

As if she knew anything about dogs. "I'll call around nine, okay?"

"Okay. Thanks, Cory. I feel a lot better now."

When Cory hung up, she found Wade sipping his coffee, quietly attentive. After a moment's hesitation, she decided to explain.

"My friend Marsha. She got one of those calls, too."

"Why did it frighten her?"

"Her ex was abusive. Very abusive. She's afraid he might find her."

He nodded slowly. "So she's hiding here, too?"

"Too?" She didn't want to think about what his use of that word meant, how much he must have figured out about her.

He said nothing, just took another sip of coffee. Then, at last, "What did the caller say?"

"Just 'I know where you are.'"

Another nod. "That would be scary to someone who doesn't want to be found."

And she'd just revealed a whole hell of a lot. She ought to panic, but somehow the panic wouldn't come. Maybe because having listened to Marsha, some steely chord in her had been plucked, one long forgotten. Prank call or not, at least two women were going to have trouble sleeping tonight, and that made her mad.

"Why would some idiot do this?" she demanded. "I don't care if it was kids. This isn't funny. Not at all."

"I agree."

His agreement, far from settling her, pushed her into a rare contrarian mood. She knew kids, after all, had taught them for years. "They don't think," she said. "They probably got the idea from some movie and are having a grand old time laughing that they might have scared someone."

"Maybe."

"They wouldn't realize that some people might really have something to fear."

"Maybe."

She looked at him in frustration. "Can you manage more than a few syllables?"

At that he almost smiled. She could see the crack in his stone facade. "Occasionally," he said. "How many syllables do you want?"

"Just tell me why you keep saying *maybe*."

"I told you, I'm suspicious by nature. Tell me more about your friend Marsha."

"Why? What? I told you her story, basically."

He set his cup on the end table and leaned toward her, resting his elbows on his knees and clasping his hands. "Try this. Have you both always lived here or did you move here? Are you about the same age? Any similarities in appearance?"

Just as she started to think he had gone over some kind

of edge, something else struck her. For a few seconds she couldn't find breath to speak, and when she did it was a mere whisper. "You think someone could be trying to find one of us?"

"I don't know." The words came out bluntly. "A sample of two hardly proves anything. But I'm still curious. Will you tell me?"

She hesitated, then finally nodded. "Marsha and I are sort of friends because we…share a few things. We both moved here within a couple of weeks of each other, almost a year ago. We work together at the grocery."

"Your ages? And your appearance?"

"We don't look like twins."

"I didn't think you did. But otherwise?"

"I think we're as different as night and day." Indeed they were. Marsha had short red hair, a square chin, green eyes and a bust a lot of women would have paid a fortune for. Cory, on the other hand, now had chin-length auburn hair—which she hated because she had to keep it colored herself to hide her natural dark blond—and brown eyes that had looked good when she was blonde but now seemed to vanish compared to her hair. The Marshals had given her a slight nose job, though, replacing her button nose with something a little longer and straighter. They hadn't messed with her bust, though. That was still average.

"Are those differences that could be easily ma-nipulated?"

She didn't like where he was going with this, didn't like it at all. "You *are* suspicious." But then, so was she. All of a sudden Gage's phone call seemed a lot less reassuring. "Marsha and I don't look at all alike." But how sure was she of that?

"Then I'm overly suspicious." He leaned back, picking up his coffee again. "Way too much so."

"Why?"

"Because I've lived my life in the shadows. Suspicion is part of my creed. I never take anything at face value." He shrugged. "Best to ignore me, I suppose."

It might have been except for her past. Had she an ordinary life behind her, it would have been easy to dismiss him as a nut. But she couldn't quite do that.

"Why," she asked finally, "would he call so many? If someone was after either of us, a whole bunch of phone calls wouldn't make sense, would it?"

He shrugged. "Like I said, just ignore me."

Easier said than done, especially when he seemed to have been following some train of thought of his own. But he said nothing more, and she really couldn't imagine any reason he should be suspicious.

But of one thing she was reasonably certain: the man who would want her dead wouldn't need to call a bunch of women to scare them. In fact, it would be the last thing he would do. Because calling her would warn her, and if she got scared enough to call the Marshals, they'd move her.

Even though moving her would take time, it would certainly make killing her more difficult while she was under constant surveillance once again, as she had been in the three months between the shooting and her eventual relocation.

So it had to be a prank. Surely. She clung to that like a straw in a hurricane.

Because it was all she could do.

# Chapter 3

In the morning, Cory decided to go for coffee with Marsha after all. She had a little money to spare because of Wade, and a cup of coffee at Maude's didn't cost that much, especially if she avoided the fancier drinks that Maude had begun to introduce, taking her cue from the major coffee chains. So far Cory didn't think there was a huge market for "mocha decaf lattes" here, even though she loved lattes herself, but they were now available if anyone wanted them.

Marsha expressed huge gratitude for the call. In her voice, Cory heard a stress that matched her own. She hadn't slept well at all last night, tossing and turning, one nightmare following another.

When she finally gave up trying to sleep, it was only five-thirty in the morning. She'd grabbed a book from the table beside her bed and had attempted to read for a couple of hours. In the end, though, the words might as well have been random letters, none of the story penetrated, and she thought she might have dozed a bit.

Wade must still be asleep, she thought when at last she reset the house alarm and slipped out the door. She'd been the only one to change the alarm settings since she awoke—she'd have heard the tone if anyone had—and she hadn't heard him moving around.

Nothing strange in that, she supposed, except she had somehow expected him to be an early riser. Why? Because he'd been in the navy? Not everyone in the navy worked days and slept nights. She knew that much. Maybe he'd had some kind of night duty. Which got her to wondering what kind of work he'd done, and how he'd gotten enough medals to paper a wall, according to Gage.

Well, she could always try asking him, but she doubted he would answer. And how could she complain about that when she kept her own secrets?

It was a lovely summer morning, and she could have walked to Maude's but uneasiness made her take the Suburban anyway. Besides, she told herself, trying to pretend she wasn't acting only out of over-heightened fear, if Marsha really did want to get a big dog, the Suburban might be the best way to get it home.

Marsha was already there at a table with coffee in front of her. Hardly had Cory slid into a seat facing her when Maude stomped by, slamming a mug down and filling it. A little bowl of creamer cups already sat in the middle of the table.

Cory actually felt a smile twitch at the corners of her mouth. In a year she'd never bought anything here except coffee, and Maude had apparently given up on talking her into anything else. Once in a blue moon, a piece of pie would be slapped down in front of her but never show up on the bill. Interesting woman, Maude. Cory was quite sure she had *never* met anyone like her.

Marsha smiled at her, but the expression didn't reach her eyes. She looked exhausted, and Cory suspected they had both spent nights filled with nightmares and restlessness.

"I'm glad that you told me a bunch of women got the same call," Marsha said.

"I don't know how many, but Gage indicated there were a few of us. That's why he thinks it's a prank."

"Makes sense." Marsha opened another little cup of half-and-half and lightened her coffee even more. "And I guess if a few reported the calls, there were probably more like me who never called him at all."

"Probably," Cory agreed. "You look like you slept about as well as I did."

Marsha's laugh was short and hollow. "Yeah, we look like a pair of zombies, don't we? I just couldn't stop thinking about Jack all night, about all the things he threatened to do to me. But it's been almost a year, so he probably never wanted to come after me. He just wanted to scare me."

And Marsha had plenty of reason to be scared, considering the things her ex had done to her. Cory wanted to say something reassuring, but couldn't. How could she reassure anyone when she was living with a similar terror herself? Her pursuers might have more reason to try to track her, since she could help identify one of them as a murderer, but did that mean Marsha's ex was necessarily less determined?

"Are you still going to get a dog?"

Marsha nodded. "I called the vet before I came here. He says he has a couple of dogs I might like and that they're naturally protective breeds."

"That sounds good."

"I told him I wanted a big dog, but he recommended against it."

"Really?"

Marsha gave a small, tired laugh. "He asked me how much I wanted to walk it, and did I want to be able to hold it in my lap…" Her voice broke, then steadied. "Sorry. I'm just tired. But anyway, the idea of a dog that would curl up on my lap sounded good, and with the hours we work, I couldn't walk a dog at the same time of day every day…" She trailed off, sighed and looked down into her coffee.

All of a sudden, Cory felt something she hadn't felt in far too long: a desire to protect someone besides herself. The urge rose fiercely, and burned away some of the fear.

Those men had stolen her life, but for the last year she'd let them steal *her,* too. She'd let them turn her into a quivering, frightened recluse whose only concern was surviving each day.

How much more twisted could she get? How could she let them keep doing this to her? She wasn't the only person on this planet with fears and needs. Look at Marsha. What had she ever done except marry the wrong man? Yet, she, too, had been driven into a hole in the ground.

Angry, Cory couldn't sit still another moment. She slapped some bills on the table, to cover both their coffees, and stood. "Let's go get your dog. You need a reason to smile."

Marsha appeared startled, but then began to grin. "Yeah," she said. "Let's go get that dog."

"Cute and cuddly," Cory said. "The cutest, cuddliest one we can find."

Because there still had to be something good in life, and a dog was as good a start as anything else.

* * *

Conard County wasn't a heavily populated place, so it had a limited tax base and had to cut some corners. Hence the vet and animal control shared property and kennels, and the vet, Dr. Mike Windwalker, was on retainer to care for the impounded animals. Like most small-town vets, he handled everything from horses to the occasional reptile.

A handsome man in his mid-thirties, he'd replaced the former vet five years ago and seemed to enjoy his broad-spectrum practice. He had one assistant, though he could probably have used more.

"You picked a good day to do this," he remarked as he led Marsha and Cory back through his office toward the kennels. "I'm not very busy so I'll have time to help you make a good match."

As they approached the wire gate beyond which lay the sheltered kennels, the sounds of dogs barking started to build.

"They know we're coming," the vet said with a smile. "But before we go in…" He turned to Marsha. "I want to know a bit more about why you want a dog. Just for protection? Or would you like a companion? And can you afford much dog food?"

Marsha bit her lip, then admitted, "I'm tired of being alone so much. Yes, I want a dog that can alert me when someone comes, but I think I'd like to have one to love, too. And play with. I'd love to play with a dog. As for food—" she wrinkled her nose "—I probably shouldn't have a dog with a huge appetite."

At that Mike Windwalker smiled. "Then I have a couple of good ones for you. Love and protection can come in small sizes as well as large."

Cory stayed back a bit, watching as Mike introduced Marsha to various small dogs. She didn't want to get too interested in the process because when Wade left, unless she got a better job or more hours at her current one, she simply wouldn't be able to take care of a pet. Nor, when she thought about it, could she have one running around at night with the motion detectors on.

But it was so hard to resist all the puppy-dog eyes. It would have been entirely too easy to choose one for herself, and she had to remind herself again and again that she couldn't afford it.

But she felt a definite stab of envy when Marsha eventually settled on a Pomeranian. "Definitely loyal," the vet said approvingly. "She'll let you know any time anyone approaches the house and these dogs can be relied on to fight for their owners if necessary." He shook his head. "People often underestimate the protectiveness of the small breeds. There are ways to get around a dog, any dog, but these small guys have hearts like lions."

Marsha definitely looked as if she'd fallen in love. And while she naturally had a cheerful nature, it was often eclipsed behind spurts of worry. Right now, she looked as if she didn't have a worry in the world.

"Just one caveat," the vet said. "I offer obedience classes for free, and with this one you'd be wise to take them."

"I will."

"I'm starting a new class Saturday morning at nine."

Marsha beamed at him. "I'll be there."

When she drove back home a short while later, Cory felt she'd managed to accomplish at least one good deed, small as it was. And it *had* been small. She hadn't been able to give Marsha the dog, or even help her decide which one was best, but she suspected Martha might not have acted so quickly on her own, simply because living in fear had a way of paralyzing you. Even small decisions sometimes seemed too big to make.

And that had to stop, she told herself sternly. It had to stop now. For too long now she'd been little more than a wasted lump of human flesh.

Wade must have heard her pull up, because he was waiting for her at the foot of the stairs. Apparently he'd been sleeping because his hair had that tousled look, and his blue sport shirt hung open over his jeans.

Cory couldn't help herself. She stopped dead and stared. That was some chest, smoothly muscled, bronzed and just begging for a touch. Oh, man, as if she needed this now.

With effort she dragged her gaze upward and then wished she hadn't, because she saw in his obsidian eyes that he hadn't missed her look. He revealed nothing about his reaction to it, though, nor did he make any attempt to button his shirt.

"Did Marsha get her dog?" he asked before the silence got long enough that she wouldn't be able to pretend he hadn't noticed what she'd been noticing.

"Yes. A Pomeranian."

"I had a buddy who had one. He called it his pocket piranha."

The remark was utterly unexpected, and it bypassed every short circuit the past year had put in Cory's brain. She giggled. Actually giggled.

A faint smile leavened Wade's face. "He liked to bite my ankles."

That seemed even funnier. "Such a stupid dog," she giggled again.

"Stupid?"

"Taking on someone your size? That's stupid."

Wade's smile widened just a hair more. "He knew I wouldn't hurt him. Dogs have good instincts."

She laughed again, still amused by the image. Then it

struck her that he seemed to have been waiting for her. "Is there something you need?"

"Well, actually…" He hesitated. "I know the deal was I would eat out. But I was wondering, would you mind if I bought groceries and cooked for myself? I'll leave things squared away so you won't even notice I was in there."

For some reason she liked the idea that he wouldn't be leaving her alone three times a day to hunt up a meal. Amazing how far she had come in less than a day. What had initially seemed like a threat now seemed like a bulwark. Nor was this a matter she wanted to take issue over.

"I don't mind." Although she was a little surprised that he'd felt it necessary to say she wouldn't even know he'd been in the kitchen. Most people wouldn't have bothered to mention it, unless asked.

She drew a sharp breath, and all of a sudden her heart tugged. She'd heard promises like that before, unsolicited ones. *You'll never notice I was in there.*

A few faces floated before her eyes, youngsters all, former students all. And she knew what phrases like that really meant. Could this big, powerful man with all his medals still carry scars like that? After all this time?

But she couldn't ask.

"Is something wrong?"

His question shook her back to the moment. "No. Really. My mind just wanders sometimes. I think I spend too much time alone." Her laugh this time carried no mirth, but was more of an apology.

"I'll just go get some groceries then."

She shook her head. "It may go against your grain to look for help, but you shouldn't try to carry groceries home when I can drive you. Just let me get a glass of water, and then I'll take you."

For an instant she thought he would argue. Something about him said that he didn't relinquish autonomy easily, or accept help easily, at least not from virtual strangers. But then he nodded. "Take your time. Obviously I'm in no rush."

Wow, she thought as she headed toward the kitchen, at this rate they might even start to converse in whole paragraphs. She took her time drinking her water because she heard him climb the stairs again, probably to brush his hair, button his shirt and pull on some shoes.

Sure enough, five minutes later she heard him descend again. She finished her water and went out to the foyer. "Ready?" she asked, though it was clear that he was. His boots had given way to some comfortable and battered deck shoes, and he'd buttoned and brushed.

"If you are," he replied.

She grabbed her purse and keys, saying, "Let's go then."

"You're sure you don't mind?"

There it was again, a niggle. A hint. She looked at him, wishing she could just come right out and ask. But that might be a mistake, because he'd probably just get angry at her prying, and rightfully so. He hadn't poked into her life, so she should give him the same respect.

"I don't mind at all," she assured him, and summoned a smile. Aware now of what might lurk in his past, she felt old lessons rising up to guide her. And the thought that she might, through her training, help this man feel a bit more comfortable made her feel better than she had in a long time. She might not be able to teach anymore, but it would be so good to *help*.

Always assuming, of course, that she wasn't totally wrong about him.

The drive to the store was silent, but she was getting

used to that with him, and didn't feel as uncomfortable as she had just yesterday.

When she pulled into a parking slot, though, he spoke. "You don't have to wait for me," he said. "If there's something you need to do."

She shook her head. "Not a thing. Maybe I'll check and see if they can give me any extra hours."

She climbed out and locked the car. Another car pulled in nearby, and the driver, a man, appeared to be fussing through some papers. Probably lost his shopping list, Cory thought with a small sense of amusement.

Wade waited for her, then walked beside her across the parking lot, measuring his stride to hers.

"You work here?" he asked.

"Yes." Then she volunteered, "We all had our hours cut back a couple of weeks ago."

"That hurts. No wonder you need a roomer. How's Marsha managing?"

"Somewhat better. She gets an alimony check."

He paused just after they stepped through the automatic doors and looked at her. "Then her ex knows where she is."

"Theoretically not. The court sends the checks and is supposed to keep her address private."

He nodded. "Good thing."

She headed for the manager's office at the customer service desk while he got a cart and started down the aisles. Interesting that he'd expressed concern for Marsha, she thought. Apparently a real heart beat behind the stone.

The manager, Betsy Sorens, greeted her with her usual wide smile. "Sorry, Cory. No extra hours. Not yet anyway. You're at the top of my list though when we can start adding them."

Cory felt almost embarrassed. "Why should I be at the

top of the list? That doesn't seem right, Betsy. So many others need hours, too."

"We all need hours, some more than the rest. You're self-supporting. A lot of the other employees have other sources of income."

Cory felt her cheeks color a bit. "Still…"

Betsy shook her head. "You're a good employee. If I can do a little something for you, I will."

A customer came then with a complaint, so Cory smiled, waved and left. Wandering around the store with nothing to buy and nothing to do felt odd. Almost without thinking, she paused occasionally to straighten the stock on the shelves.

She hated to have time hanging on her hands, and she'd certainly had too much of that in the past year. She'd once been busy almost every second of the day, between Jim and her job. Now she had endless hours of free time, and that meant too many hours to think.

Hours to think about the past, about that phone call yesterday, hours to let her fear and anxiety build when there was no real reason for it. Certainly they would have found her by now if they were going to.

She met Wade in one of the aisles and glanced into his cart. There wasn't much there yet.

"Having trouble?" she asked.

One corner of his mouth lifted. "You might say that."

"What's wrong?"

"I've been mostly eating in mess halls or eating out of boxes for years. I know the basics about cooking, but shopping for one person isn't as easy as I thought."

That was a whole lot of syllables, she thought, and for some reason that made her smile. "I have an idea."

"What's that?"

"I hate cooking just for myself. Why don't we take turns cooking for each other?" she suggested.

"Are you sure? You could be taking an awful gamble."

"On your cooking?"

"What else would I mean?" he asked.

"I'm willing to take it. And if it doesn't work out, well, I could teach you to cook. Or you could just let me do it."

He shook his head. "No way am I going to let you cook for me every night. That wasn't part of the deal."

She could almost see him closing down again, as if the idea that he might lean on her concerned him. "Okay then, cooking lessons if you need them."

That seemed to satisfy him. Armed with the idea that they'd take turns cooking seemed to loosen him up though. He started tossing more items into the cart.

"I should go buy some more groceries," she said suddenly. "I just realized, I only bought enough for myself for a couple of days."

"Let me," he said. "It'll cover the cooking lessons I'll probably need."

She opened her mouth to argue, but then shut it. This man absolutely *needed* to feel as if he wasn't a burden. That much was clear to her so she endured it as he spent money on foods she would have ignored because of the price.

But the thought of cooking some of the dishes she had once *loved* to cook and eat soon had her thinking of ingredients she should buy.

"I don't know what's needed to cook some of this stuff," Wade said. "Grab whatever you need." It was enough to get her going.

Along the way she saw the man from the parking lot again. He was pushing a cart and carrying a piece of paper, and nodded when he saw her. She managed to smile back. Evidently he'd found his list.

Before they even reached the checkout, two more people had smiled and nodded at her. She was used to that when she was working and in uniform, but for the first time it struck her that folks around here might be friendly as a matter of course. Maybe she ought to make a bigger effort.

By the time they left the store with another four bags of groceries, she was looking forward to dinner.

And how long had it been since she'd last felt that way? No, she wasn't going there, not when she was actually feeling good, feeling almost *normal,* for the first time in a year. There was absolutely nothing wrong with feeling good, she reminded herself. Nothing at all. Jim wouldn't have wanted her to become the woman she had been during the past year.

The shadow that hovered over all her days tried to return when she had to deal with the alarm, but she refused to let it. No more of that, she told herself, as if something as simple as a command to herself could change her entire outlook and banish the fear that never quite deserted her.

But at least she was making an effort, and when she looked over the past day, she felt glad those kids had made that stupid call. Yes, it had thrown her into a tizzy, and yes, it had upset Marsha just as much, but in the course of reacting to it, she had helped Marsha a little bit. Now she could at least help Wade learn to cook.

Little things, but more purposeful than almost anything since that awful night. Time to cherish her tiny victories.

"When do you usually like to eat dinner?" she asked as they worked together to put things away. She stopped a moment to look at her refrigerator. It hadn't been that full while she lived here, ever. And now it held an embarrassment of riches.

He paused, a box of cornstarch in hand, and looked at her. "Ma'am, you're talking to a SEAL. I learned to eat when the food was there."

"Oh." She bit her lip. "A SEAL? Really?"

"Really."

That would explain at least some of it, she thought, how he could look so hard and dangerous at times. It might even explain his lack of expression and his disinclination to talk. Hesitantly she said, "I can't imagine what it must have been like."

"No."

And that closed the subject. Well, it would if she let it. How much did she want to risk now that they'd found some common ground? But the silence seemed heavy in some way, no longer comfortable. With one word he'd fixed an image of himself in her mind and she didn't know how to absorb it. Nor did she know why she wanted to cross the barrier he had set so firmly in place with that one word.

Recklessly, she didn't take the warning. "I've seen programs about SEALs," she offered.

"A lot of people have." He started folding her cotton grocery bags neatly.

"The training looks terribly hard."

"It is."

Volumes of information. She almost sighed. "I saw another program about an operation where the SEALs had to board a ship at sea to remove a container of plutonium that could have been used to make a bomb."

"Yes."

"It's amazing what you guys can do."

"Most people have no idea what we do." With that he put

the folded bags in a neat stack on her counter and walked from the kitchen.

She listened to him climb the stairs, listened to the creak as he went into his room.

And with him departed the little bit of positive purpose she'd found just today.

# Chapter 4

Cory felt bad. For the first time in forever, she had felt positive, felt ready to reach out, however tentatively. And she'd blown it.

She had pressed Wade, even when her instincts had warned her that might be a mistake. Apparently her skills had atrophied over the past year. There'd been a time when she would have handled that approach a whole lot better.

Or would she? How could she even know anymore? For so long she'd been curled inward in a tight ball around her own fear and pain. Maybe she would have flubbed the conversational attempt even back then. Wade, after all, was a grown man, not one of her kids. His barriers had to be even higher, even more deeply ingrained.

Regardless, she wished she'd just kept her mouth shut, because it had been surprisingly nice to do ordinary, routine tasks *with* someone else, even a someone she didn't know, and could barely talk with. Just the rhythm of it had probably been one of the most soothing experiences she could remember in a while.

Worse, she was brooding about what surely had to be the most minor of trespasses. It wasn't as if she'd demanded personal war stories or anything. Far from it.

*Let it go,* she told herself. Good advice except that perhaps the worst change in her over the past year was the way she could seldom just dismiss things. Like that phone call last night.

In her previous life, she wouldn't have given it a second thought. Once upon a time, even if it had disturbed her, she'd have been able to shake it off in relatively short order.

Events had changed her. Worry had burrowed mole holes in her mind, ever ready to grant easy access to the next concern that showed up. The stupidest things could run in circles for hours or days, and she could no longer shake them.

But today, thanks to Marsha and then Wade, she'd managed to put that call out of her mind. To put it in its proper place.

But it was still there, ready to pounce the instant she allowed it to. If she sat here too much longer brooding, the fear would steal back in and soon she'd be like a dog gnawing at a bone, unable to let it go.

Finally she stood up, deciding the best thing in the world would be to take a walk. She'd spent too many hours hiding in this house over the past year, and that had turned her into an even worse mess.

She wondered if she had failed to heal because fear had taken over to a paralyzing degree. Which was more ridiculous when she considered the entire weight of the federal government had thrown itself behind making her disappear.

Yes, she was still grieving, but somehow grief and fear had become so intertwined she no longer knew which was which. The one was a healthy thing, the other not.

Today she seemed to have taken two successful baby steps in the right direction. It was time, she decided, to step back out into the sunlight, to start living again the way most other people lived: without the constant expectation of the terrible happening.

Nobody got a guarantee, after all.

Grabbing her keys, leaving her purse behind, she slipped into her jogging shoes then turned off the alarm. She had to turn it off, because once it was set and had been on more than forty seconds, opening and closing the door without triggering the alarm sequence became impossible. Failure to turn off the alarm within forty seconds meant that the police would be called.

So she punched in the code to turn it off, listening to the near-squeal it made. As soon as it was disarmed, she could reset it and safely leave.

But she didn't get to the rearming part.

"Where are you going?"

She turned and saw Wade at the top of the stairs. A spark of annoyance flared, a welcome change from the steady diet of fear she'd been living with. "Out. What business is it of yours?"

"None." His shirt was unbuttoned again, but he still wore his jeans and deck shoes. This time she noticed more than the broad expanse of his chest. She noted his flat belly, the fact that he had the coveted "six-pack" of abdominal ripples, though not overdeveloped. She had to drag her gaze away, back to his face. He started down the stairs. "I'll go with you."

Her jaw dropped a little, and her annoyance grew. "Why? I'm just going to walk around the block."

"I'd like a walk."

But he didn't have to take it *with* her. She almost said so, quite sharply, and then realized something. Her fear hadn't just dissipated on its own today. No, *he* had driven it back.

Now what? Would she insist she go on the walk alone? When she might well get scared again halfway around the block? Was she going to take the offered crutch?

She ought to say no, for her own good. It was high time she started conquering her fears. But then remembering how she had felt when she'd made him leave the room earlier, she decided she didn't want to needlessly offend him again.

It was as good an excuse as any, she supposed, because now that she actually thought about it, she wasn't sure she yet had the courage to take that walk alone. Especially after that phone call last night.

"Damn!" she swore.

He was now at the foot of the stairs, buttoning his shirt, and looked at her. "What?"

"I'm so confused I can't stand it."

"About what?"

She hesitated.

"You don't have to tell me. Walking helps quite a bit."

Giving her emotional space, but not physical space. She looked at him, and for the first time got past the sheer impact of his solidity and strength to notice that he was a handsome man. Very handsome, in a rugged, healthy way.

She sighed. *Not now. Please.* But it was a simple fact that the frisson he made her feel was not fear for her life, but fear of dangerous sexual attraction. With a man as closed off as Wade Kendrick, there could only be pain on that path.

But she was still young enough and healthy enough to feel those urges. Well, maybe that was a good thing. Another part of her coming back to life.

"Are we taking that walk?"

"Uh, yeah." She punched in the codes again and together they stepped out onto the small porch. She set out purposefully in the direction of the town park, thinking it would do her some good to see kids at play again. Among the many things she had avoided in the past year was children, because they reminded her of things lost. But she might be ready to let them remind her of some of the goodness in life.

Once again he measured his pace to hers, as if it came automatically. And once again, he said nothing.

The summer afternoon was warm, the sun as brilliant as it could get this far north. And without warning she found herself talking, although she had to catch herself frequently so she didn't reveal too much.

"I used to live in...down south. Almost in the tropics, actually. I notice the difference in the sun here."

"It is different," he agreed.

"The days are longer in the summer, but the sun never gets as high or bright. And the winter nights are so long here."

"Yeah."

"But at least I don't burn as easily." She managed a small laugh. "In the summer down you can get a tan walking across a parking lot."

It was his turn to give a small laugh, as if he, too, were trying. "I've been in all kinds of climates."

Well, that was a positive step, she thought. "I imagine so." She was careful not to question. Instead she chose to talk a little more about herself. "I've had a lot to adjust to, and I haven't been doing a very good job of it."

For a few paces he didn't say anything. Then, "I guess it's harder to adjust when you're afraid."

"It's that obvious, huh?"

"Like I said, only to someone who would know fear."

"I don't know whether that's a compliment or a criticism."

"Neither. Just an observation."

"Do you ever get afraid?" As soon as the words were out she realized she might have trespassed too far again, but it was too late to snatch them back. She almost held her breath, wondering if he would turn and walk away.

Instead, he astonished her by answering. "I'm human."

Sideways, but still an answer. She relaxed a bit and looked around, taking in the old trees that lined the street, their leaves rustling ceaselessly in the summer breeze. Nobody else seemed to be out and about, but that wasn't unusual. Here, as everywhere, most couples both needed to work.

"In the evenings," she remarked, "there will often be people sitting out on their front porches. Different from where I used to live. Most of the neighborhoods around me back home were built relatively recently, when it was important to have a privacy-fenced backyard. You'd almost never see anyone out front unless they were doing yard work."

"In most places in the world where I've been, a house is where you sleep or shelter from the elements. The rest of life happens in common areas, on the street, in front of the house. Not for everyone, of course. There are always some who want to keep the unwashed masses away. And in some cultures an enclosed courtyard is considered necessary, but given that several generations of a family live together, it's not exactly isolation."

That was practically half an encyclopedia coming from this man. "Do you think we're losing something with those fenced backyards?"

"Depends on what you want out of life. But once you build that fence, if you're having a barbecue you're not going to have a neighbor who might drop over for a chat and bring a six-pack, and wind up staying on for dinner."

"True." She turned that around for a few seconds. "I don't really know how different it *feels* to live in a place like this," she finally admitted. "Basically, when I come home from work I pass all these probably very nice people on their front porches and go inside and lock myself in."

"Maybe you have good reason."

Maybe she did. Or maybe she'd been acting like a wounded animal that wanted to be left alone in its burrow. The whole point of the Marshals moving her here had been so that she didn't *have* to live this way. Another sigh escaped her.

"I thought," she said reluctantly, "that I was breaking out of the cycle earlier today. I even told myself to go take a walk."

"But?"

"But then I realized that I'd just been distracted. That despite everything, I'm still worried at some level because of that call last night. Oh, I can't even explain it to myself."

They reached the park and found a bench not far from the sidewalk. Nobody else was there, so Cory's hope for distraction was disappointed.

Wade let the silence flow around them with the breeze for a few minutes before he spoke again. "Sometimes," he said quietly, "we get confused because we're changing."

That made her look at him, and for an instant she wished she hadn't because she felt again that unexpected, unwanted attraction. What was going on with her? Why did she suddenly have the worst urge to put her head on the shoulder of a stranger? To feel his arms close around her?

She jumped up from the bench and headed home. Walking it off seemed like the only sane course available to her. "We need to start dinner," she said, the sole explanation she could offer for her behavior. Because there was no way she could tell him that the feelings he awakened in her were nearly as frightening as that phone call had been.

Despite her sudden takeoff, he fell in step beside her before she had made two full strides. Glued to her side. Part of her wanted to resent that, and part of her was grateful for it. Confusion? She had it in spades. At least her fear and grief had been clear, so very clear. No questions there.

Now the questions were surfacing, the conflicting feelings, all the stuff she'd avoided for so long. She forced herself to slow her pace to an easier walk. She'd been running again, she realized. Had she forgotten every other mode of existence?

"Darn," she said under her breath. All of a sudden it was as if someone had held up a mirror, and painful or not she had to look at herself. She wasn't seeing a whole lot that she liked, either.

"Something wrong?" Wade asked mildly.

She stopped midstride and looked at him. Mistake, because the truth burst out of her and she wasn't sure she wanted it to. What did she know about this guy after all? "Has something ever made you stop and take a good look at yourself?"

"Yes."

"What if you don't like what you see?" She didn't wait for an answer, just started walking again. She didn't expect an answer, frankly. It wasn't the kind of question anyone else could answer.

But he surprised her. "You make up your mind to change."

"Easier said than done."

"Always."

Some inner tension uncoiled just a bit. Change? Why not? After all, she'd allowed herself to be changed by life, had just rolled along like a victim. That did not make her feel proud. "Sometimes," she said more to herself than him, "you just have to grab the rudder." She hadn't done that at all since the shooting. Not at all.

"Grabbing the rudder is easier to do when the seas aren't stormy."

She glanced at him again. Oh, there was a story there, and she wished she knew what it was, but she didn't dare ask. This man could disappear even in plain sight, and she didn't want him to disappear again. At least not yet.

For some reason the invader had ceased to be an invader. Maybe just his presence had reminded her that she still had a life to live. Maybe his obvious protectiveness had made her feel just a little safer. Or maybe the attraction she felt was overcoming all the walls she'd slammed into place.

Because she *had* slammed those walls into place. She hadn't built them brick by brick. No, she'd put up the steel barricades almost instantly in the aftermath. Huge parts of her had simply withdrawn from life, no longer willing to take even small risks, like making a friend.

She stole another glance at Wade and wondered at herself. If ever a guy looked like a bad risk for even something as simple as friendship, he was it. Yet for some reason she was opening up to him. Not much, but enough that she could get herself into trouble if she didn't watch her step.

She ought to be afraid of him, the way she was afraid of everything else. Instead all she could do was notice how attractive he was. Wonder if that hard line of his mouth would feel as hard if he kissed her. What that hard body would feel like against her soft curves.

Ah, she was losing her mind. For real. It had finally snapped. After a year of inability to feel anything but grief and anguish, she had finally broken. Now she was looking at a virtual stranger as a sex object.

*Way to go, Cory.* Very sensible. Clearly she couldn't trust herself at all anymore.

Two cars came down the street toward them as they rounded the corner right before her house. She lifted her hand to wave, deciding it was about time to make a friendly gesture. The woman in the first car smiled and waved back. The man in the second car didn't even glance at them.

They reached the door and went inside, resetting the alarm. Without a word, he followed her into the kitchen, evidently ready to get his first cooking lesson. She started pulling things out, preparing to make a dish with Italian sausage and pasta and fresh vegetables. The recipe was one that had emerged one day from a scramble through the cupboards and the realization that the only way she could put together dinner was the stone-soup method.

"I can't trust myself anymore," she muttered, at first unaware that she was thinking out loud. When you lived alone long enough, having conversations with yourself often moved from the mind to the mouth. "Everything's been so screwed up for so long. But then how do I know my thinking wasn't screwed up before? I was living in some kind of enchanted universe before. A place where bad things didn't happen."

She turned from pulling a package of frozen Italian sausage from the freezer and saw Wade standing there, arms folded, watching. And that's when she realized her muttering hadn't been private. Her cheeks heated a bit. "Sorry, sometimes I talk to myself. Bad habit."

"Don't mind me."

"Well, you don't want to hear it. And I'm not sure I want anyone else to hear the mess that's going on inside my head."

"I can go upstairs if you like."

She shook her head. "Stay. I promised to teach you some cooking, and this is a great dish to start with." She passed him the package of frozen sausage. "Microwave, hit the defrost button twice, please."

He took the sausage and did as she asked. Soon the familiar hum filled the kitchen. Green peppers and tomatoes were next, a true luxury these days, washed in the sink and readied for cubing. "Do you like onions?"

"Very much."

So she pulled one out of the metal hanging basket and peeled it swiftly before setting it beside the other vegetables. As soon as she reached for the chef's knife, though, Wade stepped forward. "I can slice and dice. How do you want it?"

"Pieces about one-inch square." She passed him the knife and as their hands brushed she felt the warmth of his skin. All of a sudden she had to close her eyes, had to batter down the almost forgotten pleasure of skin on skin. Such a simple, innocent touch, and it reminded her of one of the forms of human contact she absolutely missed most: touch. Even simple touches. She almost never let anyone get that close anymore, certainly not a man.

A flood tide of forgotten yearnings pierced her, and she drew a sharp breath.

"What's wrong?"

He was so near she felt his breath on her cheek. Warm

and clean. A shiver rippled through her as she fought the unwanted feelings, and forced her eyes open, ready to deny anything and everything.

But the instant her gaze met his, she knew she could deny nothing. His obsidian eyes darkened even more, and she heard him inhale deeply as he recognized the storm inside her. There was a clatter as the knife fell to the counter, and the next thing she knew she was wrapped in his powerful arms.

He lifted her right off the floor and set her on the counter, moving in between her legs until she could feel his heat in places that had been too cold and too empty for so long. This was not a man who hesitated, nor one who finessed the moment.

He swooped in like a hawk and claimed her mouth as if it were rightfully his. An instant later she learned that thin mouth could be both soft and demanding. That his hard chest felt every bit as hard as it looked, and felt even better as it crushed her breasts. His arms were tight and steely, and she should have been afraid of their power, afraid of what he could do to her whether she wanted it or not.

But all she could feel was the singing in her body as it responded to needs more primal than any she had ever imagined. Somehow the dissenting, cautious voices in her head fell silent. Somehow she lifted her arms and wrapped them around his neck, holding on for dear life.

Because this was life. Here and now. Like Sleeping Beauty awakening from a nightmare, she discovered she could want something besides freedom from terror and pain, and that good things were still to be had despite all.

Her body responded to life's call as her mind no longer seemed able to. His tongue passed the first gate of her teeth, finding hers in a rhythm as strong as her heartbeat, a thrusting that echoed like a shout in a canyon until it reached all the way to her very core and came back to her in a powerful throbbing.

A gasp escaped her between one kiss and the next. Her legs lifted, trying to wrap around his narrow hips, trying to bring her center right up against his hardness, trying to find an answer to the ache that overpowered her. Any brain she had left gave way before the demands of her body for more and deeper touches. Her physical being leaped the barriers that had existed only in her mind.

He moved against her, mimicking the ultimate act, not enough to satisfy, but enough to promise. She wanted every bit of that promise. Every bit.

He drew a ragged breath as he released her mouth, but he didn't leave her. No, he trailed those lips across her cheek, down the side of her throat, making her shiver with even more longing, causing her to make a small cry and arch against him. One of her hands slipped upward, finding the back of his head, pressing him closer yet. She wanted to take this journey as never before.

Then the microwave dinged.

All of a sudden, reality returned with a crash. He pulled away just a couple of inches and looked at her, his eyes darker than night. She stared back, hardly aware that she was panting, suddenly and acutely aware of how she had exposed herself.

As if he read her awareness on her face, he stepped back a little farther. The absence of pressure between her thighs made her ache even more, made some part of her want to cry out in loss. But with the return of awareness came a bit of sense.

He didn't pull completely away, as if he knew how sensitive this could become. How dangerous for her, and maybe for him.

Instead, even as she let her legs fall away, he reached out to gently brush her hair with his hand.

"You're enchanting," he said huskily.

Enchanting? No one had ever called her that. She remained mute, unable to speak, knowing that her eyes, her face, her breathing must be telling a truth she didn't want to hear herself say. Not yet, maybe never.

"I forgot myself."

He wasn't the only one. She didn't know what to say, could only stare at him, torn between yearning, loss and the returning shreds of common sense.

He leaned forward, giving her the lightest of kisses on her lips. "I think," he said, "that I'd better cut those vegetables."

She managed a nod, awhirl with so many conflicting feelings she doubted she could ever sort them out. He turned to pick up the knife, and moved down the counter about a foot to the cutting board and vegetables.

"You don't have to be afraid of me," he said, his voice still a little thick. "I'll behave."

Another odd choice of words. As she fought her way back from the frustration of awakened, unmet desires, she tucked that away for future consideration. Right now, the thing she most needed was some equilibrium. Thinking could come later.

Wade, just about to start slicing the vegetables, put the knife down and turned toward her. He gripped her around the waist and set her back on her feet. "Sorry," he said. "Should have thought of that."

She could have slid off the counter on her own, but hadn't because she still felt so shaky. Unable to tell him that, she mumbled her thanks and turned desperately in another direction, away from him, seeking something to keep busy with. This was a simple meal, and he was about to do the major part of the work.

Finally she measured out the penne into a bowl, then walked around him to get the sausage from the microwave. Just act as if it never happened, she told herself. Maybe it never had.

But her traitorous body said otherwise. Oh, it had happened all right, and she suspected the internal earthquakes had just begun. Even the light brush of her own clothing over her skin, especially between her legs, reminded her that something primal had awakened.

She coated the bottom of a frying pan with olive oil, then began to slowly cook and brown the sausage on medium heat. Her hands still shook a little when she pulled out the stockpot she used for cooking pasta. A cheap pot, it wouldn't have served well for anything that wasn't mostly liquid, and she found herself pausing, suddenly locked in the most ridiculous memory of her previous pasta cooker, an expensive pot with a built-in colander and a smaller insert for steaming vegetables.

It was an odd memory, coming out of nowhere. She had long since ceased to care about the things she had lost during her transition to this new life, but for no reason she could almost feel the weight of that pot in her hands and with it the tearing edge of memories, ordinary memories, the simple kinds of things that should hold no threat whatever. It wasn't a memory of Jim, of their life together. It was just a memory of a damn pot, one she had bought long before she married Jim. Nothing but a memory from the life of a woman who had once slowly built up a kitchen full of all the best cooking utensils because she loved to cook, and part of that expression was using the best of everything.

On a teacher's salary, many of those items had truly

been an indulgence. She had scrimped to buy them, until she had had a kitchen that would have pleased a world-class chef.

And now she was using a five-dollar aluminum stockpot and a chef's knife she'd bought on sale at the grocery store.

How odd, she thought, looking at the pot. How very odd what had once seemed important to her. And how little she usually missed those things now that they were gone. In fact, even had she been able to afford them, she doubted she would have replaced them.

They didn't matter any longer. Who had that woman been, anyway? Had she ever known? She certainly didn't know who she was now.

A faint sigh escaped her, and she put the pot in the sink to fill it with water. Indulgences. Her past life had been full of them, her new life was empty of them. In the midst of the storm, all she could say about it was that she had never known who she was? Had no idea who she had become?

When she started to lift the heavy pot full of water, Wade stepped in and lifted it for her. "Don't call me a pig," he said. "I've just been trained to act a certain way."

She arched a brow at him. "So a woman can't lift anything heavy?"

"Why should she when I'm standing right here?"

Once again she was left wondering how to take him. But this time she asked, emboldened, perhaps, by the fact that he had called her enchanting. "What exactly do you mean? That I'm too weak to do it?"

He shook his head. "No."

That awful answer again, the one that told her nothing. "Then what?" she insisted, refusing to let him get away with it.

He put the pot on the stove. "Would it make you feel better if we had an argument?"

That yanked her up short and hard. Was that what she was doing? Trying to get angry so she could forget the other things he made her feel? Or was this some kind of insistence on independence that actually made no sense? She bit her lip.

He faced her again. "It's my training. It's my background. Call it a simple courtesy."

And he'd done it even though he'd expected her to object. In fact, he'd tried to deflect the objection before it occurred. Would she have even thought he was being chauvinistic if he had not shot that defense out there to begin with?

"You're a very difficult man to understand," she said finally. "Not that you try to make it any easier."

"No. I don't."

"Thank you for lifting the pot."

"You're welcome."

Feeling a bit stiff and awkward now, she returned to cooking. Maybe she should never have agreed to this whole cooking thing. Maybe she should have kept him at a distance, as a roomer she hardly saw.

Because right now she felt too much confusion for comfort.

Confusion and fear. Great companions.

# Chapter 5

Wade went to ground for the night. He had no problem staying out of the way upstairs until sometime in the morning. He had a finely honed instinct that warned him when it was time to become part of the background. Wallpaper. Just another tree in a forest. Now was such a time.

The hours ticked by as he read a novel he'd bought during his bus trip but had never really started. He had plenty to think about anyway as the hours slipped toward dawn. The past he still needed to deal with, the future he needed to create out of whole cloth and finally because he could avoid it no longer, a woman who slept downstairs.

Not quite two days ago, he'd met Cory Farland for the first time. There had been no mistaking that she lived in a constant state of fear, though he didn't know why. Now, in an extremely short space of time, she had made several attempts to break out of that fear, to become proactive, to take charge of even little things. And she had come perilously close to having sex with a total stranger.

He recognized the signs of someone emerging from a terrible emotional trauma. Her actions were a little off center, her reactions misaligned. He didn't even have to try to imagine the kind of confusion she must be experiencing within herself because he'd lived through it.

He wanted to kick himself, though, for giving in to the sexual desire that had been so plainly written on her face in the kitchen. Yeah, she was a helluva sexy woman, but she wasn't a one-night-stand kind of woman. If he'd pursued the matter any further, he might have given her another wound to add to the seemingly heavy scars she already carried.

His own actions had taken him by surprise, though. He usually had much better self-control, and he couldn't imagine why she'd gone to his head so fast. Yeah, it had been a long time, but that was a poor excuse. He'd quit enjoying pointless sexual encounters many years ago. Lots of women were eager to hop into bed with a SEAL, and there'd been a time when he had been glad to oblige.

Not anymore. Not for a long time now. The hero worship, the sense that he was another notch on a belt, had palled ages ago. Nor did he have the least desire for notches of his own.

What he wanted was a connection. And he knew he couldn't make them. As he'd already told Cory, he didn't make them at all. Couldn't afford them, sure. But couldn't make them, either. And he'd long since given up trying to pretend he could. Best to just hold the world at a distance.

But trying to hold the world at a distance didn't mean he could ignore that fact that Cory might need his protection. She seemed afraid in a way that suggested the threat, whatever it was, still lurked somewhere, that she had found no resolution.

It also fascinated him that while she had shared Marsha's story of an abusive husband, she had shared nothing at all about why that phone call had terrified her so. Secrets meant something. And in this case, since her first call had been to the sheriff, he doubted she was on the run from a legal problem.

Which left…what?

And then something clicked together in his brain.

He sat up a little straighter as the circumstances he had so far observed came into focus. Moved here about a year ago, deliberately censored her speech when she spoke about where she came from. Her silences were more revealing than her speech. No offered comparison of her situation to Marsha's. High-tech alarm system when she had little money. And terrible, terrible fear. Collapsing because some anonymous person had said, "I know where you are."

WITSEC. Witness Protection.

He knew the protocols, had been part of WITSEC teams abroad. Usually the protected person was in some kind of trouble up to his neck, and was being protected because he'd agreed to inform against his own cohort.

But he'd bet his jump wings that this woman had never done anything more illegal in her life than speed on the highway. Which meant she had been an innocent witness to a crime and her life was in danger because of it. A crime that had yet to be solved. Nothing else would put her in the protection program. And nothing else would have caused the Marshals to spend so much money on that alarm system. Your average confessing criminal didn't get that kind of care.

He swore under his breath and stared at the closed door

of his bedroom. Every instinct and every bit of his training rushed back to front and center.

No wonder that call had terrified her. No wonder she seemed as jumpy as a cat on a hot stove. No wonder she hadn't been able to create a life for herself here.

Then he remembered something from their walk home that afternoon, and gave himself a huge mental kick in the butt.

Without a thought, he jumped to his feet, dressed in his darkest clothes and his favorite boots. Then he switched off the motion sensors, wishing there was some way to silence the squeal, and headed downstairs. Six months of trying to be normal vanished in an instant.

He barely reached the foot of the stairs before Cory came staggering from her bedroom, her eyes heavy-lidded with sleep, a blue terry-cloth robe held tightly around her with her arms.

"Sorry," he said. "I just needed to move around." *Check the perimeter.* "I didn't think it would do much good for your sleep if I clomped around upstairs."

Her brown eyes regarded him groggily. "What time is it?" she asked finally, smothering a yawn.

He glanced at the highly complex dive chronometer on his arm. He hadn't worn it in months, but for some reason he'd put it on during the night. As if something had niggled at him, saying it was time to go on duty. "A little past five," he answered.

"Good enough time to start the coffee," she said, yawning again.

"I can do it. Why don't you go back to bed?"

"I'm one of those people. Once I'm awake…" She gave a shrug and shuffled toward the kitchen.

"I'm just going to walk around the block," he said.

"Fine." She didn't even look back, just waved a hand.

So he turned off the alarm and turned it back on again so he could slip out the door. He was going to hate that alarm before long. It hampered him. He should have been able to do this without waking her at all.

On the other hand, he was glad he didn't have to leave her unprotected in there. Outside the sun was rising already, casting a rosy light over the world. He walked around the house, then set out to jog around the block.

He should have noticed it sooner, but the guy who had parked beside them at the store, then met them in the aisle had been the very same man who had driven past them on Cory's street in a *different car*. Evidently he'd relaxed more over the past six months than he'd realized, because he *never* would have failed to notice that immediately when he was on the job. Now that he'd made the connection, he had to know if they were still being watched. Had to make up for lost time.

But neither the mystery man nor either of his cars showed up.

Which of course meant nothing except that if the guy was indeed shadowing Cory, his prey was in for the night. Reaching the house again, his breath hardly quickened by his fast jog over such a short distance, he stepped inside once more, tended the squealing, annoying alarm and made his way to the kitchen.

Cory sat at the table, chin in her hands, eyes half-closed as she waited for the coffeemaker to finish.

"Do you ever hate that alarm?" he asked as he pulled mugs out of the cupboard and put one of them in front of her.

"Sometimes." She gave him a wan smile. "I never love it, that's a fact."

"I'll get used to it," he said as he reached for the coffee

carafe and filled both their mugs. Then he got the half gallon of milk out of the fridge for her and placed it beside the carafe on the table.

"Thank you. You do get used to it."

"Sorry I woke you," he said again. "But I just couldn't sit still another moment." Not exactly as simple as that, but just as true.

"No need to apologize. I may not get back to sleep now, but I usually can manage a nap in the afternoon if I need it. I'll be fine." She poured maybe half a teaspoon of milk into her coffee, then raised the mug to her lips and breathed the aroma in through her nose. "Fresh coffee is one of the greatest smells in the world."

"It is," he agreed. He pulled out the chair across from her, but looked at her before he sat. "Do you mind?"

Something crossed her face, some hint of concern, but it was gone fast and he couldn't make out what it meant. She waved toward the chair. "Help yourself."

He turned the chair so he could straddle it, then sat facing her. "Looks like it's going to be a nice day out there."

"Probably. I miss the rain, though."

"Rain?"

She covered her mouth, stifling another yawn. "Back in…back where I used to live, this time of year we'd be having afternoon thunderstorms almost every day. I miss them."

"But you get some here, too, right?"

"Sometimes. Not nearly every day, though. In a way, they're prettier here."

"How so?"

"You can see so far you can almost watch them build out of nothing. Sometimes anyway." She gave a little shake of her head. "No trees to get in the way if you drive out of town."

"True."

"But there's not as much lightning with them. I used to love the lightning shows in—" Again a sharp break. An impatient sound. "We used to watch them some nights. One storm in particular, there must have been a lightning bolt every second or so. And when they'd hit the ground, you could see a green glow spread out from them and rise into the sky. I only saw it in that one storm, but I was fascinated enough to research it."

"What was it?"

"Corona discharge. It's actually quite common in electrical discharges, but often we don't even see it. The air around gets ionized as the charge dissipates. Most corona discharges aren't dangerous, but when lightning is involved, it can be."

She sipped her coffee, then held the cup in both hands with her elbows on the table. "You must have seen storms all over the world."

"I have. Monsoons, hurricanes, typhoons and then just the regular buggers, which can be bad enough."

"Yes, they can. There's so much power in a thunderstorm. Incredible power. I used to te—" Another break. She looked down, effectively hiding her face behind her mug.

Teach? he wondered. Deliberately, he let it pass. The last thing he wanted to do was cause her fear because she'd revealed something she felt she shouldn't. Not yet anyway. It wouldn't serve any useful purpose to make her more afraid.

He fell silent, enjoying his coffee while his mind turned over the things he should do, and might do, to help protect her. Maybe one of the first things he should do was find a way to speak to the sheriff. But given WITSEC procedures, he doubted Dalton would give him anything useful. No, he guessed he was on his own with this, at least until he had something more than suspicion.

But he was fairly decent on his own. And he was intimately acquainted with his own abilities and weaknesses. After all, he'd spent twenty years honing those abilities and weeding out those weaknesses.

So the question now was how much he should share with Cory. Should he let her know what had coalesced everything for him? Or should he let it ride to avoid making her any more frightened? That was always a difficult question in WITSEC ops. You needed your protectee to be as cooperative as possible, as helpful as possible, but you didn't want to scare him or her needlessly because that could result in actions born of fear that could endanger the entire operation.

Cory still had her head down, her face concealed. He studied her, trying to see her as a mission, not as a woman who had stirred some long-buried feelings in him.

He needed to gain her confidence, sufficiently that she would trust him if he told her to do something. That was primary. But how? This was no ordinary operation where being bulked-up in body armor and armed to the teeth would do the job.

Well, he couldn't let her know how much she had betrayed by her silences. That would scare her into wondering if she'd left a crumb trail for someone to follow.

Yet, he feared someone had found her. That phone call, he was now certain, had been no innocent prank. Someone was sounding out women who fit a certain profile. Waiting to see if something changed after the call. He could explain it no other way. Certainly you wouldn't warn your intended target if you were certain you had the right one. Instead, and he had done this on an operation or two, you would try to precipitate revealing action.

The person or persons who hunted Cory might still be wondering. That would depend on how many changes the other women who got those calls made. Marsha had adopted a dog, making no secret of the fact that she wanted it for protection.

But what had Cory done?

The rest of the picture slammed into place. She'd taken in a boarder. One who could easily look like a bodyguard.

Cripes. Was he himself the link that had led the hunter to her? That would depend on whether the hunter learned of him before or *after* the phone call, and for security purposes, he had to assume the worst.

The thought sickened him.

But still, sitting right before him was the woman whose trust he needed, a woman who knew nothing about him, and was likely to know nothing about him unless he started opening up the coffins of his past enough that she felt she knew him.

He swore silently, and poured more coffee into his mug. He needed to go totally against his own nature here. Needed to expose himself in ways he never did.

In that regard, this was a very different type of operation. But where to begin?

He cleared his throat, trying to find words. She looked at him immediately, which didn't really help at all. But he had to take the plunge, sort of like jumping out of a helicopter into a stormy sea and falling sixty or more feet into water that had turned into bricks.

Her eyes looked more alert now, pretty brown eyes, naturally soft and warm, especially right now when fear hadn't tightened them.

"I, um, told you I'm not good at making connections."

She nodded, but didn't try to say anything.

"Truth is, I feel like an alien."

Her eyebrows lifted, but her eyes remained warm, and even gentled a bit. "How so?"

Well now, that was hard to explain. But he'd been the one who brought it up. "Because I've been places ordinary people don't go."

She gave another nod, a slow one. "I take it you don't mean geographically."

"No." And leaving it there wasn't going to get this part of his mission done. He could almost hear the vault doors creak as he opened the crypt of feelings he didn't care to share. "I've done things, seen things, survived things most people can't even imagine. I know what I'm capable of in ways most people never will, thank God. And I can't talk about it. Partly because most of it is classified, but partly because no one will understand anyway."

"I can see that."

"The only people who truly understand are the people I served with. And we all have that sense of alienation. Some are proud of it. Maybe even most. But there's a cost."

"I would imagine so."

"So we can't make connections. We try. Then we watch it all go up in smoke. Our wives leave us because we can't talk, our kids feel like we're strangers who just show up from time to time, even parents look at us like they don't know who we are. And they don't. We pretend, try to appear ordinary, but nothing inside us is ever ordinary again. And finally we realize the only people we can truly connect with anymore are our fellow team members."

He watched her eyes glaze with thought as she absorbed what he was saying. "I guess," she said slowly, "I can identify with that just a little bit."

He waited to see if she would volunteer anything more,

but she didn't. So he decided to forge ahead. "I'm not saying this out of self-pity."

"I didn't think you were."

"I'm just trying to explain why I'm so difficult to talk with. Over the years, between secrets I couldn't discuss, and realities I shouldn't discuss, I got so I didn't talk much at all."

She nodded once more. "Did you have a wife? Kids?"

"I was lucky. I watched too many marriages fall apart before I ever felt the urge. That's one closet without skeletons."

"And now your only support group, the rest of your team, has been taken away from you."

He hadn't thought of it that way before, but he realized she was right. "I guess so."

"So what do you do now?"

"I'm trying to work my way into a life without all that, but I'll be honest, I'm having trouble envisioning it."

"I'm…" She hesitated. "I guess I'm having the same kind of problem, generally speaking. I can't seem to figure out where I want to go, either."

He waited, hoping she'd offer more, but she said nothing else, merely sipped her coffee. So he tried a little indirect prompting. "Big changes can do that. You'd think, though, that since I knew I was going to retire I could have planned better."

A perfect opportunity to say her changes had come without time to plan, or even any choices, but she didn't say anything. Which left him to try to find another way in.

For the first time, it occurred to him that talking to him must be as frustrating for others as talking to Cory was for him. Okay, regardless of his reasons for preferring silence, that wasn't going to work this time. If he was right, and he was rarely wrong about things like this, she had to learn to trust him.

But he'd never had to win anyone's trust in this way before. Oh, he'd gained the trust of his team members in training, during operations and eventually even some of it by reputation. But none of those tools were available to him here. A whole new method was needed and he didn't have the foggiest idea how to go about finding it.

Nor, if he was right, did they have months to get to that point.

Maybe he had to keep talking. He sure as hell couldn't think of any other way. The problem was that most of the past twenty years of his life contained so much classified information, and so much that he couldn't share with the uninitiated, that his own memory might as well have been stamped *Top Secret*. And what did you talk about besides the weather if you couldn't refer to your memories?

But then Cory herself opened the door to a place that wasn't classified but that he wished could be. She asked, "Do you have any family?"

His usual answer to that was a flat no. But given his task here, he bit the bullet. "None that I speak to."

"Oh. Why?"

"It was a long time ago." Which meant he ought to be able to elaborate. It had nothing to do any longer with who he was. In fact, he'd removed them almost as cleanly as an amputation.

Then she totally floored him. Before he could decide what to tell her, and what to omit, she said gently, "You were abused, weren't you?"

Little had the power to stun him any longer, but that simple statement did. "What, am I wearing a mark on my forehead?"

She shook her head. "I don't mean to pry. But just a

couple of things you've said… Well, they reminded me of some…people I worked with."

Still hedging her way around her past, while asking about his. The tables had turned, and he'd helped her do it. Didn't mean he had to like it.

"Well, yes," he finally said. "What things did I say?"

"It doesn't matter, really. You're not that child any longer, but there were just some echoes of things I've heard before. Most people wouldn't even notice."

The way most people wouldn't notice her omissions. His estimate of her kicked up quite a few notches. In her own way, she was as observant as he.

She reached for the carafe between them, and poured a little more coffee into her mug. Then she added just a tiny bit of milk. "Sometimes," she said, "I guess things stay with us, even when they've been left far in the past."

"I guess." How could he deny it when she had picked up on something he'd buried a long, long time ago? "Yeah, they were abusive."

"Physically as well as emotionally?"

"Yeah."

"I'm sorry." Her brown eyes practically turned liquid with warmth and concern. "Did that play a part in you becoming a SEAL?"

He was about to deny it, because he had, after all, been out of the house for nearly a year before he joined the navy. But then he realized something, and saw how it dovetailed into what was going on here, and he made a conscious decision to breach a barrier so old and so strong that he was hardly aware of it any longer.

"Yes," he said finally. "In a way I suppose it did."

"How so?"

Well, *he'd* opened the vault. "After I got out of high

school, I couldn't shake them off fast enough. I worked my way through a few jobs, feeling at loose ends. Confused."

"Confused?" She repeated the word, and he could tell she felt the connection to her own situation. He could have waited for her to add something, but he suspected she wouldn't.

"Confused," he said again flatly. "I'd lived most of my life with one goal, to survive and to get away from them. And once I was away, I didn't have a goal anymore. I felt like a stranger to myself. I finally realized that the way I was drifting I wasn't going to get anywhere, so one morning I walked into a recruiter's office. Then I had a goal again, something more than merely surviving. They gave me one."

She nodded. "I can understand that. I really can. I'd like to have a goal again."

He took a gamble, sharing a little more of himself. "When you've lived for so long thinking of yourself in one way, looking at life in one way, and then something dramatic changes, it's like the earth vanishes from beneath your mental feet. Your whole identity can vanish."

"That's exactly how it feels." Her face reflected pain.

"Especially when everything you thought you were was a reflection of the life you were living."

He heard her draw a small, sharp breath. So he plunged on, laying himself out there. "For so long I'd identified myself in opposition to my parents, partly by denying all they told me I was, and partly in reaction against them and everything they did and believed. And all of a sudden I didn't have anything to push against anymore. Any goal to fight for. Well, I'm kind of there again."

Her head jerked up and she looked straight at him. "Because you retired?"

He nodded. "For twenty years, the navy gave me an identity and a goal. Now it's all gone again."

"Oh, Wade," she said quietly. "I know how hard that is."

"Somehow," he said pointedly, "I think you do."

Her eyes widened a shade. Then she confided something for the very first time. "I was…my husband died a little over a year ago. Before I came here. Everything went up in smoke."

Still evasive, but at last a nugget of the truth. He waited, hoping she would say more, but she didn't. And he'd said about all he could stand about himself. Admitted more to her than he had really wanted to about himself. Voiced out loud the struggle he'd been facing for six months now without any success.

God, he felt exposed. And life had taught him that when you exposed yourself this way, all you did was give someone ammunition to use against you.

He could have used a ten-mile run right then, but he fought down the urge to get up and walk away. Only two things stopped him: this woman might be at risk, and he realized he couldn't keep running from himself any longer.

He'd been running an awful long time. All the way back to the age of four. Running inside his head, running with his career, always running.

One of these days he needed to stop, and apparently today was going to be the day.

*Chapter 6*

Wade excused himself to go shower. Cory placed the coffee carafe back on the warmer, put the milk away and washed their mugs. She smothered another yawn, considered getting dressed, then discarded the idea. It was just too early to bother, especially when she didn't have anywhere to go.

But she did have a lot to think about. Wandering into her living room, she curled up on one end of the couch, tucking her robe around her legs, and put her chin in her hand thinking over all Wade had shared with her that morning.

She wished she knew what had unlocked his silence but she had to admit it was good to know something about him even if it wasn't a whole lot.

But she wasn't at all surprised to find out he'd been an abused child. Nor did it surprise her to learn that the navy had given him what he needed. Often abused children needed order in their lives, clear-cut rules to follow, after being subjected to the unpredictable whims of mean adults. The regimented lifestyle took away the fear of never knowing what would bring retribution down on their heads.

And apparently he'd needed to take charge at the same time, or he never would have gone into the SEALs. Maybe there'd even been an element of *nobody's ever going to get away with treating me that way again.*

She didn't consider herself an expert, but in eight years of teaching she'd certainly seen enough kids fighting these same battles, and few enough who were willing to talk about it. It was sad how they became coconspirators with their abusers, protecting their tormentors with silence and even outright lies.

And often, even when she thought she had enough to report it to the authorities, nothing came from it. Without physical evidence, as long as the child denied it, there was little enough anyone could do.

The thing that had always struck her, though, was the incalculable emotional damage that must come from being so mistreated by the very people a child by rights ought to be able to trust.

Well, she'd always wondered about that, and now she was looking at it. He seemed to blame his job for his inability to make connections, and perhaps it was responsible in large measure, but she suspected the seeds of the problem lay in his childhood. If you couldn't trust your own parents, who could you trust?

She closed her eyes, chin still in her hand. As always, when confronted with something like this, she wanted to help, but in this case she didn't see how she possibly could. This was a man who must be what? Thirty-eight? Thirty-nine? She couldn't just step in like some delivering angel.

He wouldn't want it, and honestly, she didn't know enough to be much help. The best she could do was listen when he was willing to talk.

He had turned out to be a good case for not judging a book by its cover, though. If her ears hadn't become properly tuned through teaching, she probably would have thought all along that he was a hard, harsh man, sufficient unto himself, needing no one and nothing. That's certainly what he had tried to become, and the image he tried to perpetuate.

And she had to admit she felt a lot more comfortable now knowing that he wasn't the stone monolith he had first seemed.

Listening to him had also made her think about her own situation, and doing so made her squirm a bit. Yes, terrible things had happened to her, and her entire life had changed as a result, but how could she truly excuse her waste of the past year? Terror and trauma could explain only so much. The woman she had once believed herself to be had turned out to be a weakling and a coward.

She gave herself no quarter on that one. Some of it could be excused, but not all of it. After all, look what Wade had managed to achieve out of his own trauma as a child. He may have drifted for nearly a year, but then he'd taken a stand to make something of himself.

She hadn't even tried.

But even as she sat there trying to beat herself up in the hopes that she might regain some sense of purpose or direction, she found herself remembering that episode in the kitchen yesterday, when he had lifted her onto the counter and kissed her.

Oh, man, that had started some kind of internal snowball rolling. Just the memory of those all-too-brief moments was enough to make her clamp her thighs together as the throbbing ache reawakened. She had thought that part of her dead and buried for good, only to discover it could come back to life at the merest touch.

Like a daffodil determined to bloom even though snow still lay on the ground in an icy blanket, her body responded to the memory as surely as the touch. She could only imagine what it might feel like to be claimed by such a man, one so powerful and strong, one so confident in his own desire. Sex with Jim had been good: loving and tender. She couldn't help but feel that the entire experience would be different with Wade: hot and hard.

And maybe that's what she needed now, someone to push her past all the invisible lines she had drawn around herself, someone to knock her off center enough to emerge from her cocoon.

Because she sure as hell needed some kind of kick.

Wade returned downstairs eventually, waking her from a half doze where dreams of hot kisses had collided with inchoate fears, the kind of feeling that something was chasing her, but she couldn't escape it, and the kisses felt like both protection and trap.

Freshly shaven, smelling of soap even from several feet away, he sat facing her. "Sorry, woke you again."

"I didn't want to doze off. If you want some, the coffee should still be hot." The memory of her odd half dream made her cheeks equally hot. She hoped he couldn't see and thought he probably couldn't since she kept the curtains closed, and the early daylight out.

It was time to start opening those curtains. Time to allow the sunlight into her house, something she hadn't yet done in all this time.

She rose at once and went to the pull cord. The instant her hand touched it, Wade barked, "Don't."

With that single command, he drove all her resolutions

out of her head and brought the crippling fear back in a rush.

She froze, feeling her knees soften beneath her. She wanted some anger, even just one little flare of it, but it failed to come. Instead she reached for the wall beside the curtain, propping herself against it and closing her eyes.

When her voice emerged, it was weak. "Why?"

"I'm sorry." As if he sensed the storm that had just torn through her, leaving her once again gutted by fear, he came to her, slipping his arm around her waist, and guiding her back to the couch. "I'm sorry," he said again as he helped her sit, and sat beside her. He kept her hand, holding it between both of his, rubbing it with surprising gentleness.

This had to stop, Cory thought. This had to stop. One way or another, she had to find a way to get rid of this fear. Else how was she ever going to do anything again? "I can't keep doing this," she said to Wade, her voice thin. "I can't."

"Keep doing what?"

"Being afraid all the time. And I was just starting to do things to fight it back. Like letting you move in here. Like helping Marsha yesterday. Like opening the damn curtains for the first time in a year! And you told me to stop. Why? *Why?*"

At least she didn't dissolve into tears, but she felt on the brink of it. Ever since that phone call, she'd been teetering as she hadn't teetered in a long time. Before that she'd lived in a steady state at least, even if it was one of grief and fear.

Wade surprised her by drawing her into his arms and holding her. "I'm sorry," he murmured, and stroked her hair gently. "I'm sorry."

"After...after..." The thought fled before a renewed

rush of terror as something struck her. "What do you know?" she asked on a whisper. "What do you know that I don't?"

His hand hesitated, then resumed stroking her hair. "I'm not sure I know anything."

"Tell me!" Her hands balled into fists, and she pounded one of them against his chest, not hard, but enough to make a point. That chest yielded to her fist about as much as cement.

He sighed, tightening his arms around her.

"Wade, don't do this to me. You either know something or you don't."

When his answer seemed slow in coming, she stiffened, ready to pull away. "You can't do this," she said, anger beginning to replace fear, and weakness with strength. "You can't! You can't just waltz into my life and then do things to make me afraid all over again. Not without a reason. I won't stand for it."

"All right. Just keep in mind this may be meaningless."

"Just tell me."

"That man we met at the store yesterday morning? The one we ran into later in the aisle?"

"Yes? What about him?"

"Early this morning I realized he was driving the car behind the woman who waved to us as we were walking back to the house."

She hardly remembered the incident and had to make herself think back. Yes, a man had driven past them, right after that woman. She tipped her head back, trying to look at him. "But it was a different car."

"Yes, it was. But it was the same man. Maybe he just owns two cars."

No matter how hard she tried, she couldn't remember

the face of the man in the car during their walk. "How can you be sure? I can't even remember what he looked like."

"Training. If I hadn't gotten so lazy over the last six months, I'd have picked up on it right away. And he might just have two cars. A lot of folks do."

He looked down at her at last, his obsidian eyes like chips of stone. "I can't ignore it. Coincidence or not, I *cannot* ignore it."

She bit her lip, then said, "That's what made you come down so early this morning. Why you went out to jog. You were looking for him."

He nodded. "I didn't find him."

"So it could be coincidence."

"Maybe."

She shook her head a little, trying to sort through a bunch of conflicting thoughts. Finally she came up with one question. "That phone call couldn't be part of it, could it? I mean…" She wanted to believe it was all random chance, but the phone call kept rearing up in her mind, some part of her insisting it was no prank. "It doesn't make sense. Why call me if you know where I am?"

"Because maybe you don't know exactly which of a handful of women is your target."

"And how would that prove a damn thing?"

He loosened his hold on her, giving her space, but she didn't move away. She didn't want to. Odd considering that he was busy ripping her newfound courage to shreds. Not that it had been much to begin with.

He spoke finally. "Sometimes the only way to identify a target is to do something that makes them take a revealing action."

She searched his face, but it remained unreadable. "You've done that?"

"A couple of times."

"It works?"

"It did for me."

"But I haven't done anything since the call! So that can't be what's going on."

"Maybe. Maybe not."

"Stop being so elliptical. Just tell me what you're thinking. Please!"

"I moved in here right before you got the call. What if the person trying to locate you saw me only after the call?"

Her stomach sank, and right along with it her heart. "Bodyguard," she whispered. Then she had another horrifying thought. "Marsha got a dog."

"If I were them, I doubt I'd pay much attention to a dog."

She was feeling sicker by the second. "No. Especially not when they could trace her back if they want to. If they can."

"Can they?"

In that question she heard the million unanswered questions her own life had become. She had as good as admitted what was going on here. And he had apparently figured out plenty on his own. Now what? Tell the truth, or leave the lies hanging out there. The omissions. The secrets.

Then she had another thought. "What if..." This one really sickened her. So much so she wrenched away from him and jumped up from the couch. She backed away, wrapping her arms around herself, staring at him, feeling horror start to grow.

"What if I'm the one hunting you?" he asked. "Good question. Call the sheriff right now. Tell him to come get me. Tell him whatever you want."

"And then what?"

"And then I'll leave. I'll be gone from this county as fast as I can pack my duffel."

Did she want that? No...no... Not if he was who he was really supposed to be. "You know too much about me."

"Lady, I know nothing about you. I've guessed some things, but you sure as hell haven't told me anything."

"What did you guess?"

He passed a hand over his face. "Will it scare you if I get up and pace? I'm not really good at holding still unless I have to."

She waved a hand, indicating permission. God, when he stood he seemed to fill the entire room.

He started pacing, but slowly, taking care not to come too close to her. "You know I noticed how afraid you are."

"Yes."

"Well, I noticed some other things, too, and last night it just all kind of came together for me. The way when you talk about things from your past you hesitate and then skip anything that might actually give away where you lived before. I also noticed that when you got scared by the phone call you turned to the sheriff."

"What does that tell you?"

He looked at her. "That you're scared and on the run from some threat that still haunts you. But you're not running from the law, or your first response wouldn't have been to call Gage Dalton."

She nodded stiffly. "Okay."

"I noticed the security system. You can't afford it."

"No," she admitted.

"I've been involved in WITSEC ops overseas."

"WITSEC?"

"Witness security. Witness protection."

"Oh...my...God..." She sank onto the rocking chair, arms still tightly wrapped around her.

"All the signs are there for someone who can read them. Which most people can't. It took me more than a day to figure it out, so don't worry that you've tipped off everyone in the county. I'm sure you haven't. But it's the only picture that fits. Am I wrong?"

She shook her head stiffly. "It was that easy?"

"Actually, you made it very hard. Like I said, I didn't glom on to it immediately. But when I put a few things together, it was the only explanation I could think of. The alternative was to think you're just crazy, and you're not crazy, Cory."

She felt numb, almost out of her own body, with shock. This man had figured her out so fast, and yet he said it had taken him too long. How did that add up?

But if he'd figured it out, how many others had? No one, he said. But could she safely believe it?

"Trust me," he said, "it wouldn't occur to anyone not familiar with the protocols. You don't give anything away."

"I...find that hard to believe, now."

"Well, believe it. WITSEC is not the first thing that would occur to anyone about you. It would probably be the last."

"Why?"

"Because no one would suspect you of being a criminal, even if they suspect you have some secrets."

"I'm not a criminal!"

"I know that. It's obvious. And since everyone thinks that only criminals get witness protection, you're even more covered. Very well covered."

Her eyes burned and she felt hollow as she looked at him. "What now?" she asked, a bare whisper.

"Well, all I have is a suspicion. But you can choose how to act on it. Call the sheriff, I'll tell him everything I noticed about the guy. Call the Marshals and they'll move you again. Or…I can try to protect you until we get something solid."

She'd already made up her mind she didn't want to move again. Once was enough. What few tenuous connections she had managed to make here were more than she wanted to sacrifice. She couldn't face another blank slate in a blank town, couldn't face having to start all over again, small though her start here had really been. After all, there was Emma, Marsha, Gage, Nate and Marge Tate. While she hadn't exactly gotten close, she had come to know them a bit. And she discovered she wanted to know them even better.

She raised her eyes to his, resolve steadying her. "I'm not running again."

He nodded. "I kind of decided the same thing this morning."

She nodded slowly. "I guess you did." Her decision made, her muscles began to uncoil slowly, one by one. "I guess I need to tell you the story."

"Cory, you don't have to tell me a damned thing. I can work this without knowing. Your secrets can remain your secrets. But I gather, since you didn't recognize the guy at the store, that he's not someone you're afraid of."

"No. Actually…I saw only one man. The man who killed my husband and shot me."

"Shot you?" He stopped short.

She nodded, and for some reason she didn't understand, she opened her robe and tugged her pajama top up enough to reveal the scar across her midriff. "He killed my baby, too."

He swore, a word she wasn't used to hearing, and the

next thing she knew he'd gathered her up off the chair and was carrying her through the house toward her bedroom. There he laid her down on the queen-size bed, and stretched out beside her. Without another word, he drew her into a close embrace, as if he wanted to surround her with the shield of his body. As if he wanted to shelter her from it all.

But nothing could. She stared blindly at his chin as her head rested on his upper arm, feeling as if a wind had blown through her and left her empty in every way, empty of her past, empty of her hopes and dreams, empty of feeling.

Something in her had died all over again.

In the hollowness that seemed to engulf her, she heard her own voice. It sounded dreamy, disconnected, as if it belonged to someone else and she wasn't in control. And maybe she wasn't.

"I didn't really grieve about the baby," she heard herself say. "I'd just found out that morning. Not enough time for it to become real."

"Mmm." A sound to let her know he was listening, indicating no reaction whatever. She didn't want a reaction. She couldn't have handled one just then.

"What *was* real was that when I woke up from surgery they told me that the only part of Jim I had left was gone, too. I miscarried because of the trauma."

"I'm sorry."

"I was…I was at the best and brightest point of my life that night. The happiest. I had Jim, we were going to have a baby. Maybe no one is entitled to that much happiness."

"Everyone is entitled to that kind of happiness."

"Really? Even you?"

He didn't answer, his silence speaking volumes.

"We went out for dinner to celebrate the news, came

home and…made love. I was so happy I couldn't even sleep. And then some son of a bitch came through our door and took it all away with a gun."

He murmured something, but she didn't try to make it out. She didn't care. Numbness still wrapped her like cotton wool.

"I saw the man. They couldn't find him, though, couldn't identify him. We think…they think…he was working for a drug gang that Jim was about to bring in indictments against. A hired gun, probably. They put me in protection from the instant I got to the hospital. They wouldn't even let me go to Jim's funeral."

His arms tightened a bit, but he said nothing.

"Then, after three months in a safe house, they told me I had to relocate because the word on the street was there was a contract on me because I could identify Jim's murderer."

"Not penny-ante criminals then."

"No. Sometimes I think they were bigger fish than even Jim realized."

"Maybe so."

"There wasn't even a threat beforehand. No warning of any kind. The grand-jury testimony was sealed, the indictments were going to be sealed until they'd rounded everyone up. Maybe there was a leak from somewhere. No one seemed to know. I'll probably never know."

"So three months in a safe house, and then the beginning of the journey to nowhere."

"First, first they did a little plastic surgery. I had a nose job. Just enough to make me look different if anyone had a photo of me. My hair…I have to color it. I wear it differently now. Not big changes."

"Big enough changes. The nose especially. Minimal change, maximum impact."

"That's what they said. Change a nose and you change the whole face."

"That must have been hard for you."

"Even now I sometimes jump when I look in a mirror. Anyway, they moved me through three towns before the nose job. After that, it was another six towns. We'd stay for a while, then they'd pack me up and move me again. They said they were making sure nobody could follow me."

"That's right."

"So you've done that part, too?"

"I've done it all, from the moving to the safe-house protection. Of course, I had the disadvantage of having to protect a couple of really bad guys. Sometimes it seems hardly worth the trouble."

"But it is, right?"

"If they have enough information, yes. In your case, it would have been an honor."

She reached up with one hand and touched his chin. At once he tipped his head to look at her. "I hated it."

"I imagine so."

"But they were really doing everything they possibly could for me. Even while I hated it, I understood it. They went out of their way for me."

"Because you were innocent."

"Because my husband was an assistant U.S. attorney. Because he was one of theirs. I don't kid myself that I would have gotten the same kind of care except for Jim. The only man I could put behind bars is the man who killed a federal prosecutor."

Something in his dark eyes seemed to soften just a hair, but he didn't argue with her, probably because he knew she was right.

"Those kinds of resources," she said, "don't get spent on just anybody. I could have witnessed almost any other murder, been the only one able to identify the killer, and I'd have been on my own before long."

"Seems like you're kind of on your own now."

"That's the way it works."

He nodded. "Most of the time. Are you angry about that?"

"That I got first class instead of coach? How could I be angry about that? What I'm angry about is that every single thing I cared about was stripped away from me. My family, my friends, my career. Sometimes I get angry at myself for letting them take me away."

"Be sensible. What good would it possibly have done to get yourself killed?"

"It might have spared me the limbo I've been living in."

He sighed and cupped her cheek with his warm hand. "Now that's crazy talk. Somehow we'll get this guy and then you can get on with your life."

"Can I? I'm not so sure of that. I was supposed to be safe ever since I got here, but I haven't spent one hour of one day without looking over my shoulder."

"All I can tell you is that things may be coming to a head finally. And that I'm trained for this kind of stuff. And that the last year…Cory, think about all you went through. Of course you couldn't get your bearings, especially when you had good reason to be terrified."

"Apparently so, since I seem to have been found."

He fell silent for a half minute, then said, "You're going to hate me for this."

"For what?"

"Maybe it's a good thing you've been found. Maybe we can deal with this mess for once and for all. Maybe we can get your life back."

"I don't exactly have a life to get back anymore."

"Maybe you could even go home and resume your career."

"I don't know about that. I'm not sure I want to." She was sorry then, sorry because the numbness wore off suddenly and she started feeling again.

And what she felt was a pain deeper and wider than the Grand Canyon. When she started to cry, he just gathered her closer.

As if that would help. As if anything could help.

# Chapter 7

He wiped her tears gently away when she finally quieted. For a long time he just held her, but finally he spoke. "We have to talk about how to deal with this."

"What can we possibly do?

"Well, I'll have to think about that some, but we've still got to talk. We have to sort through your options and my options, and see what we can come up with. There's a lot I can do, but I don't usually plan entire operations by myself."

"Teamwork?"

"Yes. And you're my team. And the sheriff, too. We've got to talk this all over with him."

"I don't want to! What if he calls the Marshals? I don't want to do that again."

"Easy now. I'm sure we can convince Gage not to do that. But as good as I may be, I'm still just one man, Cory. We're going to need some help."

She pressed her face into his shoulder, hating all of this, from the fear that tingled along her spine to the sense of being trapped in a nightmare. Why couldn't she have even an hour of forgetfulness? Was that so much to ask?

Then he shifted her, so that she lay even closer to him. His hand began to run over her back, in steady, soothing circles. At least she thought he meant them to be soothing, but after a few minutes they had a totally different effect. Their passionate kiss yesterday had made her aware of her own needs again, and it didn't take long for her body to remind her that there was still something good in life, something that could be hers for the asking. Something that would make her forget.

But forgetfulness quickly took a backseat to a slowly building heat. Even if her mind and heart quailed, her body wanted to spring back to life, to grasp it with both hands and revel in it.

The softest of sighs escaped her, and she tried to wiggle closer, to say with her body what she could not with words.

His hand paused. As soon as she realized he must have received her silent message, she caught and held her breath, torn between an impulse to pull away and hide, and an almost excruciating hope that he wouldn't turn her away.

She should run. Now. Because she couldn't handle the rejection. Not now. Not after all she had exposed about herself.

*Turn away* now, *don't give him the chance to say no.*

But her body refused to obey her brain. It wanted something primal, something more elemental, an affirmation of life that bypassed all those messed-up circuits in her brain.

His hand left her back. She tensed in expectation of the rejection. But instead he caught her chin and turned her face up so they were looking at one another, only inches apart. His dark eyes searched hers, then moved over her face, as if seeking an answer to some question.

Then he swooped in like a bird of prey and took her mouth in a kiss that stunned her with its intensity, as if he wanted to draw her very soul out of her.

Oh, he knew how to kiss. His tongue mated with hers in a rhythm that exactly matched the pulsing it set off in her body. Fireworks sparkled along her nerve endings, making every inch of her so sensitive that the merest brush of clothing against her skin seemed overwhelmingly sensual and sexual.

He shifted, tugging both her legs between his, so they were locked together and her throbbing center was out of reach even as it grew heavy and aching with need.

All from a kiss.

Her body wanted to fight the imprisonment until she felt his hardness against her belly. She understood then. He wanted her every bit as much as she wanted him, but he would make her wait, slow her down, force patience where she felt none.

And that understanding made her relax into his arms, and let him have his way. *No need to rush.* No need at all. Somehow that freed her in a way desire alone couldn't have.

He continued to hold her close with one arm as he kissed her, but his other hand began to wander. He slipped it under her robe, leaving only her pajamas in the way, and stroked her side from breast to thigh, to the point where his leg trapped hers, then swept it up again, slowly...oh, so slowly.

And as it returned upward, it slid beneath her pajama top, and she gasped. She arched a little, breaking the kiss as she felt his callused palm touch her bare skin. He stayed there for a while, drawing slow, lazy circles on her middle while his mouth claimed hers again, this time more gently, echoing the touch of his fingers.

Impatience started to build in her again, causing her to squirm a bit against his bondage, but he didn't release her. Her breasts ached for a touch, a kiss, until she thought she would go out of her mind from the longing.

Yet still he withheld it.

Tearing her mouth from his, she gasped for air, then reached with one hand to undo the buttons of his shirt. If he wasn't going to give her more, she would take more.

He didn't stop her when she pulled open his shirt and pressed her palm at last to his chest. She thought she even heard a deep sound of pleasure escape him as she began to trace the contours of those hard muscles, glorying in the smoothness of his skin, in the ripples across his belly, in the small points of his nipples. Exquisite. Perfect. As much a feast for her hands as he had been for her eyes.

Then without warning, his hands gripped her around her waist, he freed her from the prison of his legs and leaving her almost dizzy, he lifted her over him, so that she straddled his hips.

A groan escaped her as he tugged her down until her moist yearning depths met his hardness through layers of denim and cotton. What was he doing? She needed to get rid of the clothing that interfered.

But when she reached for the snap of his jeans, he stopped her and murmured roughly, "Just ride me, Cory."

She didn't know what he meant until his hands gripped her hips again and he moved her against him. All of a sudden those layers of fabric didn't seem to matter. Her hips helplessly rocked against him, demanding a solution to the problem of need.

And as she rocked, he slipped his hands up under her nightshirt and cupped her breasts, rubbing his thumbs over her nipples.

He might as well have plugged her into an electric socket. Shocks zinged through her, setting her alight, then zipped to her center, creating an ache that made her forget everything, everything except her need.

"That's the way…" He groaned the words, urging her on, tormenting her even as he encouraged her to ride the cresting wave. And somehow, by keeping them both clothed, he had set her free in an unexpected way.

Set her free to take what she wanted as she rubbed herself against him over and over. Set her free to give in to her need without thought of anything or anyone other than herself.

Free to be.

Free to ride the crest of the wave all the way until she tumbled wildly into the warm waters below.

And knew peace.

She lay on Wade's chest, his arms around her as aftershocks made her tremble. Her legs sprawled on either side of him, leaving her open, and each aftershock caused her to tighten them just a bit against his hips.

She felt more safe, more secure and more relaxed than she had since…the shooting. And she couldn't even rustle up a smidgen of guilt about it.

Well, except that she didn't know if Wade had enjoyed it quite as much as she had, didn't know if he'd found completion himself. And had no way to ask.

Silly, after what they had just shared, an experience all the more exhilarating because of the way he had brought it about, that she should feel a bit shy. But there it was.

But oh, she never would have believed that having sex

while fully clothed could actually enhance the experience, could arouse her so much, could give her such a sense of primitive freedom. In a way, she supposed, it had been an updated version of dragging her away to a cave by her hair. Little finesse, a lot of hunger, and *bam!*

He'd lingered just long enough for her inhibitions to weaken, and then he'd forced her to shed them all. Quick, hot and ready.

And damn, it felt good.

He moved at last, just a bit, lifting a hand to stroke the back of her head, then wind a strand of her hair around his finger.

"You okay?" he asked gruffly.

"I'm fine," she murmured. "You?"

"Pretty amazed, actually."

At that she lifted her head and looked at him. His hard face looked softer now, and even his obsidian eyes seemed less like rock and more like deep waters. "How so?"

"I couldn't begin to explain."

She laid her cheek on his chest again. "Some things beggar words, I guess."

"Maybe so." He released the strand of her hair, and ran a fingertip along the curve of her jaw. "Were you a teacher, before?"

This man had a gift for putting a few pieces together into complete a puzzle, so she guessed it shouldn't have surprised her that he had figured that out. "Why do you ask?"

"Something you said. Well, actually, something you started to say and never finished. You caught yourself just as you started to say the word."

"And you finished it."

"I do that sometimes."

"God, you're incredible. It's like you read minds."

"I'm just observant. You don't have to tell me."

"No, it's okay. I was a teacher. Maybe I'll teach again someday."

"Was there a reason they didn't just get you a certificate here?"

"They felt it would leave too much of a trail." And here was reality, intruding again. She almost wanted to beat her fist on something.

"Sorry, guess I'm ruining the moment."

She must have grown tenser, she thought. In some way he'd picked up on her reaction. He was amazing. In so many ways. Jim had been a sensitive guy, but not this sensitive. "No, I can't hide for long from reality. Not now," she admitted finally. "Not when there may be a threat."

"No." A word of agreement.

Her stomach chose that moment to growl loudly. No more breaks for her today, she thought almost ruefully.

"I think," Wade said after a moment, "that you ought to take a shower while I go make us some breakfast."

"You're going to do the cooking?"

"I told you I know some basics. I may not be able to turn out that pasta thing you managed last night, but I can make a mean scrambled egg, and I can cook it with anything from sunlight, to a flameless ration heater, to a candle to a stove."

"I recommend the stove."

"Since it's available."

She lifted her head and looked at him again. "How do you cook with sunlight?"

"We carry mirrors for signaling. All you have to do is set it up right."

She nodded. "Someday you'll have to show me."

He rolled then, dumping her off him onto the bed. He smiled, actually smiled down at her as he raised himself

on one elbow. "Shower," he repeated. "I'll go make some
edible scrambled eggs."

Then he gave her a quick hard kiss and was gone.

For the first time in forever, Cory thought about what
she was putting on. Ordinarily she grabbed a uniform from
her closet, or just a shirt and jeans, not caring which. But
this morning she dithered over whether she should wear a
denim skirt, the brown plaid shirt with the piped yoke, or
a plainer polo shirt.

Finally she told herself to stop being ridiculous, pulled
on fresh jeans—in Florida jeans were rarely worn except
when it was cool, but here everyone wore them even if
it was hot—and the gold polo shirt. She even added a
bit of lipstick and mascara, from among the few personal
possessions she'd been able to bring with her: nothing that
wouldn't fit into a suitcase.

Good smells reached her as soon as she opened her
bedroom door. Apparently Wade had added some bacon
to the menu from the groceries he had bought yesterday,
and from the aroma she could tell he'd brewed fresh coffee.
Not only a second cup today, but a second pot. Now that
was an extravagance she hadn't enjoyed in far too long.

When she entered the kitchen, she found the table
already set. The bacon was draining on a paper towel over a
plate on the table, and a stack of toast stood on the counter
beside the toaster, already buttered.

"You can cook," she said with surprise.

"Told you. What do you think happens when we're at
some small firebase on our own? We take turns, and God
help the guy who can't even make a decent breakfast."

A little laugh escaped her.

"And here it's easy. You even have a toaster. Take a seat.
I'll bring you coffee."

She sat, saying, "I thought you guys had prepackaged meals. What are they called?"

"MREs. Meals, Ready-to-Eat. Three lies in three letters. I won't give you any of the slang names for them."

"But you cooked anyway?"

"When we move, we move fast and travel light. Try to live off the land. Besides, what you eat affects how you smell, so it's best to eat local diet as much as possible."

She noticed his consistent use of the present tense, and wondered if he really found it that hard to put his years as a SEAL in the past, or if the present situation had just put him back in the mental mode as if he'd never left.

"I never would have thought of that," she said as he joined her at the table with the toast and eggs.

The eggs were perfectly cooked, not too dry or moist, though he evidently hadn't whipped them. But why would that occur to him, considering he had done most of his cooking in the field? He'd spiced them with just a hint of cayenne, too, making them more savory.

"Perfect," she said, complimenting him.

One corner of his mouth lifted in a smile. "Thanks. I hate overdone eggs. I'll eat them, but I won't like it."

For a man who said he didn't know how to converse, he was doing a darn good job of it. Maybe something in him had begun to open up, too, as it had inside her.

Almost as soon as she had the thought, he clammed up again. They ate breakfast in silence and hardly said a word as they washed up afterward.

But then, after they moved back into the shadowed living room, he said, "I'm going to call the sheriff."

And ugly reality came crashing back down.

Wade called Gage then excused himself to jog around the block. He didn't say why he was going, but Cory figured it out without having to ask: he was going to make sure the guy he'd noticed yesterday wasn't hovering around. She spent the time pretending to tidy up the house, although all she really needed to do was some dusting. She'd done all her major housework just a few days ago, and while the dust hadn't really built up since then, it gave her an excuse to keep moving, and moving seemed like a good way to hold her fears at bay. Barely.

Wade returned to the house at the same time Gage arrived. They entered together, Gage in civvies, and joined Cory in the living room. Before she could even greet Gage or put down her dustrag, Wade said, "I didn't see him."

Cory wasn't sure that eased her mind at all, given what Wade suspected. She dropped the rag on the table, brushed her hand quickly against her jeans, then shook Gage's hand and invited him to sit. "Coffee?"

He shook his head. "I'm fine. Thanks, Cory. So let's cut to the chase. Wade said next to nothing except you needed to see me."

Cory nodded, then sank slowly onto the Boston rocker. Gage took the easy chair again, and Wade the end of the couch nearest to her. She looked at Wade. "You explain. Please."

"Okay." Wade leaned forward, resting his elbows on his splayed knees, and folded his hands. "I knew from the outset Cory had something to be afraid of. I was here when she got that call, after all, the one she called you about."

Gage nodded. Cory noted he wasn't giving a thing away. He wasn't likely to speak a word until he was certain who knew what, and what they thought was going on. Protecting her secrets.

"Anyway, I won't bore you with all the irrelevant details, unless you think you need them. I've been on WITSEC operations overseas, and by early this morning I realized that Cory must be in Witness Protection."

Gage immediately stiffened. "I don't think…"

"Relax," Wade said. "No one else would guess. I figured it out because I was here, I could see the fear, and some of her omissions were glaring, to say the least."

Gage swore and looked at Cory. "I'm sorry. I never would have brought Wade here if I'd ever thought someone would figure this out."

"It's okay," Cory said. "I'm not upset that he knows. Far from it. And honestly, I think he's right when he says no one else would guess. He figured it out because he had the experience to put the pieces together."

"I hope so," Gage said flatly. Right now he wasn't looking too friendly.

Wade appeared untroubled by the reaction. Or maybe he had just gone back to his inner fortress. Cory surprised herself by hoping like hell that he hadn't. She didn't want him to go back to that. She kind of liked the man he'd revealed himself to be, even though he had as yet revealed little.

"Anyway," Wade continued with little expression, "I also figured out why someone might have made that phone call, and I remembered something I would have caught on to immediately if I hadn't spent the last six months trying to lose most of what I learned as a SEAL."

"And that is?"

"First let me explain a method we used a time or two in operations. You don't always have a clear idea of who your target is. Sometimes you don't have a photo, or even a decent description. So what we would do was try to scare a group of potential targets, then watch who took the most revealing action."

Gage nodded slowly. "So you're saying you don't think that phone call was a prank."

"It might well not be. And the reason I'm suspicious is because we saw the same guy at two different places yesterday. He followed us into the parking lot at the grocery, then we ran into him again in the aisle."

"That doesn't mean anything."

"That alone wouldn't. However, when we were walking home from the park together yesterday afternoon, I saw the guy again. Driving a different car down the street out front."

"Hell." Gage scratched his head almost irritably.

"I realize, of course, that some people have more than one car. I realize that call may indeed have been a prank. But when you put it all together with Cory's being in protection because she's the only person who can identify the man who murdered her husband, it doesn't pay to ignore coincidence."

"No. No, it doesn't. But what would you say is the revealing action Cory took? Because I don't see that she did a thing."

"Except take me in. And the guy who's watching might not have seen me arrive before the call. Actually no reason he should have, because he wouldn't have been looking for telltales until *after* the call…and I arrived basically right before it."

Gage nodded slowly. "It's possible."

"The thing is," Wade continued, "if you assume he's got his eye on, oh, say half a dozen women who've moved here sometime over the last year, and he has to watch all of them, he's going to be looking around at one after another to see who did what after the phone call. And after the call he sees two things: Cory and her friend Marsha go to the pound and pick out a dog for Marsha. That might have been enough to point a finger at Marsha except that then Cory comes home and a very short time later she emerges to go to the grocery store with me."

"And you could easily look like a bodyguard."

Cory spoke. "I think Wade is right, Gage. Especially when you consider that I not only suddenly have Wade living here, but we went shopping together. Ordinarily when people do that, they have a long-term relationship of some kind. But Wade wasn't in my life until the day before yesterday. In fact, when I look back at it, it could easily have appeared that I was doing the shopping and Wade was just *there*."

"Okay," Gage said. "And then you saw him again in the afternoon. In a different car."

"And he didn't even glance at us," Wade remarked, "while the woman in the car ahead of him smiled and waved."

"Most folks in Conard County smile and wave. We're pretty sure someone is an outsider when they don't." He rubbed his chin then looked at Cory.

"But you can't identify him as the man who killed your husband?"

"No, he didn't look anything like that man. I'd have noticed instantly if he had."

Gage cocked one eyebrow and looked at them both. "You know how thin this is?"

"Very," Wade said immediately.

"But it's still not something I can overlook. Give me a minute to think."

For an instant, crazily, Cory heard the *Jeopardy* music in her head. Where had that come from? She looked at Wade and saw a man who was infinitely capable of waiting when necessary, one who might prefer to be moving, but one who could also sit as still as a statue when he chose. He chose to be a statue right now.

Finally Gage spoke. "Okay. The way I see it is that while we can't be sure, Wade is making a good point about revealing actions. The guy who is after Cory may not know her appearance has been changed. They don't often do that in Witness Protection, but given that he can't find anyone who matches her appearance exactly, that kind of provocation would make sense, assuming he somehow found out where she is. And the only way I can think that he would have learned that is if he got the info from someone who works for the Marshals."

Cory's heart skipped a beat then climbed right into her throat. "I didn't even think of that," she whispered hoarsely.

Gage's dark eyes turned her way. "It's been a year, Cory, so it's obvious the Marshals succeeded in making sure no one followed you. So the only way this guy could have any idea you're here is if someone in the program talked. Some kind of leak."

"My God," she whispered. Her skin started to crawl with fear and anxiety again. "What else might he know?"

Gage shook his head. "I don't know, but if Wade is right about that call, then he didn't manage to find out your new name. So whatever someone leaked, it was minimal, or this guy would have your name and address."

"Yes, that's true."

"And it would be my guess that you didn't follow the usual protocol of using the same first name you had before, along with a last name that starts with the same initial, or he'd just as good as have your new name and address."

"No, they told me that's what most people do but one of the Marshals…" Her voice broke, then steadied. "One of the Marshals was a good friend of my husband's. He seemed more worried than the rest, and he was the one who suggested I come up with a totally different name."

"Did you?" Wade asked suddenly. "Totally different? Or could there be a link between your name now and your past?"

Cory bit her lip. "My mother's name was Cory. And her maiden name was McFarland."

Wade looked at Gage. "He could find that out, now that he thinks he might have located her."

Gage nodded. "All too easily. Assuming he bothers to look."

"Why wouldn't he look?" Cory asked, her heart still beating a nervous tattoo.

"Because, assuming this guy does indeed know where you are, he may feel he's already got all the information he needs. I can't read his mind, Cory. I just know we have to take steps."

"What kind of steps? Are you going to call the Marshals?"

Gage shook his head. "Why in the name of all that's holy would I call them? If this isn't just some kind of weird coincidence, then we're dealing with an organization that has already leaked information about you. They're the last ones I'm going to call now. Unless that's what you want me to do."

Cory shook her head quickly. "No. No. I don't want to run again. I can't do that again." Her entire soul seemed to be screaming that another round of running and hiding would break her forever. Clenching her fists, she said again, "No."

Gage's face gentled. "Not even to save your life?"

"What life? If I don't make a stand now, I'll never have one. I'm tired of always being frightened, of always looking over my shoulder. This guy is a killer and I'm the only one who can put him behind bars. If he's found me, then I want to finish it now. I can't…I can't keep living this way. I just can't."

"All right then." Gage stood. "I won't even call the Marshals for a sketch of the murderer. I'm going to send an artist over here to do one just for us. I'd also like a sketch of the guy Wade thinks was following you. Are you up to that, Cory?"

"Definitely." The decision was made. She would stand her ground.

And amazingly, that decision calmed her. The calm probably wouldn't last, but for now it felt wonderful to have finally made the choice. "I'm through letting that guy ruin my life," she said, looking from Gage to Wade. "And frankly, the way I've been living is no life at all. So let's finish it, one way or another."

The police sketch artist turned out to be nothing like Cory had imagined. Esther Nighthawk was a beautiful redhead who wore a long skirt and leaned heavily on a cane. Under one arm, she carried a sketchbook.

"Oh, I just do this to help out," Esther said as Cory invited her into the kitchen so she'd have a table to work on. "I'm a full-time watercolorist, but I enjoy the challenge of doing these sketches for the sheriff."

She settled on the chair facing Cory, and opened her sketchpad to a blank page. Then she pulled a box of drawing pencils from the large woven bag she carried. "I'm sorry we haven't met before. My husband and I live on a ranch—he raises sheep—and I only get to town every couple of weeks for shopping. Or when one of the children needs to come in for something."

"That sounds like a nice life," Cory said almost wistfully.

"It is." Esther's gaze softened a bit. "My life sure changed radically after I met Craig. Before then I spent most of my time hiding."

"From what?"

"Life. I had myself convinced that my art was all that mattered, but basically I was just afraid of a whole bunch of things. *Neurotic* would probably be a good word."

"And now?"

"Now I love every minute of every day." Esther smiled. "So, you're going to help me draw a picture of a man Gage seems to be worried about?"

"Yes. I'll try, anyway."

"You talk, I'll draw."

So Cory closed her eyes for a minute, and tried to summon her memory of the man who killed Jim. "It's hard," she said after a moment. "You know how faces seem to skate away when you concentrate on them?"

"I know. That's why you're not going to concentrate. You're going to give me one detail to start with. I'll draw it, and you watch. As you watch me, tell me what's right and what's not. It'll work. Trust me."

So that's what Cory did. She started with the general shape of the guy's head, and after a few erasures she decided it was correct. Then a nose, and that needed only three iterations. Little by little, the image built, and Esther was right, it was easier to say when something was wrong than to give an exact description of what was right.

A half hour later and she was looking at an eerily familiar face, one she couldn't have pulled out of her memory any other way.

"That's him," she said. "You couldn't possibly get any closer."

Esther nodded, smiling. "It's never as hard as people think it will be."

"Only because you're such a good artist."

Wade joined them, and together he and Cory helped create a sketch of the man they had met at the grocery.

"This is truly amazing," Cory remarked again as she looked at the second sketch. "I thought I'd forgotten him entirely, but this is him."

"You're very gifted," Wade told Esther. "Very gifted."

Esther laughed. "Keep stroking my ego. More is always better." She began to pack up her materials. "Listen, why don't you come out to the ranch for dinner some night? I'd like a chance to get to know you better, and maybe someday you can tell me what this is all about."

"I'd love that," Cory said immediately, realizing she would. The urge to put down roots here had become almost compulsive since just a few days ago. It was as if warning flags had started to pop up in her psyche, telling her that if she continued on her current course she might as well die.

And along with all those warning flags, a desire to start making connections again, a real life again, pushed her.

Possibly into a very dangerous place, the dangerous place she'd spent more than a year hiding from.

Cory said goodbye to Esther at the door, then stepped back away from the opening as Wade ushered the woman to her car.

"Lock up and set the alarm after me," he murmured as he passed. "I'm going to scout a bit before I come back."

She did as told, then went to sit in the living room and wait. How had she survived the past year living this way? Waiting for a doom that never came, too afraid to lead any real kind of life, trying to be invisible even at her job.

With absolute certainty, she knew she couldn't return to that way of life. She'd been dying by inches for too long. She couldn't do it anymore. No way.

And if that meant possibly sticking her head into a noose, then that was what she would do.

Wade returned about twenty minutes later, quieting then resetting the alarm before he joined her.

"You're going to go crazy," she said when he sat beside her.

"I am? Why?"

"Because I just looked in the mirror."

"Meaning?"

She gave a little shake of her head. "Inside this house is limbo. I sit here doing next to nothing, worrying, grieving, afraid. You're going to go nuts locked in here with me."

"I see." He drummed his fingers briefly on the arm of the couch. "I won't go crazy. I've been known to sit in hides for days on end waiting for the right moment, or the target, to appear. I can do it."

"Well, I'm tired of it. I was just sitting here wondering how I'd managed to do nothing for so long."

"Aww, Cory," he said quietly. "Give yourself a break. You went through a terrible trauma, and then you got dumped on a foreign shore where almost nothing was familiar anymore. You needed time. You took it."

"You're very generous."

"Just calling it the way I see it. If you'd lost your husband but been allowed to remain with your friends and family, to keep your job, you could have coped with your grief better. If you hadn't lost your husband but had simply been obliged to move, you would have coped with that, too."

"So sure?"

"I've watched your transformation over the last two days. I'm sure. What's more, I think you need to cut yourself some slack because you experienced two major traumas, both of them stressful to the extreme. And then you had a killer to fear. Most people would have dug a hole and pulled it in after themselves."

"That's basically what I did."

"But look at you now. For whatever reason, you've reached the point where you're ready to take action. But that doesn't mean the time you took to hide and lick your wounds was wrong."

She would never have imagined this man could be so kind. Or that he would be willing to put himself out there the way he had today. He'd seemed so self-contained, so impervious, so...rocklike. Yet while she still felt the almost insurmountable strength in him, she had found a kindness and understanding that seemed like a gift.

It was likely that if she'd ever put herself out there over the past year, she might have found that kind of kindness and understanding from other sources, but she'd been terrified into silence not only by the fact that a killer might be hunting her, but also by all the strictures the Marshals had placed on her. All the warnings. They had meant well, she was sure, but how do you pick up a life that had been so completely and totally interrupted?

"It was like they wanted me to erase myself and start out like a baby all over again."

He nodded. "From their point of view, that seems like the best way to handle it. But it also leaves you without much of a starting point for anything."

"Others are probably more resilient."

"Most of those others didn't see their husbands murdered and lose their baby at the same time."

The stark truth of that bowed her head. She drew a shaky breath, hoping she wouldn't dissolve into tears again.

He slipped his arm around her shoulders and squeezed gently. "Just grant that you've been doing the best you can."

"I want to do better."

"You've made that clear." He paused for a moment, then said, "The way you need to think about the last year or so is that you were wounded. And it takes time to heal. So while you're recovering, there are lots of things your body won't let you do. Or in your case, your mind and emotions. Things that need to rest will rest."

"I hardly think being totally terrified was much of a rest."

"How can you know?"

"What do you mean?" She turned her head to look at him.

"Maybe the fear was a rest from things that were even harder for you to bear."

That drew her up short. She hadn't thought of it that way before, not at all. "Maybe," she said finally. "I know how it's been feeling, though."

"How's that?"

"Like I've been stuck in a quagmire of awful feelings with no way out."

"And now?"

"I see a door. I don't like what might be on the other side. It scares me. But, like I said, I've got to crawl out of this swamp or I'm going to die anyway."

"We'll get you out."

He sounded so confident. She wished she could be as sure. But life offered absolutely no guarantees, and if she had just accepted that months ago, she might have already started to construct a new life.

Of course, if she had done that, she'd still be sitting here worried that the killer might have found her. Would it have made it any easier for her if she'd allowed herself to put down all those roots she was thinking of now? Not one bit.

In fact, it might have become even scarier. And this was already going to be scary enough.

# Chapter 8

She tried to pass the time reading a book, but that didn't work at all. Wade prowled the house from time to time only to return to the living room and sit for a while. She had no idea if he was peering out windows or what. Maybe he just couldn't hold still.

She could barely stand it herself. Finally she closed the book and looked at him. "Are we supposed to just sit here indefinitely like bumps on a log?"

One corner of Wade's mouth lifted and he came to sit beside her on the sofa. "What would you ordinarily do?"

"Exactly this," she admitted. "Only now I'm too antsy."

"Well, I don't think we should do anything until Gage tells us he has his ducks in a row. Waiting is always the hardest part."

She pursed her lips, trying to find some way to anticipate what might come next. "This guy, this killer, he wasn't afraid to come to our house in the dead of night, knock on the door and shoot everything that moved."

"Apparently not."

"So what's to keep him from doing the same thing here?"

"Nothing, except that I'm an unknown in the equation. That won't hold him back indefinitely, but I'm sure it's giving him pause."

"What kind of pause?"

"He's probably wondering just what kind of protection I can provide. Whether there's a way he can separate us. All of which is based on the assumption that he's really found you."

She sighed. "I wish I knew for certain."

"There are times when you can act, and times when you simply have to *re*act. This is one of those times that we have to wait to react. Because we don't know anything for certain."

She felt a crooked smile twist her lips. "Listen to me. I spent more than a year just letting myself be pushed one way or another and now all of a sudden I want to do something. Anything."

"I know that feeling."

"You probably do." She looked down at the book she was still holding. "I still can't understand what they thought they'd accomplish by killing Jim. It's not like they could erase the grand-jury testimony, or prevent indictments from being handed down."

"I don't know. Maybe they thought that if they removed one prosecutor, the government would have a hard time finding someone else to take over. Intimidation is the only reason I can see."

"I doubt it worked."

"But you don't know?"

She shook her head. "Jim didn't talk about his cases with me. He couldn't. So even if I tried to check newspaper stories or court records, I couldn't tell which case was his."

"But you knew he was after a drug gang."

"That was all I knew. And I'm sure he wasn't the only prosecutor working on a case like that. In a way it's hard not knowing if all his work put those guys in jail. But at the same time..." She shrugged. "What difference does it really make? It won't change anything. Not for me, or Jim, or our baby."

He turned her a little, cupping her chin with his hand, and kissed her gently. "I'm so sorry."

If he meant the kiss to be comforting, it went beyond that. Way beyond that. She wished she knew how his kiss could drive everything else from her mind in a flash. And this one hadn't even attempted to be sexy.

She searched his dark eyes and caught her breath as she saw the heat there. She wasn't alone in her sudden desire, not alone at all. Yet he didn't press her, didn't even try to tip her in that direction.

His hunger for her went straight to her head, lifting her out of herself so that she forgot everything except this man and the heaviness growing between her thighs, a heaviness that demanded an answer.

There was something incredible in arousing a man so powerful and self-contained so easily and quickly. Maybe it was the only way he felt he could truly connect anymore. Maybe he would have responded that way to any woman.

She didn't care. She knew what she wanted, and it was right in front of her. In his eyes she could see that he wanted it, too.

Her fingers moved before she realized it, reaching for

the buttons of his shirt. He waited, letting her unfasten
them, watching her face intently the whole time. When
the last button was undone, she looked down at this chest
and sighed.

"You're beautiful," she said, meaning it. Pressing her
palms to that wonderful, warm skin, she ran her hands
over him, feeling the rocks and rills of honed muscle,
glorying in the sensations and in the way he indulged her
exploration.

A slightly ragged breath escaped him. "Are you sure?"
he murmured. "Very sure?"

"Yes." The word came out on the last puff of air in her
lungs, and hardly had it escaped her, than he scooped her
up in his powerful arms and carried her back toward her
bedroom.

"I won't stop this time," he warned her. "No half
measures."

"I don't want half measures." The truest words she had
spoken in a long, long time.

"No quarter," he said.

She wasn't sure what he meant by that, but she was
eager to take this ride all the way to the end. Not only did
she want this, she needed this. All of it.

He laid her on the bed in her half-darkened room and
stood over her like a hero of myth, so big, so hard, almost
unreal in his strength and power.

He shrugged off his shirt, then made it clear what was
coming when he reached for his belt and the snap of his
jeans.

Was she sure? Oh, yes. She watched with hungry
fascination, hearing each tooth in the zipper as he drew
it slowly down. It was the sexiest sound she had ever
heard.

"Stop me now," he said, pausing. "Now."

"No." His own word flung back at him.

She dragged her gaze up from where his hands rested against his fly and saw a lazy smile start to curve his mouth. His eyelids drooped a little with passion, but the rest of his face hardened with hunger.

He kicked off his shoes, then in one smooth movement shoved his pants down and discarded his socks. When he straightened, he was naked to her gaze, and what a breathtaking sight he was.

Michelangelo had never carved a more perfect male body. Nor had anyone to her knowledge ever carved a statue with an erection like that. He was big, he was hard and he was ready.

And the sight of his readiness made her damp, so damp she might have been embarrassed if she weren't already in thrall to her needs. And his. For his need excited her even more than her own.

He bent over her, his fingers pausing just briefly as he once again warned her. "Last chance."

She had begun to pant with the hunger he had already stoked in her, and it was hard to say one word, just one word: "Yesss…"

He stripped her clothes away impatiently, tossing each piece across the room until she lay naked. He paused a moment, drinking her with his eyes, leaving her feeling at once utterly vulnerable and utterly beautiful. No one had ever looked at her like that before, not even Jim, as if she were the most desirable woman he had ever seen. Just that look was enough to make her nipples harden and her center throb so hard it almost hurt.

In that instant, she became woman primal. Everything else vanished entirely. Nothing mattered except this man and this moment. She hardly noticed that he used the few seconds to don protection, because she watched his eyes as they traveled over her like a caress.

Lying over her, his leg pinning hers, his arms holding her tight, he plundered her mouth with a kiss so hungry and needful it echoed all the pain inside her. His hands began to knead her flesh with a heat and longing that just missed being painful. She didn't care. Each touch made her feel so wanted, and oh, heavens, how much she needed to feel wanted.

His mouth closed on her nipple, sending spears of longing straight to her womb. His hand stroked the smooth skin of her hip, and then dived impatiently between her thighs, seeking her heat, her moisture, her life-giving core. She was caught in a storm, with no desire to escape. Whatever he took seemed rightfully his.

Raising his head, he muttered guttural words of encouragement as his touch lifted her higher and higher. Too fast, she thought dizzily, but even that objection drifted away as he took her closer and closer to the brink she dimly sensed was waiting.

"So sweet," he muttered in her ear, and yet another river of excitement poured through her. "Come on, Cory, that's the way."

When her hands clawed at him and the sheets, needing something to hang on to, he grabbed them and moved them upward, wrapping her fingers around the spindles of her headboard. "Hang on," he muttered roughly. "Don't let go." Then he settled between her legs.

Gasping for air, clinging so tightly to the headboard that she dimly felt her hands aching, she opened her eyes and looked up at him. He loomed over her in the dim room, huge and powerful, so strong. She had never imagined, never dreamed, that anything could be as overwhelming as these moments. Every cell in her body was begging for him, begging for completion, for the answer to the screaming ache he had awakened in her body.

He touched her, gently. He found that delicate knot of nerves, then rubbed so carefully, lifting her higher and higher until she hung suspended in exquisite agony and nearly screamed his name.

"Now," he demanded. Slipping an arm beneath her hips, he lifted her to him and took her in one swift, deep thrust, filling an emptiness she had forgotten could exist.

The precipice was close, so close, and his every movement drove her nearer the edge. Letting go of the headboard, she grabbed his shoulders, digging her fingers into smooth, muscled flesh, drawing him down, needing his weight on her as she had seldom needed anything. Needing him.

"Let it happen," he growled in her ear. "Damn it, let it happen!"

Then, with a single, long, deep thrust of his hips, he pushed her over the edge. Moments later his face contorted and he followed her over.

Cory thought the explosion inside her would never end.

They lay tangled together, sweaty and exhausted. Too weary and sated, Cory thought, to work up even a smidgen of fear. The best medicine in the world.

When Wade tried to lever himself off her, she grabbed his shoulders, afraid he might leave.

"I'm not going anywhere," he murmured. He slid off her, to lie beside her on his back, still breathing heavily.

The air felt cool against her hot, damp skin, another delicious contrast. Yes, they needed to cool down, but she hated not feeling the touch of his skin. When she blindly reached out with her hand, his was there to grip hers and hold it. When she gave his fingers a little squeeze, he squeezed back.

"Why can't life always be like this?" she asked softly. As soon as the question emerged, she knew reality was returning, and there was no way to hold it off.

"If life were always like this, we'd never do anything else." He surprised her with a note of humor in his voice.

She turned on her side and smiled at him, a smile that felt easier than any she'd tried to frame in fifteen months. "Would that be so bad?"

A small chuckle escaped him. "No way."

Reaching out, she trailed a finger over his still-damp chest and downward to his hip bone. His manhood responded with a small leap. "Mmm, I could get used to this."

"Used to what?" he asked.

"Having you at my mercy."

"Ah!" In one swift movement, so fast it caught her utterly by surprise, he pushed her on her back and leaned over her, his leg imprisoning hers, his dark eyes holding her. "Who is at whose mercy?"

A truly silly smile rose to her lips. "I like it either way."

"Good." Now he ran a fingertip over her, tracing circles around her breasts and down to her belly, causing her to shiver. "We'll take turns."

"Soon?" she asked hopefully.

"Soon," he said, one corner of his mouth lifting. "But maybe not right now."

She sighed. "Okay."

He lowered his head and brushed a light kiss on her lips. "I'd like nothing better, Cory. But Gage will probably call soon."

She couldn't argue with that, though she wanted to push

back the dark shadows that edged into the corners of her mind. Yes, there were things they had to face, maybe had to face soon, but she felt a huge tide of resentment, something she'd never felt before. Before it had always been the fear and grief, leaving room for little else.

"I resent this," she announced, then instantly regretted her words as she saw him pull back a little. Of course he would misunderstand. "Not you," she hastily said. "I just hate that I'm feeling good for the first time in forever and now I have to think of...of..."

"I understand." His infinitesimal withdrawal vanished as he moved closer, and dropped another light kiss on her mouth.

"How bad was it?" she asked, stroking his short hair as he laid his cheek on her breast.

"What?"

"Your childhood."

He stiffened a bit, and said nothing. Time seemed to drag as she held her breath, wondering if she had pushed too far into tender territory. It really was none of her business, and she suspected this was a man who didn't like admitting his vulnerability, despite what he had tried to share with her over coffee in the wee hours.

"It was bad," he said finally. "I spent a lot of time locked in closets. My dad was fond of whipping me with the buckle end of his belt."

"My God!"

"I survived."

"But..."

He reached up and laid a finger over her mouth. "I survived," he said firmly. "What doesn't kill you makes you stronger."

"You really believe that?"

"Yes."

Perhaps, she thought. Perhaps. But surviving didn't necessarily mean the scars were gone, either emotionally or physically. She had sensed the emotional ones quickly, in some of his almost apologetic statements. As if he felt a need to erase himself. Another thought occurred to her.

"Do you feel like a fish out of water now, away from the SEALs I mean?"

At that he lifted his head. "Lady, if you're going to ask a man to bare his soul, it might be best to let him choose the time and place."

She felt hurt. Unreasonably so, she tried to tell herself, but it didn't quite erase the pang. Logically she knew that women were more likely to become emotionally attached through the act of lovemaking than men, and logically she realized the experience they had just shared had probably made her feel a whole lot closer to him than it had made him feel to her. They were strangers, after all, brought together by a coincidence, and now held together by a threat. He undoubtedly planned to move on as soon as he sorted out whatever it was he had come here to deal with.

And she would be left alone again. Common sense dictated that she not allow herself to grow close to this man. She needed to think of their lovemaking as merely a way to affirm life, and not one thing more.

She ought to know better, and clutching at straws just because a man was decent enough not to leave her in the lurch with this mess was dangerous. She didn't think she could take another loss, so why set herself up for one?

She tried to smile at him, but her face felt pinched. "I need to get dressed. Gage might call at any minute."

"Ah, hell," he said and rolled onto his back.

She looked at him and saw he was staring at the ceiling now. "What?"

"I just hurt you, and I really didn't want to do that."

She felt another pang, this time for him. "No. Really. It's just a girl thing, expecting confidences at a time like this. I know better."

He turned his head to look at her. "I should know better, too. I'm sorry."

Then he jackknifed up off the bed and started hunting up clothes. Hers he dropped beside her on the bed. He climbed into his own swiftly, and left the room before he even finished buttoning and zipping.

One hot tear rolled down Cory's face. She had tried to reach out, and had reached out in exactly the wrong way at the wrong time.

Why would any man want her anyway? She had become a terrified husk of a woman, with nothing left inside her that anyone else would want.

She definitely ought to know better.

Wade stood in the kitchen, filled with self-loathing. He had started another pot of coffee brewing, because coffee had fueled him through some of the most difficult times in his life and had become a habit he clung to the way some people clung to a cup of tea or a blanket for comfort.

He'd drunk it instant, mixed with water barely safe for drinking. He'd sucked it down hot and thick on shipboard. He'd guzzled it thin and watery when what few grounds he had needed to be reused. It didn't much matter how it tasted as much as it mattered that he could cradle a cup in his hands and take comfort in one of life's small habits.

Despite warning himself, he'd taken the step: he'd made love to the woman. And despite warning her and himself that he couldn't make connections, he'd taken the one action most likely to create a connection. You didn't make love to a woman like that and expect her to treat it as a form of entertainment.

So he'd taken that all-too-critical step, he'd started forming a connection, a connection he absolutely believed himself incapable of sustaining. If he had an ounce of common sense, he'd rupture it right now, pack his bags and get out of here before he did some real harm.

He couldn't do that, not with the threat he believed to be lurking. Yes, he knew the sheriff and his entire department would be keeping an eye on Cory. No, he didn't have an inflated sense of his own importance.

But he *did* know how the best net in the world remained a sieve simply because you couldn't plug every hole, and unless Gage meant to assign someone round the clock to stick to Cory's side—and he doubted that because this was a small county and probably had a force just big enough for the ordinary tasks it faced—then someone had to be pinned to Cory's side. Someone who knew how to handle threats like this.

That left him.

Even if others had such training hereabouts, he doubted it was as fresh as his own. He doubted their reflexes remained so honed that the merest glimpse of something moving out of the corner of their eyes could shift them instantly into hyperdrive.

It was true that you never forgot your training, but you could slow down. Hell, hadn't he come here intending to do just that?

So that likely made him the meanest, fastest SOB around here right now. Walking away was not an option.

What to do about Cory? She'd naturally felt their lovemaking had brought them closer, and to be fair, he kind of felt it, too. Not like with the women who'd just wanted to sleep with a SEAL. This was different. Different kind of woman, different kind of experience.

Hell, he wasn't even proud of the way he'd made love to her, so rough and ready, without any of the hearts-and-flowers-type stuff she deserved.

He'd been strung out on need in a way he'd never felt before, and all the self-control he owned seemed to have been focused on giving her a chance to say no. When she hadn't, his self-control had vanished.

And then, after his caveman routine, all she had wanted was to feel closer to him. To know that she hadn't been used like some plastic fantastic lover.

Cripes. He leaned his forehead against the cabinet, waiting for the coffee, and asked himself how he had just managed to mess up two people with one thoughtless act.

But that was him, wasn't it? The whole relationship thing was beyond him, always had been. The relationships he had managed over the years had been built on shared experience and trust within the boundaries of his job. With Cory he had no rules, no guidelines, no purpose other than making sure she survived until they figured out what was going on here.

And he didn't know how to handle it. The only thing he knew for certain was that Cory was as fragile as fine glass emotionally, and he'd probably just added a ding, if not a crack.

He ought to be hanged.

"Wade?"

Her tentative voice reached him from the kitchen entryway. He screwed his eyes shut and tried to get a grip on his self-disgust. "Yeah?"

"I'm sorry. I shouldn't have asked."

He whirled about to find her standing there, clothed

once again, her eyes pinched and lost-looking. She was apologizing when *he'd* put that look back on her face.

"Goddamn it," he said.

Her head jerked. "I'll just leave you alone."

"No."

She hesitated, wrapping her arms around herself as if she needed to hold something in, or hold herself together. "No?" she repeated.

"No. Grab a seat. Stay."

Still she hesitated, but then, after what seemed an eternity, she moved to the table and sat. She kept on hugging herself though, a sure indicator that all was not right in the world of Cory Farland.

He turned his back to her. "I stink at this," he said. Once again he pressed his forehead to the cabinet, glad the coffee hadn't finished yet because it gave him time not to look at her.

"Stink at what?"

"I told you. Connections. Relationships. Whatever the current terminology is. I'm the guy sitting alone at the back of the bar with a beer while the others shoot the breeze. I don't talk about much that isn't mission specific. Nobody really knows me, and I like it that way."

"Because you can't be hurt."

An impatient sound escaped him. "Don't give me the psychobabble. Even if it is true."

"Okay."

The coffee finished, and his excuse was gone. He pulled two mugs from the cupboard and filled them before he carried them to the table. Then he got her milk for her and put it in front of her.

He straddled the chair facing her, but didn't look at her. He didn't want to see that pinched expression again.

"I'm a minefield," he said finally. "Loaded with emotional trip wires. Yeah, I was abused as a kid. So were lots of other people, so don't give me any special passes because of it. I got away as soon as I could, and I promised myself I'd never get into that position again, a position where anyone could beat me up like that. The navy picked me up out of the mud, basically, restored my self-confidence, gave me a purpose and a goal. But they couldn't take away the trip wires. So I learned to keep them buried because they're absolutely useless. What the hell good does it do to keep reacting to things that happened twenty, thirty years ago when they're not still happening?"

She made a little sound but he couldn't tell if she was agreeing.

"What matters," he said finally, "is who I am now. What I became over the years. Unfortunately, I never got around to the part about dealing with people I didn't have a professional relationship with. So I stink at it."

"Mmm." Totally noncommittal. Well, what did he expect when he'd basically told her to shut up while he spewed?

Finally he raised his eyes and looked at her. At least she didn't look ready to shatter any longer. If anything, her face had grown calmer.

"I don't want to talk about when I was a kid," he said. "I don't *need* to talk about it. I got past it the day I realized that if my old man ever came at me like that again I could snap him in two."

She gave a little nod.

"I got past the fear. I got past most of the anger. I got past the feeling of helplessness."

"Good." She lifted her cup and sipped her coffee. "Good."

"Anything that's left is my own fault, not theirs in any way."

"Really."

"Really." And he didn't want to argue about this. "Anything I'm dealing with now is baggage I picked up all on my own."

"Such as?"

"Things I saw, things I did, things I chose not to do. If there's one thing I learned from being in the service, it's that ultimately I'm responsible for myself. The past is past, and it's useless except as a lesson for doing it better next time."

She drew a long breath. "You really believe that?"

"Yes. I do. And I'm quite capable of looking at the things I chose not to do over the years and taking responsibility for them. I chose to let my professional life consume me, I chose not to try to branch out into some kind of normal life. Admittedly, watching my buddies, I eventually concluded it wasn't worth the trouble. At least not while I was still on the job. So it's my fault and nobody else's that I chose not to learn how to build day-to-day relationships apart from the job."

"So you take that whole burden on yourself?"

"Of course. I made the decisions."

"That's a pretty heavy load. Most of us at least accept that our pasts played a role in making us who we are."

"I'm not saying it didn't play a role. But I'm the one, in the end, who says how much and what kind of a role. I'm not arguing that I'm not a product of my past, I'm arguing that I'm a product of the decisions I made in my past."

She nodded slowly, and his gut clenched a bit when he saw her face tightening up. "What?" he asked. "What did I say?"

Her lips tightened. "I'm just thinking about what you said. So you don't even think that as a child you were a victim?"

He shook his head impatiently. "I'm not saying that. When I was a kid, I handled what was dished out to me the best way I could figure out. Every kid does. And when we're kids, we don't have the breadth of experience that comes later, so we're easy to victimize. But later…no. Which is not to say no one is ever a victim. I'm not saying that at all."

"Then what *are* you saying?" she asked, her voice stretched tight.

"I'm saying that it's what we choose to do with it that puts us in control. It's the choices we make, and the lessons we choose to take. And I made some god-awful choices, and maybe I took some of the wrong lessons. That's what I'm saying, and I'm not going to blame any of it on the kid I used to be, because I was a man when I made a lot of these decisions."

She gave a single, jerky nod.

"Cory…what? Am I hurting you? Crap, I don't want to do that."

"No…no. You're making me think."

Oh, hell. He suddenly realized how she could be taking this. "I'm not criticizing *you*. I'm not saying you weren't a victim."

"I know that. I get that. It's just that…"

He waited, and when she didn't speak, he finally prodded. "Just that what?"

"Just that you're right. I've kind of been thinking along the same lines over the past couple of days. That bastard stole my husband, my baby, my old life. But I'm still breathing. So what did I do? I crawled into a hole in the ground and stopped living. I chose to let him take away even my hope."

"Aw, hell." He couldn't take any more of this. He rose from the table, knocking over the chair and ignoring it. He rounded to her and scooped her right up out of her chair, carrying her to the living room where he sat with her in his lap.

"You don't get it," he whispered, hugging her close. "You didn't do anything wrong. Everyone needs time to heal before they can get going again. You needed the time. You *needed* it. I keep telling you that. What if you'd had your leg blown off? Do you think you could skip surgery and rehab? Of course not. All I'm trying to tell you is that I take responsibility for the fact that I chose not to learn basic life skills. Like how to talk to a lady. Like how to reach out. Like how to share myself."

"Actually," she said brokenly, "I think you're doing a damn fine job of it right now."

"Not good enough. I've hurt you twice in the past half hour. I'm ham-fisted at this."

Her hand gripped his shirt, balling it. "Listen to yourself. Just listen. You'll make all kinds of excuses for me, but none for yourself. Think about that, Wade. The people who used to beat you up are gone from your life. So what do you do? You beat yourself up *for* them."

He grew so still and silent that she almost panicked. Had she done it again? Pushed him to places he was unwilling to go, to even look at? She tensed herself, in expectation that he'd toss her off his lap and walk out the door never to be seen again.

But then, finally, she felt him relax. His hand covered hers, where it knotted his shirt, and held it.

"Maybe you're right," he said gruffly.

"Maybe you think you can't make connections, but have you ever tried? You're doing just fine with me."

"But I hurt you."

"So? That's part of any relationship. People hurt each

other. When it's unintentional, it's okay. I don't think you want to hurt me. Do you?"

"Hell no."

"Then okay. It happens." She sighed. "Do you think my marriage to Jim was pure perfection? We had our fights. We hurt each other sometimes. The important thing is forgiving and forgetting when the hurt wasn't intentional. *That's* how you make a relationship that works."

He turned that around in his mind, giving her credit for being far more adult in some ways than he was. "With me a person would need the patience of a saint."

"Same here." She squirmed a little on his lap, reminding him that he still wanted her like hell on fire, then rested her head against his shoulder. "We've all got trip wires, Wade. Fact of life. And when those wires get laid by terrible emotional experiences, they're hard to get rid of."

"Well, I laid a lot more of them over the years." He didn't have to look very far back to see where they'd come from. "Combat vets get lots of them. A sound. A sight. A smell. Even a word. I told you I can't hold still. That's not purely my training at work. It's my learning."

"Learning?"

"How long do you think you can live on the edge before living on the edge becomes the only way to live? You think you can unwind just because you're home, out of the zone? Too many of us drink too much because it's the only way to wind down. Others of us just live with the constant skin-crawling feeling that something is about to happen, that we can't relax for even a minute."

She nodded against his shoulder, just a small movement. "I've lived that way for a little over a year. You've lived that way your whole life. Insecure, sure something bad is always just around the corner."

"Yeah. It makes me explosive, like a bomb." He sighed,

not sure where he wanted to take this, not sure why he was spilling his guts like this. Maybe he was hoping that his warning would get through, that she'd back away. Or maybe he was hoping that the next time he did or said something wrong she'd understand he didn't mean to hurt her.

But regardless of what she understood, he would hurt her. He'd slam an emotional door in her face, or retreat behind his personal drawbridge. In one way or another, he'd go into self-protection mode, and once he got into that mode, he might well stage a preemptive attack.

"You've got to understand," he said roughly. "You have to."

"Understand what?"

"That protecting myself is automatic. Regardless of the kind of threat."

She tipped her head against his shoulder and he knew she was looking up at him. He refused to look back at her. Let her read what she could from his chin; he wouldn't give her any more than that. Not right now. Maybe never.

"Okay," she said finally. "You protect yourself. I understand that."

A frustrated sound escaped him. "Do you understand what that might mean?"

"Maybe not in every detail. But I get the general picture."

He envied the note of confidence in her voice, but he didn't believe it. Whatever this woman had been through in her life, and the little she had told him had been bad enough, he didn't think it could possibly prepare her for what he could dish out. She had absolutely no idea of all that he was capable of.

But he did. That was the curse of so many years in Special ops. You knew what your limits were, and worse, you discovered you didn't have a whole lot of them. Whatever the mission required. And sometimes the mission was your own self-protection.

That didn't mean he was ashamed of himself, because he wasn't. But it did mean he knew himself in ways most people never faced. Most people never needed to look into the darkest parts of human nature. And people like him were the reason they never had to. But those who had looked…well, they lived in an uncomfortable world with all the rosy tint stripped away.

It was a sad fact of life that someone needed to visit those black places, that someone needed to come face-to-face with the ugliest things in the human heart and soul.

But those who went there remained apart and different because once you'd looked into the abyss, it became part of you.

She thought she understood, God bless her. She thought because she had seen the terrible thing the night the killer came to her house, that she had some idea. But she had no idea at all, because seeing was not the same as doing. Sometimes a person like Cory glimpsed the abyss. But folks like him not only glimpsed it. They walked into it. They melded with it.

And when they returned they were forever changed in ways only someone who had trod the path with them could imagine.

So how the hell did you get around that?

*Chapter 9*

Gage called during the early afternoon. Cory got the cordless-extension phone from her bedroom so they could both listen to him and talk as necessary.

"Okay," Gage said. "I've got both pictures going out to all deputies. They're not being told anything about you, Cory, just that I want these guys hauled in on sight for questioning in a possible homicide case. They're to be treated as armed and dangerous."

Cory caught her breath inaudibly at the description, then wondered why. It wasn't as if she didn't already know how dangerous these guys were. But somehow hearing it from Gage's lips made the threat seem more imminent. He had removed it from the realm of speculation and put it out there as reality.

Only as she felt her heart slam in response did she realize just how much denial she had been living with. Yes, she'd been afraid, maybe even ridiculously afraid all this time, but at some level she had desperately believed this moment would never come. And even now a part of her brain insisted on saying, *We don't know for sure*.

And that was true. They were acting on little more than suspicion and a confluence of coincidences. As Jim had so often said of such things, "It won't stand up in court."

Gage knew that, surely. Yet he was moving forward as if a real threat had been made.

And maybe it had, in that phone call. It had certainly been made a year ago when the Marshals decided they had to put her into permanent protection. After all, it wasn't as if they were manufacturing a paranoid conspiracy out of whole cloth.

She barely listened to the discussion the two men were having. It was as if a switch had been thrown at the instant she had faced the naked threat yet again. Once again she felt numb, utterly numb, perhaps even hollow. Yet there seemed to be no place left inside her for the fear, or even anger. In fact, even the spark of hope that had ignited in her over the past couple of days had deserted her.

There was nothing, could *be* nothing for her ever, unless she got this threat off her back for good.

Sitting there, hardly hearing as the two men talked, she faced the dismal reality of what her life had become and what it would remain as long as that killer was after her.

There would be no recovery, no hope, no future. That was what that man and his vendetta had done to her. He might as well have finished her off with a bullet to the head.

She couldn't go back to the woman she had been just a few days ago. Because over the past few days, she had tasted hope and life again, however briefly. She might have found just the illusion of it in Wade's arms, but it was enough to make her realize she could not go back. Whatever the cost.

Into the emptiness crept a steely resolve unlike anything she had ever felt before. Death, she knew in her heart, was infinitely preferable to the way she had been existing. She could not, would not, go back to that.

Nor did she pin her hopes for a future on Wade. She understood that he was a troubled, complex, complicated man who had come here seeking some kind of release, but he would have to find that on his own. Just as she would have to find her own resolve to live again, for *herself.*

No crutches, for they were unreliable, and temporary at best. So, she thought, as ice seemed to settle over her, she would deal with this mess. Then she would look for the woman she wanted to become. The woman who had once loved being a teacher. The woman who had enjoyed cooking as if her own kitchen was part of the finest restaurant.

And perhaps she'd discover other parts of herself in the process, parts she'd never had a chance to find before because she'd been too preoccupied with her goals, and then with Jim.

She was, she resolved, going to find her own two feet.

And the first step was getting rid of this threat. Allowing it to steal not one more day of her life.

She hung up the phone before the two men even finished their conversation. The details of what they planned really didn't matter.

All that mattered was that she was going to face down her husband's killer or die trying.

It didn't take Wade long to notice the change in her. She sensed him start watching her more closely a couple of hours later. She didn't care. He could watch her all he wanted. If she'd had a psychological break of some kind, it was a beneficial one.

She had had enough.

If that meant turning into an ice queen until this was over, then that was fine by her. Remembering how she had collapsed only two days ago after that phone call, she looked at herself and decided ice was infinitely preferable to that. Death was infinitely preferable to that. She had paid the price for someone else's criminal act long enough.

She started dinner at her usual time. Wade joined her, but didn't say anything. Nor did she have much to say, except to give him directions, since he seemed determined to help. Nothing personal. Nothing emotive. Just dry, flat instructions.

She felt no particular desire to eat, recognizing her hunger only as a sign she needed fuel. She didn't even allow herself to enjoy the tasks in the kitchen. Not now. No way.

Not even in the littlest way did she want to feel regret for what was gone. No room for that now.

Finally, over dinner, he asked,"What's going on?"

"What do you mean?"

"You've got a thousand-yard stare."

That at least caught her interest. "What's that?"

"It's the way men look coming out of battle. Distant. Shut down."

She forked some salad and ate it, pondering the comment as an intellectual exercise, having no other reaction to it. "I guess that would about cover it," she finally said.

"Did something happen?"

She barely glanced at him. "I've had enough. That's all. This gets finished if I have to hunt that man myself."

"I see."

He probably did. She returned to eating.

He resumed eating, too. But after a few minutes he spoke. "I get worried when I see that look."

"Oh? Why?"

"Because when I see it, it means someone really *has* had enough. That the only way they can keep from breaking is to totally withdraw. It's usually a sign of post-traumatic stress disorder."

"Hmm. Well, I probably have that, too."

"Probably."

Again silence fell. Then, "Cory?"

"What?"

"It's not good."

She raised her gaze from her plate. "What's not good? That I've decided enough is enough? That I've decided I'm going to get my life back or die trying?"

He shook his head. "That's not what I mean."

"Then what do you mean?"

"Shutting down. Not caring. That's dangerous. I've seen men do stupid things and get themselves killed when they have that look in their eyes."

She simply looked at him, then resumed eating. Go back to what she had felt before? No way. This was infinitely preferable to feeling.

Wade didn't say any more as they finished the meal. She barely tasted it. Fuel, nothing more. He joined her in the washing up, so it didn't take long.

Then there was nothing to do except wait. The thing was, she didn't want to wait. Not anymore. The Sword of Damocles no longer frightened her, but it was still hanging over her head.

"I'm going to take a walk," she announced.

"Not without me."

"I didn't say I was going alone."

"Okay," he said. "Okay."

* * *

Oh, he didn't like that look in her eyes at all. He pulled on his boots, lacing them tightly, readying himself. He even went so far as to put his sheathed knife on his belt, then let his shirttails hang out over it. He could throw that knife with as much accuracy over short distances as he could hit a target with a gun from seven hundred yards. These were some of the skills he'd learned, used and had to live with.

And since he couldn't carry a rifle with him on the streets, the knife would have to do. As would the garrote he stuck into his pocket, and the three plastic ties that could double as handcuffs.

Even if he went to prison for the rest of his life for it, he would allow nothing to harm Cory. Nothing. The certainty settled into his heart with entirely too much familiarity. It was not a new feeling, and he knew to the nth degree what he could do when he felt like this.

He supposed he was now wearing his own thousand-yard stare. The calm of imminent battle had settled over him.

The feeling was as familiar as a well-broken pair of boots, like those he had just donned. Comfortable, but that didn't mean he liked it. He'd been in enough battles to know better. Even success seldom left a good taste in his mouth. Or a totally quiet conscience.

Even less did he like the way the skin on the back of his neck crawled. It was back, all of it, just like that: everything he'd tried to shed and untangle over the past six months resurrected as if it had never gone away.

The man he wanted to leave behind took over now, emerging front and center almost mockingly. It didn't matter, though. This was the man he had chosen to become over many years, and now he needed to be that man again. For Cory's sake.

Whatever it took. Mission-specific goals became paramount, pushing everything else into the background. The man he had hoped he might become would just have to wait for another day.

Even in battle mode, however, he wished Cory wouldn't take this walk. It would create unnecessary, uncontrolled exposure. Things like this should be planned in advance, contingencies reviewed.

But much as he wished she wouldn't do this, he could see that nothing was going to stop her short of breaking the law and keeping her a prisoner in her own home. As he had said, when he saw that look in someone's eye, he knew they were capable of doing something stupid.

All he could do was call Gage and tell him what he and Cory were about to do.

"Are you out of your minds?" Gage asked.

"I can't stop her short of imprisoning her. You want to come argue?"

"Hell. All right, I'll see if I can get some people in the vicinity fast."

After he hung up the phone, he went to meet Cory at the front door. Her eyes remained flat and empty, but her body was moving impatiently. God, he knew that feeling all too well.

"I can't talk you out of this?" he asked quietly.

She just looked at him and switched off the alarm. He was the one who had to punch it to reset it before they slipped out the door.

This was definitely not good.

She paused on the front porch as if deciding which direction to take.

"You need to think," he said.

"I *am* thinking."

"No, you're trying to take the bull by the horns without any adequate preparation. You should stay inside and let me scout first."

"I want my life back. And I'm through waiting for that bastard to give it back."

He could understand that. He could even identify with it. What worried him was the flatness of her statement. If she'd been angry or upset, he'd have had a chance to reason with her. But in this state, there would be no reasoning.

She turned away from the park. He took it as a good sign. She might be utterly reckless with her own safety, but not even in her present mood was she prepared to risk the families and children who might be in the park.

She walked briskly, as if she had somewhere to go. That was fine by him. His own senses went on high alert, his field of vision widening as he slipped into the mode where his brain paid as much attention to his peripheral vision as to his central field. Maybe more. For most people that happened only with an adrenaline rush. For him it happened from long practice.

The same thing with his hearing. The brain usually filtered most sounds, prioritizing and even making people unaware of background noise at a conscious level. But like a person who'd been hard of hearing for a while and had just gotten his first hearing aid, when he went into this mode every sound became equally important, and none were dismissed as mere distraction.

Hyperaware, hyperalert. All without a whisper of adrenaline. Unfortunately, Cory had none of his training, and in her current state, she most likely wouldn't have adrenaline to sharpen her senses.

Which made her a liability.

Cripes, he hoped she walked off this mood. It wasn't

that he wanted her to be terrified, but a reasonable caution would be nice. A person couldn't make good decisions without even a modicum of fear in a dangerous situation.

Which was what he had been trying to tell her a little while ago. And she just plain wasn't listening.

Well, it wasn't as if he hadn't seen this before. Hadn't dealt with it before. It could happen to a man at any time: after his first battle, after a particularly nasty or long-lasting fight, or for no discernible reason at all. It just happened. Some cog slipped and everything shut down.

He supposed it was a form of self-protection and probably had its uses as long as it didn't go on too long, or start happening inappropriately.

They took a power walk, as he'd heard some describe it. Not quite running or jogging, but it would have been impossible to move any faster and still call it walking. When he glanced at Cory, he saw her face was still set in a blank expression, and perspiration had begun to give her skin a dewy look.

But he didn't look at her often. With his senses stretched he was trying to take in and process every sight, sound and smell within reach.

And he memorized the layout of the area for several miles around Cory's house. It pleased him about as much as the mountains of Afghanistan had. This might not be mountains with boulders and caves to hide behind at every turn, but the houses, garages, cars, trees and shrubs served the same purpose, and like many older towns, the houses nearly hugged each other. The people who had originally built this area had been looking for comfort in numbers, not privacy by lawns.

He wondered if she had any idea that pacing up and down every street as she did was a good recon. Probably not. Such things were undoubtedly far from her mind.

And as they walked, he noticed an increasing number of patrol cars. Nothing truly obvious, but probably more of a show of force than this neighborhood routinely saw.

He honestly didn't know if that was good. Scaring these guys off temporarily would only delay the problem. But one thing he was sure of by the time they marched back up onto Cory's porch was that he'd caught no sight of the man, or either of his cars, that had set off his internal alarms.

What did that mean? He could think of answers both good and bad.

Inside the house, once he reset the alarm, he watched Cory march down the hallway to her bedroom, then he heard her shower come on.

Damn, this house was stuffy. It held the day's warmth close, and the smells of their meal still filled the air. Imagine having lived like this for the past year, afraid to even open a window.

On impulse, he switched off the alarm, and opened a window in the living room, and another in her kitchen, allowing the freshening evening breeze to blow through. He could keep an eye on both while she showered, and the breeze would clear out the downstairs in only a few minutes.

Then it occurred to him that by shutting down the alarm system, he had left every window in the house unprotected against intrusion.

Well, hell. Sighing impatiently, he went back to the keypad and looked through all the warnings it gave him and finally got to the question about bypassing zones. He hesitated only a moment, taking time to scan the list of zones on the plastic card behind the keypad. Okay. He could switch off the living room and kitchen, and leave the rest of the house online.

He hit the bypass for each zone, then re-enabled the

alarm. Now all he had to do was keep an eye out and wait to see what emerged from the shower. A woman who had collected herself, or one who remained withdrawn.

She did emerge finally, wearing a scanty tank top and shorts. He spared a moment to notice those lovely legs and graceful arms. She seemed not to notice he had opened the windows, nor to care, although she probably would shortly. The dry air held heat poorly, and as the sun sank the breeze had just begun to take on a chill.

Cory seemed oblivious, however, going to the living room and sitting on the couch, staring at nothing in particular.

He decided he needed to try to engage her again. Try to draw her out of that netherworld where the brain and emotions went when they felt overwhelmed.

"Cory?"

She barely glanced at him.

"What happened?"

"What *do* you mean?"

At least she was answering him. "I mean what made you…" He hesitated, not wanting to use the word *snap*. A person in this state could switch from withdrawal to rage in an instant. "What pushed you over the edge?" he said finally, realizing there was no delicate way to phrase this.

"All of it."

"Well, yes." This was like walking through a minefield. "But something particular happened to put that look in your eye."

The slightest movement of her shoulder suggested a shrug. "You and Gage were talking on the phone. That's when I realized that I don't want to live this way anymore. I refuse to live this way any longer. I'm done with it."

Good. She was talking. "That's understandable."

"There's no point in living if I have to live this way. So I just won't do it anymore."

And that was where the danger lay. That came awfully close to suicidal thoughts. He sought a way to get through the cloak of detachment that shrouded her. "Making up your mind that you've had enough shouldn't lead you to act rashly."

"Why not?" Her hollow eyes regarded him unblinkingly. "Why should I put up with this one day, one hour, longer than necessary?"

"Because once we deal with this, it would be nice for you to be around to try building a new life."

"What am I supposed to build a new life with? That bastard took everything that mattered to me, directly or indirectly. Survival is not enough."

"Then what is?"

Finally he saw a spark of life in her gaze. Just a spark. "I don't know. I don't care anymore."

"Yes, you do."

She looked away, saying nothing.

"Admit it, Cory. In the past couple of days you've started to feel a little hope again. A little pleasure. You've tasted the idea that life could be good again."

"No." She turned to face him, and now she was angry. Good and angry. Part of the reaction, but in its own way as difficult to deal with as the distancing.

"Do you really think," she said, "that sex with you is enough to make life good again? Do you really think a hasty tumble in the hay is all I need to make things better? God, even a man should know better than that."

He didn't argue. She was right. Even if it stung.

"For the love of heaven," she said, jumping to her feet. "I'm living in a prison! I got a couple of hours of parole but that's all I got. And then I asked myself why I should start hoping again. What makes me think this mess is going to get any better? That there'll be anything left for me except ashes even if we do catch this guy."

She rounded on him. "The Marshals haven't caught him in all these months. Fifteen months the Marshals and FBI have been hunting this man and they can't find him. In fact, I bet if I checked with them, I'd find out he's moved down their priority list to a level below some escaped felon or some bank robber. Just another ice-cold case."

He remained silent, letting her rant however she needed to.

"If they ever find this guy, it's going to be because he comes after me. And now you and Gage even suspect that somebody must have revealed my location. Some protection. All they did was take away the little I had left. They should have just let me go home to my blood-soaked condo. At least I wouldn't have had to endure a year of this!"

She wrapped her arms around herself and began pacing the small living room. "What they did was put me in solitary confinement. You say you can't make connections? I haven't been able to because getting too close to someone increased the possibility that I'd say something I shouldn't. Look at how fast you picked up on it from things I didn't say. They told me I'd be safe once they moved me, but I never believed it. How could I believe it when they couldn't catch the gunman and I was the only one who could identify him? How could I believe it when that monster who killed my husband put a contract on me?"

"I don't know," he said quietly, mostly to show that he was listening.

"You know what I think?" she demanded.

"No."

"I think they put me into Witness Protection because I

was an ongoing embarrassment. They couldn't catch the bad guy, they couldn't send me back to my life for fear I'd become a front-page scandal if I turned up dead. So they sent me away. Far away. And once they got me settled in this rundown house with a minimum-wage job, they handed me a couple of business cards and never looked back. Problem solved."

"You believe that?"

"What else am I supposed to believe? Here I am, a year after they dumped me, and that killer may be after me because of them. He may have found me because of them."

"We don't know that."

"How else would he have found me here? Look around you, Wade. Does this look like the kind of place you try to hide a witness? Newcomers here stick out. So why the hell did they pick this place? Why not some major city where I'd be just one of millions?"

It was a good question and had already occurred to him. "Maybe they thought no one would ever look in a place like this."

"Clearly they may have been wrong. Regardless, here I am, all alone, facing the thing they said they were protecting me from."

He lowered his voice even more. "You're not alone."

"Not now. Because you just happened to land here looking for peace. Bet they didn't count on that."

Uneasiness began to creep through him. "Do you know what you're saying?"

"Yes!"

"There's just one problem with that. A phone call."

She threw up a hand. "So? Like you said, the guy needed to figure out which of a number of women who moved here in the last year was the right one. But if you're at all right about that call, and that guy we ran into, someone put him on my tail. And the only people aside from Gage who are supposed to know where I am are the Marshals."

He didn't speak, just turned her paranoia around in his mind, testing it for validity.

"I mean, how am I supposed to know that Seth Hardin sent you here? Because Gage said so? Because Gage said you've got a wall full of medals and you check out? That doesn't mean you didn't come here for some other purpose. I can't even trust you. You're a trained killer yourself and you figured out my situation pretty darn fast."

At that, everything inside him went still, cold and silent. Everything she said was true, insofar as it went. But it was twisted through the lens of fear and paranoia and trauma. Regardless, he never again was going to let anyone kick him this way. Bad enough he had to live with what he was, without someone using it against him to claim he was untrustworthy.

He stood. "I'll leave."

She didn't answer, just continued to stand there hugging herself and glaring.

"But let me make one thing clear to you, lady. I don't lie, and good men in far worse situations than this have trusted me. I never betray a trust."

He turned, then remembered the windows. Without a word, he slammed the living room window shut and locked it. Then he went to do the same in the kitchen and came back to reset the alarm. Cory suddenly appeared beside him.

"I'll be gone in less than thirty minutes," he said tautly.

"Wade…"

"No, Cory. Not another word. Nobody talks to me that way."

He was halfway up the stairs when he heard her start sobbing.

# Chapter 10

Oh, God, what had she done? The numbness that had sheltered her most of the afternoon and evening had vanished, first leaving her furious, then filling her with despair as she heard her own words about Wade play back in her mind.

As she started sobbing, he just kept climbing the stairs, never looking back. And she couldn't blame him, she could only blame herself. Where had that ugliness come from, all that suspicion? How could such words have passed her lips? How could such thoughts have entered her mind, especially when she knew something of Wade's background.

It was as if an evil genie had taken over her tongue, spewing vile words as if they had some basis in truth.

But they had none. Only moments after having said those things, she had realized she didn't believe them. Not about Wade. And now she couldn't call those words back.

She returned to the living room and curled up in a ball on the couch, letting the tears flow. Facing the fact that she had become some kind of emotional cripple. Nothing worked right anymore. Nothing. Her whole psyche was so messed up that the normalcy she'd been pining for over the past few days would probably escape her forever.

If she survived this. And the really scary thing was that she didn't even care anymore if she did. She just wanted to be done with it.

So what had she done? She'd struck out at the one person who had managed to make her want to live again. That was the real threat he posed: that he had made her want to move past this nightmare into a future of some kind. That he had made her want to start looking forward again, rather than back.

And she had struck at him in the way she had guessed would hurt him the most: attacking his honor.

What kind of person had she become? She didn't like herself at all anymore, not one little bit. Turning over, she buried her face in a throw pillow and wondered if she'd ever again be able to justify the space she took up on this planet. Because right now she had to face the fact she was a waste of life. A mean waste of life.

These weren't the lessons she should take from what had happened to her. My God, she'd been a teacher. How many times had she tried to help students learn to grow from their bad experiences? How many times had she painted object lessons in how even a bad experience could be turned to something good?

Now look at her. She couldn't even take her own advice.

Finally the tears stopped, simply because there were none left. The storm had moved through, but this time it hadn't left her feeling totally numb. No, she still hurt, and she despised herself. No convenient, comfortable numbness now.

She sat up finally to find the house dark. Even more surprising, however, was that she saw Wade sitting in the recliner across from her, a bulky shadow among shadows.

"I thought you were leaving."

"I don't abandon my post."

Totally neutral. As if he had put his own feelings away in a vault somewhere, as she had for hours today.

"I'm sorry," she said. "I can't tell you how sorry. I don't know where that ugliness came from."

"Doesn't matter." Indifferent. Unrevealing. The way he had seemed when he first arrived.

She had done that, she admitted. She had driven him back into that place where the walls were high and the battlements well guarded. And there was no way she could call back those words. "I'm sorry," she said again, useless words once the wounds had been inflicted. "I didn't even mean it. I don't know what I was thinking."

"You weren't thinking."

"Obviously. I was acting like an animal, striking out at everything indiscriminately."

"Maybe so."

Oh, he was giving her nothing, not one little thing. Could she blame him? "I was afraid."

"No, you were angry."

"They come from the same thing."

"Mmm."

God, it was like talking to a brick wall again. And now it was not just annoying or disturbing. Now it hurt. It was almost enough to make her mad again, that he could hurt her this way.

She sat silently for a while, scrubbing the dried tears

from her face. Finally she decided the only way to get past his walls was to lower her own. Her heart accelerated a bit at the danger in exposing herself this way. But she owed it to him, especially since after what she had said he was still in this house, still ready to protect her even with his life. Didn't such a man deserve the truth?

"I was…I was striking out because you made me start to hope again. I was afraid because you made me feel that a normal life might be possible for me. And I don't believe that anymore. I can't believe that. Look at me. I'm damaged goods. I'll never be normal again."

"It's unlikely."

Damn! She couldn't believe she had done this to him, and it was too late to rip out her own tongue.

Then, finally, in the dark so she couldn't even attempt to read his face, he began to speak. His tone was measured, his words slow.

"Nobody," he said, "who has seen and experienced what you and I have seen and experienced will ever be so-called normal again. It's an impossible thing to ask."

"I guess so." A hot, stray tear trickled down her cheek and she dashed it away.

"There will always be scars," he continued. "Things will never look the way they used to before violence entered our lives."

"No." Now she sounded like him.

A few seconds ticked by. Then, "But just because we carry scars, just because we've lived through things a lot of other people don't, doesn't mean there's anything wrong with us. Far too many people in this world have experienced violence in one form or another. Maybe that makes us more normal than those who haven't."

"What an awful thought." One that caused her a pang, not only for all the others of whom he spoke, but because it reminded her just how much self-pity she'd indulged, maybe was still indulging. He was right, and she knew it. One only had to turn on the news to see what millions of others suffered, many on a daily basis.

"Maybe. Still true. I've seen a lot of the world, and violence touches more lives than you can imagine. I'm not saying that's right, I'm just saying it is."

"You're right." Her voice broke a little. "I was protected from it all my life."

"Some people are. Some of us are lucky enough not to live in war zones, or among thugs. But an awful lot of us, sooner or later, taste the ugliest side of human nature. Unfortunately, you didn't even have a support group of friends and family who shared your experience. Maybe that's the worst thing WITSEC did to you. It protected you physically, but left you with no help to heal emotionally."

She caught her breath. "Maybe," she agreed.

"Most of us are luckier than you. We have all kinds of social support."

"You didn't, when you were a child."

"No, but I sure as hell did after I grew up. But the scars are still there. All of them. Unlike you, I've had decades to deal with my crap. You haven't. And you can see what a stellar example of healing I am."

"Don't knock yourself. I already did that, and unfairly, too."

"I'm just trying to make a point. You *can* have a life again. It's just that sometimes you're going to hurt. Always."

"I guess so."

"With time the hurting comes less often. But it never entirely vanishes. Sorry, but I can't offer more than that."

"It should be enough."

"It's life. Whether it's enough is something only you can decide."

"I'd almost decided. Then…well, you saw what happened."

"Yeah." He was silent a moment, then with a surprising note of humor he added, "You tried to build your walls back up with dynamite."

She winced, because the description was so apt. And the only person who'd been hurt by her explosion was him. She'd had no idea she could turn so ugly, and the knowledge didn't comfort her at all. "My explosion didn't work very well. I'm sorry."

"It's okay," he said finally. "I understand, believe me. I've seen it plenty of times, even done it myself a few times. That's what I meant about trip wires. You just start thinking you might reach for the brass ring, and then everything inside you starts shrieking warnings. Hell, you probably don't even believe you're entitled to live a normal life."

She honestly hadn't looked at it that way before, but the sinking in her stomach acknowledged the truth of his words. "That's a place I haven't gone."

"Not yet, maybe. You will. At some point, if it hasn't already, survivor guilt will give you a rough ride. If it does, and I'm around, talk to me about it. Been there, done that."

*If* he was around. That word caused her another sharp pang. "God, I'm a mess."

"No more so than anyone else in your shoes. Try to find some comfort in that."

"I can't believe you're trying to make me feel better after the way I treated you. You're being awfully generous." And that made him a truly remarkable person, in anyone's book.

"Don't beat yourself up." His tone had grown softer,

kinder than when they had begun this conversation, and that only made her feel worse.

"But the things I said!"

"I don't blame you for them. After I got upstairs and cooled off a bit, I realized you touched one of my trip wires. At least one. I overreacted."

"I don't think you did." She was still aching over the things she had said and implied about him. "You offered to protect me when you didn't need to do a thing. You deserve better from me."

"You didn't say anything so god-awful, in the circumstances. Just let it go. I have."

But had he? He might say so, but given the way he had responded, she knew full well her angry words must have cut him to the quick in the places that mattered most to him, like his sense of duty and honor. Ideals to which he'd devoted his entire adult life. Maybe he wasn't proud of everything he'd had to do. She could scarcely imagine the kinds of jobs SEALs must be sent on. Maybe some of those things even stuck in his craw. But she was fairly certain he'd never betrayed one of his buddies, and had never failed in his duty. And she'd made him sound like nothing better than a hired gun.

God, she wished she could erase the memory of her words.

"Ah, damn, lady," he said on a sigh, "just let it go. Don't you think you already have enough baggage?"

"Maybe, but that doesn't give me the right to hand out more of it to anyone."

"You didn't hand me any baggage. Period."

Of course not. She didn't matter enough to him to be able to hurt him that way. In one sense she felt relieved that her shrewing hadn't hurt him in any lasting way. In another, awfully selfish way, she didn't like that she mattered so little to him. But why should she? Two days did not a relationship make. Not even good sex could make up for lack of time.

And, as he had told her more than once, he didn't make those kinds of connections anyway. So maybe she shouldn't feel bad about what she had said, at least as far as hurting him went. He didn't allow himself that kind of vulnerability.

Judging by the way he had initially reacted to her rant, she supposed he wasn't totally impervious. At least not at that moment in time, although she would guess she had sent him back to that place where he let nothing touch him.

But there was more at issue here than whether she had hurt him. She had behaved deplorably, according to her own standards whether she had wounded him or not.

He surprised her then by rising and crossing the room to stand in front of her. It was still dark, the room illuminated only by the faintest light from outside streetlamps that managed to creep around cracks in the corner.

"I want you," he said baldly.

Her heart leaped instantly. Something about her loved the way he was so open and honest about his needs, the way he voiced them without varnish or hesitation. Best of all, without embarrassment. That freed her from all those things, too.

She lifted a hand to take his. "Just don't carry me."

"Why not?"

"Because just once I'd like to get into bed with you under my own steam."

At that he laughed. "It's a deal. Sorry, I guess I've been picking you up a lot."

"Only a few times." She answered the gentle tug of his hand and rose to her feet. "Why do you do that?"

"I don't know." He said nothing for a few seconds, still

holding her hand. "Maybe," he said finally, almost breaking her heart in the process, "it's the only way I know to keep you close."

Ah, God, that was such a revealing thing for him to say, as if he had stripped his mind and emotions bare. It was one thing to say you wanted someone sexually. It was entirely another to admit you wanted to keep them close but didn't know how. Her throat tightened so that she couldn't even speak.

All she could do was stare starkly at the fact that they were both wounded souls, each in their own broken way trying to make some kind of connection again, regardless of what either of them might claim. He sought physical connections because he didn't know how to make the other kind. She fought emotional connections because they hurt too much, and found the same solace he did in the physical.

Was that wrong? No, it wasn't. And maybe it was the first step on a much longer path they both needed to walk, whether together or separately. She squeezed his fingers to show her understanding, then cleared her throat, finding her voice again.

"I, um, guess it's okay if you carry me then."

A little laugh escaped him. "Oddly, I think I'd prefer it a whole lot more if you came with me, Cory. Come lie with me, lady."

He couldn't have chosen words more likely to ignite her desire, though she couldn't have said why. Heat spiraled through her to her very core, making her feel heavy with longing. Already her body ached for his touches, for his weight, for the fullness of feeling him inside her. She'd felt desire before in her life, but never this hot and this fast.

And he did that with simple words. Somehow that *come lie with me* affected her more viscerally than, *let's make love,* or many of the other affectionate or teasing suggestions she used to hear from Jim. *Come lie with me.*

The words made her nerves hum, and she had no desire to analyze any further. She was tired of being under a microscope, his or her own. Wade offered her the freedom to be, just be, in this moment and no other. And she reached out with both hands for the gift.

This time he evidently felt no desire for the rough-and-ready matings they'd had before. This time he stood beside the bed with her, and began to remove her clothing slowly, almost as if he were unwrapping a present and wanted to savor the anticipation a little longer. To draw out each moment of expectation.

He took his time even with things that should have happened quickly, like lifting her tank top over her head. Trailing his fingers up her sides as he did so sent ripples of longing through her for more. Oh, she felt so greedy, and he made her feel that way.

Then he followed the movement all the way up as he lifted the top, tracing the most sensitive parts of her inner arms all the way to her fingertips. When he at last tossed the top aside, she felt almost worshipped.

Nor did he stop there. He cast aside his own shirt, and the darkness in the room added to the mystery of all that was happening inside her. When his hands gently gripped her waist and pulled her close, there was something inexplicably exquisite about the feeling of his skin against her belly, except for her breasts, still shrouded by her bra. Then he bent and took her mouth in a kiss that stole her breath, and seemed to touch her very soul. His tongue mated slowly with hers as his fingertips drew gentle patterns on her back and sides, promising so much, taking nothing at all. He merely ignited her cells one by one until she felt alive with fire.

Then his mouth left hers, trailing slowly down her neck, causing her to arch and moan softly with delight.

"You are so sexy," he murmured against her neck, his breath hot and moist. A shiver rippled through her. Had anything ever felt this exquisite?

On a wisp of breath she answered, "You make me feel so sexy."

"Good. Good." His mouth trailed lower, lips and tongue outlining the cups of her bra, promising but not giving. Not yet. She shivered again and lifted her arms, looping them loosely around him in offering. When she felt his muscles bunching beneath her palms, she stroked them, following hard curves and hollows down toward the small of his back, where she marveled over a new discovery. In the dip there, she felt a soft, thin tuft of fur, so masculine, so perfect.

He trembled a bit as she stroked him there, then dipped one finger beneath the waistband of his jeans.

He mumbled something against the upper curve of her breast, and then with a quick movement, he released the clasp of her bra, allowing her to tumble free.

The throbbing at her center reached new heights as lightning seemed to zing along her nerves, every new sensation headed toward her core as if it was all that existed.

The air grew thin in the room, and she panted helplessly, her head falling back, her eyes closing, giving herself to the moment and to him as she had seldom given herself before: mindlessly, helplessly. If any part of her didn't ache in that throbbing, primal rhythm, she had long since ceased to be aware of it.

Here and now. Everything else vanished.

* * *

Wade felt the moment when she left the world behind, her entire consciousness focused on what was happening inside her. He wasn't far behind, but he struggled against his own hardening body, the pounding demands of his own needs.

Because he wanted to be sure to give it all to her, everything. He couldn't explain it, maybe didn't want to look too closely. All he knew was that he wanted to brand himself on this woman, right here and now in a way she would never forget.

So when she reached for the clasp of his jeans, moaning softly, he stopped her. Instead he reached for her shorts and panties, and tugged them down with one hand just as his mouth found her pebbled nipple and drew it deeply inside. He sucked gently at first, but as she pressed herself harder against him, he threw gentleness to the wind and sucked on her as if he could draw her right inside him.

The groan that escaped her fueled his own needs, and he had to push them back. If this woman remembered nothing else about him, she was going to remember this night, these hours.

Something even more primal than need for satisfaction drove him. This was a claiming of some kind, a claim he had never tried to make before. And for some reason, that need to claim added to his passion, making him almost as desperate as he was hungry.

The damn shorts and panties flew away at last, tugged off her ankles as he swept her up in one arm, his mouth still latched to her breast, each movement of his tongue and lips sending a fresh quiver through her.

She was clinging to him now, clinging as tightly as she could manage to his back, and the feel of her arms hanging on to him was surely the most wonderful thing he had ever felt. More wonderful even than the acts to come.

He'd have gone to the stake before he would ever admit how long it had been since someone's arms had been around him, or how good it felt, or how much he needed it.

He almost didn't want to lower her to the bed.

But his body had already made promises to her, and he was going to keep every one of them.

He laid her down, cast aside the rest of his clothing, pausing only to tug some protection from his pocket. He hadn't anticipated this, hadn't anticipated any sexual relationship at all, but the military had taught him well. He always carried protection, and for the first time he was truly grateful for it because it would ensure no harm came to Cory from him.

He tossed the packets on the bedside table. Then he wrapped his arms around the naked beauty beside him, and felt her arms wrap around him, and had the craziest feeling that he could stay right here, right now forever.

Their bodies met, warm smooth skin against warm smooth skin, their legs tangled, working for even greater closeness.

But he had promises to keep. With mouth and hands he began to explore her, every inch of her, stealing all her secrets even as he lifted her to moaning heights of passion. Then his mouth followed his hands, across her belly, her hips, down the insides of her thighs to the delicate arches of her feet.

He could think of no better way to worship her than by kissing her every inch.

The pounding in his loins now hammered in his brain. Slowly he slipped up over her, smelling her wonderful musky scent, then dipping his mouth and tongue into her most private places.

Claiming. Branding. Possessing.

Causing her to arch upward with a soft scream as he touched the delicate knot of nerves that gave so much pleasure-pain. She tasted good. So good. This was something he had almost never shared, it seemed so intimate to him, and he knew just the barest moment of fear he might not be doing it right, but her body immediately answered as if it had heard his question.

Oh, it was so right. So good. He licked, nibbled, tasted, even plunged his tongue deep into her, and felt a smile stretch his lips when her hands grabbed his head, pressing him closer still, then clawed at his shoulders as if she could barely stand the pleasure.

He felt the ripping shudder as an orgasm took her, listened to her moan helplessly, then before the riptide had fully passed, he pulled on a condom and moved up over her, staking his claim completely as he slid into her warm, welcoming depths.

"Wade!" Half sigh, half cry, and never had his name sounded so beautiful. Triumph filled him in that moment, because she was his, all his.

Then the throbbing in his body demanded more, her hands tugged at him, trying to move him, and when at last he began to thrust, she sighed his name again, wrapped her arms around his back and her legs around his hips.

Holding him. Hugging him with her entire being. Making him welcome in every way as she carried him with her to the stars.

For that little while, he even allowed himself to believe he could belong.

# *Chapter 11*

They lay together for a long time, just cuddling. That was something new to him, too. And he liked it. Finally he decided to tell her so, even though he was aware it could make her dislike him, to know how casually he had treated sex in his past. But for some odd reason, he was telling Cory lots of things he'd never told anyone else. Maybe because she always seemed to understand.

"This is the first time," he said slowly.

He felt a ripple pass through her and when he peered at her face in the nearly total dark, he thought he saw a smile. "What's so funny?"

"Turn on a light," she suggested. "I want to see your face, too."

Exposure. Confidences were easier in the dark, as he'd learned sitting in an awful lot of hides in alien lands. But he obliged her, turning on the small lamp beside the bed. It was dim, just enough light to read by.

She was smiling at him with puffy lips and puffy eyes, and he had to admit she looked happier than he'd yet seen her. "Nothing's funny," she said in answer to his question. "I just don't think this is the first time you've made love to a woman."

"Oh. That isn't what I meant." And now he half wished he hadn't mentioned it at all.

"Then what?" Her smile slipped away, her gaze grew gentle.

He hesitated. "First time I ever cuddled after."

Her eyes widened, and for an instant she looked as if she didn't understand. But when she did, something happened on her face that seemed to reach out and touch his heart.

"Oh, Wade," she said softly, and all of a sudden her arms wound around him, hanging on tightly, so tightly, and giving him that feeling again. "Oh, Wade, I think that's the saddest thing I've ever heard."

"No…no, don't be sad. Be happy. I am."

She burrowed her face into his shoulder, and he felt her kiss him there. "You," she whispered, "are more special than you know."

"So are you."

She didn't answer, just tightened her hold on him even more.

He would have liked to stay there forever, and maybe if he'd been an ordinary guy, he could have done so. But he was a former SEAL, and coded into him now was a mission clock, one that wouldn't stop ticking. He couldn't forget reality for long, couldn't forget there might be a killer out there circling in even now. Couldn't forget that even alarm systems were little protection against a determined assassin. He ought to know: he'd disabled more than one.

So finally, feeling as if he were ripping off his own skin, he gave in to the demands of reality. "Let's take a shower," he said. A gentle way to ease them back. To stay as they were left them with few defenses. He might not be at a total disadvantage naked, but he couldn't say the same for Cory. And if they got distracted again—a very tempting possibility—they could miss something important.

So they showered together, playing games with a bar of soap and a nylon puff that neither had been designed for, but that made them both grin, and elicited some pleasurable sighs.

He helped towel her dry, then slipped from the bathroom while she worked a bit at her hair. His internal clock and other triggers were beginning to drive him nuts. He'd allowed himself to be off duty for too long.

A quick check of the alarm showed him nothing amiss, but he crept through the house anyway, once again putting his knife on his belt, donning boots because protecting the feet was so essential. He skipped the shirt, though, as the house was warm enough. Cory would just have to live with the sight of the knife.

When he was sure the house was still secure, he followed the glow of light to the kitchen and found Cory making coffee. He glanced at the clock. "A little late for coffee. Or maybe awfully early, depending."

She shook her head, and when she faced him, he could tell that reality had settled in once again for her, too. All the softness was gone, except, perhaps, for her eyes when they brushed over him.

Until they came to rest on the knife.

"I see," was all she said, and turned her back again, waiting for the coffee. "I didn't think we'd get much sleep. One way or the other."

"No," he admitted. "Cory, I'm sorry."

"Stop apologizing, damn it. It's not your fault all this is happening. It's not your fault I'm such a mess. So we took a vacation. At least I did. For a little while I felt normal, I'm not going to apologize for it, and okay, now we face the real world again."

"You *are* normal."

"Oh, let's not get back on that again. Look at what I did today. I freaked out, basically. I totally shut down. Then I took it out on you."

Turning, she grabbed two mugs and put them on the table. Then she got out the milk. A burst of steam announced the coffeemaker was pretty much done.

He watched, feeling an unaccustomed pain in his chest. A few minutes later, when they sat at the table, he spoke again. "Quit feeling bad about what you said to me."

"Why shouldn't I feel bad? I was horrid. I'm surprised you could even want to make love to me after that."

This was not good. He didn't want her to feel this way about herself. Not at all. Not ever. How could he make it clear to her that he really had forgotten what she had said?

Finally he chose his words with care. "I've had a lot of time to develop confidence in myself and who I am. The names don't stick anymore. I've been called far worse. I'm not saying I'm perfect. God knows, that's the last thing I'd say about myself. But I have had time to build and internalize a lot of confidence over the last twenty years. You haven't. You got stripped of everything, and now you've got a bunch of broken pieces to work with. Of course you're going to strike out sometimes. But you'll do just fine. You'll find a new version of yourself. If anything, I hope you do it better than I did."

"Meaning?"

"Maybe you can get rid of some of the trip wires."

At that she laughed unsteadily. "I don't even know where any of mine are."

"Sure you do. You know what makes you uneasy, you know what scares you. You even told me what made you feel threatened."

"I did?"

"Hope," he said simply. "You're terrified to hope."

Long minutes passed in silence as Cory faced what he was saying. It was as if his simple statement had stripped away everything else and forced her to look at what might be the deepest wound of all. And it hurt. She finally covered her lower face with her hand and closed her eyes. "I used to take hope for granted."

"I know. You will again."

He sounded so sure, but considering how long she'd been living without it, and how much its reemergence scared her, she wasn't sure about that. What did she have to hope for, after all? That one morning she'd wake up and discover that her life was free of threat, that she could then take up the strands of the woman she had once been?

She'd never be that woman again. Ever. And in the murkiness of now, she couldn't even imagine who she might become if the threat was removed.

"First," he said, "it's little things. Immediate things. Little hopes. Just seeds."

"Do you hope?"

"Hell yeah. I hope for lots of things, some big, some small."

"Such as?"

"I hope I can settle into civilian life at least enough that I'm not a ticking time bomb just waiting to be startled. I hope someday I get past this edginess and stop seeing every shadow as a place of concealment. I hope that I can sleep without waking in a cold sweat from nightmares."

"You do that, too?"

"All the time. Not as much as even a few months ago, but yeah."

"Me, too. For a long time I was afraid to sleep."

"I can imagine."

"For a long time I nearly jumped out of my skin at the sound of a knock."

"But it's better now?"

"Yes. It is."

"You see?" He spread his hands. "Baby steps, Cory. You've already started to take them. It's been my experience, though, that you'll take a few backward steps along the way."

"I think I took a big one today."

"No."

"No? What do you call what I did? That…that thousand-yard stare you called it. That numbness. That recklessness. Then yelling at you."

"The yelling was you coming back. I've seen guys go a lot deeper and stay there a lot longer. You actually had a pretty fast turnaround."

"And that's good?"

"You bet. There's a lot of life left in you, Cory. You're starting to kick the traces of fear and despair. It'll be rough for a while, but I believe you'll do it."

"I hope so." Then a little laugh slipped out of her. "I hope so. Listen to me."

"Sounds good." He stirred in the chair, and he seemed to lean forward, toward her. "You may have gone through more healing in the last year than you really realize. I don't know. I'm no shrink. I can only tell you what I've seen, and what I've learned from my own experience."

"I'm tired of being such a mess all the time."

"Tell me about it. But look at you. You're still here.

You're still trying to deal. You could have quit a long time ago."

"I don't know."

"No way I can judge. But ask yourself, have you been living in terror every single minute of the last year you've been here?"

She started to say yes, then realized that wasn't entirely true. Her heart skipped a beat with the understanding, for it surprised her. Maybe what she thought of herself wasn't exactly true. "At first, yes. But then only when something happened to worry me. I can't say I spent the whole year in shaking terror."

"No, I'd bet most of the time you let it slide to the back of your mind. When nothing threatened you directly, when you were working."

She nodded slowly. "That's true."

"So the idea that you spent a year doing nothing but living in terror is your perception. Basically it was the story you told yourself, but maybe not exactly what you were doing."

"No, it's true," she said, straightening a little. "I'd forget about it. Maybe not for too long at one time, but I did. I *had* to."

"Of course you did. So give yourself a little credit here, Cory. In some pretty awful circumstances, having lost everything that meant anything to you, you managed to function. To hold a job, pay the bills, read books, maybe go to a movie. You kept going. You were probably doing a whole lot better than you thought."

"No. No, I wasn't." She still remembered all too vividly her many failures. And there were scores of them. Things undone, things unsaid. If she sat down and made a list, she'd hate herself.

"So sure? You didn't quit. A lot of people would have.

Granted, healing probably would have been easier, maybe even happened faster, if you hadn't been cut off from everything. But that only makes what you've achieved all the more admirable."

"I haven't achieved anything!"

"Getting through the past year on your own is a huge achievement. Why don't you count your strengths instead of your weaknesses for a change?"

That comment drew her up short. Her strengths? She'd been looking at herself for a year as a quivering blob of fear, incapable of answering her own door without peeking out first to see who was there.

"You went to work, didn't you? You went to the bank, and the grocery store. You even made a few friends."

"Not really. I couldn't let anyone get too close."

"But was that a failing or a reasonable caution given what you went through?"

She almost wanted to protest that he didn't know her well enough to guess what she had been like for the past year. And yet, she found herself drawn up short by awareness, a shift of perspective on her own actions and behavior. Yes, she had lived with fear, but not enough fear that it had prevented her from functioning. Not enough that it had kept her locked in this house.

Going to work hadn't caused her a nervous breakdown, although she'd never dropped her guard about what she said. Yes, answering her door had been difficult, but considering what had come through her door that night fifteen months ago, maybe it was surprising she could answer a door at all. She'd had dinner a few times with Nate and Marge Tate, with Gage and Emma Dalton. She went to the library regularly, and never considered avoiding it, at least not since the first few weeks.

Maybe she was confusing heightened caution with

terror, at least later. There was no question she had been terrified right after Jim was killed. No question she had been terrified when she had finally been dropped here on her own. But of course she had been. For the first time in months she didn't have a Marshal at her elbow, had to venture out on her own, pick up the threads of the basic necessities of life.

And she had done it. Unhappily, with her heart so broken it sometimes seemed too painful to draw a breath, hating it and fearing the unknown that loomed before her as much as the past that might try to follow her. But she had done it.

"You see?" he said, almost as if he sensed the shift in her. "What happened today has probably happened to you a number of times since your husband was killed. You disconnected because it was too much. The past, the present, all of it converged on you again when you listened to Gage and me talking. So you shut down. That's an important protective thing. Sometimes it's the only way we can deal."

"You do it, too?"

"I thought I said so. And God knows I've seen enough people do it. You see it in survivors all the time. Survivors of battle, survivors of natural disasters. That's the thing. It's like the brain gets so overloaded it just says *enough*. It can't deal, so it basically removes you as far as it can. It's not a failing. It's not something wrong with a person. It's *survival*. It's only a bad thing when it takes over for too long and too completely."

"But you said post-traumatic stress disorder. Isn't that an illness?"

"But that's not what I saw today, Cory. PTSD, yes, but the useful, coping kind. I guess what I'm trying to get at is that after watching you, especially today, I don't think you're as bad off as you think."

She sighed, letting his words sink in slowly, rearranging her mental and emotional furniture, trying to see herself in a more positive light. The change left her feeling uneasy. Then a new thought occurred to her, one that caused her a pang.

"Maybe you're right about survivor guilt."

He stirred again. "What do you mean?"

"It hasn't been just fear and grief. Maybe I've been punishing myself with both of them." Even as she could accept the emotional logic of that, she didn't like the idea much. She almost hoped he would deny it.

"Could be, I suppose. But now you're getting into shrink territory, and I've probably already ventured too far that way. I'm just talking from what I've seen and experienced over the years."

She turned the idea around in her head, though, weighing it against her emotional response. The Marshals had tried to give her everything she needed to move forward in a safe life. If she looked at the past year honestly, they had succeeded. But she had refused to fully accept the gift. Grieving had been one thing. Even some initial fear at being on her own. But at some point had she started using fear as a way to flagellate herself and limit her options because she was still alive when Jim and her baby were not?

It was as if doors were finally opening in her mind, giving her a different view than the box she had tried to paint around herself during the past year.

Plenty of food for thought, and plenty to leave her feeling adrift inside herself. Who was she, actually? And what had she really been doing with herself over the past year? She suspected these new ideas of herself might be closer to the mark than the abbreviated form she had adopted previously. Grief and fear did not begin to explain it all.

She sighed. "I've got a lot of thinking to do. But I'd appreciate it if you would accept my apology for what I said earlier. I'm horrified at myself."

"I thought I already had. Apology accepted."

"You're a very kind man."

He said nothing for a while, and she wondered if she had offended him somehow. Then he said, an almost rueful note of humor in his voice, "I think I need to learn how to accept a compliment."

"Does it bother you that I said you're kind?" How awful if it did, because he had certainly been kind to her, kinder than she had any right to expect.

He answered, still sounding rueful. "My mind is trying to remind me of all the times I wasn't kind."

At that a forlorn little laugh escaped her. "Yeah, the way I'm sitting here remembering all the ways I wasted the last year. All the things I could have done but didn't."

"I'll cut myself some slack if you will."

"Deal." But was it? Could she really see herself through his eyes, rather than her own? He certainly made a compelling case for a Cory who had acted the way most people would after what she had been through, rather than the Cory she had talked herself into thinking she was.

Then she asked a question that she knew was freighted with baggage. But it was a question that needed an answer because it might help her plant one of those seeds of hope he had talked about, give her something to hang on to.

"Wade?"

"Yes?"

"Tell me just one little hope you have right now. Just one little thing, not the big things."

She watched as his face started to freeze, but before

he could turn completely to stone again, she watched him relax his expression muscle by muscle. For a full minute, he didn't say anything.

"Wade?"

"I hope that you'll hug me again sometime," he said finally.

He couldn't have sent a surer shaft straight into her heart. Aching for him, for his isolation and loneliness, she rose and rounded the table. He pushed back as if to rise, but before he could she slid onto his lap and wrapped her arms around him tightly.

"I hope," she whispered tremulously, "that you'll let me hug you again lots of times. It feels so good to me."

He wrapped his arms snugly around her in answer. "Anytime, Cory. Anytime."

The skin-crawling sensation came back, possibly because he'd gone AWOL for a few hours. Or it returned because he sensed something internally. Some inner clock was ticking, counting out the minutes and hours it would take for the killer to respond if he had identified Cory.

The sensation had never failed him when there was danger, had rarely been wrong about danger that didn't exist.

The sun would rise in less than an hour. This was the time of attack, when darkness still provided a cloak and most humans were at their weakest. This was the hour when many a guard lost his alertness, when sleep stole awareness no matter how hard one tried to stay awake.

The hour before dawn.

Maybe that's all it was. But he counted back through his mind, first the phone call, then the stranger who drove two different cars. Maybe he was to be the killer himself. Or he was merely the assassin's lookout, an unidentifiable face that should have passed unnoticed while collecting information.

Damn, he wished he knew.

He had at last persuaded Cory to doze on the couch, promising he would be right there and awake. But he wished he could slip out and sweep the perimeter, because no matter how well the sheriff's deputies did the job, he could do it better himself.

He checked the alarm more than once, making sure it hadn't been disconnected. No warnings showed on the status display.

The phone rang. He grabbed it immediately, hoping the single ring wouldn't disturb Cory. She sighed but remained asleep, exhausted and trusting him.

God, he hoped he was worthy of that trust.

He slipped into the kitchen with it, after the barest of greetings, and heard Gage's voice. Through the kitchen curtains, he could see the pale light of dawn.

"We identified the guy you saw with the two different cars," Gage said. He sounded barely awake himself.

"Yeah? Who?"

"A private detective out of Denver."

"Hell."

"Exactly. I've got the Denver P.D. going to roust him and find out who he was working for."

"Like I can't imagine."

"This could be good. At least we'll know exactly what info he passed on, and who he passed it to."

"Yeah. Maybe we can even use him." Wade's brain slipped into high gear and he refilled his coffee mug. The more he thought about it, the better he liked this setup.

"That was my thought," Gage said. "If it's not too late. But first I have to question him. He'll be cooperative if he wants to keep his license."

"How long is that going to take?"

"I'm going to start with a phone interview once Denver picks him up. I'll let you know. Don't let her out of the house for now."

"I won't. Listen, Gage?"

"Yeah?"

"I gotta get some sleep, man. Four hours."

"I'll send Sara Ironheart over in mufti. Like for coffee. Give me an hour. I can also put eyes on the house, but that might take a little longer so we don't give the game away."

"Absolutely don't give the game away. We've got to end this."

"I agree. Can you make it another hour?"

"I'm fine. But I'll be better on a little sleep."

He hung up and rubbed his eyes. A private dick, huh? Someone who wouldn't know the story, could be fed a line of bull. Someone unrelated to the case who could be sent here to find Cory without setting off alarms. In theory, anyway.

This killer was no tyro at this. No tyro at all. The palms of his hands started itching as he thought of all the things he'd like to do to the assassin. Things he knew he'd never do because he was an ordinary citizen now.

But there were hundreds of ways a man could die, and in his experience few of them were quick or merciful.

With a shake of his head, he pushed the thoughts away. He wasn't that man anymore. In fact, he was trying to become a very different man. One who might actually be worthy of breathing the same air as a woman like Cory Farland.

One thing he did know for certain. He would do whatever it took to keep Cory safe. Even if it meant spending the rest of his life in hell.

# Chapter 12

Sara Ironheart arrived with the gentlest of taps on the window beside the front door. She wore a heavy jacket, overshirt and jeans, and from its concealment flashed her badge. He also caught a glimpse of a 9mm semiautomatic in a shoulder holster.

Cringing because it would undoubtedly wake Cory, Wade turned off the alarm and let her in. Then he turned the alarm on as quickly as possible, hating that damn beep.

"Wade?" Cory called drowsily.

"I'm here," he called back. "Everything's fine. Get some more sleep."

She mumbled something, and from the doorway he watched her turn a bit on the couch and slip back into slumber. This woman, he thought, wasn't anywhere near the scared kitten she thought herself.

He motioned Sara to follow him into the kitchen,

and closed the door on the hallway so their conversation wouldn't disturb Cory more.

"Thanks for coming."

"Least I can do." A beautiful woman with raven-black hair that was highlighted by just a few threads of silver, she gave him a half smile. "Gage filled me in. You go to sleep."

"Coffee's over there, mugs in the cupboard above."

"Thanks."

"Four hours max," he cautioned her.

She nodded. "I'll wake you."

Then, sentry in place, he went back to the living room and made himself as comfortable as he could on the recliner.

An adrenaline jolt tried to keep him from sleeping, but this was a battle he'd fought and won many times. A man couldn't survive his job without learning to sleep anytime, anywhere, even standing bolt upright. And the recliner was a hell of an improvement over that.

A couple of minutes later he'd quieted his body, and sleep slipped over him. A light sleep.

For even as he dozed, his ears never quit working, cataloguing every sound as either normal or not.

It was another one of those survival things.


Cory awoke, a warm, lovely dream giving way to instant panic. Someone was in the house.

"Shh," a voice said quietly, and she opened her eyes to see Sara Ironheart squatting beside her. "It's okay. I'm spelling Wade."

Cory drew a shuddering breath, managing a nod as her racing heart started to settle from a terrified gallop to something closer to normal.

"Coffee?" Sara whispered.

Cory nodded and pushed herself upright. When she saw Wade dozing in the recliner, everything inside her turned warm and soft. The gifts he had given her during the night hours seemed to have settled in and taken root. She felt good, despite the reminder of the threat that Sara represented.

She rose as quietly as she could and followed Sara to the kitchen.

"He sleeps lightly," Sara remarked. "Reminds me of my cat. His ears almost twitch at every sound, even when his eyes don't open."

Cory smiled. "He's amazing."

"I could tell you were starting to wake, getting restless. I didn't mean to scare you, but I didn't want you to realize someone else was here without knowing immediately who I was."

"Thanks. I appreciate that." She filled her own mug and topped Sara's. They sat together at the kitchen table. "So what's going on?"

"Wade said he needed to catch some sleep, so Gage sent me over. That's all."

"Yeah, he was up all night." She didn't explain her part in that, but she supposed Sara could put the pieces together.

Then another thought struck her. "If he didn't feel comfortable sleeping without someone here on guard, something must have happened."

"I honestly don't know." Sara smiled ruefully. "My brother-in-law—you've met Micah?"

"I've seen him around."

"Well, he used to be special forces, and I've seen him get antsy at times, as if he senses something but doesn't quite know what. Even after all these years he'll still go into a hypervigilant mode at times. Don't ask me to explain what gets them going. It's like they have some kind of internal radar for when something is off-kilter. Or gathering."

"Is he often right?"

"Let's just say I've been glad more than once to have him on my team, as well as a member of the family."

Cory nodded slowly. "It must be hard on them, though."

"I can't say. It's been my experience they don't talk a whole lot about it." Sara's smile was almost wry. "Sometimes I think they get hooked into some kind of mystical cosmic-information highway. Like when my son broke his arm. Micah started getting worked up the day before Sage fell out of the tree. Said he could feel something was going to happen."

"Wow." Cory tried to imagine it.

"Other times, on the job mostly, he's tried to explain it as some kind of internal countdown clock. If $X$ happened, then $Y$ should happen within a certain time frame." Sara shrugged. "I don't know. I'm just a cop, but I guess I have my own form of the same thing. Hunches. Little niggles. The feeling that something isn't right."

"Good intuition."

"Whatever you call it." Sara glanced at the clock. "Wade made me promise four hours and not a second longer. So I'll wake him a little after ten."

"He could sleep longer," Cory protested. They were still keeping their voices low, so it was hard to put enough emphasis into the words. "He needs it."

"When a man like that says four hours, he means it. I'm not going there."

Nor, Cory decided, would she. Wade could be determined about some things, and she had already nearly made him walk out with some nasty words. Who knew how he'd respond to direct defiance, even a little one like this.

Only he probably wouldn't see it as little. He had undertaken to protect her, and she supposed he would have good reason to get hopping mad if she broke his rules.

And she'd be foolish not to cooperate with her protector, even over something so small.

A sigh escaped her, and she began to feel a bit as she had when the Marshals had kept her in the safe house those three months. Trapped, watched, with no volition. At least this time she had moved past mourning. Mostly.

But events roused the old memories, and she sat there with her hands wrapped around her coffee mug, forcing herself to sort through them.

The loss of Jim and the baby still ached, but more like a tooth that had been treated than one that had a raging infection. It would probably always hurt. But as Wade had showed her, she could live again, if she committed to it. Committed to moving on and taking whatever little joys came her way, instead of feeling guilty about them.

Once she got this killer off her back.

Even that, she realized, was a choice she was making. Would she let that man's desire to protect himself keep her always one step removed from truly living? Or would she take charge of her own life again?

Because nobody, nobody, had a promise that they would see tomorrow. She surely ought to have learned that the hard way. She was here now only because a gunshot had failed to kill her, too.

Borrowed time? Maybe. Or maybe this was just life and it was time to stand up and participate again.

A half hour later, Cory went in to wake Wade. It was the first time she had seen him wake, and she was fascinated. At first his eyes snapped open and he tensed, as if ready to spring, but the instant he saw her, his face softened. "Everything okay?" he asked.

"Everything's fine. Sara's getting ready to go."

"Okay." He passed his hand over his face and sat up. Then he wrapped his arms around her hips and pressed his face to her belly. Instantly warm tingles awoke in her center. Reaching out, she ran her hand over his short hair.

"One of these days," he muttered.

"One of these days what?"

He sighed, then tipped his head back and smiled at her. "One of these days we're going to have all the time we want alone together."

She smiled, liking the sound of that. "I'll hold you to it."

"Good."

But then he let go of her, and the guardian returned, flattening his face, steeling his eyes. He pushed out of the chair and went with her to the kitchen, where Sara was donning her jacket to conceal her gun. She looked like just anyone, nothing giving away that she was a deputy.

"Okay, then," she said with a smile. "I'll be off."

At that moment there was a knock at the door. They all stiffened. Cory's heart slammed. That sound would probably always make her heart slam.

"Let me get it," Wade said.

But Sara was right on his heels, gun magically appearing. She stood back, holding the pistol in a two-handed grip, waiting, while Wade looked out the window beside the door. Cory peered around the edge of the kitchen door, gripping the frame so tightly her knuckles turned white.

"Gage," Wade said.

He opened the door to the sheriff, and Cory almost gasped in amazement. Gage didn't look anything like himself. No, he looked like a man who could have lived on the streets undercover for DEA, as he once had: utterly disreputable in a worn leather jacket, stained jeans and a ball cap rather than his usual Stetson.

"Hi," he said as he stepped inside. "Sorry, but I didn't want it to look like the sheriff was stopping in."

"You sure don't," Cory managed.

Gage chuckled. "Good. Okay, we've got plenty to talk about now."

Sara spoke. "Want me to stay?"

"Oh, yeah. We've got some planning to do."

The living room was the only place where they could all sit. Gage took the recliner, Sara the rocker, leaving the couch for Cory and Wade.

Cory's heart had begun to beat a little nervously, knowing Gage wouldn't be here unless he had learned something.

"Okay," he said. "I told Wade earlier, and I don't know if he had a chance to tell you, Cory, but the guy he saw that he thought might be tailing you was a private detective from Denver." Reaching into one of his pockets, he pulled out a notebook and flipped it open. "I'll try to stick to just what you need to know."

"Okay." Her heart skipped then beat a bit faster. Her mouth started to dry with anticipated fear.

"His client, who is going by the name of Vincent Ordano, hired him to find you under the pretext that you had embezzled a huge sum of money from him. He claimed he could track you only as far as this county, that you seemed to have changed your appearance and name, and the only way to flush you out was to make you think you'd been found. Just as Wade suggested might be the strategy."

Cory felt her stomach turn over, and she covered her mouth with her hand, as if that could somehow help.

"Anyway, as Wade suspected, again, the investigator, Moran, scoped out women of a certain age group who had moved here within the last year. He found eight of you, and since Ordano couldn't be sure which of you it was, Moran made the phone call and watched the reactions. He settled on you and your friend Marsha, for exactly the reasons Wade suspected. Moran saw that Marsha got a dog, but he was far more concerned about Wade appearing out of nowhere in your life. That struck him as a whole lot odder than buying a dog. My apologies."

"There's nothing to apologize for," Cory said.

"No? Maybe not. None of us thought you taking a roomer would be pulling some kind of trigger. Regardless, Moran then started some background checking. Marsha, of course, had a trail he could follow all the way back. Yours was sketchy enough to make him think you might be the one hiding."

A soft sound of distress escaped Cory. Wade immediately took her hand, but at the moment it proved to be scant comfort. "It was that easy?"

"Only because someone, somewhere, pointed Ordano to this county," Gage reminded her. "And that's something we are definitely going to deal with as soon as we get Ordano."

"How are we going to do that?"

"That's what we're going to discuss. But let me finish up here, because there's actually some good news in this morass."

Cory managed a nod, and tightened her grip on Wade's hand.

"Moran hasn't reported back yet to Ordano that he's sure you're the woman Ordano wants. He only finished his background checks late last night, and we caught him this morning before he even got to his office. To say the guy is appalled would be an understatement, so we have his full cooperation."

"But if he knows where Ordano is…"

"He doesn't. Their communications have all been by phone and email, and services were paid for with a credit card by phone. We assume Ordano must be nearby, but we don't know exactly where. I'm tracing activity on the credit card Moran was given, but the information may well be out-of-date by the time we get it. If there is any. He might not even be using that card anymore, or any other cards under that name. Hell, we don't know that he really *is* Vincent Ordano. I've got folks researching him, but they may well come up empty-handed."

Cory tried to swallow but her mouth was too dry.

"And I am not, I repeat *not,* going to call the Marshals on this." Gage's frown was deep and dark. "I don't know who talked, but someone evidently did, and until I find out, this stays here, in this county, among my people."

"I agree," Wade said flatly. "The least little slip could start the clock ticking again. I don't want Cory having to live any longer in fear."

"Absolute agreement here," Gage said. "We take care of our own in this county, and Cory has been through more than enough."

Cory actually felt her throat tighten. She was part of this county now, this place she had tried not to connect with. An unexpected homecoming in the midst of this mess. Yes, she wanted to stay here, and she would do whatever was necessary.

"For the moment," Gage continued, "we have an advantage. Moran hasn't identified Cory to Ordano.

That means we can arrange an ambush and substitute a stand-in."

"No." The word came out Cory's mouth almost before she was aware of it.

Everyone looked at her.

"No one is going to risk their life for me. Absolutely not."

"Cory," Wade started to say.

"No." The determination that filled her now was unshakable. "Don't you see? I have enough to live with. I couldn't live with it if someone was hurt or killed in my place. What's more, I think I need to do this. I need to face this guy. I'll never be free of fear again unless I do this." She wondered if she could even convey how strongly she felt that this was something she had to do to lay to rest some of her demons for good. How could you explain that you had run long enough, and now it was time to stand your ground?

But instead of endless argument, she was surprised because all three of them seemed to understand what she was trying to say.

"Okay," Gage said, and Wade nodded, albeit with obvious reluctance. "We'll set up an ambush. Since I want Cory in armor, we need to set it up to occur at night when she can reasonably wear a jacket to conceal the armor. I'm thinking the supermarket parking lot. It would be reasonable for Cory to leave work a half hour or so after the store is closed, and to leave apparently alone. Yet there are plenty of places around where we can conceal ourselves. There are always cars out there overnight for example. A Dumpster. Some trees. Rooftops. The trick will be making sure we don't pick a hiding place that Ordano would choose."

Wade spoke. "Give me a thousand-yard sight line, and I won't miss."

Gage's head tilted a bit. "Are you asking me to deputize you?"

"If it'll make this work better. At least make sure I'm on a roof somewhere with an unhindered sight line. In case."

Cory shuddered helplessly at what he was proposing. She didn't want him to have that on his conscience because of her. She didn't think she could stand it.

Sara spoke. "Micah's a trained sniper, too."

"So put both of us out there. It'll reduce the number of people you need on the ground, and thus reduce the number of people who might give us away."

Gage nodded slowly. "Okay. I like it. I'll go set it up, and give Moran his story to pass along. I'll see if I can't get him to do it in a way that'll push Ordano to move quickly. We can't afford to give him a lot of time to plan."

Cory spoke through stiff lips. "If what happened that night he came after my husband is any indication, he's not one for a lot of planning. He may be good at covering his tracks, but there were so many other times he could have gotten Jim when he was alone…" Her voice broke. "He didn't have to come into the condo when we were both there."

"Good point," Wade said, squeezing her hand gently. "The guy's an opportunist, and a bit careless. He chose an easy way to get at your husband at a time when escape would also be easy, with no one out and about to notice him. And he didn't care about collateral damage, obviously."

He paused a moment, then added, "This Ordano may think of himself as an assassin, but I'd give him low marks. My bet is he's an ordinary thug who took the job for money, and that he doesn't have a whole lot of experience."

Cory looked at him. "How could you know that?"

"Because I would have done it cleaner, and you wouldn't have been around."

The words chilled Cory, but she looked into those dark eyes of his, and she saw a whisper of the pain he felt because he had been required to do such things in his past. She ached for him, for the burdens he carried in silence, for the duty that had scarred him. It raised him even higher in her estimation that he couldn't shrug off such things, that she could see the ghosts in his gaze.

"All right," she said, as if everything had been settled. "Just tell me where to be, and when, and exactly what you want me to do. But let me make it perfectly clear, I will not let anyone take the risk in my place. I cannot live with that. I will not live with that."

Gage sighed and nodded. "I get it, Cory. And sometimes we have to face our demons head-on. It's the only way to be free."

That was it in a nutshell. It didn't mean that she'd sleep any better until this was over. It didn't mean her heart would stop galloping.

But she had to stand up for herself. Now. This time. No matter the cost.

Gage and Sara left like a couple, arms linked, heads bowed together and talking as they walked down the street a little way to Sara's battered pickup. Keeping up the pretense, just in case.

*Just in case.*

The words seemed to hang in her mind like smoke long after a fire has burned out. They had to assume that Moran was Ordano's only information source, but they had to assume at the same time that he was not. No chances, no unnecessary risks.

And Cory felt as if the house were closing in on her, just as those safe houses had a year ago. Only now that she had lost it completely did she realize just how much freedom she had exercised in the past year despite her fear. Freedom to run to the store. Freedom to sit in her backyard on a warm evening. Simple things, but huge in their absence.

"We'll take care of this soon," Wade told her. They were both pacing like caged animals, which might have amused her at another time. Right now it wasn't even remotely funny.

"What if he gets away?"

"He won't."

She faced him. "You can't promise that."

He stilled, becoming as motionless as a statue. "If he gets away, I promise you I will hunt him to the ends of the earth. He will not escape me."

Her chest tightened and began to ache. She reached out and seized his hand, clutching it between both of hers. "No, Wade. Promise me you won't do that. I couldn't stand it. I couldn't bear you to turn into that kind of hunter for me."

His gaze remained hard. "It wouldn't be the first time."

"Maybe not. But you've already done it for the last time. Promise me you won't do that for me. You've already served your time and done your duty. Now…now is for building, not destroying. Promise me, please."

His gaze never wavered. "I can't."

Then he turned from her and resumed his pacing.

Oh, God! She stood still, watching him, knowing there was not a thing she could say or do. This man would do his duty, however he perceived it, and that was that.

The only question was if she would accept it. Accept

him. As he was. As he had been. As he might have to become again.

And somewhere deep inside, she knew she already had.

# Chapter 13

Wade figured at most two days. His reasoning was straightforward. If Ordano was anywhere in the vicinity, he would move fast. Probably the very next night when Cory went to work. If he was halfway across the country, he might take another day.

"But no longer," he said. "This guy wants the threat removed, the faster the better."

Gage agreed.

Cory went to work at her usual time. Her shift seemed to drag. Gage had talked to her boss, so arrangements had been made so that Cory would leave the locked store alone at about a half hour past closing, while others remained inside, out of sight.

Even though she worried about the other employees, Cory was grateful that she would not have to spend that hour alone in an empty store, locked though it would be. Gage felt the presence of the other employees would prevent Ordano from trying to break in and take her out inside the store.

They were doing everything they could to ensure the attack happened in the parking lot. And all they wanted her to do was go in the back room, put on the body armor, pull her jacket over it, then leave the store. And if she saw Ordano, all they asked was that she drop to the ground and roll. Making herself small. Getting herself out of the way.

Walking bait. Exposing herself completely. Her skin crawled in anticipation, and as the hour grew closer, her heart accelerated and her stomach filled with nervous butterflies. She must have made a dozen trips to the fountain to ease the dryness in her mouth, but it only returned minutes later.

She knew the deputies were out there. She knew Wade was on some rooftop, deputized at least for a few days.

But worst of all was the way Wade had withdrawn again, turning into the stony man she had first met. No smile lightened his dark eyes. No unnecessary word passed his lips. He was gone from her as surely as if he had left town.

That hurt. It hurt so much that she now would have new baggage to deal with if she survived the next few days: the baggage of having fallen in love with a man who could shut her out as surely as if he had closed a door and locked it.

And she hurt for him, for the places this must be taking him back to, for all the memories it must be evoking. Right or wrong, duty or not, no soldier survived without scars. And every single one of his must have been ripped open by having to once again slip into the role he had chosen to protect her: Sniper. Killer. Hunter.

God, she almost wished Ordano had found her before

Wade ever appeared. She couldn't stand the thought of what he must be dealing with now.

The hour came at last. Her heart climbed into her throat as she looked at Betsy, her manager. The woman nodded, her face conveying fear and sorrow.

"Be careful."

Cory nodded. She went to the back room, climbed into the body armor and jacket then headed for the front door.

Betsy had given her a key so she could lock the door as she left. Gage didn't want to risk anyone else being visible through all that glass, because Ordano had proved he didn't care who he shot in addition to taking out his target.

The hair on the back of her neck was standing on end as Cory stepped out into a night that seemed strangely chilly for summer. Her entire back prickled with the sense of being watched as she turned and locked the front door from the outside.

But of course there were a dozen eyes on her right now, at the very least. Wade and Micah on the rooftops somewhere. Other deputies hiding in cars or elsewhere. Gage hadn't shared the details, nor did she especially want to know them.

Maybe those were deputies she spied sitting on the sidewalk in front of the pizza place four doors down, looking like two drunks sharing a bottle, totally ragged and sharing a torn blanket. How would she know?

They certainly sounded drunk, and argued over who had drunk the most of the bottle they passed between them.

Slowly she began to cross the parking lot. Per direction, she had left her car at the farthest end so she would have a longer walk. Giving Ordano more opportunity.

There were a half dozen other cars in the lot. Some probably occupied by deputies. All appearing empty.

She'd been ordered to avoid walking anywhere near any of them. Stay in the open. Stay away from those places of concealment.

Step after step she walked, her legs feeling like lead, her heart beating so loud she couldn't hear much else. Wandering a little to avoid the cars. Making loose shopping carts her excuse for the meandering walk, giving the attacker more opportunity to approach. Trying to make it necessary for him to leave his vehicle. If he was in one.

She glanced around again, but could see no heads in any of the cars. And of course, there was her own Suburban, a threat in itself, although she was sure it had been watched continuously since her arrival. She doubted anyone could have managed to hide himself in or around it.

At least, she had to believe that.

Another step. Grabbing another cart and shoving it toward a corral. Annoy the man, Gage had said. Make him impatient.

Well, there were certainly enough forgotten carts out here to help her do that.

She began to shiver, though she couldn't possibly be cold. Her legs went from lead to rubber, and she began to wonder if she would be able to make it all the way to her car.

Another cart. Turn around and walk it back. She clung to it for support even as she pushed it.

How had Wade lived like this for so long? She didn't think she could stand it for another ten minutes.

Maybe it wouldn't happen tonight. She was getting closer to her car, farther from the two guys sitting out in front of the pizza place. More isolated with every step.

"There you are."

She didn't recognize the voice. She froze, her fear ratcheting up to full-blown terror. Stiffly, she turned.

She recognized the face the instant she saw it. It was him. And he was pointing a gun at her from within the confines of a loose jacket. "You!" She gasped the word as she looked into a face that had haunted her nightmares.

"We're going to take a ride," he said. "A nice little ride, just the two of us."

That gun was pointed straight at her. Fear clouded her brain for a few seconds. Paralyzing her, making her forget what she was supposed to do.

"Move it," he said, his voice low and threatening.

But she couldn't move. Then, almost automatically, like any person faced with a gun, she started to obey.

No! The word shrieked in her brain. Drop and roll away. Drop and roll away.

For a few seconds she didn't think she'd be able to. It was as if her body had become a statue. But she might be blocking the sight line they had warned her about. And how would they know this was the guy if she didn't drop and roll? That was their signal that this was the one.

All of a sudden Wade's face popped into her mind. Somehow, thinking of him reminded her that she was capable. Not merely a frightened mouse, but a capable woman.

From his rooftop, Wade watched the encounter. He couldn't tell from the way Cory was acting if this was the guy, or just somebody who wanted to ask for directions. She stood there, still but yet standing, not doing the one thing they had told her to do.

Looking through the scope on the sniper rifle Gage had given him, he couldn't see enough. Cory blocked part of his view. And he couldn't shoot unless he was sure.

Damn!

He held his breath, hoping he didn't watch her get

murdered while he dithered about whether the target might not be the right guy. But he couldn't shoot until he was sure.

He glanced across the way to another rooftop where Micah lay, triangulating on the parking lot. The man seemed undecided, too.

Not enough info. He looked through his scope again, focusing, trying to see some defining detail. Only long experience kept him calm, his heartbeat steady. Forget it's Cory, he told himself. Don't let emotions get involved.

Stay calm. Steady breaths, finger on trigger, waiting. *Become ice.*

Then the two deputies in front of the pizza place started arguing loudly, in slurred voices. The man facing Cory turned just a bit. And Cory dropped to the ground.

It was him.

He held his breath and began to squeeze. But before he got off his shot, the loud pop of Micah's rifle pierced the night.

The guy dropped like a marionette whose strings had been cut. Wade waited, keeping a bead on him as the two "drunks" dropped bottle and blanket and charged across the lot toward Cory.

Only when they got there, and he could see through his scope that they kicked the guy's gun away and bent to cuff him, did Wade ease off on the trigger.

An explosive breath escaped him and he rolled over on his back, staring up at the star-studded heavens.

Thank God. Thank God.

Then the night erupted with colored lights and the sounds of sirens.

He could only lie there drained, thanking God. But a minute later, the adrenaline hit and he was up. He had to get to Cory. *Now.*

* * *

Cory was on her feet by the time Wade came charging up. Shaking from head to foot, she was staring down at the man who had killed her husband. It seemed he was still alive. She didn't know how she felt about that.

But then Wade's arms closed around her, and she was sure she had never felt anything more wonderful in her life. She sagged into his embrace and said his name over and over.

"Are you okay?" he demanded, clutching the back of her head and pressing her tightly to his chest.

She managed a nod.

Gage's voice reached her. "Take her home, Wade. We'll talk after I take care of this creep."

There wasn't an ounce of protest in her, and this time she didn't at all mind when Wade scooped her off her feet and carried her to her car. She hated it only when he let go of her after putting her in the passenger seat and buckling her in.

But when he climbed in beside her, and had turned over the ignition and shifted into gear, he reached over and grabbed her hand as if he were afraid it might slip away.

He carried her into the house, too. And this time when he turned off the alarm, he didn't turn it back on. No need now. From somewhere deep inside, a smile nearly rose to her lips. No more living in fear.

Wade stripped her of her jacket and the armor, then wrapped her chilled body in a blanket and settled her on the couch. "You need something hot to drink. Coffee? Something to eat?"

She doubted she could eat a thing. She still felt adrift, apart, as if she didn't quite belong in the here and now. "Coffee," she managed.

He went to start a pot, but came back immediately to sit

beside her, wrap her in his powerful arms and rub her to stimulate circulation. "Do you feel dizzy? Weak? Maybe you're in shock."

"I'm fine." Slowly, but surely, she realized she was. By the time the coffee was ready and he returned with two mugs, she actually smiled at him.

"I did it," she said.

And slowly, slowly, he smiled back, leaving the stony Wade behind, maybe for good. "You certainly did."

And for that moment, it was enough.

They cuddled throughout the night. First on the couch, then in her bed. Not making love, just cuddling and hugging. Little talking even, but as dawn began to lighten the world beyond the windows, Cory felt something she hadn't felt in a long time.

Pride. And exhilaration. She had done it. She had faced the killer. She had helped catch him.

It was her final act for Jim and their baby. The best memorial she could give them. But it was also the first act in her new life.

She bounded out of bed, and headed for the kitchen to make a huge breakfast, feeling hungry for food, but also hungry for life.

Wade followed, muttering something about a woman who didn't know when she had it good in a warm bed, but she laughed at his grumpiness until he laughed, too.

Oh, it was so good to hear him laugh. So good to feel like laughing.

She made mounds of scrambled eggs and hash browns, poured tall glasses of orange juice. And when they sat to eat, Wade said something that made her feel as light as a helium balloon.

"I'm so proud of you."

From him, that meant a whole lot. "I'm pretty proud of me, too."

"You should be."

She grinned at him and was thrilled when he grinned back.

"You make a mean hash brown, lady."

"Anytime." It felt good to cook for him, good to be doing something for someone else again. At the back of her mind lurked a little rain cloud, warning that there was no permanence here, that Wade would inevitably move on once he had settled whatever he had come here to settle with himself. But she didn't want to think about that now.

No, she was willing to toss her heart over the moon, and take the pain later, because it felt so good to be truly alive again, and life was nothing at all if you wouldn't take risks. A lesson she had learned all too well over the past year.

After they cleaned up, they took a walk together, and for the first time in forever, Cory noticed all the beauty around her, from the birdsong to the ceaseless breeze that whispered through the old tress lining the street. For the first time in a long time, she noticed that life was all around her.

Later they dozed for a while on the couch, for they'd been up most of the night, but then Gage dropped by, and the first of many questions got answered.

"Ordano is in the hospital under guard. The Marshals arrived this morning and the FBI will be here in a little while. The guy started talking as soon as he came out of anesthesia. If you care, Cory, we now know who hired him to kill your husband. And we know who gave you away."

"Who?"

"A secretary in the Marshals' office. All it took was some

sweet-talking, some wine and a few dinners to convince her she was in love with the creep. She managed to find out where you'd been placed and passed the information to him, but nothing else. She didn't have access to begin with so she shouldn't have even been able to learn that much."

"Wow," said Cory. "The things people do for love."

"Or when they think it's love. Anyway, she's been arrested, and procedures are going to be changed, or so I've been promised, although that's not going to be a problem for you anymore."

Cory smiled at him. "No, I guess it isn't."

Gage smiled back. "You'll still have to make a sworn statement for the FBI, and identify Ordano as the man who killed your husband. And there are going to be some other charges related to what happened last night. But one thing for absolute certain, you are never going to have to worry about that man again."

She couldn't stop smiling. "It's a wonderful feeling. I can't tell you how wonderful."

"I think I can imagine." Then Gage looked at Wade. "We've got a place for you as a deputy if you decide you want to hang around. Just think about it."

Rising, he picked up his hat and nodded to them both. "I'll call when we need your statement. It'll probably be later today or early tomorrow."

"I'm free." Free. At last. And how good it felt.

When Gage left, however, other thoughts tried to crowd in. Feeling suddenly nervous, and not sure she even wanted to hear the answer, but needing to know how many possibilities might lie before her, she said to Wade, "Will you take the job with the sheriff?"

"I don't know. I'll think about it. I guess it depends."

Her heart slammed uncomfortably. "Depends on what?"

Wade turned toward her, looking suddenly remote. Or was it something else she saw in his dark eyes. Concern? Unease? She couldn't quite read him.

"On whether you want me to hang around."

She caught her breath and her mouth went dry. Speech seemed impossible. But as she remained silent, she saw his face start to harden into stone again, and near panic struck her. She couldn't let him do that. No matter how hard it was for her to make herself utterly vulnerable to the wound he could inflict on her heart.

"I want you to hang around," she said almost breathlessly.

At once his face began to thaw. "Do you mean that?"

She took her newfound courage in her hands. "I mean I never want you to leave."

"Ever? You hardly know me."

"I know you well enough to know I don't want to give you up. Maybe you don't believe in love at first sight. I'm not sure I used to. It took me a while to fall in love with Jim. But with you…" She hesitated. "Wade, I've been in love before. I know what it is. All of it, good and bad. And I know for certain that I am in love with you."

For a moment he remained perfectly still. Her heart began to beat a nervous tattoo, for fear she had tried to claim something he wasn't prepared to let anyone claim. After all, he'd said he couldn't make connections.

"I think…I think I'm in love with you, too," he said. "I never felt this way before, so I'm not sure of anything except…I always want to be with you. Nobody's ever made me feel what you make me feel. I never knew a hug could mean so much or feel so good. I never knew I could get so intensely preoccupied with another person that I hang on to every word, every look, every gesture. I want to make you happy, if you'll just show me how. I want never to hurt you. Is that love?"

She leaned toward him and wrapped her arms around him. A moment later his closed around hers. "I want this forever," she whispered.

"Me, too." A sigh escaped him. "I want to marry you. I want to know that you want to marry me. For the first time in my life, Cory, I want the ring and the promises. Do you?"

She tilted her head up and looked at him, hoping her heart was in her eyes. "I want them, too, Wade, and I thought I'd never want them again. But I want them with you."

"So will you marry me?"

She watched the sun dawn on his face as she answered, simply, "Yes."

Then he pulled her onto his lap and kissed her, making this deepest of connections in the best way he knew how.

And with that kiss, they ushered in the dawn.

\* \* \* \* \*

"Just being there through how much she'll want me to turn this to than later?"

"It sounded like she could withstand her argument and he'd be proud of her or at least because I want this because he still loved her."

"So am I. And so does Dan. I want to marry my own prince? We're engaged to marry the Deputy Chief of Halton. Everyone's heard of him now."

She'd stopped staring at all of it at me, concern for Dan was in her eyes. "I don't know how can I manage if anything if every morning you print, but I want Dan, I will never."

"Maybe, you many are."

"No, no," she replied quickly because of my words and he simply said.

Then Dan pulled me to him tightly and I saw the outline difference of the wondering him in the way we, we know how.

And with that, Dan's smile seemed to the shower.

# SECRET
# AGENT SHEIKH

BY
LINDA CONRAD

All the characters in this book have no existence outside the imagination of
the author, and have no relation whatsoever to anyone bearing the same name
or names. They are not even distantly inspired by any individual known or
unknown to the author, and all the incidents are pure invention.

First published in Great Britain 2011
by Mills & Boon, an imprint of Harlequin (UK) Limited,
Eton House, 18-24 Paradise Road, Richmond, Surrey TW9 1SR

© Linda Lucas Sankpill 2010

ISBN: 978 0 263 88550 7

46-0911

Harlequin (UK) policy is to use papers that are natural, renewable and
recyclable products and made from wood grown in sustainable forests. The
logging and manufacturing processes conform to the legal environmental
regulations of the country of origin.

Printed and bound in Spain
by Blackprint CPI, Barcelona

When asked about her favorite things, **Linda Conrad** lists a longtime love affair with her husband, her sweetheart of a dog named KiKi and a sunny afternoon with nothing to do but read a good book. Inspired by generations of storytellers in her family and pleased to have many happy readers' comments, Linda continues creating her own sensuous and suspenseful stories about compelling characters finding love.

A bestselling author of more than twenty-five books, Linda has received numerous industry awards, among them the National Reader's Choice Award, the Maggie, the Write Touch Readers' Award and the *RT Book Reviews* Reviewers' Choice Award. To contact Linda, read more about her books or to sign up for her newsletter and/or contests, go to her website at www.LindaConrad.com.

To Shelley and Peggy, the most ingenious
website and newsletter creators ever!
You two are the greatest!

# Chapter 1

Swinging in midair under an endless star-filled sky like some kind of superhero, Tarik Kadir held his breath until his feet reached the solid surface of the ledge.

Monte Carlo's tourists went about their business at sea level twelve stories below—oblivious to the drama unfolding high above their heads. Steadying himself, Tarik released the thin metal rappelling cable attached to the safety harness under his specially outfitted tuxedo shirt.

He let the line go loose and flattened his body against the stucco wall, stopping to let his pounding heart calm. But his heart continued thundering in his chest. Dropping over a dark abyss with nothing but air between your very existence and certain death was not his idea of smart.

The best part of his job had always been hiding in plain sight. Preferably at the nearest casino table.

Becoming a different personality and handing people bold-faced lies was much more in keeping with his lifestyle than any crazy high-flying acrobatics needed to reach hotel ledges. After all, his brothers had always maintained that as the baby of the family, he'd excelled from earliest childhood at being a chameleon and making up stories.

He was born for his old job as a covert agent. But the Kadir family had recently asked all their sons to assume the responsibility for their growing war with ancient enemies, the Taj Zabbar. Out of loyalty, Tarik resigned his commission with the United States Army immediately upon learning of his family's need for him to lead their intel-gathering efforts.

His foot slipped on the slick ledge and Tarik lost his balance. Grabbing hold of the uneven brick wall with his fingertips, he tried balancing on tiptoes. Looking out at the black expanse of ocean in the distance and the ant people strolling the seawall directly below, he swallowed back his panic and relied on innate athleticism to regain his balance.

Breathing slowly in and out, he made his way along the twelfth story ledge of Monte Carlo's Le Meridien Beach Plaza hotel. His thoughts turned to his former work as a member of a special para-military task force—a cross-branch compilation of Army Special Forces, Navy Seals and CIA spooks. He regretted having to quit and he missed working with some of the most elite men and women in the world of covert intelligence. His old unit had been special, known within the Department of Defense for its ability to track down international mobsters and terrorists while staying in the shadows.

With his heartbeat stabilized again, Tarik cleared his

head, inching along in the darkness. As he reached the balcony of the penthouse suite, he slipped over the open railing and the half glass-wall enclosure and crouched down to conceal himself behind a potted palm. The balcony doors had been closed against the chilly night air, but he'd paid the maid a small fortune to see that the sliding glass was left unlocked for the night.

A secret power-broker meeting was supposedly about to take place in the suite on the other side of these glass doors. He needed to be in position with his high-tech surveillance and listening equipment before any of the action began.

Tarik peered past the edge of the glass. The room was an enormous space, set up with a temporary conference table surrounded by six captain's chairs. A handful of men had already gathered and were standing at a bar with drinks in their hands.

He recognized the Russian gangster who'd reputedly organized this little get-together from his CIA dossier. The gangster was Karolek Petrov, a renowned physics genius before the fall of the Soviet Union who had since amassed a $300 million empire based on illegal banking ventures and arms deals.

Tarik had to hand it to his older brother, Darin. His intel about this meeting had been spot-on.

As Tarik quietly set up the micro recording/receiving device Darin's geek department had come up with, he rifled through his memory trying to put names to a couple of the other faces he'd recognized around the bar. Clearly none of the men were members of the Taj Zabbar. He and his brothers had turned themselves into experts at facial recognition when it came to their family's enemies. At this point he could pick out a Taj Zabbar face from any crowd.

Apparently not everyone had arrived for the meeting yet. The Taj Zabbar participant was the only one Tarik cared about, and he'd better show up soon.

Darin's technicians had gathered secret intelligence about this private auction a few days ago. It had been one of many dirty dealings the Kadirs had been anticipating from their enemies. The Taj Zabbar were going back into the international black market to buy arms. According to Darin's sources, the arms for sale at tonight's auction would be more along the lines of weapons of mass destruction.

Judging by Petrov's background, the evening's prize would involve advanced technology. Either biological or nuclear.

Adjusting his earpiece, Tarik finished setting up and settled in to wait for the meeting to start. Crouching in the dark, he listened for anything important.

Tarik thought of Shakir, his middle brother, and of how he had recently destroyed an underground nuclear reactor plant in Zabbarán that had been designed by the Russians for the Taj Zabbar. The Kadir brothers had figured then it was only a matter of time before the Taj Zabbar tried to buy the nuclear capability they needed in the open market.

When the Kadirs had learned of tonight's private auction, Tarik had gone to his old boss at the Department of Defense, trying to enlist the Americans' help in gathering intel about the Taj Zabbar. Buying nuclear technology seemed a clear threat against the entire world rather than simple revenge against old enemies. But the DOD had been reluctant to commit, saying their resources were thin at the moment.

"Get me something tangible I can use to convince my superiors that this new third world nation of the

Taj Zabbar is anywhere close to obtaining nuclear capabilities," General Wainwright had told him.

Tarik had tried to explain about the auction and had asked for help from his old unit in putting together a sting. Instead, when the general had turned him down flat, it had been a hard lesson in the futility inherent in a major bureaucracy.

One of the men in the room moved to the glass next to Tarik's head and stared out toward the moonlit sea. Tarik held his breath and eased farther back in the shadows, quickly coming up with a name for the face. The man was one of the Nigerian terrorists his old unit had recently been trying to locate. Here in Monte Carlo and about to bid on weapons of mass destruction?

Wouldn't the DOD love to know about the Nigerian's participation.

Tarik checked his equipment and made sure the video was being transmitted back to Darin's computers. This Nigerian terrorist alone would have been worth his old boss's attention.

As Tarik sensed the auction was about to start, a rap came at the suite's door. A heavyset man who looked a lot like the movie version of a Russian bodyguard went to answer.

Tarik's pulse rate picked up again. This had to be the Taj Zabbar representative at last.

Instead of a Taj Zabbar agent, a thin man sporting a mustache and wearing a gray tuxedo waltzed into the room with three beautiful women on his arm. Tarik was stunned. Expensive call girls at a secret auction like this?

His gaze flicked to the Russian, whose expression had gone cold. But the man did not make a move to expel the newcomers. Instead he offered them all drinks. It was odd behavior. Tarik studied the new arrivals a little further. Something was not right.

One of the women laughed at the Russian's greeting, the sound of her voice reverberating deep and erotic in her throat. Something about that laugh...

He narrowed his eyes and looked closer, but she didn't look familiar. Her blond, pixie-cut hair was thick and shiny. Too shiny to be real. Her eyes were a violet color not often found in nature. Obviously the lady was trying to disguise herself and not doing it very well. But then, Tarik supposed, if he were a high-priced call girl, he might want to change his identity for each job, too.

He let his gaze rake down over her tight, compact body and the too-exposed expanses of exotic, tanned skin and felt a surprising thrill of recognition. Those curves had appeared in his dreams often enough.

What the hell...?

Another knock on the suite's door grabbed everyone's attention. When the new man and his entourage entered, Tarik sucked in a breath. Not only had the Taj Zabbar sent a representative to the auction, this one was none other than the Elder Nabil bin Khali Taj Zabbar—the general in charge of Taj Zabbar armed forces. With him was a bodyguard and another man Tarik believed to be the new head of Taj Zabbar secret police, Malik Kasim Taj Zabbar. The Taj Zabbar had sent their big guns.

CIA covert agent Jasmine O'Reilly worked hard not to fidget in her too-tight, scratchy dress while she surreptitiously checked out the men in the room as they greeted the newcomers. Who knew rhinestones could be this uncomfortable?

She was accustomed to wearing six-inch stilettos on special missions, but the flashy hooker-style dress was turning into more than she'd bargained for. How did women wear all these spangles and zippers? The simple answer came to her before she finished the question. The dress was not meant to be worn for long.

Pulling her attention back to the targets, she catalogued what she knew of them. The most important man in the room to her was not the Russian mafia character and his cohorts who'd called this meeting. No, with great glee she fixed her thoughts on the Nigerian terrorist she'd been after for the past six months.

God, was she ever good at her job.

Who else could've finagled their way into a room full of third world terrorists and wannabe bad guys? Certainly not that handsome but insufferable ex-agent, Tarik Kadir. She proudly noted that Kadir was nowhere to be found—even after he'd called the DOD's attention to this meeting in the first place.

Whatever was really going down here, Jass was about to make the premier bust of her entire career. She almost rubbed her hands together in satisfaction. But first she wanted to know about the rest of the players in addition to the Nigerian.

There was Karolek Petrov, of course. And a number of bodyguards. Then the high-priced pimp she'd paid to bring her and the other two phony call girls tonight. And if she wasn't mistaken, the other bidders included an Indonesian member of *al-Qaeda,* a rogue member of the IRA, a Georgian separatist and—hmm… The two Middle Eastern–looking newcomers were men who'd not been on her radar before. Interesting.

She supposed it was possible these were the representatives from the Taj Zabbar that Kadir had insisted were coming to buy tonight. But no one in her unit or their superiors had imagined he could be right.

Okay, the people known as the Taj Zabbar, from the
new Republic of Zabbarán, had recently struck it rich
with oil. Rich enough to buy whatever they wanted. But
no rumors of their having terrorist leanings had reached
the ears of the international intelligence communities.
Why would the Taj Zabbar suddenly want to buy nuclear
arms? Certainly not to attack the Kadir family as Kadir
had insisted when he'd asked for assistance from the
unit.

Perhaps it would be worth her effort to question Tarik
Kadir at some point. However, tonight she was all about
taking down the Nigerian. She wouldn't allow any of
the other people in this room to stand in her way. She'd
been after him and his information for six months.

Jass clicked her hidden mouthpiece twice to notify
her backup that she was all set. According to the plan,
two agents would burst through the door five minutes
from her signal. That should be about right. By then
everyone would be seated around the table and she could
position herself close behind the Nigerian.

The Russian murmured to a bodyguard and a silver
briefcase appeared on the table. Petrov nodded toward
it and most of the men sauntered to their seats. All but
the Middle Eastern men.

"Why are females in attendance?" the older one
asked the Russian with a sneer.

"A prize for the losers tonight, Elder bin Khali."
Karolek Petrov beamed as though he had a secret he
couldn't wait to tell. "These are no ordinary women.
Each represents a dozen young virgins who will give a
man the night of his life before they gladly lay down their
lives and die for him. They are worth a king's ransom…
and are my gift for participating this evening."

Jass was glad the two actresses she'd rounded up

looked young and didn't speak English. She tried to move farther away from the man Petrov had addressed as *Elder.*

But before she could take a second step, the younger Middle Eastern man grabbed her by the wrist. "This one is no virgin. If I am not mistaken, she is no lady of the evening either." He swung her around to face the other men. "Look at the intelligence in these eyes. She sees too much."

Jass didn't have a moment to react before the man brought a dagger to her throat. "I will let her fulfill her contract and die for my pleasure right now."

*Oh, brother.* There went all her best-laid plans.

She gritted her teeth to notify her backup with three clicks that she was in trouble. Then she overpowered her surprised assailant by using a nifty thumb hold she'd perfected years ago. The knife went flying and he went to his knees with a yell and a thud.

Chaos erupted in the room. Shouts in several languages bounced off the walls. Guns were pulled from under jackets. The door banged open and a shot rang out. And somewhere in the back of her mind she thought she heard the balcony's glass doors sliding open.

But she was too busy to notice. She appropriated a gun from one of the hulking bodyguards with a smooth move he never saw coming and then headed through the crowd toward the Nigerian, who had been standing closest to the balcony. She caught a glimpse of him before he ducked out through the open balcony doors.

*Oh, no you don't. We're twelve stories up. You're mine, you bastard.*

Tarik was inside the room and fighting to reach Jass O'Reilly before he could think twice about it. His mind had blanked when the head of Taj Zabbar secret police had put that dagger to her throat. Tarik had been intrigued with her from afar for years and the idea of his fantasy woman going down in a slash of bloodshed had moved him to action.

But by the time he overpowered the Russian and put him out of commission, she was nowhere to be found. Had she ducked out the front? Impossible. That exit was now clogged with men in various stages of being apprehended.

He twisted around and as his eyes darted across the room, he realized two unsettling things. The suitcase was missing from the table and the two Taj Zabbar reps were gone.

Worse, with another sweeping glance, he noted both the Nigerian and Jass had also disappeared. But they could not possibly have gotten past him. They'd both been too close to the balcony when the sting went bad.

He would have to consider the Taj Zabbar later. Right now he needed to back up his former comrade in covert operations.

When he barged through to the balcony, Tarik was hit with another shock. Jass and the Nigerian were leaning over the balcony wall, wrestling over a Ruger .357 Magnum. The Nigerian had a good fifty pounds and six inches on her.

Tarik's weapon was useless under the circumstances. He couldn't get off a clean shot. He held his breath and moved in closer, waiting for a moment to let the Nigerian learn of his presence—the hard way.

But the longer their struggle went on, the more he could see Jass weakening. The Nigerian had her bent over backward with her upper body hanging out over nothing but night air.

Tarik couldn't wait. He had to make a move now.

Grabbing the assailant by the shoulder, he tried to turn the Nigerian around to face him. But right at that moment Jass made her move, too.

She hooked her leg around the Nigerian's knees and used all her power trying to bring him down. But Tarik's shove had overbalanced the assailant and all three of them slid closer to the balcony wall.

Horrified, he watched as both Jass and the Nigerian slipped over backward and disappeared completely into the black night. With a roar, he dove over the wall, landing tenuously on the ledge beyond.

"Help me, you idiot." The small voice coming from below him finally cleared away the hazy panic in his head as Tarik spotted her fingers gripping the edge.

"Jass." He flattened himself on the ledge and made a grab for her arms.

When he felt the warm skin of her wrists and fastened his hands around them, he began to murmur quiet encouragement. "I've got you. Take it easy."

She groaned. "Stop talking and pull me up."

Earlier the breeze off the ocean had been benign and gentle. Now it felt like a full-force gale. He latched one arm around the balcony wall and hoped to hell he could drag her up one-handed. It would do no good for both of them to take a header into oblivion.

Whenever he'd thought of Jass in the past, he'd never thought of her as particularly thin or small. But with a spurt of much needed adrenaline, he raised her up over the edge without a lot of effort.

Son of a gun. They were still alive.

Dragging her closer to his chest, he waited until

his breathing slowed and he could actually feel his extremities again. That was as close to death as he ever wanted to go.

Jass pushed at his chest. "How about we move to a solid surface?" She came to her knees and reached for the balcony wall. "I suppose you expect a thank-you for saving my life."

Suddenly irritated, he pulled them both over the wall to the balcony floor. "I would rather get an explanation as to why you felt it necessary to bust in on my sting."

She stood in bare feet with her wig askew and dusted off her hands. "Not your sting, pal. Mine. I've been chasing that Nigerian for months and now you've ruined our chances of ever questioning him. You owe me."

*Damn.*

"My mistake," he muttered as he turned toward the suite doors.

He left her standing there trying to figure out what he'd meant. If he'd known how ungrateful she would be, he might've left her swinging in midair.

Now he had the sinking feeling he was going to live to regret tonight's entire heroic episode.

# *Chapter 2*

She was completely screwed.

Jass ran her hands through the auburn mop on her head that laughably passed for her real hair and squared her shoulders to face the music. Ed Langdon, her CIA handler, and General Gus Wainwright, the head of their interagency Task Force, came through the conference room door. Tarik Kadir was right on their heels.

She jumped up and stood as still as if she were at attention. It was barely twelve hours since the Nigerian had gone to his heavenly paradise and Jass hadn't had much sleep. For most of the night she'd been too busy trying to interrogate the men who'd been captured in the hotel room and, when that became futile, working desperately to salvage something from the fiasco of last night. She had come up empty-handed on all counts.

For the last hour she'd been sitting quietly in the American consulate's office waiting for her scheduled meeting with Ed. Jass had been going over all her moves from last evening's sting, still trying to piece together how things had gone wrong. When she'd originally designed the plan for last night, she was positive nothing could prevent it from becoming one of her biggest career highlights. Capturing a man that the Agency had been seeking for the last three years had seemed the perfect path to advancement.

The fact that General Wainwright was here in Monaco—that he'd felt it necessary to fly in from the states, did not bode well for her rising career at all. The general motioned for her to sit and she took her first breath since he'd walked through the door. Somehow she had to survive whatever came next with her job intact.

Tarik Kadir plopped down in the seat next to hers. Her senses started reeling. She could actually feel heat emanating from his body, even considering his place at the table was well over two feet away. She scooted her chair a little farther to the side, but it didn't help.

Glancing at the ex covert agent out of the corner of her eye, she found him staring back at her. Besides being insufferable, the man was also a rude bore.

He flashed her a crooked grin from behind his benign-looking black-framed glasses. Was he in some sort of disguise this morning? She knew for a fact that the man did not need glasses for his eyesight. Last night in a tux he'd been delicious to look at. Like the billionaire playboy sheik he was rumored to be. But this morning, the hand-tailored button-down shirt and soft suede jacket made him look unpretentious and conservative.

*Bull.* Did he really believe anybody would miss the aura of controlled power or the watchful intelligence hiding underneath the traditional cut of his coal-colored hair or in the eyes behind those ridiculous fake glasses?

"You still waiting for a thank-you for saving my life?" she asked while trying hard to sound unaffected.

"I don't waste much time on fantasies." The look he gave her was so full of erotic meaning it sent her pulse racing and made her mouth go dry.

She tried to inch farther away but found herself hugging the wall as Ed and General Wainwright seated themselves across the table.

The general's forehead furrowed as he began, "Well, Special Officer O'Reilly. It seems your crack plan for capturing the Nigerian turned into a royal cluster f…" He stopped, looked slightly flustered about almost using the crude military expression meaning disaster, and then cleared his throat. "Either of you two have anything more to say about what happened last night?"

"Everything would've worked out if *he* hadn't stepped in."

"If the DOD had listened to me about the Taj Zabbar building weapons of mass destruction in the first place, *we* could've worked this sting together and nothing would've been lost."

They'd both spoken at the same time and their words were more or less blown away in the confusion. Exasperated, Jass folded her arms over her chest and sat back.

The general pinned her with a steely gaze. "Did it once occur to you to ask what item could've been big enough to induce the Nigerian to come out of the shadows and attend last night's sale?"

"I figured it was big drug deal or maybe U.S. counterfeit currency plates, sir. Rumor has it the Nigerian has been raising funds and buying into moneymaking schemes all over Europe." Jass was becoming more uncomfortable by the second.

The general waved his hand dismissively. "My fault. I should've seen this coming when I approved your plan."

Next he turned on Tarik. "You thought you recognized Special Officer O'Reilly in her disguise. Is that right?"

Tarik nodded once.

"And yet you went out on the balcony to rescue someone you knew to be a competent officer and turned your back on the briefcase containing a nuclear device."

Tarik's face paled and his jaw became impossibly hard.

The general surprised him by flashing a grin. "I guess we're all treading in deep water over this screwup. Let's see what we can do to make it right."

Jass didn't like the sound of that. She had no intention of ever doing anything with the infuriating *sheik* Kadir.

Tarik could see the frustration building on Jass's face. He knew what that was like. He'd been trying for months to convince the DOD, and General Wainwright in particular, that the Taj Zabbar were a serious and growing danger to the world. Up until this morning, he hadn't succeeded.

He forced his attention back to the general. "I just finished speaking to my brother at Kadir headquarters, sir. The briefcase has disappeared—along with the Elder bin Khali Taj Zabbar. We'll pick him up again, though it might take some time. But Darin did get a line on that other matter you asked about." He took a breath.

"Seems our technical unit has been hearing the same rumors over the social networks that your units have, and we're fairly sure the Taj Zabbar will be involved in that upcoming auction, too."

"Then that gives us a place to start fresh together." The general tilted his head to address Jass. "We caught a break when another DOD split task force captured an *al-Qaeda* operative in Pakistan last week. The Pakistanis have been interrogating the man and yesterday obtained a major piece of intel."

Tarik watched as Jass's expression went from resigned and frustrated to hopeful and eager. She was arresting to look at with her exotic mix of cultures. Not classically beautiful, but expressive and fascinatingly intense when she thought she wasn't being observed. A man couldn't avoid keeping his eyes trained on that face. At least, not this man.

"It seems our Russian from last night's auction had another partner," the general continued. "Someone still operating in the wind who supposedly has one more auction scheduled for next week."

"Another briefcase bomb? Surely not. That's—"

The general's hand chopped the air to stop her words. "No, another bomb would've been impossible to sneak out of Russia, even for a genius like Karolek Petrov. But it seems there is one more item up for bid that's worth paying a king's ransom—at least for terrorists."

Jass sat up a little straighter. "A detonator or timing device of some sort?"

"Good point. It's possible. We don't know for sure." General Wainwright folded his hands on the desk and stared down at them. "Whatever it is, it's big. All we know are the identities of some of the bidders and the approximate location and date. We need to know the rest."

Jass's eyes rounded and dilated. Bless her fiendish little heart. Tarik could see she was almost drooling over the potential of being given such a plum assignment. When she learned the truth, that this was going to be his sting—not hers—he had a feeling her expressive face would be speaking a different language.

"Do we have a way to firm up the location?" Jass asked the general.

She was starting to believe this would be more of a golden opportunity rather than the end of her career. She snuck a look at Ed, her handler, and was puzzled by his narrowed expression. He apparently knew something she did not.

"The auction will definitely be taking place in Brazil," the general answered with authority. "The Russian's partner, also one of the Russian mob but not as clever as Petrov, has developed a network headquartered in Rio. That much we know for sure. The Kadir family's intel unit has put feelers out and we expect to have better information as we get closer to the date."

The *Kadir family* intel unit? What the heck was that? And what the devil was wrong with their own CIA intelligence? No wonder Ed was not looking too happy.

Jass pinned her lips together to keep from making a remark she might regret later. She was still convinced she was only a hairsbreadth away from being kicked out of the Task Force over last night's screwup. The way this new mission turned out would make all the difference to her career.

She had to keep her job. It was her only chance to live

up to the high standard her father set years ago. Thank God it appeared she was being given the opportunity.

"Special Officer O'Reilly, your background file says you can speak both Russian and Farsi. Is that correct?" The general had his gaze trained on her face.

"Yes, sir. My mother's family was originally from Iran and I spoke Farsi before English. I learned the Russian language for a covert op a few years back."

"Well, Farsi is not perfectly suited for this mission but we can make it work. The Russian is pivotal."

He was going to make her the operative in charge of the mission after all! Relief nearly brought her to tears. Jass was thrilled to get the badly needed superior position to make up for the one she'd messed up. Taking a deep breath, she turned to study Kadir. What was his role here? Informant? Adviser?

Whatever it was, she hoped they wouldn't have to work together too closely or for terribly long. The man rode her nerves whenever his gaze raked over her body. Which was pretty much every time she'd ever run into him.

"We've devised a sting to take advantage of a couple of lucky breaks." The general turned to Ed for an affirmative nod, then continued. "First, about a month ago, ICE agents apprehended a woman who's been on Homeland's watch list for years. She's an international illegal arms dealer with no allegiance to any country and who seems devoid of any scruples about the deals she makes."

"The *Messenger?*" Jass knew of only one woman who might fit that criteria.

The general nodded grimly. "As a favor to us, Homeland has kept the lid on her capture. We're sure nothing has leaked out to any of the intelligence community."

Jass was positive he was correct. She'd been following the exploits of the mysterious woman known as the Messenger for years and knew nothing of her capture.

Turning to Tarik, the general explained further. "This shadowy female dealer's real name is Celile Kocak. Originally Uzbekistani from Russian and Turkish decent, as I understand. Her exploits in the field of buying and selling arms have been embellished over time, yet no one had ever seen a picture of the woman.

"Now that we have her in custody," he went on. "It turns out she has a few years on Special Officer O'Reilly. But other than that, the two could easily pass as sisters."

Wow. Think of that. The mysterious woman who had captured her imagination for forever looked enough like her to be a sister. Jass was enthralled by the idea of passing for such a deadly and merciless criminal on a sting.

From his position next to her, Tarik cleared his throat. "You said there'd been two lucky breaks?"

"Indeed. Under intense interrogation we've learned that this Kocak woman has been scouring the market for the last few months, looking for special arms to buy for another mysterious character. A shady Middle Eastern sheik who goes by the name of Abu Zohdi. We've been trying to track him down, and he's recently turned up in an English jail in the Bahamas—although they didn't know who they had in custody.

"This middle-easterner is one extremely dangerous and rich terrorist," the general went on to explain. "With close ties to *al-Qaeda*. And the Bahamians were about to release him due to lack of evidence. It was only by pure luck that we obtained his whereabouts from the Kocak woman before he was long gone."

"We have Abu Zohdi in our hands now?" Jass knew that name too and was beginning to worry about where the general's explanation was heading.

"Momentarily. In the meantime we are continuing to interrogate the Kocak woman, trying to learn what kind of arms will be for sale in Rio."

Yes, the more information she had before going in, the better prepared she would be to disrupt the sale. "Excuse me, General Wainwright, but what result do you anticipate from our mission? Is it more important to capture this other Russian or to take control of whatever weapons are for sale?"

The general raised one eyebrow and she almost giggled at the silly picture he made. "I trust you will not hesitate to confiscate anything as potentially dangerous as a nuclear bomb if it's placed right in front of you, Officer O'Reilly. Not this time."

Her smile faded in that instant. She felt her cheeks warming and was glad for her golden skin tones. Fairer women had a more difficult time disguising their embarrassment.

"Yes…uh…no, sir."

"Your job on this sting is to get your partner inside that auction to meet all the bidders. Gather information. Intel is your ultimate assignment with the Task Force, remember." The general narrowed his eyes at her. "Your handler will give you further instructions once we get a clearer picture of what's going on inside."

"My partner?" Jass's whole body tensed.

"Kadir here will be going in undercover as your client, Abu Zohdi. For months he's been trying to convince the DOD that the Taj Zabbar have become terrorists worthy of our attention." He spoke in a low, measured tone. "If they do show up at this meeting ready to buy, my boss will have to accept that they're powerful enough to pose a threat to the world."

Jass's mind raced with good reasons why she couldn't take Tarik Kadir along with her on a mission. The number-one reason being that he was no longer employed by the United States government. He'd quit.

Tarik stirred in his seat beside her. They shot a glance at each other. He didn't seem all that thrilled about working with her either.

"But sir, I respectfully ask you to reconsider," she pleaded. "I can handle this mission better alone. If you want to know the identities of the people at the auction, leave it to me. I'll get names, pictures and backgrounds on everyone involved with no trouble. It's my *job*."

"Besides," she continued, desperately trying to come up with a good argument in her favor. "Doesn't the Messenger always work alone? On behalf of a client, for sure, but haven't her past clients always remained unnamed?"

"Not recently. Your intelligence on the Messenger is at least a year behind. You'd better study her files carefully on your way to Rio."

"But…"

The general tilted his head toward her as if to say he was done with her questions. But then he made one more chilling remark to top off his side of the argument and leave no doubt why this sting would go down exactly his way.

"Over the last year, Celile Kocak and Abu Zohdi have become lovers. According to her, they seldom leave each other's sides. In fact, that's how ICE got their hands on her. She made a mistake in her haste through the States to the Bahamas trying to reach her lover and bail him out of jail."

*Lovers? Oh, Lord.*

She felt Tarik go rigid in his seat beside her as he asked, "Lovers, sir? Exactly how close to that definition do you want us to stay?"

"Close enough for it to appear you can't keep your hands off each other, Mr. Kadir. This joint mission was originally your idea. And you agreed to accept one of our Task Force agents as your partner."

The general glared at both agents.

"Now stick to the plan we've drawn up. You two are going in as lovers or the whole deal is off."

# Chapter 3

Jass's knees were still trembling an hour after her meeting with General Wainwright. She'd finally shed the scratchy dress for her jeans, but her mind continued racing with possible scenarios for escape.

She couldn't imagine having to work with the irritating sheik. Now, while sitting alone across from Ed having coffee, she had the feeling she'd stepped onto a boat that was taking on water.

"I don't like it any better than you do, Jass. He's a loose cannon and I'm not sure we can trust him."

Ed Langdon, her longtime friend as well as her handler, ran a hand across tired-looking eyes. The poor guy hadn't had any more sleep than she had last night.

"But we don't have a choice." He sighed and stared into his coffee. "You have to at least go through the motions of this sting with Kadir or else Wainwright may bust us both out of the Task Force."

"Oh, Ed. No. Whatever I screwed up had nothing to do with you."

He dug his fingers through his thinning hair and then went back to drinking coffee with both hands wrapped around the mug. "You're my responsibility. When an assignment goes bad, it's my fault."

Ed was the closest thing to a father figure she'd had since her own father died on a CIA covert mission nearly ten years ago. At that time she had recently graduated college and was interviewing with the Agency for her first job. Her father had wanted her to go to law school. He'd wanted something safer and saner for his daughter than he'd had for himself.

But she'd always seen her father as the sun, the moon and the brightest star in the sky. Everything revolved around him and had since her mother died when she was a girl. What her father did for a living was exciting. Stimulating. The very idea of undercover work had thrilled her down to her bones.

Her mother had been the steady one in the family. The rock. She'd had a nice, normal job as an accountant. And what did that get her? She'd been kidnapped from her nice safe office, robbed and murdered.

No thanks. Jass would take her chances with undercover work.

"I don't like the whole idea of this Kadir character forcing himself on you while you try to make an ill-conceived plan work. He's charismatic when he wants to be."

Jass bristled. "Geez, Ed. You know me better than that. No one takes advantage of Jasmine O'Reilly."

Ed gave her a lopsided smile. "I know, honey. Sometimes I think you take yourself far too seriously. How long has it been since you've even had a date?"

"Uh, a while. I've been working. It's hard to go out when you're playing the part of a dangerous Indonesian spy or in disguise as the girlfriend of an IRA terrorist." She shrugged. "But I don't feel deprived. I like under-cover work. A lot."

Ed grinned. "Yep. Too damned independent and serious for your own good. You can't go through your whole life like that, you know."

After her father had died, Ed had gone to bat for her at the Agency. He'd been her father's partner and longtime friend and said he wanted to help her however he could. And when Ed was promoted to being SAC and a handler, he'd made sure she was under his wing and came along, too. He'd always been every bit as concerned about her as a person as he was with her as a covert officer under his control.

Jass fiddled with her paper napkin. "I have lots of time for a life later. I'm only twenty-nine. You know how important it is to me to be the best at what I do."

Ed sat silent for a few moments. Finally he said, "Look, you have to take this assignment. But you don't have to fall for whatever Kadir is selling. I believe he has his own agenda and will try to gain your trust so he can somehow get his hands on the prize." He looked at her intently. "Don't let him. As usual, I'll be standing by to remind you to keep your head in the game. Listen to me."

"Don't I always?" she murmured, smiling at Ed.

He blew out a breath and chuckled. "Okay, little girl. Good enough for now. Let's see about getting you prepped for whatever surprises come your way."

Tarik had to force his gaping mouth shut when Jass climbed into the back of their limo with him. Man, did she look hot. Not that she didn't always look terrific, with her sexy auburn hair, exotic hazel-green eyes and a body to drool over.

But this sophisticated persona of the deadly Celile Kocak sent electric shivers straight to his groin. Maybe their mission wouldn't be hard to take after all.

The CIA handler, Ed, slammed the limo's back door after her and slid into the front seat next to the driver. "You all set, Kadir?"

Tarik wasn't paying much attention to Ed. He had better things to look at. Dressed in one of those French-designed suits and Italian leather four-inch heels, Jass never turned her head his way. She kept staring out the window as the limo began to roll away from the hotel.

Tarik absently adjusted his gold-braided head scarf and spoke to Ed without turning. "Becoming a rich Middle Eastern sheik is one disguise that shouldn't be too much of a problem for me, Langdon."

He kept his eyes trained on Jass. "You look amazing. Run into any trouble with the background intel?"

She turned her head only slightly and a strand of that long, luxurious mane slid over one dark-brown contact, obscuring it from his view. "I know how to do my job."

If it wasn't a balmy, late winter day in Monte Carlo, Tarik would've expected an ice storm. Much more of that kind of cold shoulder and this assignment might be the death of him yet.

"Well, I wish one of you could speak Portuguese," Langdon added from the front seat. "A dozen languages between you and yet not the one that might save your ass in Brazil."

"Spanish is close enough," Tarik said without as much as a smirk on his face. "We can fake it."

Jass shot him another icy, half-hidden glare and inched closer to her door. "You can bet the *Cariocas* will notice we don't speak their language."

"We're going in as tourists," he argued. "Arms buyers. Not Rio natives. We'll get along."

Tarik heaved a heavy sigh and leaned back in his seat. Yes indeed, this was going to be one long, miserable assignment. And if they couldn't find some middle ground, they'd both be lucky to come away from it alive.

A few hours later, flying high above the Atlantic, Tarik loosened the seat belt in his first-class seat and checked on Jass. He thought she might be trying to sleep, but she was wide awake and working on her laptop. She had the privacy screen set on the laptop so no one could read over her shoulder and she looked for all the world like any wealthy international businesswoman.

They needed to begin bonding. He'd let her put an aisle between them for the flight. But the minute they left the relatively secluded confines of this first-class cabin and moved into the duel worlds of espionage and glitz in Rio, they would have to begin the lovey-dovey act. The snow princess would have to thaw or the entire mission would be compromised.

He cleared his throat, moved into the empty seat beside her and pitched his voice low enough to be heard only by her. "I understand you keep an apartment in D.C. How long has it been since you've been home?"

She flipped down the laptop's lid and turned her head, pushing back the thick veil of hair covering the side of her face. "You've been reading my file? Maybe it would be better if you stuck to studying the files concerning Celile and Zohdi."

"We only have a few hours to work on becoming an

intimate couple." How could she rile him this quickly? "I thought it would be smart for us to get to know each other a little better on a personal level first."

Jass frowned and drew a weary breath. "Fine. D.C. is not my home. I was raised in Chicago by my mother's family—which of course you know if you've read my file. But the apartment in D.C. is a few blocks from where my father used to keep his base while working for the Agency. As a kid I visited him between assignments and I know a little about the neighborhood. Still, it isn't what I would call a real home.

"When you come right down to it," she added quietly. "I don't guess I have what most people would call a home. Never felt the need for one."

Ah, but the wistful tone in her voice said that last statement was a lie. Tarik filed the interesting bit of information away for a later time when he'd gotten to know her better.

"But that's something we have in common," he murmured. "See? We haven't been talking for more than a few moments and already we've found a subject to agree on. None of the extended Kadir family have formal roots either. Not for a thousand years. We're…"

"Nomads," she supplied. "Originally Bedouins. Yes, I read your file, too."

He felt ridiculously pleased that she'd cared enough to read his file. Not that he should have doubted it. Whatever else Ms. Jasmine O'Reilly turned out to be underneath her many personas, she was a serious and dedicated CIA operative. She would never go on a mission unprepared, even one that had been as spur of the moment as this one.

The flight attendant brought them both glasses of

white wine. Jass took a sip before thanking the fellow and sending him away.

"Why did you resign your commission?" she asked as she studied Tarik over the rim of her glass. "The files weren't clear on that point."

*Ah yes, the billion-dollar question.* He knew the men in his old Special Forces unit and many of his former comrades in the joint Task Force were asking themselves the same thing. Well, he wanted to become closer to Jass for this mission. Might as well tell her all of it.

"I doubt my file has a notation in it explaining the five-hundred-year-old family feud between the Kadir family and the Taj Zabbar tribes of Zabbarán. It's something my brothers and I barely understand ourselves."

Jass set down her wine but kept her eyes trained on his face. "I discovered a little about the feud by doing a Google search. Originally, the Kadirs were caravan traders on the Spice Route. And around five hundred years ago the caravan was decimated by the fierce Taj Zabbar tribes. Right so far?"

He nodded, fascinated by her low, hypnotic voice.

"Yes, well. Apparently the Kadirs turned around and destroyed as many of the Taj Zabbar as they could in retaliation."

"Hold on. Our side of the story is a lot different. The Kadirs had no choice. We had to neutralize the threat in order to survive. The Taj wouldn't stop. They kept on coming. They…"

He stopped himself mid-rant and forced a smile when her eyes gleamed with humor. "Okay, I agree. That was centuries ago and no real written records were kept at the time. It could've happened the way you said. And at a much later date we weren't exactly angels when it came to our treatment of the Taj."

"Ah yes," she interrupted. "Let's jump the story ahead to fifty years ago when the Kadirs were already filthy rich in the shipping industry and looking to further their interests in the Zabbarán territory." She quirked a brow. "Didn't your family make a secret deal with the Taj Zabbar's neighbors and oppressors, the Kasht? Supposedly the Kadirs traded guns and other armaments for the sole rights to the only deep-water port in Zabbarán and the surrounding area. Right?

"Now that was really some Spice Trade." She'd added her own answer with a wry smile. "And didn't the Kasht use those very weapons to subdue a revolt by the Taj? They killed Taj women and children, put the men into slave labor and then burned and pillaged everything in sight. Nice family trade, Kadir." A note of derision filled her voice. "Why am I not even a little surprised that the Taj hate your family and want revenge?"

Tarik tamped down on the automatic rise in his blood pressure. He knew the truth of what his family had done and who they were now. The Kadir family's past was not spotless. But in more modern times they had become contributing members of civilized world society—unlike their counterparts the Taj Zabbar.

"I don't have to defend my family to anyone. Everything you said may be true, but it was done long ago. Before either of us was born. And it's no excuse for the Taj to behave the way they do today." His eyes hardened. "They're terrorists, killers and brutes. They deal with drug lords and mobsters the world over. They've tried to annihilate my family by blowing us up, and never mind that fifty innocent people were caught in the explosion."

He took a breath and let the words roll out. "They kidnap vulnerable women and sell them to the highest bidders. They run their own country like a medieval fiefdom, even with all their new wealth. And worst of all, they are secretly planning to become the world's newest nuclear power before any of the civilized nations can take notice."

"How do you know that last part? About their nuclear ambitions."

She had genuine interest in her eyes for the first time since he'd begun speaking. The new expression made her look young…vulnerable, and made Tarik damned curious about getting to know this part of her a lot better.

"My middle brother Shakir went into Zabbarán covertly a few months ago to rescue the woman who has since become his wife. She and their son were being held for trade to the highest bidder," he explained. "I was part of my brother's backup team. While we were there, we found an underground nuclear centrifuge facility and…"

"What?" Jass leaned in close and pinned him with a doubtful look. "From what I understood the Taj are too backward and couldn't possibly have that kind of scientific know-how."

"Just listen," he began, instead of counting to ten to calm his temper. "I have in my possession a few satellite photos of the area under construction. And the images seem clear enough to people in the know. But we blew the place up before we left the country. I figured why not take the opportunity and save the rest of the world a hell of a lot of grief."

Jass leaned back in her seat. "So you don't have any real proof. Only wild speculation and fuzzy pictures."

He bristled but kept his voice down. "I was there. And our family's intelligence units have been picking up further mentions of nuclear subjects in the current Taj communiqués. We're sure they haven't given up their ambitions."

"How so?" she probed.

"Look at the other night. They sent a couple of representatives to that auction and stole the briefcase bomb, didn't they?"

"Did they? We only have your word on that. I wouldn't know what they look like. The Taj aren't on the world intelligence radar screens." She smirked at him. "Those Middle Eastern men in the room that night could've just as easily been members of the Kadir clan for all I know."

Frustrated, Tarik sat back and stared out the window before he made a few remarks that would be totally inappropriate for anyone who intended to become her lover within the next few hours. He was usually much better at capturing a woman's attention and interest than this. In fact, he was *always* better at convincing people of his honesty and sincerity. Ironically, that was part of what made him such a good covert agent.

What was with Jass O'Reilly? He'd known she was slightly different than most women. But she wasn't even responding to him like a normal human being.

He was foundering here, trying to find some common ground. What the hell would happen when they had to pretend to have an intimate love affair?

Jass was a pro. She didn't need Tarik Kadir to remind her of their mission. But he'd tried to do exactly that as they left the plane and entered Rio's Galeao Airport. She'd sniffed at his ridiculous attempt to rile her and brushed out past the flight attendants.

Throwing her tote bag over her shoulder, she sidled

up close to him on their walk to retrieve the baggage and whispered low, "Don't forget Zohdi wouldn't let Celile carry anything heavy—or walk too far ahead. It's part of his macho personality."

Tarik's body jerked, almost imperceptibly, but he slowed enough to reach around and take her tote with a huge grin. "Here, let me, my darling." He used a clear, slightly accented voice. "Wouldn't want to tire you before we reach the hotel. I have big plans for us later tonight."

She ground her teeth and smiled seductively. "Of course, sweetheart. But business comes first."

Fortunately for her, another part of Zohdi's personality was deeply rooted in his Middle Eastern background. He did not indulge in sentimental bodily contact in public. No pawing or slobbery kisses for him. She almost reminded Tarik of that, but decided to keep her mouth shut for now.

Zohdi never let his gaze stray from the love of his life for long. And he never let her talk to another man without putting himself close enough to feel her pulse beat.

Jass thought that last part might've been romantic if the two people in question weren't such a dangerous duo. And if her undercover partner on this romantic assignment wasn't Tarik Kadir.

The Rio airport terminal was a madhouse. Crowds descended from every corner and surrounded them as they walked. Jass felt the tension building in her every cell. While she was undercover, she never cared for crowds. An assassin could easily attack from any direction and she wouldn't recognize the threat until it was too late.

When they finally reached the baggage carousel,

they found the crowds impenetrable around it. This much congestion in the Rio airport on a Thursday evening seemed strange—and she wondered if it could potentially signal a glitch in their mission.

The two of them stood motionless at the edge of the crowd for a moment as they silently pondered their best plan of attack for reaching the luggage.

"Ms. Kocak. Sheik Zohdi." Suddenly a man who seemed to be a native Brazilian spoke to them with a heavy accent. He'd appeared out of nowhere right beside them. "I am your driver. Your luggage is being sent ahead. Please follow me."

Jass raised her shoulders along with her gut instincts. Ed had told her they would be contacted by someone from the CIA station chief's office with further instructions. But she hadn't expected anyone this soon.

She glanced at Tarik, who also seemed to be on alert, but then he gave her a cockeyed grin and inclined his head. "After you, love. I am yours to command."

He was silently signaling that he was leaving the choice to follow this man up to her. Her whole body trembled with pride and an odd sensual awareness as she forced herself to turn and make her way through the throngs behind the stranger.

That grin of Tarik's might end up becoming her undoing before their assignment was over. The man was impossibly handsome all dressed up as a modern sheik in his Versace suit, white linen boat-necked shirt and head scarf. Jass shook off the sensual pull she'd felt and worked her mind back to the persona of Celile.

She had to remember that Ed said not to trust Tarik despite his glib manner and sincere looks.

They reached the curb in front of the airport and found a sleek black sedan waiting. Their driver paid two thugs who were obviously carrying concealed weapons and, with a few words in Portuguese, sent them on their way. Then he ushered her and Tarik into the backseat.

As they pulled into the stop-and-go traffic, she asked the driver, "What's going on here? Why all the people and congestion?"

Suddenly their driver didn't have even a slight accent. "You're kidding, right? Tomorrow is the start of *Carnivale*. The tourists are pouring into the city. Expect the crowds to get a lot worse over the next four days."

"Smart." Tarik relaxed back into his seat and propped an ankle over his knee. "The Russian picked the best time of year to hold this little auction. His buyers will be tough for us to pick out from the rest of the tourists."

She turned to see Tarik in the dim light filtering in through the car's windows. "Have you ever been to Rio's *Carnivale* before?"

"Several times. You're going to love it. All sensual music, body heat and very little clothing." He chuckled under his breath. "It's guaranteed to warm up the chilliest woman on earth. Even the ice queen Celile Kocak doesn't stand a chance during *Carnivale*."

Oh hell. The man was doing his damnedest to unnerve her. Well, no matter what Tarik Kadir sent her way, she wouldn't let him throw her. She would remain in control.

After all, Jass O'Reilly was a pro.

# Chapter 4

Tarik led the way through the grand lobby of the Copacabana Palace Hotel. The towering sixty-foot columns and ornate glass chandeliers were familiar, but the feeling of being watched was unique.

He liked crowds. Liked the anonymity of getting lost in the confusion. When their driver had first reminded him of *Carnivale,* Tarik's brain began processing new ways of completing their mission over the next few days. He'd thought of the festivities as a terrific idea for a cover.

But he hadn't counted on having the exotic and stunning faux Celile Kocak in tow. Every male head in the cavernous lobby turned to stare as she walked past. No wonder Sheik Zohdi seldom let more than a few feet pass between them in public.

Tarik tried to control the possessive urges he felt toward her. In reality the woman beside him was not the ice queen. Instead she was Jass O'Reilly, every bit as gorgeous as Celile but ten times more annoying. Everything he said seemed to strike her the wrong way. Despite his usual charm and glib small talk, she'd refused to warm up.

But that didn't mean his body didn't grow too warm every time he looked her way. Damned woman was hot. Both in the guise of Celile and out. And he figured she was going to make him sweat a lot more before this mission was over.

"We've already registered you two," their driver said quietly. "And your suite's checked and clean. We'll be able to go over mission specifics without being overheard."

So…while they'd been in the air, the Task Force had been busy devising a plan. Good enough. Tarik needed to keep his head in the game—and off his partner.

After they settled into the three-room suite and double-checked for listening devices and cameras, the driver nodded toward the dining table. "We couldn't secure a penthouse suite on such short notice at this time of year, but I hope you'll be comfortable here."

Jass removed her jacket and plopped into one of the chairs around the table. "It'll do for Celile and Zohdi. They're not on vacation."

"Well," their driver began as he set up the rest of the chairs around the table. "This is the honeymoon suite. Part of your cover story is that the two of you are taking a romantic interlude while you wait for the upcoming auction."

"Uh…" Jass jumped up, looking a little green around the edges. "Excuse me a moment." She grabbed her jacket off the back of a chair and headed straight for the bedroom.

"Do we know yet when the auction is supposed to take place?" Tarik gladly reached for any excuse to put the spotlight back on the mission and take it off his errant libido.

The driver turned to him with his hand outstretched and not a trace of accent in his English. "We haven't met, Kadir. The name's Joäo Bosque, CIA station chief. Have a seat."

Tarik joined him at the table. "What do we know?"

"Coincidentally, we've been keeping an eye on this Russian character you're after. His name is Andrei Eltsin. He blew into Rio several months ago and immediately took over the territory and operation of one of our *bicheiros*—those are the gang operators of this city's illegal lottery." Bosque scooted his chair closer.

"We inserted a man inside Eltsin's *bicheiro* about a month ago. Their headquarters is in a penthouse above a nightclub in the Lapa district." Bosque poured himself a cup of the strong Brazilian coffee that had been placed on the table along with a basket of fresh fruit. "Our inside man is there gathering intel on their money-laundering operations. We're sure some of those billions are going to fund terrorism operators in the U.S."

Tarik nodded and sat back. "Okay. But what about the auction?"

"Our man isn't positive where, but he believes it's to be held on the last night of *Carnivale*. Fat Tuesday."

"Makes sense. But…"

"It's supposed to take place in Eltsin's retreat in the mountains right outside the city." Jass added the new info as she floated back into the room, looking light and airy in a floral silk pants outfit. "I received a message from Ed. He's on his way into the country,

taking a military transport. Seems the real Celile was…
convinced…to contact Eltsin and put her name on the
bidders list for Tuesday. We're in."

"Fast work." Tarik couldn't keep from staring. His
real-life partner, the covert agent, had become a real-live
piece of art in cool shades of green and blue. And her
movements were those of a lithe dancer as she crossed
the room.

"The CIA has a convincing team of interrogators
working with Celile and Zohdi." Jass picked up an apple
and took a bite with relish.

Drooling at the sight, all Tarik could think at that
moment was that he was glad his name wasn't Adam.
This *Eve* was already tempting him enough to send him
straight to hell.

*The honeymoon suite.* Jass's knees still wobbled at
the idea, but she wouldn't give Kadir the satisfaction of
seeing her sweat. They could straighten out the sleeping
arrangements later—when she'd taken control of the
mission again. In the meantime she would sleep on the
couch or in the bathtub if necessary.

"Do we know what item we're supposed to bid on?"
Tarik looked slightly annoyed.

What did he have to be annoyed about? He was on
this mission despite her reservations. He should be
grateful.

"No," she managed past another bite of apple. "Celile
honestly doesn't know. And our interrogators couldn't
devise a way for her to ask Eltsin without sounding
suspicious either. We're going to need—"

"Reconnaissance," Tarik interrupted. "Our intel unit
will continue gathering info from the underground."

And by *our intel unit* he meant the Kadir family?

She opened her mouth to complain when Tarik stood and backed away from the table.

"Come on," he said as he took her hand and pulled her to her feet beside him. "Put on your dancing shoes."

He drew her into his arms and pulled her close. Too close.

"How rusty are your samba skills, darling?" He'd whispered those words into her temple, but she could swear she felt the pounding of his heart right through both their clothes. "Need a few quick lessons?"

With the way he was holding her, that question could have a double meaning. She tried to pull away, but he held her fast.

"I'll match my samba skills to yours anytime, *darling.*" She could barely believe how parched her voice sounded.

Tarik chuckled and released her. "We'll see about that. Now go put on your sexiest shoes—and take off most of your clothes. Nightclubbing in the Lapa district is always undertaken with a lot of skin showing. Especially during *Carnivale.* You need to be nearly naked to capture the true beat of the samba."

Two hours later, Jass decided she hated a know-it-all. As they entered the nightclub and found a table, she could feel Tarik's so-called *true beat* of the samba right through the soles of her shoes. Even with a skin-tight red dress and dangerously high stilettos, she almost felt overdressed inside Carioca da Lapa, one of the Lapa district's pioneering samba clubs and Eltsin's headquarters. People should be naked when experiencing music this sensual.

Looking around, she discovered many people in the club came close to that description. Some women wore shirts made out of thin metal strips with nothing underneath. While other statuesque *mulatas* wearing glittery *Carnivale* garb clung to their partners as if they couldn't stand on their own. Even by glancing twice, Jass would not have been able to swear to the true gender of every woman she saw on the dance floor.

As it turned out, however, it was Tarik who looked overdressed with a lightweight linen jacket covering his sleeveless T-shirt. All the other sweaty young men in the joint were clad only in their undershirts. And as the evening progressed some of those T-shirts had come off in time to the beat. Everyone in the place seemed to have begun their drinking well before noon.

Tarik ordered them the local drink: *cachaca,* sugar-cane alcohol tempered with crushed ice, sugar and lime juice. Then he held out his hand. "Couples come to Carioca da Lapa for only one reason, love. Let's check out those samba skills of yours."

She let him pull her into his arms. "I thought we were here to do recon," she whispered. He hugged her tightly against his body as they moved onto the crowded dance floor.

"Oh, but we are. Let's see if anyone here recognizes Celile and Zohdi." Tarik pulled her even tighter to him, until she felt completely surrounded by his masculine presence. Hot and spicy and full of rigid male power.

The samba in this club played in time to a reggae beat. Slow. Sensual. Steamy. Keeping the beat with conga drums, cowbells and primitive sticks that thrummed the music right to her bones. Tarik began to move, swiveling his hips like a pro. He took her by the hands and pushed her an arms' length away. But his eyes locked onto hers, sending the hypnotic rhythm straight through her veins by the force of his formidable gaze.

She felt it in every inch of her body. The sexual gaze, the heat, the noise. Her nerve endings came alive in a dull burning flame.

Jass had been in a lot of tricky situations on those missions when she was acting the part of a girlfriend. But she had never felt so completely wrapped up in the moment as she did right now. Shaking her head, she tried to throw off the spell of Tarik's personality. This mission should be no different than all the rest—despite her having to work with rogue agent Tarik Kadir. She wouldn't let it get to her.

She tried closing her eyes, but that was little better. She could still smell his virile musk and feel his gaze raking over her body, making her sweat in places no one could see.

He pulled her close again and swung them around. "Your samba act is fine, love," he murmured in her ear. "But your reactions to your lover aren't quite up to the mark. Remember to behave like Celile would on the dance floor with the man she loves. Loosen up."

*He* was telling her how to behave undercover? How dare this outwardly charming reprobate tell the best undercover operative in the business how to do her job?

Straightening her spine, Jass pulled back and smiled, though she let her eyes tell the truth of what she was feeling. "I've studied the woman for years. Celile Kocak is never loose, *love*."

She'd gritted out the words so only he could hear. But Tarik's reactions to what she'd said weren't what she'd expected.

He manhandled her back against his chest and plundered her mouth with a kiss that was deep and hard and took her breath away. "I'll bet she comes undone in bed," he whispered against her lips. "Wanna go practice?"

Jass's first reaction was to jerk away in panic, but Tarik held her fast. "Remember your act, darling."

Exasperated, Jass narrowed her eyes at him and spoke in a loud clear voice. "You'll need to excuse me for a moment, darling. I must use the restroom."

Tarik stepped back and opened his arms, holding up his palms. "Of course, my love. But hurry back. I'll count the minutes."

Swearing under her breath, Jass headed through the throng of dancers toward the back of the club. This was *mission impossible*. But their assignment should've been her salvation, making up for the fumble with the Nigerian.

Instead of her usual feelings of control and being ready for anything, when she moved across the room and looked for a back entry, she felt the solid premonition of doom.

*You're one intense little cookie, aren't you? Tough guy. One cool agent. More alpha than most of the men you meet.*

That was Jass O'Reilly. Still, Tarik had clearly felt her response to him while he was holding her in his arms. Jass might believe she was invincible and she put on a harsh front, but underneath everything else she was all woman.

The sexual tension had shimmered between them, drawing them together like a magnet. Precisely what he didn't need at this stage in his life. Loyalty to his family called for him to avoid any kind of entanglements during this all important mission.

Stalking back to their table, he kicked back to watch the crowds. But he couldn't keep his mind off of Jass.

She'd flinched when he'd touched her. Flinched like a school girl. And she'd given him a challenging look full of— As he thought about it now, that look in her eyes could've been vulnerability.

That was it, he decided. Jass was tough on the outside to hide a defenseless inside. Like one of those hard-candy-covered chocolates. She was used to taking charge, taking risks alone and getting her orders from only her bosses at the CIA. She wasn't used to anyone challenging that rigid outer shell.

Jass was an excellent operative because she was intelligent and perceptive and had nearly total recall of anything she'd ever read. But she wasn't a team player.

Then again, he didn't need a team on this mission. He hadn't even wanted a partner. But he was willing to bet his life that Jass would step up and do whatever was required to get the job done.

All he had to do was keep his own mind and hands in the game. Easier said than done.

A while later, after ordering his second round of drinks, Tarik realized she'd been gone too long. Was she doing a little side reconnaissance on her own? Or had she run into trouble?

Either way, he'd better quit sitting on his butt day-dreaming and find her.

He got to his feet and asked the waitress to direct him to the ladies' room. She threw him a skeptical look but pointed him in the right direction with a small laugh.

Yeah, he would bet she saw a little of everything during *Carnivale*.

Tarik thanked her and made his way through the

tangle of sweaty, dancing bodies all moving to a bossa nova beat. In a darkened corner of the main floor, he found a staircase to the penthouse above. He made a mental note of its placement but moved on into an alcove that held what was loosely called the public restrooms.

The alcove was crowded with lines of people waiting for a turn at the toilets. He thought about asking someone to check the stalls for Jass but decided against it. No telling who was a real patron of the club and who was here on some kind of criminal business.

As he stood toward the rear of the lines considering his next move, he heard footsteps on the stairs behind him. An argument reached his ears, and he had just enough time to duck for cover under the open stairwell. The conversation was taking place in the Taj Zabbar language and the two men speaking were making no attempt to keep their voices down.

They stopped on the landing right above his head to continue their disagreement. "I do not like the idea of staying in the country for the next four days, Excellency. It is not safe. Too much frivolity in this place."

"Nonsense." With that one word, Tarik recognized the second speaker's deep voice. "The Russian...uh... Eltsin is a powerful man. He will protect us while we are in Brazil. Has he not already told the elder that we have no risk of losing anything in this little charade of his?"

"But what about the other bidders? I am concerned about our main mission and the other item. The one we were sent to Rio to claim."

"Remember your place and trust me to do what needs to be done. We've been invited to stay for the next few days at Eltsin's retreat in the mountains not far from here. I assume that he means for us to procure that other item during our private stay. His men will escort us into the mountains tomorrow. In the meantime, let's enjoy ourselves, shall we?"

"Yes, Excellency. Whatever you say."

Tarik recognized the more formidable voice as that of Malik Kasim Taj Zabbar, head of the secret police in Zabbarán. The two men lit cigars and proceeded down the stairs, disappearing into the crowds on the dance floor.

Well, that answered one thing for sure. The Taj Zabbar were here in Rio to attend Eltsin's auction. But now Tarik had many more questions. What charade? And what was the other item they'd been talking about?

And where the devil was Jass?

A commotion erupted above his head. He heard a man growling orders in Portuguese. And he heard a woman's voice, calm and cool, returning the sentiments in Russian.

*Jass.* Tarik shot up the stairs without thinking. What had she gotten herself into?

# *Chapter 5*

**J**ass tried to keep her voice down, low and sultry like Celile would. But this idiot bodyguard didn't speak any of her languages and he wouldn't give in and take her to see the Russian. All he wanted to do was flash his knife and make threats in a slang version of Portuguese.

All *she'd* wanted to do was a little scouting around. Maybe get a line on what the upcoming auction was all about. And she'd hoped to do so unnoticed. No such luck.

Now she was going to have to use force to make the bodyguard let her go. Something she was sure Celile would never be caught dead doing. Ah well.

Flipping her head and allowing the annoying silky veil of fake long hair to fall over one eye, she aimed a come-hither look at him. She continued to work her womanly wiles as she reached for the hem of her dress and slowly began lifting it up her thighs.

The bodyguard's eyes bugged out of his head and his tongue nearly hit the floor. A little farther and Jass could reach the derringer she'd holstered between her thighs and right below her crotch. Another inch and...

"Trouble, love?" Tarik came up behind the bodyguard and pulled him into a headlock before the guy ever knew what had hit him.

One neat karate chop to the forearm and the guy's knife disappeared into the darkness. Next Tarik used a tricky pressure-point move, and in seconds the bodyguard was quietly laid out unconscious on the floor.

Jass dropped her dress and shook her head. "I was handling it, Kadir. No sense making anyone mad."

Tarik's expression went hard. Something in his gaze shook her. But she didn't have time to consider it.

He took her by the wrist and spun them both in the direction of the stairs. "Tell me later. Right now, I need to make a quick exit before the Taj Zabbar spot me in the crowd."

"The Taj are here? Tonight?" She had seen two Middle Eastern men leaving the penthouse suite as she was hiding down the hall. They were the Taj Zabbar? Couldn't prove it by her.

"Can we *please* discuss this later?" He hustled her down the stairs and pushed through the crowded lines waiting to use the restrooms and mingling around the back exit.

Next thing she knew they were shoving past another couple of sleazy-looking characters who might've been bouncers as Tarik shoved their way out into the alley behind the club. The balmy night air and the unfortunate but prevalent smells of garbage hit her smack in the face.

"Keep moving." Tarik dropped her hand and pulled

a phone out of his pocket. "We'll have our driver pick us up around the block."

*Yeah, if we live that long.* "Hold on a minute. Let me reach my weapon, before…"

Tarik elbowed her in the back and propelled her forward as he frantically poked buttons on his phone. "Keep moving if you want to stay alive."

*Of all the arrogant, testosterone-loaded—*

Jass didn't waste any breath telling him off as she pounded down the dark cobblestones in her stilettos. Not yet. First she needed to live through the rest of this night.

But afterward…rogue agent Tarik Kadir had better watch his step. She was ready to let him have it.

By the time they arrived back at the honeymoon suite, Jass was in a full snit as she stormed into the bathroom and slammed the door behind her. A tiny kernel of guilt snuck up on Tarik. As annoying as she had been on the ride home, he was still hyperaware of that vulnerability he'd spotted in her on the dance floor.

He could see how CIA covert officer Jasmine O'Reilly would be hard-pressed to accept help from anyone in the middle of an assignment. Even if it might save both her life and the mission. Irritating. And yet, Tarik also found it somehow endearing.

But he hadn't expected the private side of Jass O'Reilly to be so sexy. And a world-class kisser to boot.

The two of them still needed to arrive at a better working relationship. A good, soul-revealing conversation was in order. But not tonight. Tonight he would back off and let her lick her wounded pride.

He stepped into the walk-in bedroom closet, where the hotel valets had hung their things, and began pulling out a change of clothes for himself. The bathroom door opened and Jass walked out, completely covered in one of the hotel's full-length terry robes. She still wore Celile's hair and makeup, but in the robe she was all Jass. A little sweet and hesitant. And a whole lot spicy.

"I'll take the couch, Kadir. Give me a moment to gather up a pillow and blanket."

"No can do," he told her with a shrug. "If any of the hotel staff lets themselves in to make up the kitchen or bring in an early breakfast, it won't be acceptable for the lovebirds to be sleeping in separate rooms."

For a split second she looked terrified. He had a guilty feeling that she was remembering the supposedly fake kiss he'd given her on the dance floor. He was having some trouble forgetting the kiss himself.

He reached for a solution that would give them both space. "You take the bed. There's a decent chaise on the balcony terrace right outside the bedroom. I'll be good out there. Give me a minute to shower."

He edged around her as she stood mute where she was. "It'll be fine, partner. Don't worry. I sleep like a rock."

It was a lie; he seldom needed more than a couple hours a night and always slept lightly in case of attack. But the excuse was the best he could come up with on short notice. The one thing he hadn't lied about was that she needn't worry. As much as she turned him on in so many ways, he wouldn't be rushing into a sexual relationship in the middle of an undercover assignment. Not with anyone, and least of all not with the woman who'd flinched in response to his touch and whose kiss was one of the most sensual and memorable of his lifetime.

\* \* \*

Restless and too warm, Jass tossed the covers for the umpteenth time that night and sat up in bed. She automatically turned her head to glance toward the sliding glass doors leading to the balcony terrace, making sure Tarik was still where he'd been the last seven times she'd checked during the long night.

But this time when she looked, the chaise was empty. She spotted him then, standing with his back to her at the railing, staring out at the first rays of the rising sun.

Her body seemed to react to the sight of him all on its own. She swung her legs over the side of the king-size bed and threw open the glass doors, moving in his direction without fully knowing why.

He had to have heard her sliding back the doors, but he didn't turn and remained silent and brooding where he stood. She went to the railing too and gazed out on beautiful Copacabana Beach and beyond that across the bay to Sugarloaf Mountain shrouded in the morning mists.

Tarik didn't turn but said, "It's early. Go back to bed."

She gazed up at his profile. "I was hot and needed some air."

He said nothing more and made no move. She wanted to drag her gaze away, but couldn't keep herself from staring at his hard jawline and rigid stance. He wasn't wearing a shirt and his broad muscular chest led down to a flat belly and lower to a pair of white boxer shorts. The purely masculine and sensual sight captured her attention and imagination, paralyzing her with sudden longing.

She'd always known Tarik Kadir as the covert officer

to play the part of a ladies' man. The charmer. The agent who could worm his way inside any nest of bad guys with a few glib words and a smile.

Not her type. Not even someone she could be friends with, really.

Still, her body had reacted almost violently to his kiss last night. She'd been hyper-aware of the extraordinary strength in the arms that held her tight. Super sensitive to his calloused fingers as he'd touched the skin on her arms. And extremely susceptible to the warmth of his breath on her neck. It had so affected her that she'd run like a scared rabbit.

Inside, where all her insecurities lay, she was still running.

She thought of later last night, when there'd also been that strange way his eyes had held hers for a single moment after he'd come to her rescue. Something she saw in those dark eyes said there might be more to the man. Could it be that all his fast-talking charm hid a sensitive and intelligent person underneath?

She looked at him again. As the first rays of sun hit his face, the strong set of his chin made her want to reassess all of her initial impressions. Perhaps she and her handler Ed had rushed to judgment about Tarik.

"So," she began. "You went into Zabbarán to help your brother and found a nuclear reactor. That must've been a shock."

"Not especially." He turned and looked at her for the first time that morning. "By then I would've expected anything from the Taj. Both my brothers have firsthand knowledge of how truly terrifying the Taj tribe can behave when no one is watching."

"Tell me about them— Your family, I mean."

Tarik went to the chaise and sat, patting the spot

beside him and inviting her to join him on the wide cushions. "Not much to tell. Darin and Shakir and their new wives are everything to me. I'm the baby of our three brothers. But there's also dozens of cousins and relations and now a new nephew and another baby on the way. We're a tight group, though some of the rest of our family are spread all over the world."

"How has such an extended family managed to stay close together when you have no homeland?" Jass did settle on the chaise, but she kept a good distance between their two bodies and folded her arms tightly across her chest, her legs up under her butt.

No sense giving her own wayward body any ideas. She was curious about him and his family. About how he'd turned into the man he'd become. That's all there was to this sudden need to be close.

"Ah. Well, we're raised with a deep sense of family loyalty. It's tradition with the Kadirs. But even that didn't always keep us physically close."

He stopped talking, took a breath and glanced over at her. "Are you cold? You don't have much on. Just that T-shirt. You want to go inside or maybe grab your robe?"

"I'm fine. It's quite balmy out here." Again she was grateful for her olive complexion keeping the blush from her cheeks, but she wasn't ready to open her arms or unfold her legs from beneath her body.

Tarik gave her an odd look, but then clasped his hands and leaned his elbows on his knees. "When the family first realized we were being threatened by the Taj Zabbar, they called us all to a family conclave from our various corners of the world. Darin had been running Kadir Shipping from a Greek island. Shakir had resigned his commission from a British paratrooper regiment in

Afghanistan and was in the process of starting up his own security business. And I…well, you know where I was."

She nodded but wasn't sure he saw the movement since he was staring at the floor. "Every one of you dropped your lives and came, without question?"

"It's that loyalty thing again. Runs in the family. Identity and loyalty have been a huge part of our makeup for centuries." He stared down at his joined fingers. "Besides, I would go anywhere for my two brothers. I would die for them. They kept me going when things were rough."

"What about your parents?"

He sighed, not so loud that she was supposed to hear, but she noticed anyway. "Our mother died of cancer when I was young. It shook all of us, but especially my father. He left us with the help and dived into his businesses with his complete attention.

"Turns out, the *help* left a lot to be desired," he added with a snicker. "Oh, we were fed and clothed. But all three of us were very young and had been completely spoiled by our mother. None of us knew how to grieve and we were blindsided by the loss of our parents' love."

He shrugged and seemed to struggle for the right words. She was willing to bet that he seldom faced these old memories. They seemed to be raising a range of emotions he didn't know how to handle.

"I'm sorry," she said to fill up the silence. "I know how bad that must have been. My mother died when I was about ten. It was a difficult thing to get past."

But her mother had not been the type to spoil her, not in the least. In fact, Jass remembered a moment when

she'd felt almost glad her mother was gone, enabling her
to be alone with her easygoing father.

However, things hadn't exactly worked out that way
either.

Tarik frowned and turned his head toward her. "Yes,
it was bad enough. Did your father take up the slack in
your life after losing your mother?"

"He would've liked to. But he had to work to support
us. And his job with the CIA suddenly became all about
the covert assignments and he was gone most of the
time. My mother's family took up the slack, as you call
it."

Tarik chuckled. "You should see your face. Like
you tasted something sour. I'm guessing your mother's
family wasn't exactly what you had in mind."

Jass chuckled at her own reactions to the memories.
"Um…no. They were immigrants from Iran and very
strict. They expected me to grieve all the time for the
first year. I was only ten. After that, it was pray, pray,
pray. I escaped during breaks and in the summers when
my dad was between assignments."

She tried to push the memories aside like she always
had as a child. It wasn't working as well this time.

"Did you do anything else to escape?"

"Like what? I did read a lot. And I daydreamed about
having adventures with my father. I idolized him." When
she noticed Tarik's expression began to change again,
she shifted the focus back to him. "So what did you do
to escape?"

"Me? I made up stories and acted them out." He
stood and paced along the length of the terrace. "In
my daydreams, I became anything I wanted. I could
go anywhere in my mind that I wanted—be anyone I
wanted. A pirate, a cowboy or an astronaut. I learned I

could escape into my head anytime if I plastered a smile on my face and stayed quiet."

The man was a romantic. She never would've guessed that about him. Knowing it now, knowing he understood her daydreams, made him seem more human. Someone she could build a friendship with after this mission was over.

They were both quiet for a few minutes while Tarik kept pacing. She suspected he was as lost in his thoughts as she'd been.

"Seems we have a few things in common." The sympathy in her voice astounded even her.

Tarik stepped behind the chaise and gently laid his two hands on her shoulders. It was a friendly gesture, but the electric shock that sizzled between them caused her to draw back in surprise.

"Tense?" He began kneading her neck muscles. "You need to relax with me. I thought we were getting closer to developing a decent working relationship. We'll never pull off being lovers if you keep flinching every time we touch."

She jerked away from his hands and stood to face him. "I can pull off any covert op. Don't worry about me—I'm the best you've ever worked with. Keep your hands to yourself when we're alone and stick to your job."

"Jass…" He held out his hands, palms up, as if pleading for her understanding. "Before we're through with this mission, we may need to be seen touching and kissing while in public places. And it's even possible we may have to sleep in the same bed. We'd better come up with some solution if this thing between us is going to be a problem."

Tarik looked exasperated but went on, "Maybe what

we need is a good old-fashioned roll in the hay. To break the ice. It might conquer your inhibitions."

Speechless for a moment, Jass stared until her indignation came pouring out. "Not on your li—"

"Ms. Kocak. Sheik Zohdi." A male voice coming behind a knock on the door to the sitting room had both her and Tarik racing into the bedroom for their weapons. "I've brought your breakfast. Courtesy of Chef Langdon. Please to join me?"

*Chef Langdon?* As in Ed, her handler? Jass reached for her robe instead of the Glock and nodded to Tarik to don his robe, too.

She'd never been more glad in her whole life for an untimely interruption.

By the time Tarik drew on his robe and opened the bedroom door, the supposed waiter had set aside his breakfast tray and was standing on the dining table checking out the chandelier. The fellow turned out to be Bosque, the Rio CIA station chief they'd met yesterday.

The guy had a disturbing way of turning up at the oddest times. He was beginning to get on Tarik's nerves.

Bosque had one of those high-tech bug-detection devices in his hand. When he saw Tarik, the station chief raised his other hand to indicate Tarik shouldn't say anything until he was through with his check.

Jass came out of the bedroom right behind Tarik and stood silently while they waited. She had her arms protectively folded over her chest again, and Tarik would bet she was wishing she'd never come out on the terrace to confront him.

That made two of them. He was still battling the

coil of longing that had settled in his gut from touching her. But their situation was becoming intolerable. They needed to find a way past whatever discord lay between them.

The more he considered it, the better he liked his bright idea. They should have a quickie fling. Get past all the sexual tension and get on with their mission.

"Looks clean," Bosque said as he jumped down from the table. "Langdon's in town. And we have a couple of messages for you."

Bosque held out the hand with the bug detector. "Here, Kadir. Keep this device and check for bugs wherever and whenever you think it's necessary. Run over this room periodically."

"You believe Eltsin will listen in or record the Messenger and her sheik lover? Why?"

The station chief shrugged a shoulder. "Maybe Eltsin. Maybe your Taj Zabbar friends. The whole lot of them are paranoid as hell." He turned to the breakfast tray, pulled off a large white tablecloth and placed it over the table. "Help yourselves to coffee or açaí berry juice, while I give you the rest of Langdon's instructions."

Tarik opted for coffee while Jass picked up a toasted baguette with melted cheese and popped it in her mouth. He debated having the papaya but decided against it. He'd lost his appetite on the terrace earlier.

"We're not getting anywhere on figuring out what the item that's up for bid will be," Bosque told them. "But we have our ears to the ground. You can bet someone in the Brazilian criminal community has heard what's for sale. Particularly if it has something to do with nuclear weapons. You can't keep that kind of thing quiet."

Jass nodded and lounged in one of the dining chairs. Bosque joined her at the table. Tarik decided to remain standing. At the moment he was full of left-over nervous energy, enough to power his own nuclear weapons.

"Langdon wants you two to check in periodically with him. He's setting up a Fruti Vita stand on the beach and expects your first rendezvous this afternoon." He cleared his throat. "We're working on a plan to get you inside Eltsin's mountain retreat early. Maybe you can gather more info there."

Tarik didn't like the idea of working blindfolded. "Does the Task Force know the Taj Zabbar are already here?"

Bosque stared for a moment, then shook his head. "I have men taking pictures of everyone coming and going from the club. But there's hundreds of photos to go through. You're sure it was the Taj?"

"Definitely. I ran into a couple of them last night at the club. A man in a tux with another man dressed in a black suit. They shouldn't be too hard to spot inside that casual nightclub."

"I'll get someone on it. Meanwhile—" Bosque reached into his jacket pocket and withdrew two pairs of sunglasses. "Here. Each of you wear these at all times, even at night if possible."

Jass took hers and flipped them over, studying them in her hands. "What are these? They feel weighted."

"Signaling devices," Bosque told her. "Here, let me show you."

He stood over Jass and showed her how to slide the side piece forward. "Doing that sends us an alarm, along with your GPS coordinates. If you practice, you can do it surreptitiously without taking them off." Bosque bent close and eased the glasses onto her face. "Like this."

Tarik felt his blood pressure soar when the station

chief touched Jass's face. A green haze clouded his vision.

*Geez, get over yourself, Kadir.*

He didn't know which would become the bigger danger on this mission. The Taj Zabbar, or the tempting woman who was now his partner.

## Chapter 6

Heading for the beach, Jass darted across the boulevard in front of the hotel with Tarik in her wake. Damned man hadn't let her out of his sight all morning. She understood his possessive act was in keeping with Zohdi's character. But sometimes he laid that act on a little thick in private and it was beginning to feel all too realistic.

She was having trouble decoding her true feelings for Tarik. On the one hand, they had a few things in common. He was a dreamer and good at being a chameleon on the job. But she only wished she knew for sure when he was acting and when he was being himself.

He also seemed to have as strong a sense of loyalty as did she, though his was to his family and hers was to her country. Logically they should be able to develop a relationship based on those few facts alone.

Still, on the other hand, a couple of things about him continued to bother her. She had relied on Ed's opinions for most of her adult life. Her handler had saved her back end more times than she could count and was nearly always right. Ed remained unconvinced that Tarik was one of the good guys.

Then there was the matter of that nagging physical tug-of-war between them whenever Tarik got too close. When he touched her, those old reliable gut instincts of hers kept screaming to run away from him before he pulled her into something that was bigger than she could handle.

Frustrated and wishing she could make a decision about him and get on with their mission, she came to the conclusion Tarik may have been right about one thing this morning. Maybe what they needed was a quickie fling. *Slam bam, thank you, ma'am.* It wasn't her style. She didn't do sex for sex's sake. Yet, she needed to step out of her comfort zone with him somehow in order to get over her jitters.

This assignment was too important to her career to let a little thing like being sexually uptight ruin it.

Hanging on to the brim of her straw hat in the wind, Jass tried to act casual as she strolled the colorful and wide pavement at the edge of Copacabana Beach. She could feel Tarik walking right behind her and her nerves kept jangling with mixed messages.

He was safe and familiar. He was mysterious and a complete stranger.

She gritted her teeth as she searched for Ed's Fruti Vita stand. Seeing her handler should help calm her down and put things in perspective.

"Do we have any idea where this juice stand is

supposedly located?" Tarik came up next to her and whispered in her ear so no one else could hear.

Turning to him, Jass opened her mouth to speak, but the mere sight of him in the bright sunshine struck her dumb. He was stunning. Handsome and virile enough to make her weak in the knees. In his lightweight suit, panama hat and the aviator sunglasses that Bosque had supplied, he looked every bit the part of a larger-than-life Middle Eastern terrorist.

"Uh...uh..." She bit her tongue to keep from stuttering and tried to rein her anxiety. "No. Keep looking. It has to be up here on the beach close by."

The beach seemed almost deserted for the middle of the afternoon during *Carnivale* weekend. A few bikini-clad women sunbathers snoozed on blankets here and there, and she thought she spotted a volleyball game starting up a hundred yards down the beach. Everyone else must be napping or resting up for the night's festivities.

She took a couple more steps and found herself absently fanning her face with her hand. "It's really scorching hot on the beach today, isn't it?"

Tarik was staring out over the huge expanse of beach sand and didn't turn. "February is the hottest month in the southern hemisphere. But I noticed you still look cool and in control. Celile would be proud of you."

Jass didn't feel cool or in control next to Tarik. Not in the least. And the last thing she cared about today was what Celile would think. Celile would probably screw him and get on with her life. But that wasn't something Jass could jump into as easily as she'd learned to shoot a gun.

"The bay is a beautiful deep green today," Tarik suddenly announced in the phony half accent of Sheik

Zohdi. "Pretty, though different from the blue Mediterranean we love, yes? Nice day for a beach stroll. But I'm becoming thirsty."

She threw him a look of utter frustration, wondering what the hell he thought he was doing. But as she turned, she spotted a line of wooden stands right ahead on the sand at the edge of the sidewalk pavement.

"Oh, yes, I agree. Let's see if we can find a Fruti Vita stand that's open." She marched out onto the brilliant white sand and headed down the line of stands.

Most of the food and drink stands were closed down for the afternoon. They'd probably been jumping during the morning what with the tourists in town for *Carnivale*. This afternoon in the heat everyone seemed to be taking a break until the evening parades began and their customers returned.

She'd about given up on finding the right one when she darted around the last stand and found her handler there in disguise as the juice vendor. Immediately, Jass felt a bit more stable than she had only a moment ago.

"Everything under control?" Ed asked.

Before she could respond, Tarik came up beside her. "Isn't this spot too wide open for a meeting?"

Ed nodded his head and closed the wooden flap on the front of the stand, shutting them out. A moment later he opened a side door and shuffled them both into the tiny, sweltering space inside the booth.

"This suit you better, Kadir?"

Tarik's eyes went cold in the heat, but he said nothing.

Ed scowled at him, though when he turned to her, it was with a smile. "Still no word on what's for sale this week. But we've come up with a new plan for finding out. Tonight is the first of the *Carnivale* parades and the first of the Samba schools' competitions. A good chance to obtain intel unnoticed."

"What competitions?" Jass wasn't sure she understood.

"The whole purpose of the street parades is for local samba schools to compete with rival schools to win the title of best school of the year." When she still looked confused, he continued, "It's a big frigging deal with all the locals in Rio. Tonight the samba school that Eltsin's *bicheiro* controls will have its first shot at a parade entry. He'll have no choice but to attend."

"I get it," Tarik chimed in soberly. "While he and most of his men are gone, we break in to his offices and see if we can find out what's coming up for auction."

"Right." Ed reached under the counter and hauled up a designer, satchel-style handbag. "The Task Force lent us a few high-tech toys to assist..."

"I don't like it." Tarik interrupted him and turned to her. "Neither of us is an expert in breaking into computers and that's where our best shot of finding info in his office would be. There isn't a chance in hell of us stumbling over the item itself during a B & E attempt."

"True, the item is no doubt at Eltsin's mountain retreat," Ed agreed, taking back control of the conversation. "But the techs came up with some toys that will make your jobs in his office easier. I know Jass at least can become an expert with only a few minutes of instruction."

Ed hesitated, seemingly watching for Tarik's facial responses. But Tarik's face had become a mask of serious intent. Not even a hint of his usual grin was anywhere to be seen.

"Look, Kadir." Ed's tone changed all of a sudden

as he spoke casually to Tarik. "Why don't I give these toys and the instructions to Jass while you contact your brothers? A Darin Kadir has been calling the Task Force and is anxious to speak to you. Is it true that you have an encrypted satellite phone that you can use?"

Tarik nodded sharply in response. "Fine. I'd like to see what Kadir intel has come up with anyway. I'll step out on the beach where I can get a better signal and still keep watch in case anyone is within earshot." He turned to Jass. "Take his instructions but don't agree to anything until you talk to me. I'll be back in a few minutes."

Jass's temper flared for a split second. But almost immediately after he was out the door, she decided Tarik was being a good partner and not trying to run the show.

Ed, it seemed, was not quite as generous. "What's he been up to, anyway? Has he been trying to convince you to do something you're not comfortable doing?"

"No, Ed," she lied. "We're learning to become friends. For the sake of the mission. That's all."

No sense enflaming Ed any further. Jass would make up her own mind whether she and Tarik would become anything more than friends and partners.

"Don't try to be friends with a snake, little girl. If you try, the guy will only let you down," he warned her. "You might find yourself involved in something that could be a career-ender or something even worse—like a life-ender. Stay away from him."

Ed sure disliked Tarik. Jass could sort of understand his hesitance to trust a man who'd quit the Task Force and was heading up his own covert operation doing heaven knows what. But...

"Ed, I have to be his partner. It's in the job description.

How can I play his girlfriend and still stay away from him?"

Ed pulled off his ball cap and ran a hand over the bald spot underneath. "You're a pro. You can pull off anything. I care too much about you to see anything happen to your career." He sighed. "I do trust you, Jass. But be careful."

How could she resist when he was so concerned for her welfare?

Trying to calm his fears for her, she cooed, "I will. And I am the pro here. You know I can watch out for myself. Don't worry about me."

"I can't help worrying." Ed took a deep breath and shook his head. "But okay, for now we have work to do. Let me show you how to use these gadgets and then suggest a plan for tonight. You can run rings around that Kadir guy. But don't forget what I said."

How could she forget? Every second of this mission seemed consumed with nothing but thoughts of Tarik Kadir. Something was going to have to give soon.

She only hoped she wouldn't be the one to break first.

Tarik swallowed down his annoyance over the handler's remarks as his brother Darin picked up the call.

"Can you talk?" Darin asked.

Tarik threw a quick glance at his surroundings as he adjusted his covert earpiece. He stood near the shore on a particularly isolated stretch of beach. The nearest person was a nearly nude woman, sunbathing about a hundred yards away. He wasn't worried about anyone trying to listen in to his conversation unseen, because Kadir phones all had special encryption coding.

"Yeah. I'm good. What have you discovered?"

"We've made a couple of good initial contacts in the criminal community around Rio. I have one particularly solid lead who claims Tuesday's auction is about nuclear fissionable material." He hesitated. "But the informant also said some of the same things you overheard last night. Everyone in the know there in Brazil is aware the whole deal is a sham. Seems it's only the American Task Force and the local CIA who're supposed to believe that's what this meeting is all about."

"Do we have any idea what's really going on?"

"Not yet." Darin sounded as though he had something more to say.

Tarik waited, knowing his brother would eventually get to whatever was concerning him.

Finally Darin cleared his throat and began. "Cousin Karim asked if you had a thumbnail drive and wireless transmitter and if you know how to use it to transmit the data back to us."

"I know how to use them in a pinch. You want me to try accessing Eltsin's computer system?"

"Perhaps. If you have the opportunity and the access to the equipment. But my guess is the computer we want will not be located in his main offices. Eltsin is street smart. He would keep this kind of info close. In a laptop or a BlackBerry he carries around with him."

"Right. I'll see what I can do." It was now Tarik's turn to ask a tricky question. "What's your best guess, brother? Do you think this whole charade is for our benefit as much as for the Task Force? Is it possible Eltsin has gotten word the Kadirs are close and is waiting to ambush us somehow? The Taj secret police officer I ran into last night seemed overly confident when I overheard his conversation."

It took a moment for Darin to answer. "All things are possible. Shakir is on his way and we're putting together a stealth backup team to help with surveillance at Eltsin's fortress in the mountains. Give us a little time to see what we can come up with." Skepticism filled his voice. "I can't quite buy that Eltsin is partnering with the Taj, but we'll wait and see. In the meantime, watch your back."

Tarik thanked his brother, bid him goodbye and headed for the handler's Fruti Vita stand. He always watched his back. The trouble on this mission was centered more around keeping his eyes off his beautiful partner's back long enough to keep them both alive.

He knocked once and entered, finding Jass in the process of kissing her handler's cheek in a much too intimate manner. Jealousy ran through his mind.

Hell. What the devil was he thinking? Jealousy was out of bounds. She was his partner, not his lover.

Besides, this mission was all about the Taj Zabbar and their nuclear ambitions. Not about his partner.

Jass looked up at him with those big brown eyes of Celile's. "Glad you're back. I was getting set to take off." She patted the purse under her arm. "I have toys and instructions. And we need to go get fitted for our costumes before it gets any later."

"Costumes?"

She scooted past him and stepped out into the humid sunshine. "I'll tell you all about it after we pick up our car."

"Car?"

Jass laughed. "Come on...I've got it covered. Thanks again, Ed." She headed up the beach.

Tarik turned to follow her, but Ed's voice stopped him. "Just a second, Kadir."

He held fast at the threshold and glared at Jass's handler. "Yeah?"

"I don't know what game you think you're playing by horning in on the Task Force and taking over this mission, but I'm keeping my eyes on you. Jass is my responsibility and if you hurt her in any way, you're a dead man."

Tarik's fingers ground into the wooden doorjamb. "Without me, there would be no mission and you know it."

Ed glared at him but said nothing.

"But I've got a question for you." Tarik held his ground and quirked a brow. "Wouldn't this mission proceed perfectly well using Bosque, the station chief, as a standby go-between from the Task Force to us? Why is it necessary for a big-shot CIA officer to do the actual legwork?"

"I'm only here because of Jass," Ed grumbled. "Bosque is supposed to be a good man. But this assignment may make or break Jass's advancement. Nothing can go wrong."

Tarik didn't think that was a good enough answer, but he let it pass until he could talk to Jass. "Nothing will go wrong if you let us do the work we're paid to do. Trust your own operative to do the right thing. I'll watch out for her."

"She means a lot to me."

Tarik could suddenly see the man had real fatherly feelings for his operative. Ed wore his emotions on his sleeve when it came to Jass O'Reilly.

"Watch your back, Kadir."

Yeah, that was the second time in less than ten minutes he'd been given the same warning. But as he walked out into the afternoon sun and stepped across the smooth, white sand, Tarik figured it wasn't that his back needed watching. No, it was his raging libido that was giving him the biggest problem.

"This costume is outrageous." Tarik squirmed in the passenger seat of their tiny dark green sedan. "Why did you ever agree to anything this juvenile for Sheik Zohdi?"

"I think you look adorable. And a pirate costume is not juvenile. It's dashing." Unlike her costume, which at the moment was giving her fits. "Besides, under that *gia-normous* hat and the eye patch, no one would ever recognize Zohdi. Relax. We're not out to win any awards, but to blend in."

Tarik gave her one of his charmer-style looks. "As a matter of fact, I happen to be a big fan of *your* costume. You pick that out?"

The sparkly red bodysuit clung to her skin like a dive suit. Not a speck of bare skin showed from her neck to her ankles. Yet after she'd put the thing on, she felt sexier than ever before in her life.

"No, I didn't pick out either of our costumes. But at least mine is far better than all those sparkly thong getups we've been seeing on the streets."

"I'd give a lot to see you in one of those *getups*. But some other time. That much skin wouldn't be quite the right thing for Celile."

"Keep your mind on the mission, Kadir."

He chuckled and turned to look out the windshield. "Tell me again why you have to drive?"

"Sheik Zohdi does not drive. He's chauffeured everywhere he travels. You're not worried about my driving skills, are you?"

Tarik raised a shoulder. "No. Not unless we run into real trouble."

"Well, I wasn't planning on running into trouble tonight. Are you?"

"You never know," he retorted. "I'm not crazy about the whole idea of going back to Eltsin's offices tonight. It doesn't feel right."

"Why not? Everyone should be on the streets watching the samba parade."

Tarik folded his arms over his chest as she stopped for a traffic cop. "Maybe. But I can't believe we'll find any useful intel here without having to fight our way out. No one with any sense leaves sensitive info unguarded."

"I have a few tricks to use in case we run into security problems. Don't worry."

By the time they found a guarded parking spot a few blocks away and Jass wrestled her heavy feathered headdress onto her head, the area seemed deserted. Instead of blending in to the crowds, the two of them looked ridiculous sneaking down the darkened alley-ways.

Tarik echoed her sentiments. "I'm thinking we could do better if we both lose the headgear. You with me?"

They found an empty water barrel and stashed the feathers, the oversized pirate's hat and the fake swashbuckler's sword. "We can pick these up on the way back."

"Hmm." Tarik didn't seem thrilled with the idea.

When they arrived at the nightclub, they found guards at every entrance.

"Time for one of those toys you were issued?"

She elbowed past him and sidestepped around to the side of the building. The structure was only two stories tall on this side. And no one was guarding the alley with its lack of entrances and no windows.

"You planning on walking through the walls?" he asked with a smirk in his voice. "Those must be some high-tech toys you've got there."

"How're your mountain-climbing skills, Kadir?" She reached into her bag and pulled out what appeared in the darkness to be a flare gun. "This baby will get us inside in moments."

She nearly laughed at his incredulous look as she fired in the air. With a tiny, shallow sounding pop, the titanium grappling hook deployed and struck the tiled roof, embedding itself deep and tight. Carbon fiber threads parachuted back toward them. With another small click, she clipped an aluminum ascender to the bottom of the thread and gestured to Tarik that it was for his foot.

"A little like *Mission Impossible* and James Bond," she murmured. "I love it. Up you go. Send it back down for me."

He looked at the contraption in the shadowed light from the street lamp. "Oh, crap. You're not serious. I hate rooftops and ledges. Can't we find another way?"

"Sure. You can stay here and guard our backs. I'll handle this op alone."

"Not on your life." Tarik pulled off the fake eye patch and rubbed his hands against his black slacks. "Let me worry about my own back. And I'll be guarding your back from right behind you, my love. Lead the way."

# Chapter 7

Tarik managed to step off the tile roof and ease inside a second-story window right behind Jass without breaking his neck. Though he didn't like any part of this op, he was determined to keep up with her.

Nothing moved in the darkness of Eltsin's penthouse offices, but the smell of violence lingered in the air. What had happened inside these rooms earlier tonight?

Jass didn't seem to notice the odd sensations he was receiving and it was too dark to see anything more than shadows. She nudged his arm and crept off into the ominous black emptiness, undeterred from her mission. Tarik stood his ground for a second and listened. The sounds of a wall clock and the whir of an electric motor in the distance were all he could hear. Nothing he could put his finger on as out of place, and no hint of human activity he could sense.

Following Jass through what appeared to be a sparsely

furnished sitting room, he noted they were passing a darkened alley-style kitchen and a bathroom. Apparently she was looking for computers or file cabinets and nothing else. But the farther into the apartment they traveled, the more Tarik wanted to flick on a light and study his surroundings a bit more thoroughly. Every cell in his body tensed with concern.

Convinced that this was some kind of ambush, he caught up to Jass as she entered the first office space she came to. "Hold on." He stopped her with a firm grip to her forearm. "I think we need to get out of here. Something isn't right."

She quietly removed his fingers by using her own gloved hand. "Nonsense. We're in and no one's around. This won't take me five minutes. Why don't you look in the next room while I break into the computer?"

Their whispered conversation seemed to echo off the walls. This was all wrong.

Too easy.

Jass sat in front of a desk computer and turned a penlight on to study the drive box. Her light was bright enough for Tarik to see that the room was totally vacant of any other furnishings besides the desk and the lone computer. No, not right at all.

He backed out the door and into the hall. Reaching into his inside pocket, he pulled out a set of night-vision goggles and slipped them over his eyes to leave his hands free. No question, he had to give the place a more thorough visual check. And he'd better do it fast.

Moving quickly, he opened each of the other doors off the hall. Nothing but empty rooms and a lone disheveled cot. No filing cabinets, conference tables or office machines. What was going on?

Retracing his steps, Tarik went back toward the sitting

room. He stuck his head into the bathroom. Again, nothing. Then he turned to the kitchen and moved far enough into it to check out the whole space.

What was that, lying on the…? Damn. He nudged the object with his booted toe and found what he'd expected. A dead body.

At that exact moment he also caught the unmistakable sounds of police sirens in the distance. Great. They were being set up. But by whom? And why?

Swinging around, he made his way back to Jass in record time. She was on her way out the door of the office. He caught a smug look on her face.

"Got it," she crowed. "Found several computer files on fissionable nuclear material. We've got…"

"Shussh. Listen. Hear that?" He grabbed her by the arm and pulled her through the darkness toward the window where they'd entered a few minutes ago. "Move!"

Two steps later and the sounds of sirens were unmistakable.

"What's happening? Those can't be for us."

"We've been set up. Dead body in the kitchen." They reached the window "Out. Now!"

Jass was a smart enough operative to stop questioning and slip out into the night air without another sound. She crept along the tile roof, not waiting to make sure Tarik was behind her. But he was. He didn't let a botched job deter him from being her protector.

Determined to stand at her back regardless of what happened next, he dove out the window and caught up to her in a few seconds. Shouts were coming from the street below, and the sirens were still shrieking through the noisy night.

Jass was about to crawl over the ledge when she threw

a quick glance down to the blind alley where they'd begun their flight. "Eltsin's goons," she whispered and pointed below. "We'll have to find another way."

"Whatever we do, we'd better do it soon. The cops will be here any second."

She looked uncertain. As though this change of plans was so unexpected that she'd been thrown off track.

He imagined she would snap out of it any moment and come up with a backup escape plan. She was a pro and the best operative he knew. But he didn't wait to find out for sure.

"This way." He swung around and headed back up to the roof and then to the other side of the building. He crouched low to avoid being seen from below.

"That's the way to the side street," Jass said in a stage whisper. "A guard was there when we first entered."

Tarik kept going. "Maybe not anymore."

Sure enough, as they crawled to the roof's edge and peered over, they discovered the guards had gone. The alley was at least temporarily empty. Apparently the guards were either over at the side of the building, waiting for them to come back down that way, or they'd disappeared into the night to avoid confronting the police.

"Now what?"

Tarik nodded to the fire escape below them. "I'll lower you to the platform. Hurry."

"What about you?"

"Right behind you, love. Go now."

Jass nodded and swung herself off the edge. God, she was spectacular.

Tarik leaned down and went flat on his stomach, grabbing hold of her forearms as she clung to the edge.

The second his grip was sure, Jass took her fingers off the edge, and he eased her down into the darkness.

"Good enough," she whispered.

He hoped to hell she was right, and then he let her go. In another instant a clang and then a thump told him her feet had hit the metal fire escape.

Mumbling a curse under his breath for whoever had put him in the position of dangling over a dark abyss again, Tarik lowered himself over the roof edge and prayed he was lined up with the fire escape platform. After a big cleansing breath of air, he opened his hands and let go, dropping into yet another endless, star-filled night.

Jass managed to pull Tarik into her arms to keep him from falling into the street below as he'd dropped off the roof feet first. Out of breath and a little bruised from both her own fall and from being a cushion for his, she was grateful that they were both still alive.

But Tarik didn't give her the time to take a break or give thanks.

"Let's go." He shoved her down the fire-escape stairs ahead of him. "Keep moving. Those cops are pulling up in front now."

She scrambled down the one flight and planted her feet on the pavement. "Back to the car?"

"Yeah. But stick to the alleyways if you can. Stay in the shadows."

Earlier today Jass had memorized the streets around the samba club. Heading off now, she wished for a pair of running shoes instead of these silly heeled boots. The boots had been okay for use on the roof, but running full out in the dark on crumbling city sidewalks would've been a heck of a lot easier in a good pair of Nikes.

Tarik stayed a step behind, though she figured he could easily outdistance her if he wanted to. He was moving like a cheetah. Smooth and sleek and precise. On the other hand, she was plenty fast too as her heart pumped double-time with adrenaline. In fight-or-flight mode, she ran almost a half mile out of their way, winding through the alleys and down half-deserted streets. Still, in fifteen minutes they were nearing the car.

"Hold on a minute." Tarik stopped and jogged in place. "Isn't this where we left the headpieces to our costumes?"

Gulping in air, she wondered how he could sound this cool. She was nearly out of breath and his breathing was barely labored.

"Yes." She pointed at the rain barrel down the block.

"We can't leave them for the cops to find." He raced ahead and started pulling out feathered hats and a swashbuckler's sword.

Exactly what she didn't need—more stuff to weigh her down. But she took the monumental headgear under her arm when he handed it to her and started down the street toward their car once again.

The sound of sirens getting closer rang through the quiet, putting the hair up on the back of her neck. Then it hit her. Why did the streets seem deserted? It hadn't been quiet when they'd first come this way.

As they reached their car, she gritted out, "Where the heck is everyone? Might as well be carrying a painted sign announcing our guilt."

Tarik didn't answer but raced to the passenger door, jerked it open and jumped in. He slammed the door behind him as she managed to crawl in behind the wheel, squished her costume down at her feet and fastened her seat belt.

"Here come the good guys," Tarik said as he gave a quick glance up ahead at the flashing lights. "Move."

Jass jammed the car in gear, grabbed the wheel with both hands and did a quick one-eighty in the middle of the street. She had to get off the main road. But which way to go?

Taking three quick turns in succession, she blindly roared down alleyways and doubled back over the same streets where they'd been running. But she didn't seem to be losing the cops. There simply wasn't any way to hide without any other traffic around. Flashing lights and screaming sirens stayed right behind them.

"Take the next left," Tarik commanded.

She turned without question, sliding hard on two wheels. And drove right into the tail end of the traffic jam to end all traffic jams. Bumper-to-bumper cars lined the street and blocked the way.

"Brilliant, Einstein. Now what do you suggest?"

"Quick, change places with me. I'll drive."

"Drive where?" She gestured to the line of cars practically parked on top of each other in the street ahead.

"Just go. But don't get out of the car."

With a quick glance behind them and an exasperated sigh, she figured she had no choice. "Right."

"Thank you."

He'd better sound appropriately grateful. And this had better work to get them off the hook. She would hate facing the Rio police without any idea of who'd tipped them off or how they'd been turned in. No telling if someone had paid to get them out of the way—or if a few of those cops wouldn't be a little trigger-happy.

No, she decided firmly as she undid her seat belt and started over the console. They couldn't face the authorities. They needed to find a way out. If not by outracing the cops, then by hiding from them.

"What's with the traffic jam?" she muttered as he slid his body in under hers.

Instead of answering, Tarik sucked in a breath and stilled. Yeah, she'd felt it too as the curve of her bottom brushed over his crotch. All of a sudden she was the woman on top. And he was the utterly masculine male on the bottom.

Bad timing. She sucked in her own breath. Extremely bad timing.

Fortunately, she was a pro. "Excuse me. Uh, can you keep going, please?" She laid a hand on his shoulder to help lift her weight off of him.

But that didn't do much to help. The heat from his body seared her hand and sent an earthquake rumbling back up her arm and into her belly.

"If you'll scoot a little farther—"

"Uff." She threw her body into the seat he'd vacated.

Tarik maneuvered himself into the driver's seat and locked down his seat belt. "The traffic jam is all about the parade. See the pedestrians crowding the sidewalks trying to get a better view? Nothing's moving until the parade goes past." He gave her a quick once-over. "Hang on."

Throwing the car's transmission into low, he nosed the front bumper toward the sidewalk to their left and inched ahead into the crowd.

"Stop! Are you nuts? You'll kill—"

She stopped talking and held her breath as pedestrians

scattered. The sidewalks here had no curbs and this one wasn't quite as wide as the car.

She flicked a glance behind them and saw two cars pulling into the space at the end of the line that they'd left. The police—or someone impersonating them—jumped out and came in their direction.

Tarik kept the car steadily moving forward. Faster and faster, heedless of the human beings in his way. By now paradegoers were beginning to complain as they were unceremoniously shoved aside by a car. Shouts erupted as holes opened in front of their car's bumper and then promptly closed in behind them when they drove through. Suddenly they were completely surrounded by irate costumed paradegoers and the police were nowhere in sight.

Everyone was shouting and raising their fists. Jass wasn't thrilled about putting these people out, nearly killing them and taking the chance of a riot. But she was relieved the cops had been left behind in the process.

"Don't breathe easy yet. Those cops are now on foot. As slow as we have to go in the crowd, they'll catch up too soon. I think we should bail. We'll stand a much better shot on foot."

Jass nodded and undid her seat belt.

"Put on your hat," Tarik ordered as he turned the car off and eased open the door. "We'll blend in."

He was right. She bent to adjust her hat while Tarik jumped out from the driver's side door. By the time she turned to open her own door, an angry mob was outside the window.

Trying to open her door, she muttered, "Hey, sorry. Can't you take a joke? Isn't this a party?"

She shoved hard against the mass of humanity pushing against the car door on the other side. But the more she put her shoulder into it, the more difficult it became to move the door even an inch. She would never get out of the car before the cops arrived at this rate.

Right then the car began to rock from side to side. Jass had visions of being caught in the front seat as the crowds turned the sedan over and set it ablaze.

She grit her teeth and worked even harder to get the door open. Nothing she did would budge it.

But all of a sudden the door flew open and her body was pulled free. But how? Before she could react, she felt herself being dragged through the crowds. The police? Was she on her way to jail?

"Keep moving." No, when she looked up, it was Tarik.

She should have known.

He was propelling them through the throng faster than she would've thought possible. She chanced a glance behind them. Only a few yards from the car and it had already disappeared inside the mass of humanity.

Tarik threw his arm around her shoulders and jerked her closer to his chest. It was a protective motion that should've annoyed her with its macho implications. Instead, she was grateful for the cover.

The music and the noisy revelry grew to thunderous proportions. Yet they kept shoving their way forward through the crowds.

"You still with me?" Tarik hesitated only a second.

"Go," she screamed over the din.

He pushed them out into an opening in the humanity. And suddenly they were smack in the middle of the street—right in the midst of the samba dancers as they paraded along the boulevard doing their show.

But it was open enough here in the street to actually run. Tarik almost lifted her entirely off her feet as he dashed from side to side, dodging dancers and drummers alike.

Jass expected another riot. But this time they only received a few shouts and lots of laughter and good-natured applause. Several blocks down the way Tarik stopped long enough to take a bow along with the dancers.

"Quit being a ham," she gritted out. "Get me out of here."

He laughed and dragged them off the street on the other side and back into the crowds. "We wouldn't have gotten that far without the costumes. Thought we'd be clever and use them to the fullest."

Jass tsked at him. "Now how do we get back to the hotel?"

"Are those boots made for walking?"

"How far is it?"

"Only a couple of miles. Mostly downhill. It'll be a good chance for us to get to know each other."

Shaking her head and trying to keep the smile off her face, Jass pulled the heavy headpiece off. "My boots are perfectly fine for walking, thank you. In fact, you'd best keep up the pace or I'll leave you in my dust, Kadir."

With that, she turned in a circle, looking for a familiar landmark or street sign.

"Lost?" Tarik took her by the hand and hustled down the street. "Come on. Maybe we'll be better off with my slower pace. But whatever we do, let's move it now."

# Chapter 8

Tarik kept hold of her hand, more to settle his own nerves than for any other reason. Jass tried halfheartedly to break away. But when he refused to let her loose, she relaxed and remained comfortably beside him, keeping up with the pace he set.

"We can't run or we'll call attention to our movements," he told her. "If we stroll, we'll look like any other tourists or paradegoers. Good enough?"

"I suppose."

She sounded so petulant that he nearly laughed. Instead, he decided to give her an out and let her go back to being her sarcastic self.

"Don't I get a thank-you for saving your ass back there? My driving skills saved the day."

Narrowing her lips to tiny white lines, she simply stared at him. The quiet was unlike her and he couldn't let it be.

"Okay, maybe it was a little over-the-top for me to head right into a crowd of innocent bystanders, but it did the trick, didn't it?"

She shrugged—a totally uncharacteristic movement. That clinched it for him. He had to find a way to get her talking again.

He took a quick look around at the many other costumed pedestrians strolling along the sidewalks and heading toward the beach side of town like they were. Cars streamed by, going to different neighborhoods or possibly heading toward the parade in the other direction. No one paid them any attention. A pirate and the cat woman easily blended right into the revelry of the night.

"I sure wish I knew who set us up tonight." He kept his voice down, but he wasn't worried about being overheard. "You have any ideas on that subject?"

"Not really. The only people who could've been aware we'd be at Eltsin's tonight were the local CIA operatives and the Task Force. I'll have Ed get to the bottom of it while we stay on the job."

Now there was a subject he would bet she'd warm up to. "Speaking of Ed, he seems inordinately cautious about your welfare. Like you're more than simply a superior and his employee. You two have some sort of history?"

She gave him a wary glance before apparently deciding he had no ulterior motive for asking. "We go way back. Ed and my father were partners on covert missions for the Agency for many years. I first met Ed when I was a little girl, right after my mother died."

"I understand your father was killed while on an operation for the CIA."

She nodded quietly before clearing her throat. "Yes.

I was in my first year of college at the time. Dad and I had a huge fight right before he left for the mission." She breathed in and out. "I never got to tell him I was sorry."

"What was the fight about?" Okay, that was too personal a question for brand-new partners, but he didn't care. He wanted to know more about her.

Jass didn't seem to mind his prying. In fact, she seemed quite willing to talk.

"I was switching my major at the time. I'd been in pre-law because that's what Dad wanted. But I wanted the more hands-on approach of law enforcement. He expected a lawyer in the family. I wanted to be a covert agent like he was."

"What degree did you end up with?"

"I almost quit altogether after Dad died." She sighed and he knew she was thinking back to those terrible days when she'd first become an orphan. "If it hadn't been for Ed stepping in and offering to help me get a job with the Agency after graduation and giving me a little financial assistance, I might have ended up as a waitress or a security guard."

She screwed up her mouth and shook her head. "I graduated pre-law, in Dad's memory. But I went to work for the CIA immediately after getting my degree. Ed made all the difference. He coached me and cajoled me into graduating and then took me under his wing at the Agency." Raw emotion filled her voice. "I owe him my career. And…more. I owe him for his friendship when I needed it the most."

"Did your father ever say why he didn't want his daughter following in his footsteps?"

She took another big breath. "Not that I can remember.

He always said the job made a person hard. And too indifferent about human life."

"From where I sit, it hasn't seemed to make you hard," Tarik said with a softness in his tone that surprised even him. "You were sincerely concerned for the people in that crowd of pedestrians back there."

Instead of a smile, Jass scowled. "Right. Remind me that I'm not as tough as you are. Rub it in. I deserve it."

"What? No, I didn't mean it that way. You're plenty tough when you need to be. It's just…you're also tender—which is a good thing in my book."

"Humph." Jass lifted her chin and strode ahead with more purpose.

Tarik squeezed her hand and she slowed enough to come back to his side. "You remind me a little of my mother," he told her, more for something to say than to share something about himself.

"I thought your mother died when you were young."

"I was five." He did not want to have this conversation. Thoughts of his mother always made his chest ache with the memories.

"Why do I remind you of her?"

Okay, he'd asked for this. "Her family comes from a nomadic Bedouin background, same as my father's. But unlike the Kadirs, her family is still living in the deserts today and surviving on simple trade the way they have for centuries. They exist right on the edge of civilization, only slightly shy of savagery.

"Until my grandfather passed away a few years ago," Tarik continued. "He swore by the old ways. His sons had to be warriors and his daughters had to be tough enough to survive under the harshest of conditions."

Tarik wished he could find a way out of this, but he

knew he would have to at least be sincere with Jass—and more truthful than he'd allowed himself to be since he was a devastated five-year-old. Talking about his dead mother in intimate detail hurt.

Sighing quietly, he said the words he'd long avoided even thinking about. "My mother was raised to be tough, but she was also a princess of the tribe. Her grandmother insisted she be sent away to college, where she met and married my father." He caught her gaze. "If you'd been introduced to her, you would never have known about her upbringing. She was sophisticated and genteel. A lady in every sense of the word. And she loved her sons with a quiet ferociousness I've never seen since."

But he had a feeling Jass would love with the same kind of passionate intensity. For some crazy reason the idea made him suddenly long to be the object of all that fiery passion.

He shook off the unwelcome vulnerability. His mission could mean uncovering a threat to the entire world, and as such it was not the time or place for personal introspection and need. Maybe he should try sneaking out and getting himself laid later—in order to release the tension. In his wayward youth, a little flash-bang of a sexual nature would've taken the edge off long enough for him to finish an assignment and put his mind back in the game.

But he'd matured a lot in the last couple of years. Quick tumbles with complete strangers no longer held any appeal. He wasn't looking for any kind of commitment either—his family's covert war prevented thoughts of long-term romance. And even though both his brothers had found women to die for, he couldn't imagine bringing someone he loved into the middle of this much danger.

Still, a woman would have to mean something to him now before he fell into bed. Something more than a way to release a little tension—despite what he'd said to Jass yesterday when he'd been trying to tease her into becoming more comfortable playacting as his girlfriend.

Though at the time, when he'd said the two of them needed to have a good old-fashioned roll in the hay, he had meant every word. In fact, it still sounded like a good idea. More than good. It sounded like paradise.

But he couldn't help wondering why the conflict between what he thought he believed and what his body craved seemed wildly at odds when it came to Jass.

Compassion glistened in her eyes. "Your mother sounds like a special woman. I wish I could've known her."

"You two would've had a lot in common. You're a lot like she was. Tough when you need to be. And tender underneath."

Maybe that was it. Maybe Jass's personality felt as familiar and comfortable as cozy memories of the only woman who'd ever loved him. And therefore she must already mean something important to him and wouldn't be merely an anonymous roll in the hay. But he sure wished he could figure out exactly why that had happened so fast.

As they stepped off the elevator down the hall from their hotel room, Jass felt somebody watching. She took Tarik's arm and sidled up close to him before casually checking both ends of the hallway. She couldn't spot anyone when she looked, but someone was there none-theless.

As they neared their hotel-room door, the elevator

doors opened again and when they turned back, a waiter stepped off carrying a tray. He came in their direction but as he came closer, she saw it was Station Chief Bosque in disguise.

Jass jumped in and went with their cover story. "Ohh, is that for us?" She managed a broad smile and turned to Tarik. "Zohdi, darling, did you order a late dinner as a surprise? How thoughtful of you. I'm famished."

Tarik didn't answer but used his card key to open the door and then turned to the supposed waiter. "Bring it inside."

As Bosque brushed past Tarik, he spoke under his breath. "You've had visitors. Inside long enough to plant bugs. Stay in character, but meet me on the terrace."

Once they were inside, Bosque began setting up the dining table for two. He laid out candles, a late supper and even a bottle of chilled wine.

Her brain raced with ways to get them out on the terrace without being too obvious. She waltzed over to Tarik, went up on tiptoes and planted a kiss against his lips. She'd wanted quick and flirty. Instead, the heat and the chemistry between them flared up and nearly knocked her down.

She pulled away, but lingered long enough to lick his lips and then her own. "It's awfully warm in here, isn't it?"

Tarik look slightly stunned, but he ran with her lead. "Very much so, my love. And it's such a nice night." He shrugged out of his pirate's hat and jacket and headed toward the terrace doors. "Let's get some air."

He threw open the glass doors and stepped through to the wide terrace.

"Wait for me." She started out behind him. "What

a wonderful view. Too bad we can't have supper out here."

Bosque lifted his head and spoke while she stepped outside. "I'm sorry, madam. There is not enough room on the terrace for the setting. However—" He picked up the wine and two glasses. "You may enjoy your wine before supper outside if you prefer. If you'll allow me to pour?"

He followed both of them out through the French doors and then quietly closed them behind him. "Did you two run into trouble tonight? We found your car abandoned." He poured Tarik a full glass and handed it over. "We've received word that our man inside Eltsin's operation was killed earlier. What do you know about it?"

Tarik set the glass down on the ledge overlooking the bay. "We found the body. But somebody was trying to set us up. We barely got out before the cops arrived."

Bosque cursed under his breath. "I was afraid of that. I've already started an internal investigation, but it'll take time. Do you want to call off the mission?"

"Not a chance." Jass threw a glance toward Tarik and he nodded his agreement. "It's possible Eltsin was only fishing. Checking to see who showed up at his place. I don't believe he knows for sure it was us or he'd have sent goons to take us out, not to spy on us."

"Agreed," Tarik put in. "This mission is too important to abort. Escalating danger is all part of the job."

"All right, if you're sure then." Bosque handed Jass a glass of sparkling wine. "We'd better leave the bugs in place. We don't want Eltsin's crowd to know we're on to their game. I'm guessing they set up cameras or listening devices in the sitting room and maybe even in the bedroom." He nodded once. "Assume that's where they are for now. I'll double-check the bath and the bedroom terrace for bugs before I leave. Keep the act on everywhere but there."

*Oh hell.* Jass hadn't thought of that. *The act.* She and Tarik would have to continue pretending to be lovers even while alone. All night.

It was a good thing she believed in what Tarik had told Bosque. The mission was too important to back out of their cover story now.

But later on her resolve might prove easier said than done. Starting to sweat in the sultry sea air, she took a sip of cool wine and let it slide down her suddenly dry throat. The mission was about to become particularly difficult. A long night of sharing a single bed in front of a camera with one of the sexiest men she'd ever met might be her toughest assignment yet.

But she had to keep in mind that Tarik was not Zohdi. Tarik was out of bounds. A partner. A buddy. Not a lover. And on top of that, he was still the man her handler swore was someone she should be wary about trusting.

Ed's opinion didn't seem as much of a problem now that she and Tarik had completed one night's mission. But if she didn't watch out, Tarik could easily become too important in her life. She couldn't have that. It would interfere with her self-image as a serious, dedicated professional.

As much as he had saved their lives and she was beginning to rely on him as a competent partner, in her mind, Tarik was still kind of a clown. A gorgeous, sexy charmer who could become anything as long as it was in his own self-interest. The exact opposite of the man she'd always assumed would capture her heart. A man like her father.

Reciting once again the mantra she'd decided to live by, Jass reminded herself that despite her intense reactions toward Tarik Kadir, it was only her hormones talking. She could handle him. She could handle anything that came her way. After all, she was a pro.

Tarik tried to pretend the heat and the obvious lust between them were not serious concerns. But he knew better.

When the woman wanted to prove she could masquerade being in love, she did it in spades. His still slamming pulse did not bode well for the cover story tonight. Cool. He needed to remain cool.

A man like Zohdi did not lose his mind over a few kisses. Yet it was all Tarik could do a few minutes ago not to fall down on his knees and beg her to kiss him again.

What would he be like later? In bed with the cameras running? Could he restrain his own raging lust and yet fake making love to her? This whole business was definitely not what he'd signed up for.

Bosque feigned giving them turndown service as he checked the bathroom and bedroom terrace for bugs. But he was ready to leave them alone much too soon to suit Tarik.

On his way out, Bosque murmured in his ear, "Bath and terrace are clear. Found a hidden camera in a wall sconce in the bedroom. Good luck."

Yeah, right.

Filling his lungs with what he hoped was fortifying air, Tarik returned to Jass's side. "Let's share this meal, my sweet, and proceed to the dessert." Taking on Zohdi's persona again, he kissed her hand. "We're overdue for time alone."

He caught the quick but frantic look of panic in Jass's eyes, but when she spoke, she was all Celile. "Hmmm. I can't wait."

After they'd picked at their food for an hour and found inane subjects to discuss while sitting across the table casting lustful gazes at each other, it was time for them to play their parts as two lovers alone. He stood and pulled her into his arms, making a big show for the camera.

"Enough of this." He looked down into her eyes. "Come to bed with me."

Her gaze carried not a trace of panic this time. In fact, Jass seemed the perfect picture of a woman so much in love she would do anything her man asked. He was the one worrying about the act.

She stepped back and looked up at him through long, thick lashes. "Help me out of this costume, darling."

*Ah, hell.* He scooped her up in his arms and strode into the bedroom, slamming the door to the sitting room behind him. He would deal with the one camera in the bedroom because he knew where it was located.

Positioning himself between the wall sconce and the bed, he let Jass slide down his body until her feet hit the floor. "The only camera in here is on the wall behind me," he whispered as he helped her regain her footing. "Stay where they can't see you."

She didn't act as if she understood him, but he noticed her give the wall behind him a quick glance over his shoulder. Then twisting around, she presented him with her back.

"The zipper, love. I can't reach."

Swallowing hard, Tarik reached for her zipper but his fingers froze mid-motion. He didn't want to expose her to prying eyes this way. Was stripping her in public supposed to be part of his job description?

He made a quick decision. "My costume first, sweetheart. I want to take my time with yours."

If anyone was going to be the star of this strip show, it would be him. His naked body would be the thing they had to focus on first. And he hoped to hell they got an eyeful through that camera lens.

Pulling the pirate's shirt and undershirt over his head, he pitched them behind him without looking. With any luck they would land on the wall sconce, but thus far his luck hadn't been running hot.

Next he quickly dispensed with the pirate's boots and pants. Standing there stark naked was no big deal for him. He could care less who saw what. But once again he faced the problem of helping Jass with her zipper. Her back was still turned and he felt grateful for small favors.

Could he maneuver them under the bedcovers before she must face both him and the camera full on?

Moving in close behind her back, he wrapped an arm around her shoulders and began lowering the zipper with the other. The process seemed to take forever. His body grew harder with every millimeter.

Without clearly thinking about what he was doing and where they were, he buried his nose in her neck and breathed in the lush scent of her. Every cell, every atom in his body went on full alert and rebelled at the sudden onslaught of intoxicating need. He desired the woman under the wig and brown contact lenses. But that's not who he held.

She tugged at his arms and he let loose long enough for her to wiggle out of the cat suit. Standing there in only a red bra and thong panties, she still had her back turned. She hadn't allowed herself to be observed in anything more than what she might've worn to the beach. *Good work, partner.*

What would Zohdi do at this point?

Same thing Tarik would do if all else were equal. Groaning, he reached down and swept her up in his arms again. Without turning them around, he carried her to the bed and unceremoniously dumped her there, jumping in after her a split second later.

He threw himself over her, covering her body with his own. Holding her still, he placed both hands on the sides of her head as he insinuated himself between her thighs.

Closing in for a kiss, he whispered against her lips, "I'll cover us with the blanket in a moment. Just play along for now."

But then Jass moaned. Not out of any pain or act, but she seemed clearly lost in a real passion. Apparently she wasn't playing the same game he was.

She squirmed and opened her eyes to look up at him with a glazed look. Her expression was enough of a shock to make him forget all about his mission. All about the camera. Until finally, he even forgot his own name.

# Chapter 9

*What is Tarik saying?*

Jass struggled to come out of her haze and listen, but the blood boiled in her ears. With her pulse screaming through her veins as though she were pulling down five Gs, her body throbbed with passion. And all because of the masculine body currently lying suggestively between her legs.

Geez. She bit the inside of her cheek hard enough to snap herself out of it. They were supposedly working a sting. She was Celile. But he was not the real Zohdi.

*Work. Work. Work.* This was an important assignment and not the most intimate experience she'd ever had. Worse even than the idea of taking a risk with her career, there'd been a camera trained on them this whole time.

She'd lost her mind. But, oh man, what a terrific way to go insane. The sexual chemistry between the two of them left her soaring. Tarik's mere touch jolted her with an intense excitement, sparking a conflagration that had sent her up in flames. His naked and aroused body surprised her, but it shouldn't have. He was so much more than she imagined. The most potent male she'd ever seen.

Like spontaneous combustion, she'd found herself wet and set to explode.

But they were only acting for their mission. Right? *Remember the mission.*

"Hold on." Tarik left her long enough to drag the covers up and over their heads, covering them completely from view.

How could he remain unaffected? Well, not totally unaffected, she'd noticed. He was hot and pulsing…and huge. He'd been ready just like she was.

But his mind had stayed in the game. A trait she'd better learn how to mimic.

"Laugh," he demanded in a raspy whisper. "Or giggle. Anything that makes it seem as though we're doing what it looks like in this bed."

His words actually made some sense through her clearing fog. At last. She wiggled out from underneath his body and rolled over to face him—while both of them remained hidden under the covers.

Watching him closely, she opened her mouth and let out one of the loudest moans imaginable. "Ah. Ah. Ah." She forced the volume higher. "Oh, Zohdi. Oh. Oh."

Finally, she wound herself up and screamed incoherently. A thing she had never done during the throes of passion in her entire lifetime.

Tarik actually smiled as he murmured low, "Nice work, agent. I'd like a repeat performance someday. But not for the cameras."

That did it. He had to move away. Now.

"Get out of bed and turn off the lights, Zohdi." She gritted her teeth. "And then bring me a robe."

Why hadn't the man thought to turn out the lights in the first place?

In a hushed tone, Tarik answered. "Okay, but I'm betting turning off the lights won't help. The camera is probably NVC, night-vision capable. Most surveillance equipment is set up that way. I'll gladly get the robes." He scowled and rolled out from under the blankets, leaving her covered and furious.

Seconds later he pulled down the covers and immediately threw one of the terry bathrobes over her. "Get up, Celile," he announced in a loud voice. "You need a shower and I have work to do on the laptop."

"What did you say?" It was easy to fake a little indignation. She felt every bit of Celile's part.

Tarik turned his back. "Get up."

"Well, isn't that romantic? You bastard." She shoved her arms into the robe and stood. "I'm going. But if you think for one minute that you're in for a repeat performance tonight, you are out of your mind. You and your damned laptop can sleep out on the terrace."

Grasping the robe around her like a shield, Jass marched into the bathroom and slammed the door. Once alone and out of camera range, she leaned both hands heavily on the countertop. Hanging her head and breathing in and out through her mouth, she tried to calm her shaky nerves.

Realization began to sink in. He had actually picked a fight in order to save them from having to sleep together tonight. The whole scene back there suddenly became clear. Everything he'd done in the bedroom—stripping himself and not her, carrying her to the bed and covering them from view—all of it was done for her benefit. To save her from embarrassment.

Tarik Kadir had honor. He'd wanted her as much as she'd wanted him, but he wasn't going to give in to it in front of an audience. Amazing.

She tore off the Celile wig and popped out the brown-colored contacts, ready to scrub off all traces of the bitch who was currently ruling her life. A hot shower was definitely in order.

But then again, maybe Jass would be a lot better off taking a cold shower. The more she thought about Tarik in the buff, the more she wished he hadn't been quite as professional and thoughtful. She was starting to believe that he'd been right and they would indeed have a repeat performance someday.

But at that time he would *not* be dressed in sheik's clothing and she would *not* be wearing a brown wig and brown contact lens or answering to the name Celile. And there would definitely not be any cameras allowed.

It might've been one of the longest nights of his life. Grumpy and stiff, Tarik sat across the breakfast table from Jass, drinking coffee and feeling miserable about ever opening his big mouth last night. If he had only shut up, stayed in bed and not deliberately picked that fight with her, it could have turned into one of the best nights he'd ever had.

The only thing saving him from abject misery this morning was Jass's expression. She still resembled Celile, but there was something about the way she looked at him that told a different story. When she'd apologized for the argument that had kept him out on the terrace all night, she'd used Celile's voice. But the emotion in her eyes said his real partner was every bit as sorry for their difficult circumstances.

He reached over and took her hand, also feeling a little sorry that he still couldn't speak from the heart. "You are forgiven, my darling Celile. And I apologize for being an ass. Let's spend the day making it up to each other."

Jass opened her mouth, but right then a loud knock on the suite door captured their attention.

"I'll get it." She stood and went toward the door.

He watched her move, fascinated by the sure and steady stride. And by the curve of her hips. The way she filled out her blouse. And by the ever-so-slight pout she always wore on her lips.

God help him, but he was becoming helpless to think of anything else when he was around his partner.

Before Jass could make sure it was Bosque, the door burst open and a couple of well-dressed goons barged into the room as if they'd had their own key. They both pulled snub-nosed Uzis from under their suit coats and pointed them at Jass.

"You will come with us." The more heavyset one of the duo spoke in Russian.

Tarik was on his feet in an instant and moving toward Jass before he even realized what he was doing.

She didn't seem fazed. "Put those weapons away, you imbeciles." She made the demand in the best Russian dialect he'd ever heard.

Tarik froze where he stood. She was handling it far better without him.

The man with the gun suddenly looked as if someone had punched him in the gut. He shook his head as though he were a prize fighter who'd heard bells ringing.

"But the boss…he requests your presence for *Carnivale*

this weekend." The other man's hand began to shake as he slid the Uzi back under his jacket.

"Mr. Eltsin will not be happy to learn you treated his guests and customers in such a manner." Jass threw her hands on her hips in a perfect imitation of something Celile would do. "We'll accompany you to Mr. Eltsin's. But we will only leave after finishing our breakfast and packing an overnight bag."

She turned her back on the men as though she could care less about their weapons. "Wait out in the hall."

Tarik fought to keep the grin off his face. Man, she was spectacular. He followed her into the deep, walk-in closet in the bedroom and found her shoving high-tech gear into a collapsible backpack.

"Aren't you going to need some clothes, too?"

She glanced up at him and scowled. "A couple of sexy outfits and a few cosmetics, maybe. But this equipment is much more important. You pack the weapons."

"Okay, boss lady." With a silent chuckle, he went to work.

All the passion and romance, even the friendship, was buried for now. The covert agents were back on the job.

They rode through the streets of Rio in the backseat of a silver Mercedes sedan. Tarik's gut instincts were shouting that this was the wrong move for them to make. He didn't believe starting out with two well-armed goons, without first having contact with either the Task Force or his brothers, could lead to anything good.

As their sedan climbed into the hills above the city and drove past the shantytown areas known as favelas, his bigger worry became how to control Jass. Since Eltsin's henchmen had shown up, she'd become Celile in a deeper way than ever before. He could no longer find Jass inside her eyes. But even with his unease, he still trusted her to do whatever necessary for the mission. She was a professional and his partner.

All along the scenic drive at the crest of the mountains, Tarik stared out his window at the city and the bay spreading below them. Tiny white sailboats floated on the turquoise blue of Guanabara Bay. Sparkling white sands blistered in the hot sun of Ipanema Beach. The greens and grays of Sugarloaf Mountain in the distance were silhouetted like a picture postcard against puffy lavender and pink clouds.

Everything seemed painted in Technicolor.

His senses tended to remain on full alert during any mission. But for some reason today, on this mission, the world was brighter, sweeter than ever before.

The big hitch in the perfection, of course, was knowing Jass could be stepping into a rat's nest of trouble at Eltsin's place, completely unprepared for what Tarik felt was coming. Yes, she'd fallen deeper into her cover and had become Celile, the Messenger. But Tarik knew the Taj would be there. And they were trouble with a capital T everywhere they went.

Worse yet, he would have to avoid being around the Taj as much as possible. Since he was disguised at Sheik Zohdi, Tarik didn't imagine the Taj Zabbar officials would immediately recognize him as a Kadir. But he would have to be particularly careful with his accent, and under no circumstance could he let on that he understood their language.

One slipup would mean disaster for the Kadirs, for this mission and for Jass. That meant he was left dealing with the fact that she would have to be the public face of their mission. Tarik took a breath, wishing he could talk to her privately.

After another half hour of silence, Andrei Eltsin's gated villa appeared like a castle in the lush green mountainside overlooking the sprawling Rio metropolis and picturesque ocean far below. Tarik steeled himself to arrive in the manner of the mysterious terrorist he'd been playing. Rearranging his head scarf to partially block his face, he reviewed his game plan. Covert work was all about showmanship. And becoming a dangerous and volatile Middle Eastern terrorist meant shutting his mouth and keeping to himself. Despite the circumstances and the danger to Jass.

The Mercedes passed through a heavily guarded gate and rolled up the long drive past multicolored flowers, evergreen shrubs and a manicured green lawn. They pulled up in front of a sprawling and opulent Moroccan-style building and stopped before twenty-foot-tall, mahogany doors. It was one hell of a dramatic entryway with ornate grillwork and terra-cotta tiles on the steps. Yes, indeed, this Eltsin character had a penchant for high drama.

The two goons bailed out of the car as soon as it came to a stop and opened the back passenger doors. "The boss wants you to relinquish your weapons before you enter his private quarters. Turn them over to us now and avoid being frisked inside."

Jass came out of the Mercedes like a queen. "Not a chance, big boy." She held on to her wide-brimmed straw hat with one hand and put the other on the goon's chest. "Now do I look like I have any weapons on me?"

The Russian's face colored with embarrassment as his eyes raked down her tight-fitting zebra-print dress, long legs and strappy sandals. "No, ma'am. But it's my job."

She waved him off. "Nonsense. And as for Sheik Zohdi, I would not advise anyone to try taking his weapons. Not if you wish to live to see tomorrow."

Tarik took that as his cue, eased out of the backseat and stretched his legs. The goon by his door backed up out of his way.

Jass moved a step closer to the villa's front door, speaking over her shoulder as though she must be obeyed without question. "Take us to see Mr. Eltsin immediately. He will straighten all of this out. I'm sure he does not want to offend one of his best customers." She sighed devisively. "Oh, and you boys better bring the bags inside."

Yeah, the lady was good.

Inside the house, Tarik had some trouble keeping his mouth from gaping open. Talk about ostentatious wealth. Crystal chandeliers, which looked as if they belonged in a palace rather than in a villa, hung from forty-foot ceilings. Hand woven Persian carpets adorned the travertine tile floors. A hand-carved, exotic wood staircase soared up three flights in the grand entrance hall.

Everywhere he looked was gold leaf. Gold on the woodwork. Golden goblets and golden threads in plush fabrics.

The Kadir family had done well in their businesses over the years. But Tarik couldn't remember ever seeing wealth on crude display this way. Business must be better than good for the suppliers of weapons of mass destruction these days.

"The boss is waiting." One of the goons pointed his weapon toward a sunken living room off to the left.

Jass spun and strode down the few steps as if she owned the place. "Mr. Eltsin," she said in Russian. "How nice of you to invite us to spend a few days with you. This is such a lovely villa."

Eltsin stood alone by a bar, with a cocktail glass full of either vodka or tequila in his hand. "I'm pleased you could join me, Ms. Kocak." He'd spoken in lightly accented English and made it clear that he would prefer carrying on in that language.

Once again Tarik became wary. Did the Russian have some idea that his guests were fluent English speakers and not who they claimed to be?

Fortunately for Tarik, Sheik Zohdi was more conversant in English than he was in Russian. Perhaps Eltsin had investigated and found that out.

As if the man was answering his unspoken questions, Eltsin said, "Thank you for coming, Sheik Zohdi. My humble home is open to you. We will speak in English this weekend to make my guests comfortable. Not all of them are as at ease with Russian as you are, Ms. Kocak."

Tarik believed the Taj Zabbar would be in attendance since he'd overheard them talking about coming. Would anyone else be there? Of course, knowing the Taj as he did, they would probably refuse to speak in Russian even though he was positive they understood it perfectly well.

"It does not matter," Jass told him offhandedly. She'd made sure to heavily accent her English.

"Good. Now, before I offer you my hospitality, I would prefer it if you'd disarm yourselves."

Jass opened her mouth to make a response, but Eltsin held up his hand and interrupted. "I had sincerely hoped you would voluntarily give up your weapons while in my home. But I'll have them taken from you if that's your choice."

Tarik didn't want Jass to endure either a search or an argument. Stepping closer to Eltsin, he carefully withdrew the Walther from his jacket pocket.

"I will voluntarily give mine up." He hesitated with his fingers on the butt end of the gun. "To my knowledge, Ms. Kocak is unarmed, but no one touches her. Understood? In addition, I expect your word on our safety while we remain under your roof."

Eltsin ignored him and nodded to one of his henchman, standing in the doorway. The man gingerly approached Tarik and put his hand out for the gun.

"Your word, Eltsin?"

"Of course. But Ms. Kocak…"

Jass moved closer to Eltsin, nearly rubbing up against the Russian. "I carry a small weapon in my briefcase. It is for self-defense only. And it is tiny, really. Nearly useless."

"No weapons in my home."

"Certainly," Jass said dismissively. "As you wish. We are all civilized here."

She reached into her bag and turned over the smaller-sized Ruger she'd stashed there. Tarik handed over his weapon to the henchman at the same time.

"When do we get to meet our competitors, Mr. Eltsin?" Jass moved closer to Tarik and farther away from Eltsin. A telling move that Eltsin clearly understood.

After the tension surrounding the weapon transfer, Eltsin suddenly looked at ease. "Do not think of this weekend as only business, Ms. Kocak." His mouth actually turned up in a strange version of a smile. "I want you two to enjoy yourselves. I think you'll find the pool and gardens are quite delightful. Please take advantage of them with my compliments."

Jass lowered her shoulders and smiled back warmly. "Why thank you. We'll do that."

Tarik wanted to make a couple of things clear first. "I am not much on leisure time, Mr. Eltsin." He used the low, threatening voice of the sheik to make his point. "I expect the privacy to conduct my business and to spend time alone with Ms. Kocak."

He put his hand possessively on Jass's shoulder. "And, I expect that our personal business papers and computers will be protected from prying eyes."

"There is a safe in your room," Eltsin said without any trace of rancor. "And I give you my word neither you nor your things will be bothered while you're at my home. But I sincerely hope you and Ms. Kocak will spend at least a little time relaxing while you are here. All work and no play, you know."

*An American cliché? Eltsin must be suspicious.*

"All work and no play—what could that mean, Mr. Eltsin?" Jass had caught the odd remark and with a glance at Eltsin, casually wound her arm through Tarik's.

Eltsin smiled full-out this time and Tarik was reminded of the grin on the king cobra right before it struck. "Do not concern yourself, my dear. It is nothing. My man will see you and the sheik to your room now. But please do join us for a late lunch at the pool."

Jass laughed and shrugged a shoulder. "I'll try. But I cannot guarantee an appearance from Sheik Zohdi. He is, what was it you said? No play but all work? That is why I am acting as his agent for the auction."

Eltsin gave an elegant wave of his hand. "The auction

is two days away yet. In the meantime, I do hope to see you later. Until then?"

Jass nodded pleasantly and they took their leave, following the henchman up the staircase. Tarik could feel her trembling beside him, though her head was high and her chin strong. He wanted to wrap his arm around her shoulders to give her added strength. But he didn't want to call attention to her distress—or give her the idea he thought she was weak in any way.

No one on the outside would ever have guessed how difficult that scene must've been on Jass. He certainly hadn't noticed until now.

He hung back, leaned over and whispered in her ear. "Was the Ruger your only weapon?"

"Was the Walther yours?"

"Not a chance."

"Me neither." She'd made the reply in her own hushed tone as a twinkle appeared in her eyes. "What do you say we find someplace private and I'll show you mine if you show me yours?"

A chuckle escaped his lips. What better partner could he have than Jass? She, who joked in the face of danger.

Now all he had to do was keep her safe. From Eltsin. From the Taj. And most of all, from himself.

# Chapter 10

"**W**hat if they've already been through our luggage?" Jass raised her voice to be heard from the closet while she removed the derringer from under her dress.

Tarik had finished checking their room for bugs and cameras and declared the place clean. Now he was rifling through her duffel and his briefcase in the bathroom.

"I'm sure they made a cursory inspection, but they didn't have the time to uncover what I hid. It would take a better man than anyone Eltsin's got to find…"

As she ducked out of the closet, Tarik stepped out of the bathroom, assembling a revolver. "All the weapons we're carrying now are made of special plastic and won't show up on any metal screening. Don't be surprised to find ammo in with your underwear."

"You broke the weapons down into pieces?"

He grinned like a Cheshire cat with a bowl of milk.

"Sure. A barrel in with the swimsuits. A grip in my briefcase with my laptop. A firing pin in with shaving cream."

Shrugging, he went on, "It's not hard to disguise and smuggle weapons if you know what you're doing and have the proper equipment."

"No wonder that duffel is so heavy. I've done the same kind of thing with the surveillance toys Ed supplied. I'm surprised the luggage doesn't clank when it's carried."

"Plastic, remember?" Tarik's face suddenly sobered. "Do you think your handler knows where we are? Could he have followed us?"

The smile spread across her face as she prepared to give up the secret she'd been carrying. "He knows. I'm tagged."

"What? They implanted a GPS on you? Where is it?"

"It's a chip no bigger than a grain of rice and it's right under the skin in a spot that's— Well, let's say you'd never notice the mark."

The thought of him touching her there, or maybe putting his lips to her skin over that spot, gave Jass an unwanted chill. But she swore not to let it lead to something more.

Yes, the man gave her serious chills—and then made her hot enough to sweat bullets. But he was only a partner on the job. A good partner, she was coming to believe. But not the kind of man she'd ever imagined falling in love with. He was a player—and a man who gave up on his sensitive job with the United States government in order to prove a theory she still wasn't completely convinced could be true.

Her father would never have done such a thing. He

was her gold standard of behavior. No one else had ever measured up.

Besides, she wasn't looking for a relationship. Her career was far more important to her than throwing caution to the wind and having a good time in bed.

Oh, but she had a feeling Tarik could provide a woman with a real good time.

"Well, using your own words," he said with one of his whimsical smiles and raised eyebrows, "I'll show you mine if you show me yours."

"You're chipped, too? By whom?"

He lifted his arm and pointed to a spot under his armpit that was currently hidden by his shirt. "My brothers and I each carry a chip under the skin. Our operations people came up with the idea in order to keep track of where we were going. It's been a lifesaver on several occasions."

"So the Kadirs know where you are now?"

"I hope so. My brother Shakir should be in the area by now. I'm counting on him being close enough if we need his help."

That meant he could probably contact his people somehow.

Deciding not to ask him about communications yet, Jass posed another more pertinent question. "You didn't see any of the other guests when we were coming in, did you? I didn't. I wonder who the other bidders are and if they're here already, too."

"They're here. But no, I didn't see anyone on the way in either. Are you confident you know what's going to be up for auction?"

"It must be the fissionable material like on the file I found on the computer in Eltsin's office." After she'd posed the theory, the expression on Tarik's face led her to believe otherwise. "Why? What do you think?"

He tilted his head noncommittally. "The 'fissionable material' notation you saw was probably a red herring. And if you say anything about it, Eltsin will know it was us in his office."

She blew out a breath. "Good point. Do you have any suggestions for finding out what we're after?"

"I want to do a little snooping around. Maybe I can figure it out."

"And that's why you made such a point with Eltsin about your privacy and working from your room." What a terrific partner he made. The man could think on his feet far better than anyone she'd ever seen. "I take it you have a plan for scouting the area without being noticed?"

"Maybe. But I'm counting on you to keep Eltsin and the other guests occupied. Or at least be in a position to warn me if they're coming back to this wing of the house."

"I believe I have an idea for handling such a diversion." She could think on her feet fairly well, too. "But first I want to give you a quick lesson on the toys I brought along. Some of the surveillance equipment could prove useful for a snoop."

Tarik nodded and winked at her. "Okay, boss lady. I'm ready for instruction."

She sniffed at the term he'd used. Things had changed in her mind. They were partners. Neither of them was the boss of this operation.

But rather than raise a fuss, she retrieved her duffel and dragged it onto the desk. She turned back to him, ready with a dose of his own medicine.

For the first time in her entire life, she winked at a man. "Okay, class. Get ready to listen up."

*Good God.* Tarik felt his body go rock hard when Jass walked out of the closet a little while after their lesson dressed in the smallest damned thong bathing suit he had ever seen. And damned if it wasn't neon lime-green.

"What…" He choked on his own tongue. "Uh, what the devil do you think you're doing in that…that… thing?"

"*This* is a Brazilian-style bathing suit, not a thing. And it's part of my plan to keep the men busy while you scout around upstairs."

"Uh…" *Down boy.* "Yeah, I'd say your suit will capture everyone's attention all right. But where's your weapon hidden?"

"Not carrying one. But I'm not worried. I can take care of myself."

"Hope so," he grumbled under his breath.

"What?"

"I said I hope you can take care of yourself because you'll be fighting the men off like flies around a garbage dump."

Jass scowled. "Nice analogy, pal. How I dearly love being compared to a smelly landfill. That's a new one."

He wouldn't tell her what he truly thought about how she looked. She looked good enough to eat and he wasn't at all happy about terrorists, or any male, drooling over her nearly nude body.

He tried to remind himself she was only his partner, not a love interest like Celile was for Zohdi. And that this plan was part of her job, not a plan to make him jealous. Tarik fought to keep from demanding she cover up.

Instead, he said, "Do you think Sheik Zohdi would ever allow Celile out of his sight dressed in something like that?"

"No way." She rolled her eyes, turned and disappeared back into the closet.

A minute later she reappeared, shoving her arms through a wraparound dress. "I brought this beach cover-up along to make the sheik happy." She grinned at him.

The dress wasn't much better. Made out of some flimsy, see-through material with green and blue swirly patterns, nothing of importance was obvious underneath the so-called dress. But that only made it worse somehow. Male imaginations would run wild instead.

Tarik narrowed his eyes. "It's still…" At a loss for words, he waved a hand in the air.

"Isn't it just." Jass laughed and twirled around, letting him see her from all sides. "Still no place for a weapon. But this should do to keep Eltsin and his male guests' attention focused somewhere else besides on you. Don't you think?"

God help him, she was right. He didn't like it. Hated the idea, in fact. But it would probably work.

"When are you going to execute this plan of yours?" Tarik hoped her answer would be tomorrow or maybe the next day. *Never* would've been his first preference.

But she said what he'd feared. "In a moment, if you're ready to do your job."

The words didn't want to leave his mouth, but he pushed them out with a groan. "Ah…I'm ready. I guess."

Jass ducked back into the closet but almost instantly

reappeared having added a pair of sexy, lime-green stiletto heels and a pair of sunglasses to the outfit. "Okay then. Me, too."

Tarik groaned again and swiped a hand across his suddenly dry mouth. Damn, she was hot.

This operation wasn't turning out the same way he'd had in mind. He'd pictured her in a black catsuit and him in his NVGs, riffling through computer files and listening in on conversations together.

Now the two of them would be going in alone. But, he knew part of his mind wouldn't be concentrating on the job. Not with the constant worry over how Jass was faring on her end.

Hell. He slammed one fist into the other and Jass raised her head in surprise.

"You okay?"

"Fine." If…he could manage to control his raging out-of-whack emotions and get back in the game. "I'll give you fifteen minutes to get down by the pool. If Eltsin isn't there yet or if anything else looks amiss to you, send a pool boy or valet up here with a drink for Zohdi. I'll abort."

"Right." Jass turned and headed out the door. "Be careful," she called as the door closed behind her.

Swamped with jealousy and tingling with desire, Tarik fought to maintain some semblance of control. His unsuitable responses to a female partner were simply becoming over-the-top and crazy as hell. He was acting more like a man in love than a man on a mission.

It wasn't as if he'd never worked with covert female operatives before. But somehow Jass was different than all the rest.

He thought again of her in that teeny, tiny bikini

and felt his pulse begin to race. Yeah. She was a lot different.

*Damn it.*

Jass lifted her chin and purposefully strode down the staircase one foot in front of the other, swinging her hips. Once on a long-ago sting, she'd portrayed a European swimsuit model, and she tried to put her mind back in that place and time.

But it was tough going when images of Tarik kept creeping into her consciousness and throwing her off-balance. The man was seriously hot. With her next step, she found her imagination transporting her back to last night when he'd been naked, wanting and hard as a rock.

Forced to put a hand on the banister now, she tried to steady herself as mental pictures of those broad, supple shoulders of his holding her down caused her to miss a step. His extraordinary chest had pinned her to the bed, while his lean hips and broad thighs had moved suggestively between her legs.

She'd felt his erection. Hot and pulsing. Exactly where she'd needed to feel it the most.

Stopping to take a breath, Jass ordered herself to quit daydreaming this instant and pull it together.

She had work to do. Important work that might mean life or death for Tarik.

Someplace along the line, the idea of putting her own career in high gear with this mission had begun to pale against the idea of helping Tarik prove his family's accusations. His mission had worldwide implications. Her career could hold for another day.

Yeah, he still irritated her to no end sometimes.

The grin. The casual attitude masking a much deeper conviction. It all drove her nutty.

Worse, her own reactions to him on an intense, sexual level constantly made her angry with herself. Why now? Why suddenly find an unavailable and totally unsuitable man so attractive that she lost her mind whenever he was around? It didn't make sense.

"Ah, Ms. Kocak, is it?" A Middle Eastern–looking man hailed her as he came around the corner from the other wing of the house. "We've not had the pleasure of meeting. The name is Malik Kasim Taj Zabbar. I understand we are to be competitors at the auction."

Oh my god, this guy was one of the men at the table in Monte Carlo. Tarik and the Kadirs had been correct and the Taj Zabbar were seeking some kind of weapon of mass destruction. Of course, simply showing up for an auction was not conclusive proof to take to the international community. But it was good enough to make Jass a true believer.

Hoping to heaven her disguise would hold up under his scrutiny, she took the hand he held out. "The pleasure is all mine." Giving him a flirty gaze through her lashes, she squeezed his hand suggestively. "Are you representing yourself? Or an absentee buyer? I've found it pays to get to know your competition—very well."

He tilted his head as he studied her with a sober expression. "I am but a humble servant. And you, madam, are not the casual flirt that your expression and attire would suggest."

*Oh, crap.* "Me? But I am—"

"Please. Your title as the Messenger is well known and respected the world over. You are reputed to be a shark in the arms negotiations business." Malik tsked at her. "Do not try to fool me with your sweet smile and a stunning body. Let us begin on more equal footing—as true opponents."

Her whole body wanted to cave in with relief. He still believed she was Celile.

She pulled her hand free from his and set her jaw in true Celile style. "Agreed. I will be representing Sheik Abu Zohdi in this matter. Whom do you represent?"

He gave her a half smile. "Better. But I already knew your buyer. And I have to say Zohdi may not have the wherewithal to compete effectively. At least not with the resources of the new nation of Zabbarán behind my bids."

Man, she sure wished she had a digital recorder getting this conversation down. But there hadn't been any place to hide one. Tarik would have to find something else to incriminate these bastards.

And she needed to shift the current conversation out to the patio right this minute. Her job—and Tarik's life—might depend on her keeping an eye on all the others who should be out at the pool by now. Especially Eltsin.

She nodded her head and slipped her arm through the Taj Zabbar agent's arm, swinging him around and moving them both in the general direction of the patio. "We shall see, Malik. Um, it is all right for me to call you Malik since we'll be such close competitors, isn't it?"

"Of course. If I might also call you Celile."

*Oh, you bet yer boots, babes.* "That will be fine. But please don't use my given name around Zohdi. Not if you care about living long enough to place your bid, that is."

After hiding their weapons and equipment around the room and waiting a full fifteen minutes, Tarik changed into a black T-shirt and jeans and began scouting the rest of the residential wing. It didn't take him five minutes to befriend one of the uniformed valets, who spoke Spanish instead of Portuguese and didn't seem to think asking detailed questions about the other guests was strange.

Sure enough, Tarik discovered several of the others were also Middle Eastern like he was. The valet even pointed out a couple of rooms belonging to men whose last names were both Taj Zabbar, though he added the two weren't brothers.

After their conversation, Tarik followed the valet and uncovered a treasure trove. A large linen closet containing not only freshly washed and stacked towels and bed linens but also freshly washed valet uniforms. It didn't take him thirty seconds after the valet left to slip into a uniform and grab a handful of towels. He was headed back down the hall toward the first of the Taj's rooms before the valet was even out of sight.

Using a new high-tech master set of keys Jass's handler had provided, he got through the locked door a lot faster than if he'd had to rely on obsolete lock picks. The first thing he did was set the towels in the bath and then scour the bedroom for any hidden surveillance devices. He'd been ready to believe the Taj might even try to protect themselves by setting up some way of checking who entered their rooms.

But the place was clean. Not for long, though.

He put a listening device in both the bedroom and the closet, in case. While he was in the closet, he checked the safe but decided it would take too long to open it. The room itself held nothing of interest. No files, PDAs or laptops.

Were those things in the next room over? He grabbed up the old towels and replaced them with new ones as he prepared to leave. But when he opened the outer door, he heard voices coming from down the hall—and drawing closer.

Maybe he'd get lucky and it wouldn't be the Taj returning to their rooms. He stood at the threshold long enough to know it was not his lucky day. The male voices were speaking quietly in the Taj Zabbar language. He even recognized them as the same men from the club the other night.

Closing the door and locking it behind him, Tarik glanced around the room looking for someplace to hide. The drapes had been pulled, but hiding behind drapes was far too obvious.

He dashed back into the bathroom, wondering if he could pull off playacting as the real valet in front of the Taj Zabbar. Quickly deciding that would be pushing his nonexistent luck too far, his frantic glance landed on a tiny window in the shower enclosure and at the deep bathtub, half-hidden by frosted glass. He made a leap for the tub—at the exact moment someone entered the bedroom.

# *Chapter 11*

Jass paced the floor of their room, fighting the urge to bite her nails—a habit she'd shed as a teen. Tarik had disappeared to heaven only knew where. A little while ago she'd noticed the two Taj Zabbar men leaving the patio for their rooms and had instantly sent the pool boy up with a drink for Zohdi. But the boy had come back within minutes claiming no one answered the door.

Where the hell was Tarik? Had the Taj caught him snooping in their rooms? Was he in danger somewhere and in need of her help?

Damn it, the two of them should have a better way of communicating if they were going to keep working separately.

Nearly frantic and too hyped up to think clearly, Jass began to wonder if she shouldn't go looking. She ripped the beach cover-up over her head and threw it toward the bed. Not sure what the proper attire would be for snooping around Eltsin's huge mansion, she untied the straps to her halter and slipped out of it. Catsuit or Celile disguise? Holding the scrap of material loosely in her hand, she headed toward the closet, still wondering what to put on.

At that moment she heard a sound. Muffled and indistinct, the noise sounded like someone scraping on a faraway door. But why could she hear it from here? She and Tarik had checked the acoustics of the rooms earlier and discovered you couldn't hear a thing from directly outside the door. The walls between rooms were also insulated far better than most five-star hotels.

Jass moved to the hall door and listened, in case someone was trying to break in. But the sound wasn't coming from that direction.

The scratching noise had to be coming from right outside the windows. But right outside the windows they were three stories off the ground. Was someone washing windows? Did this have anything to do with Tarik?

She went closer to the sliding glass door leading to their own tiny private balcony and peeked out past the heavy drapes that had been drawn to block the heat from the sun. The knock came again, and when she peered down the balcony, she saw Tarik, kneeling at the door and working at the lock with one of Ed's high-tech toys.

Oh my God. She grabbed the drapes and ripped them back.

"Get inside before someone spots you." Hissing with fright and wanting to remain quiet, she unlocked the latch and slid open the glass door.

Tarik stepped inside looking disheveled and obviously out of breath. "Thanks. I wasn't having much luck with that lock." He reached up and wiped the perspiration from his forehead.

She stood shaking her head at him. "What on earth are you wearing?" He was dressed like one of the valets—only he looked much better.

With the button-down shirt open, his T-shirt clung to his taut muscles. She ached to touch him.

Tarik shook his head too but held his forefinger up to his mouth to indicate he wasn't going to answer.

Then he narrowed his focus on her as flames suddenly jumped into his eyes. "The question is, my dear Celile, what are you wearing?"

Jass froze, belatedly remembering she still held the top to her bathing suit in her hand. A shiver of sexual heat raced from her fingertips to her breasts. She closed her eyes, hoping he would disappear, or that a hole would open up in the floor and swallow her whole.

No such luck. When she opened her eyes he was blatantly watching. A hungry stare. She became painfully aware of her nipples hardening. Taking a breath didn't help. As her chest swelled, the look in his eyes took on an intense quality—like the wolf gazing at Red Riding Hood.

Her nipples grew even harder. She was in deep trouble.

The memory of the kisses they'd shared came back to haunt her. She licked her lips once and Tarik moved closer, pulling her into his arms.

"Don't say anything until I check the room for bugs again," he whispered as he searched her eyes.

What was he looking for in her eyes? Fear? Rejection?

She wasn't feeling either one. Lifting her mouth to

his, she told him what she wanted with her lips and tongue.

He tightened his hold on her, mashing her breasts against his chest as he participated in the kiss in every conceivable way. This wasn't an act. It was an astonishingly realistic move from a flesh-and-blood man who wanted *her*—not Celile.

Tarik no longer hid behind the mask of someone else. He was for real. The moment was for real. And she'd suddenly discovered some part of herself that had been hidden away wanting now to come out and play. Play only with Tarik.

Pressing on her bottom with his broad, hot hand, he jammed her tightly against his erection. Then he hummed, deep in his throat, as if this was the sweetest experience of his lifetime. To her ears, his murmur sounded of longing and pleasure, so closely matching what she was experiencing that it almost brought tears to her eyes.

She wanted to move even closer. Yet there wasn't so much as a breath of air between them. Throwing one leg up, she wound it around his hips and tried to climb right inside his body. She couldn't seem to get enough of his taste, and wished he had a lot fewer clothes on. She was dying to rub her tongue all over his skin.

He broke their kiss and lowered his head to her throat, moving his mouth in wide-open abandon toward the base of her neck and the pulse beating wildly there. She rocked against his hard erection, growing ever more desperate for a release of her tension.

His hand slid between them then and his palm cupped her with erotic warmth. She gasped, ready to explode.

Suddenly, he stopped. Froze. And swore quietly under his breath.

Her desire flamed, and then burned out in a rush of vulnerability, confusion and finally embarrassment. She stepped away and tried to cover herself with her hands.

"Go take a shower, Celile." Tarik looked embarrassed too as he nodded his head toward the bathroom. "We'll talk later."

The bugs. The mission. All of what had been lost in her lust-filled haze came back with the splash of a prickly air-conditioned chill.

She was such an idiot. Turning on her heels, she dashed out of the room to the relative safety of the bathroom and slammed the door.

Breathing deep and rushing to turn on the hot water in the shower, Jass swore at her own stupidity. Yet with each breath of air, she realized Tarik had become more than a partner and a friend. He'd become her everything, all within a few days. Furthermore, if he ever made a move in her direction again, she would fall into his arms without a moment's hesitation.

The woman she had always thought she'd been, the woman cautious with her emotions, was now gone for good.

Tarik stumbled around the room, ripping off the valet's coat and searching for the bug-detection device.

Holy hell. What had hit him?

As he found the detector and began running it along the four walls and checking the house phone, he thought back to a few moments ago when his hands were roaming over Jass. It had been pure heaven when his tongue slid into the warm, honeyed depths of her mouth. Exploring. Taking her with a savage kiss. Holding her tighter. Kissing her harder and harder while his heart went off like a time bomb in his chest.

She was so sweet. Her breasts so beautiful and her lips soft. Her tight, rounded ass felt solid as he filled his hands with her flesh. Her whole exquisite body was everything a man could ever want. Then, when she'd wrapped one of her slim, toned legs around his waist, he'd completely lost his mind.

It took her gasping out a breath as he'd touched her and found her wet, to make him remember they could be the starring attraction on some bad guy's headphones at that exact moment. It was possible the Taj or one of Eltsin's men had entered the room while they were gone and planted bugs. Earlier Tarik had set a thread over the door as a trap and to let him know if their privacy had been breached while they were out of the room. But Jass had entered through the door first and ruined his trap.

So, he'd forced himself to stop one of the most intense sexual experiences of his life.

Now he was checking for bugs. But still felt overheated and remained harder than he'd ever been.

He couldn't shake the image of Jass, nipples peaked and looking up at him with a combination of desire and vulnerability in her eyes. A potent look, it had turned his knees to mush and his brain to ash. And nothing short of making love to her would help.

But that wasn't going to happen. Couldn't happen. *Shouldn't...*

After silently declaring the room to be clean, Tarik lifted his head and listened to the water as it continued running in the bathroom shower. He *should* clear the bathroom too—to be safe.

After shucking the rest of his clothes, he went to the door and hesitated, leaning his forehead against the air-cooled wood. If he opened this door, what would she do? What did he want her to do?

He knew what *he* wanted. He wanted to touch her again. And to run his mouth and tongue along every inch of that perfect body. She wanted that too, he was almost positive.

The indecision and options were killing him.

Making a deal with himself, a deal with the devil in his soul, he finally decided to try the door handle. If he found it unlocked, then that meant Jass had deliberately left it open as an invitation. If the door was locked, he would turn away, satisfied she had left him a message that she didn't want him.

Holding his breath, Tarik's hand closed around the handle. What would come next?

The door opened with a tiny squeak of hinges. He stepped into the room with his heart jackhammering in his chest. Shower steam clouded his vision, but it didn't keep him from seeing Jass looking out at him through the glass enclosure. Another moment of indecision had him blinking and swallowing hard. She had yet another shot at turning him down.

But as he closed the door and took a step toward her, she opened the shower door and held out her hand to him. She looked beautiful. Hot. He could weep with joy.

Physically, she was perfect. But it was the look in her eyes, saying she felt as hungry for him as he felt for her, that knocked him back a step. This exquisite and strong woman knew what she needed. And it threw him to find that what she needed was him.

More than anything, he needed to make love to her and watch her come apart in his arms. To pull down the moon and put that glow in her eyes whenever she looked at him.

The vulnerability he'd seen on her face earlier had disappeared. The heat and the need were back, lighting up the hazel-green eyes of Jasmine O'Reilly—not Celile Kocak's dark browns.

Tarik knew for sure what, and definitely who, he wanted in his arms.

Stepping into the shower, he took her hand. "We're in the clear. No bugs."

She smiled up at him but didn't make a move.

"Are you sure?" he asked, with his heart in his throat.

Instead of answering, Jass moved closer, went up on tiptoes and without touching anywhere else, pressed her wet lips to his.

"Why me?" he gasped.

"Because I need you." As simple and as complicated as that.

He could no more have found the will to turn her away after that than he could have sprouted angel wings and flown out the window. Dragging her hard against him, he buried his hands in the wild tangle of her short auburn hair and kissed her again. A kiss that spoke of desperation and a surprising kind of trust.

Without question, he trusted her not to disappear from his life the way other women he'd cared about had, the same way his mother had. He needed Jass to trust him as well. It was important, not only for their mission, but for her well-being. He wanted her to feel a real emotional connection to someone who had nothing whatever to gain by caring.

Standing flush against him and throwing her arms around his neck for balance, she kissed him back with equal desire. The water cascaded down on their heads. He pushed his thigh between her legs, backing her away from the direct spray and up against the tile wall. Because he couldn't stand being close and not touching. And because he was growing more insistent by the moment. Skimming his fingers along her ribs, he thrilled to the touch of her soft-as-a-cloud skin. He let his fingers roam lower, until his greedy hands palmed the sweetest bottom in existence.

Meanwhile he kissed her neck, gently nipping and then soothing with his tongue. Sliding his lips across her chin to capture her mouth, he kissed her deeply, angling his head to get a better taste.

Perfect curves. Slick bare skin. He broke the kiss and took a half step back to take her all in. She was a goddess.

He knelt to worship her body, wrapping his arms around her thighs and burying his face in her belly. The loveliness and the feminine scent of her went to his head, steaming his senses. Warning himself to take it slow, he eased open her legs and pressed his tongue to the hot, wet center of her desire. Teasing her. Licking her.

She moaned, softly grinding her hips to give him access to her velvet folds. Then she tunneled her hands through his hair to hold him in place.

Nothing short of death would've moved him away. Not yet. Not when this was what he'd wanted since the first moment he'd ever laid eyes on her.

"Tarik." The sound of his name on her lips whispered like a tangible force through his brain.

She spread her legs a little wider and he used the opportunity to slip his fingers up inside. Tight. Wet. What a gift she was, turning him harder than ever and electrifying his every cell. Plying her with his tongue and loving every taste, he reveled in the way she kept holding him tighter and snugger to her. He listened as the tiny little catches in her throat came closer together.

*Come apart for me, love.* He badly wanted to feel her flying. To give her a small part of the fantasy she was giving to him. He needed desperately to be the man who took her higher than she'd ever been.

Her guttural murmurs grew rougher as she forced his name from her lips over and over. He continued pleasuring her, on and on, endlessly sliding his fingers in and out and teasing her with the tip of his tongue.

He lost track of time until she tensed underneath his hands and her murmurs grew to soft cries. But as he felt the contractions of her release rippling through her body, she spat out a curse.

*Yeah, sweetheart.* The climax of a lifetime.

Her knees buckled and he rose to his feet to hold her upright in his arms. "Okay?"

She leaned in, put her mouth to his ear and groaned, "More."

Mindlessly, he covered her open and pliant mouth with his own and filled a hand with her breast. *More.* The word echoed through his mind as he tweaked one of her nipples.

Her moans grew more insistent. His mind twisted and bent in response. He pushed her back against the wall, his body taut and out of control.

Wrapping his free hand under her thigh, Tarik lifted her leg around his waist. With his tongue in her mouth and a hand still on her breast, he drove into her.

How easy it was to have found a reckless pleasure deep and true enough that he never wanted it to end. Like this. With this woman. For the rest of a lifetime.

He thrust into her. Higher. Deeper. Again and again.

Her body drew him all the way inside when she moved her hips in time with his. The heat and the rhythm urged him toward the ultimate edge.

Diving deep inside her one final time, he was grateful to feel her coming apart along with him while the extreme pleasure blasted at his body with a fiery heat. Her gasping breaths were hot against his mouth. Perfect.

Breathing in heavy pants, he remained inside her, listening to the sounds she made deep in her throat. He could do this all night. Stay right here with her in his arms.

Finally, she rocked against him. Only the slightest of movements, but it sent shock waves careening through his veins.

He tightened his arms around her and nuzzled her neck, breathing in her scent and savoring the wondrous sensations of the soft and limp body wrapped around his. Did they have to move? Would either of them make it to the other room if they did?

"Oh, Tarik. That was so good." She ran her fingers through his hair and as she sucked on his earlobe.

She was the most responsive, giving woman he had ever encountered. No one else would ever come close to matching her in the future.

The ramifications of that thought had yet to sink in. They were only vague ideas, little ripples of unease in his subconscious mind. Later. He would give them further consideration later.

Slowly, and with more care than he thought he had in him, he pulled out of her. Lifting her in his arms, he reached around and flipped off the water. He stepped from the shower and, kissing her full on the mouth, carried her to bed.

*Again,* was all he could think. Under him. Surrounding him. Hovering over him while she rode him to bliss. Until they both went mad.

He wanted her again. And again.

## Chapter 12

Jass sat upright against the headboard with the sheet pulled up under her armpits.

She glanced over at Tarik and found him asleep on his stomach, naked and stunningly male. And still looking good enough to make her head spin after two hours of lovemaking.

Golden skin and long black lashes gave his face an almost beautiful quality. The dark hair covering his chest ran down across tight abs and a flat stomach. Sleek and sinewy legs plus a good, strong butt drew her attention, holding her gaze immobile until she thought she might go cross-eyed. Raking her glance upward, she focused on his full head of tousled dark brown hair that had the sweetest way of curling along the edge of his neck. Her fondest wish was to never stop gazing at the man exactly like this.

But she could just imagine how *she* looked. No makeup.

Sweat-dampened hair sticking up in spikes from Tarik running his fingers through it. Eyes probably a little bloodshot from her pulse rate soaring over the moon every time he made her come.

But Tarik hadn't seemed to mind how she looked. He'd held her and cared for her and gazed into her eyes with such hunger that he didn't even need to touch her in order to send her sailing.

And, dear God, she wanted him to do it over and over again.

One look at him brought on a rush of pure arousal. She dragged her eyes away and stared straight ahead. For now she needed to put her head back together and shape up. What had taken place between them had to be set right.

They were partners. Though how would they ever be able to work together again?

She couldn't look into his eyes now and pretend to see Sheik Abu Zohdi. Tarik would never touch her again without her seeing images of what they'd done; the way his clever fingers had touched her and his tongue had been compelling and erotic.

If she told Tarik nothing like that could ever happen between them again, would he pay attention? Maybe not. Would her own mind listen to reason? Probably not.

Desperate to find a solution to the dilemma she saw ahead of her, she tried a little rationalization. Asking herself if only one spectacular afternoon in bed could possibly make for a forever relationship, she determined that she wasn't a casual love 'em and leave 'em person. Tarik seemed more the explode and burn type rather than the steady, ever-after hero of her dreams. He was all fireworks and flames—for a time. Judging by his staying power in bed...perhaps a long time. But he wasn't someone who could make her happy over an entire lifetime. Was he?

He couldn't be her type. He was far too casual and easygoing. Almost too accommodating. Yes, it was nice having someone show such concern over her welfare. He'd been the most solicitous lover she'd ever had. Waiting until she was satisfied before—well, before satisfying himself. But…how many others out there in the world also thought he cared only for them?

The idea that dozens of other women could be waiting for him to return was exactly the jerk on her chain she'd been needing to move her to action. Shoving the sheet back, she swung her feet over the side of the bed and stood.

As naked as the day she was born, she felt someone watching her and turned around to find Tarik's eyes open and a huge grin creasing his face. "You okay, love?"

"Stop that." She turned her back on him and found her robe. But she could still see him in the mirror.

"Stop what?" He sat up and leaned on his elbow, watching her shrug into the sleeves.

"Number one: Stop calling me *love* in private. You don't know me well enough for gooey stuff like that. We're partners on a mission. Period."

The silly grin never faltered.

"And number two: Stop asking me if I'm okay. I'm a big girl. If I wasn't okay, I would speak up and tell you so."

"Sorry. But you can't put the genie back in the bottle, *partner*." Tarik tilted his head as his eyes softened. "Why don't we discuss this later? Right now, come back to bed."

The gorgeous bastard actually had the nerve to hold

out his hand as though he expected her to obey and blindly fall all over him.

"We're partners," she insisted. "What happened can't happen again. This is a mission, not playtime."

That broke the grin and brought him up out of the bed in one fluid motion. "Number one," he ground out as he headed around the bed in her direction. "We're undercover as lovers on this mission. Zohdi and Celile will be kissing, touching and in bed together again before we're finished with the job."

He reached for her and pulled her into his arms as she tried to step back. "And number two—" His dark gaze pinned her with steely intent. "You think we can ignore the raging passion between us for the rest of this mission? I believe you're wrong, but let's say you're right. I promise you that *after* the mission, we will be revisiting not only what happened between us, but also this whole conversation. Take those words to the bank."

She opened her mouth to disagree, but he leaned in and hungrily glued his mouth to hers. As they tangled their tongues together, he clutched her hips and dragged her close. She'd already noticed how hard he was again, how much he wanted her. Now she felt the truth. It was impossible to miss. Her body yearned to take him in, to welcome him right back inside where she wanted him to stay.

Taking a breath, she murmured against his lips, "Why me? Why now?"

He pushed her away and ran a hand through his hair. "I don't know why this had to happen now. But I do know *why you*. Because you're important. Because... we fit."

She was speechless as her eyes filled with tears.

They did *fit,* but what the hell was she supposed to do about that?

As he reached for her again, the room phone rang. Both of them jerked around to stare at the offending object as if it were a king cobra.

Tarik snagged the receiver and murmured something she couldn't make out. He spoke a few more soft words in the broken English of Sheik Zohdi while she tightened the robe around her waist.

After he hung up, he ignored her and went to the closet. "We're expected downstairs for dinner in an hour."

The mission. Her head went back into the game in a flash. "I had supposed they would skip dinner altogether tonight. It's late."

"It's only ten." When Tarik reappeared he was wearing his robe and had a tiny laptop in his hand. "We're in South America, remember."

Yeah, she was having a hard time remembering anything since he'd kissed her to the point of delirium and told her she was important.

Tarik set the laptop up on the desk and hit a few keys. All of a sudden a vaguely familiar voice came through the speaker. It was the Taj Zabbar agent who'd stopped her on the stairs. She would never forget that gravelly voice. What was he saying?

After about a half an hour of listening to drivel while the two Taj Zabbar agents argued in their own language, Tarik finally heard something worthwhile.

"I told you before not to concern yourself with the other bidders." Malik Kasim, head of Taj secret police, was not happy with his underling.

Tarik had no trouble translating the words he was

receiving from the device he'd planted in the agent's room. What he was having trouble with was getting his mind and body back under control. Still hungry for Jass and becoming more frustrated by the second, he clamped down on his teeth and forced the delectable image of her in the shower out of his head.

Malik continued haranguing his counterpart. "All of this…the dinner, the supposed auction on Tuesday. All of it is for show." He drew a breath and clicked his lips. "Finish packing our bags. We leave here before morning."

"But, Excellency, Eltsin told the woman she had as good a chance as any of making the winning bid. I heard him."

"Stop being such a fool. Once more, there will be no bids. Eltsin has already sold me a piece of what we came here seeking. As soon as he verifies our cash has been deposited to his bank later tonight, we will have everything we need."

"But the others…?"

"While we disappear with our prize, the other supposed bidders will be eliminated. It is part of our deal with Eltsin."

Dead air came through the listening device as the other man apparently questioned his boss without words.

"Our deal with Eltsin," Malik repeated with force. "No one leaves here who can identify us or make any connection to the Taj Zabbar."

Tarik listened another minute or two, but all he heard was Malik leave the other man with instructions on what to wear and when to appear downstairs. Shutting down the receiving device, Tarik stashed it away. He needed to talk to his brothers. Was Shakir nearby?

"What were they saying?"

He gazed up at Jass and his chest burned with the pain of how beautiful she looked. "Get dressed. And pack whatever you think you'll need for a quick departure."

She came closer. "Talk to me. Tell me what's going on."

How could he tell her she was already marked for death because of the parts they were playing? It wouldn't happen of course. He wouldn't let it. But he was having trouble forming the words.

"You just told me I was important. If that's true, if you think of me as more than a partner, then tell me what you overheard. Was it about whatever is supposed to be auctioned off?"

Shaking his head, he swallowed the unwarranted fear gripping his gut and thought only about Jass being a professional covert agent. "The Taj Zabbar are preparing to leave later tonight. They were talking about Eltsin killing off the rest of the bidders after they go."

Instead of fear or even apprehension in Jass's eyes, he saw understanding and determination. Inexplicably his chest swelled with pride. *There you go, my covert love.*

"The auction is a ruse, then," she said almost to herself while she shook her head thoughtfully. "Of course it would be. But Eltsin has a lot of nerve to off Celile and Zohdi. It'll ruin his reputation for any arms business he might want to do in the future."

"I suspect he'll be getting paid enough from the Taj that he won't mind."

"Must be liberating to control that much money." Jass shrugged a shoulder. "Or very seductive. Money can be the ruination of otherwise decent people."

He nodded.

"Sad but true."

"So what's your plan?" she asked.

"One of my brothers and a few men are supposed to be standing by. Probably in the forest within sight of Eltsin's mansion right now. We need a way out of here and a way to follow the Taj." He breathed deeply. "Plainly, we need help, and I don't think we can wait until the local CIA troops make it up here."

"Agreed. But how do you intend to reach your brother? Part of our instructions were not to use the internet or wireless communications while inside Eltsin's compound. He could easily intercept any of those kinds of signals and kill us without a second thought."

"True." He went into the closet to check the weapons and his Zohdi suit, still capable of talking to Jass without seeing her. "I have to find a way to step outside the mansion walls alone. Maybe into the patio and pool area while everyone else is in the dining room?"

"Hmm."

Okay, he needed to see her face. That didn't sound good.

Sticking his head out the closet door, he watched as she put a thoughtful finger to her chin and tapped a foot on the carpet. "What's going on in that tricky little mind of yours?"

"Little mind?" She gave him a joking smile but raised her eyebrows as if she were truly questioning his words.

"Come on, give. You know what I meant."

"Yeah, I know. And I think I have a plan." She started toward him. "But there's one major problem to work out first."

He leaned back as she brushed past him into the closet. "What's that? Maybe I can help."

She started digging through Celile's clothes. "I'll tell you all about it in a minute. Right now you would only slow me down. I have to decide on the right thing for Celile to wear. That's going to be the key."

With her head held high, Jass strode into Eltsin's huge, gilt-edged dining room on Tarik's arm. She knew her partner still wasn't crazy about her plan. But it *would* work, and he had finally agreed that it was all they had.

On their way across the foyer, she'd stashed a collapsible backpack with their weapons and a change of clothes behind a mahogany grandfather clock decorated with gold leaf details and hand-tooled scrolls. The clock was one big, ugly son of a gun, but it would be stable when she was in a hurry. And it stood close to the front doors, where she could grab the pack on the fly.

Tarik, in his Zohdi suit and thick head scarf, had armed himself to the teeth with concealed weapons. But his most important accessories were the communications devices he'd planted in both his ears and then covered with the white cloth.

She knew he'd been concerned about the Taj showing up for dinner and getting a good look at his face. It was a chance they had to take. If her plan worked the way she hoped, no one was going to be paying much attention to Zohdi before he left the house anyway.

As they walked into the dining room, fashionably late, Eltsin was standing near the door, speaking quietly to the Taj Zabbar agents. All three men had drinks in their hands. She couldn't make out their words, but everyone stopped speaking and turned to stare at her and Tarik as they came closer.

The expressions on the men's faces were plain

enough. The Russian and the two Taj agents silently gazed at them as though they were looking at two dead men walking. Or one dead man and one dead woman, as the case may be.

Shivering through the thin linen jacket she'd worn, Jass resisted the temptation to run. She would've preferred to wear a nice pair of jeans and running shoes for a quick getaway later. But that would not have worked well with her plan. Instead, she stabilized on her four-inch spike heels.

"Good evening," Eltsin mumbled at last. "We've been waiting for you to arrive. Would you care for a drink before we sit down to table?"

Tarik kept his mouth shut. He was still worrying about the Taj recognizing him under his disguise. But that was okay, because his supposed angry silence would match her plan quite well.

She dropped Tarik's arm and moved closer to their host. "I'm so sorry we're late, Mr. Eltsin. Forgive us. We…uh…the Sheik and I were having a slight disagreement upstairs."

"We're serving *caipirinhas* this evening," Eltsin said formally. "They're delightful. Can I interest you in joining us?"

"Why yes, drinks sound lovely."

The Taj agents remained silent in the corner as Eltsin turned to a servant and took a couple of drinks off a silver tray. He handed one to Tarik and then turned to hand one to her. When he did, the deadly look that had occupied Eltsin's eyes before suddenly became a creepy leer.

"You look magnificent tonight, Celile. In the past I have heard much about your reputation in business. But

I never heard anything about how beautiful you were. Welcome." He lifted his glass in toast to her.

She lifted her glass too and gave him the most come-hither look she could manage. Toughest part of her job.

"Why, thank you." She even forced herself to bat her eyelashes at the bastard.

Tarik stepped closer to both of them, turning his back on the Taj Zabbar. He cleared his throat to notify Eltsin of his presence.

Jass pretended to take a sip, ignoring Tarik. She even inched slightly to one side, lifting her shoulder to close Tarik out of the circle of the conversation.

"This is delicious." She laid a hand on Eltsin's chest. "But doesn't it seem too warm in here? Would you mind holding the drink for me while I remove my jacket?"

Eltsin's leer became more pronounced. "Of course, my dear. Would you like to have the fans turned on? We don't want you to be uncomfortable."

"Don't trouble yourself." She pulled off the jacket, revealing the silky halter top and matching tight skirt she'd worn.

Tarik hissed out a breath and reached for her arm. "Dress yourself, Celile."

She reared her arm back and gave him a small shove with the other. "Don't tell me what to do, Zohdi."

Tarik spat out a curse in Arabic, something about her burning in a thousand hells, and threw the liquid in his glass at her chest. "Cover up!"

"Ahhh. Damn." Jass's specifically chosen top immediately became see-through. Instead of covering up, she narrowed her eyes at Tarik and threw back her shoulders. "How dare you? Get out of my sight, Zohdi. Now. Before it's all over between us."

"Gladly," Tarik said in Russian. Then he pitched his empty glass against a wall and stormed from the room, being sure to keep his head down and allowing his face to remain concealed by the head scarf.

Jass made no attempt to cover up; instead she turned to Eltsin with a sheepish grin and her breasts clearly outlined beneath the sheer material. "I must apologize for the Sheik, Mr. Eltsin. He…he…" She sniffed and stepped in closer to Eltsin as though she would like to lean against his shoulder for support.

Both the Taj Zabbar agents walked closer to where she and Eltsin stood, shaking their heads solicitously.

"Would you like someone to walk you back to your room to change?" the Taj agent she'd met before asked.

Jass blinked and shook her head. "Thank you, but it's nothing. I'm fine this way." She threw her chest out and stood tall. "The material will dry soon enough. I wouldn't want to ruin your dinner."

*The dinner you expect to be my last, you bastards.*

Turning back to Eltsin, she glanced up at him with a shy smile. "You don't mind if I come to the table slightly damp, do you, Mr. Eltsin?"

The Russian dragged in a gulp of air and reached for her hand. "Not at all." Riveting his gaze on her chest, he gave her fingers a squeeze and then folded her whole hand between both of his in a too-familiar embrace. "Would you like me to send someone to bring back the Sheik?"

"Thank you, but no. He'll probably sulk outside in the fresh air for a bit, smoking one of his smelly cigars. No doubt he'll show up at the table in time for the dessert course. Do you mind entertaining me alone until then?"

Eltsin threw a quick glance at the Taj, then put his free hand around her shoulders. "Not at all. You are much prettier to look at than he is. Let us see if we can't distract you over a meal until the Sheik returns."

*Yeah? And exactly who is distracting whom here?* she wondered with an imaginary roll of the eyes.

*Go bring the cavalry to the rescue, Tarik.*

# Chapter 13

Tarik turned his back to the wind and lit one of the Padrón panatelas he carried as part of the Zohdi disguise. Smooth and complex, the limited-version cigar was a true cigar lover's brand. Not to his taste, but it would give him a good excuse for going off by himself and moving closer to the cover of the rainforest surrounding Eltsin's mansion.

Once he felt comfortably alone, Tarik noiselessly clicked open the comm to Shakir and whispered, "You nearby, bro?"

Shakir's deep voice flowed through the comm like a fine wine. "NVGs trained on your position. Location two hundred feet northwest in the tree tops. What's up?"

"All hell is about to break loose. Taj have secretly procured whatever they came to buy and are taking off later tonight for parts unknown. We need rein-forcements."

"Got your back. Tell me what you need. We've been negotiating with one of Eltsin's henchmen for info on the Taj deal. Should have him opening up within the hour. And there's a scientist training his MASINT machines at Eltsin's place as we speak."

"A device for Measurement and Signature Intel on nuclear radiation? What's your geek gotten so far?"

"Nothing." Shakir made frustrated noises over the comm.

"Not surprised. I'm beginning to think that whatever is being traded here tonight, it's not another nuclear weapon. I haven't seen anyone who looked the least bit nervous or ill at ease as if they knew something radioactive was on the premises."

"Bloody hell." Shakir drew in a breath. "You have any other ideas about what's going down then?"

"No, but I do know it's something big. Eltsin gave the Taj agents his word he would eliminate all the other bidders once they were on their way out of the house."

"All the other bidders? As in Celile and Zohdi, too?"

"That's right," Tarik confirmed.

"Must be costing the Taj a pretty penny for that kind of promise. How much time have we got?"

"Not long. What I need from your team are eyes and ears trained on the Taj agents. I'll deal with Eltsin, but I don't want to alert the Taj to what we're doing. Someone needs to follow them. Preferably you." He sighed deeply. "See where they're headed. We can't lose contact with them. We have to find out what the Taj are planning before it's too late to stop. It's something huge. I can feel it in my gut."

"Right. I'll go down now to…uh…convince Eltsin's chauffeurs and any outside bodyguards that our men should be the drivers for the Taj when they leave. You want anything else?"

"A car gassed and ready to travel in a hurry might be nice."

"Your wish is my command. You…" Shakir seemed to hesitate about something, which was quite unlike his big brother. "You having any trouble with your partner?"

Tarik bristled but bit his tongue. "None. Why?"

"Someone overheard one of Eltsin's men talking about the sexy female. About how he'd been told not to touch, that she was special. Eltsin's private stock. You sure she's a hundred percent, bro?"

"Let me worry about Jass. You do your part and don't let the Taj out of your sight."

Shakir grunted a response. "Whatever you say. But watch out for yourself, brother. Things could go sour in an instant."

Tarik clicked off and ground his panatela into the wet earth, thinking about Jass. Eltsin's men were right about not messing with her. She'd as soon shoot their balls off as she would smile at them. But they didn't know that.

Why would Eltsin warn them off? It was possible he wanted her for himself. Or, perhaps Eltsin could have another agenda.

Was something else happening behind the scenes that Tarik didn't understand? Bouncing on the balls of his feet, he turned back to the main house, ready for anything.

He didn't see his attackers until they were already on top of his position.

"Come on, you assholes," he growled as he flipped

the first man on his back and reached for his weapon. "Show me what you've got."


"Would you like an after-dinner drink with your dessert, my dear Celile?" Eltsin hadn't stopped leering at Jass since Tarik had left the table nearly an hour ago.

She was starting to itch. Most of the other guests had already retired. And the two Taj agents sitting beside her at the table also seemed ready to be on their way. They were about as fidgety as she was. Where was Tarik?

"Why yes, Mr. Eltsin, I would like another drink. Thank you." It was all she could do to sit still and smile.

Eltsin patted her hand and told the waiter to bring her whatever she required. "Please call me Andrei, Celile. It's a shame Sheik Zohdi has not returned to the table. But these gentlemen—" he gestured to the Taj agents "—and I have a little business we must attend to. It will only take a short while, but I dislike leaving you alone."

"Don't worry about me." She waved her hand as though she was already tipsy and not quite in control of her senses. "You gentlemen go right ahead."

She rose from her seat and all the men immediately stood, too. "If you don't mind, I may step out on the patio for a moment and see if I can find Zohdi while you're gone."

Eltsin's eyes took on a wary and dark expression. "All right, but don't go too far. Your lover doesn't deserve your concern. He doesn't seem to show you the same respect."

Jass nodded and deliberately stumbled.

"And stay on the patio." Eltsin made the demand in

a harsh tone, but then seemed to think better of it. "I wouldn't want anything to happen to you. The jungle can be quite dangerous at night."

*So can your mansion, my dear creep.*

She put a hand to her breast and wobbled on her heels as though the idea was a bit daunting for a woman who'd had too much to drink. The elder of the two Taj agents came to her rescue and put his arm around her shoulders.

"Aren't you feeling well, Ms. Kocak?"

It was the perfect opportunity. The one she'd been waiting for. She slipped the microscopic GPS chip off her underarm and put her hand against the elder Taj's, pretending to steady herself. From that position, it was a snap to secretly paste the extra chip to the elder's wrist without him being any the wiser.

"I'll be fine," she told him with the imitation of a shy smile. "Do not worry over me. I simply need a little air. But I'll stay where I can see back inside this room. I'll know when you return to the table from your business."

She turned to Eltsin with wide eyes. "Surely you will have another moment for me then, won't you, Andrei?"

"Count on it, Celile." Eltsin picked up her hand and kissed the fingertips. "Until then."

*Ewww.*

Eltsin and the Taj agents left the room. She watched them go. Then she weaved her way to the French doors leading to the pool area, still acting tipsy for any watchful eyes. She had a bad feeling about this. What if Eltsin had already ordered Tarik's execution? Her partner had been gone too long for comfort.

Jass hesitated at the patio door, while various scenarios raced through her mind. And then she turned to the nearest waiter.

Speaking to him in broken English, she said, "I'd like the use of a powder room before Mr. Eltsin returns. Is there one I can use that's closer than our room in the other wing?"

The waiter directed her toward the foyer, exactly where she'd hoped to go. Once she was near the grandfather clock, Jass checked over her shoulder. When convinced no one was watching, she dug into her backpack. Again thoroughly checking her surroundings inside the grand, shadowy foyer, she pulled out the phony cell phone that secretly doubled as a communications unit direct to her handler. If anyone spotted her, she would say she was trying to reach Zohdi on his cell.

This call was against orders, but she was sure the sting would soon be collapsing anyway. With the cell in her hand, she ducked into the powder room underneath the stairs and touched the button to raise Ed.

In less than two seconds, he answered. "Where are you?"

"Eltsin's mansion. But the sting's going south." She hated saying this to Ed; hated hearing the disappointment she knew would fill his voice. "Kadir is missing, and we're supposedly on Eltsin's hit list for later tonight. Something's bad with the whole deal. I need more men or we'll lose our chance at the Taj Zabbar."

"It'll take too long to put a force together." Ed's tone did not sound disappointed, nor even surprised. Yet her old friend sounded less than pleased. "Scrap the mission. Find a way out of the house and put miles between you and Eltsin as fast as you can."

"What about Kadir? I can't…"

"Leave him and get out. He's probably long gone by now."

"He might be in trouble," she said.

"Look, Jass, I told you the man has his own agenda. He wouldn't give you a second thought if your positions were reversed. Leave now."

Knowing her time was short, she didn't argue. She ended the conversation and cut the comm line to Ed without asking all the questions rolling in her mind. Standing still for one more second to think, she tried to focus on what to do next. She didn't believe for one moment that Tarik would leave her to save himself. More than that, something in Ed's tone sounded way off.

Suddenly all the things that had been bothering her rushed to mind. But she was sure Tarik wasn't keeping anything from her. She'd come to know him, almost too well, over the last few days. And he'd been open and honest with her. Jass assured herself she couldn't care for him if he was anything but a good man. Her gut instincts on such matters had kept her alive many times in the past.

Yet, she was equally as sure that someone in this operation was betraying them. Someone she'd missed. First, the betrayal of the other night at Eltsin's office. And now she was having a bad feeling that Eltsin already knew she and Tarik were covert agents. The Russian was playing a much bigger and more deadly game with them than he let on. The tentacles of his operation must be far reaching. Maybe even into the local CIA?

She needed to find Tarik. Despite what she'd said to Ed, she had no doubt her partner was alive and in control of his situation. Maybe he'd managed to reach his brother and they were working out a plan.

Jass peered past the powder-room door and glanced into the adjoining room. She found the foyer and grand hall as quiet as when she'd come in. Eltsin should still be in his meeting with the Taj.

Now if she could make it through the front door without arousing any suspicions, she'd be free to scout around outside and locate Tarik. Together they would have no trouble overpowering Eltsin's guards and could come up with a way of stopping the Taj Zabbar. The most important part of the whole mission was not letting the Taj agents get away with their prize.

She tiptoed across the shadow-filled room, snagged her backpack and opened the front door. But the telltale click of a silent security alarm alerted her to the glaring mistake she'd made before she could even set one foot outside.

*Damn.* The front door was armed. But there hadn't been any alarms on that door earlier. Eltsin must have been expecting some kind of move from them. Things were turning from bad to worse by the minute.

Feeling it was too late to turn back, and hearing the running footsteps closing in from behind her, she scurried outside into the sultry night. She couldn't outrun a turtle in these heels. Her best move had to be hiding.

Dashing to the left, Jass tried to stay within the shadows of the mansion while she headed for the forests. But almost instantly, glaring bright security lights lit up the entire night sky. *Rats.*

She wouldn't get another twenty feet before Eltsin's men caught up. Her breathing labored and heavy from the tension, she squeezed into a blind alcove and leaned against a half-hidden stucco wall. Reaching into her backpack to pull out one of Tarik's specially made revolvers, she hefted it in her palm, getting the feel of a weapon that resembled her favorite Ruger .357 Magnum. Then she made sure the gun was loaded.

Now, which way would be her best bet?

Suddenly the sound of cars starting up caught her attention. The engine noises came from the garage area. Someone, probably the Taj Zabbar, was preparing to leave the mansion. She should stop them.

But her lone weapon was not going to get her far. And she was beginning to worry about Tarik—though she still felt certain he was holding his own.

Her best move for locating him would lie with finding the Taj. She imagined Tarik hiding somewhere near the garage side of the house. Maybe he was even waiting there for her help.

Determined to make the right move and not let herself get caught first, she stashed her backpack again and eased out of the alcove with weapon in hand. But she had hardly taken two steps when someone grabbed her by the shoulder and turned her around.

"Tarik!" She rounded on him and hissed, "You scared the life out of me. Was it you following me out of the house?" Lowering the gun, she took a deep breath and tried to calm her pounding heart.

"It was me. I've been looking for you." He had his hands on both her shoulders and was gazing at her with question in his eyes. "When I made it back to the dining room and found you gone...I...I..."

He'd been worried about her? Her first reaction was indignation. She was a pro, damn it. But the sudden flash of hurt to her pride only lasted a second or two before being replaced with a gooey, warm feeling that had nothing whatever to do with the mission or their jobs. And everything to do with the besotted look in his eyes as he stared deep into hers.

"I'm okay." She slipped out of his hold so as not to be distracted by either his warmth or those sexy, bedroom eyes. "But the Taj. I think they're getting away. Let's find a way of following them."

Tarik shook his head. "Shakir's handling the Taj. I want Eltsin. That Russian knows more than simply what was supposed to be sold here tonight. He knows a name. And he's going to give us that name."

*Name?* Tarik had been thinking the same thing that she had? "Yeah. I'd like the identity of the traitor, too. Let's go."

"Find a place to hide your weapon first." Tarik raked her up and down with an exasperated look before holding out his palms with a questioning expression in his eyes. "Well, do *something* with it. And fast. Surprise works a hell of a lot better than a full-frontal attack."

The game was over. But Tarik didn't want to think too long about who might be the traitor. It had to be someone connected to the Task Force, and the idea that someone he knew—someone he'd trusted—was in league with the Taj seemed so outrageous he refused to consider the possibilities.

He would wait and hear the name from Eltsin's own lips.

Meanwhile, Tarik fought his conflicting emotions over Jass. She was the smartest, most capable agent he'd ever encountered. But he wished he could shake the images of her naked—in the shower…in the bed… and in his dreams.

Earlier, even when they'd both been sated and exhausted, he'd laid across the bed trying to find enough reserve energy to do it again. He refused to close his eyes; he'd rather think about her and the way they'd fit together. Instead of gazing at her amazing body while she slept, he'd stared at the ceiling and listened to her breathe.

After most of a lifetime spent playacting as the chameleon, wanting people to love him for who they thought he was, he'd finally found someone who knew the real person underneath. And she actually cared for him anyway.

It felt as though he'd taken an emotional exhale.

She was…like coming home. There wasn't any other word but home that matched the feeling.

But Jass was not convinced. He'd seen it in her eyes. Deep down she felt scared. Afraid to take a chance with her emotions. She'd held herself apart from any real human contact for so long that she didn't know how to stop protecting herself from the possibility of being hurt.

That was no way for such a loving person to exist. He hurt for her. Hurt for the relationship she would eventually throw away. Yeah, he knew she wouldn't stick around forever. At least not physically. She was like a frightened rabbit who would run for the cover of her work at the first scary emotional moment.

But it would be harder for her to shake the memories of the two of them and the very real sense of belonging that they'd built over the past few days. They did belong together, damn it.

She couldn't forget that.

Nothing would happen to her while they finished the mission. He wouldn't let it. As tough as she was, the professional covert agent still needed him beside her to keep her safe. They were partners. And she wouldn't forget that either.

At the building's edge, Tarik halted with Jass right behind him and peered toward the garage area. The Taj were long gone. But the car Shakir had promised to leave sat in the open driveway, hopefully with the keys in the ignition.

Tarik had changed his mind since he'd last talked to his brother. After being attacked out beside the pool by a couple of Eltsin's incapable henchmen, he'd learned they already knew they were dealing with covert agents. But he hadn't learned how they knew. He'd made up his mind that when he and Jass left Eltsin's mansion in a few minutes to catch up with the Taj, Eltsin would be coming along.

And the Russian would sing his guts out, telling them all about how he'd known who they were.

Tarik gave a quick thought to the weapon he'd stuck in his waistband. It had originally belonged to one of Eltsin's men. Now it would be the tool he used to bring down Eltsin himself.

"We're going in through the kitchen area," he told Jass. "We can raise enough of a ruckus there that the kitchen help will call on Eltsin to come remove the guests. We'll ambush him as he enters the room. That's the only way to take him alive."

"I'm not sure about this plan," Jass whispered. "Where are all his gunmen? It seems too quiet out here. They should be looking for us by now."

"I'm sure we've already neutralized most of Eltsin's men. I took out a couple by the pool and Shakir probably took out the ones who were stationed outside near the garage area. Besides, this is the best plan we've got." He added one more thought for good measure. *"Trust me."*

Jass rolled her eyes, but nodded her head in agreement. "Okay. Let's go see if we can surprise the man who thinks he has all the answers."

Tarik had previously scoped out the kitchen entrance and knew most of the layout. Keeping to the wall, he took Jass by the hand and opened the servant's door to the pantry.

"Why isn't this door on the alarm system?" Jass wanted to know.

"Shush. The servants use this entrance and they probably keep the alarm turned off to make it easier for them to go in and out."

But by the time he and Jass entered the kitchen proper, Tarik's gut instincts were screaming in protest. Too quiet. The lights were dimmed and not one soul was still at work. The place was empty.

"Where is everybody?" Jass echoed his sentiments. "How are we going to make that *ruckus* of yours now?"

She was right. As Tarik reached for his weapon, he nodded for her to turn back. They needed to get the hell out of here.

"There you two are." Eltsin's voice came from right behind them. "Drop the weapon, Sheik Zohdi, or whatever your name is. I've been expecting you."

Tarik swore under his breath. Bad move. But thank heaven he was already standing between Eltsin and Jass. She would have a better chance of staying alive if she hid behind him. Tarik bent and gently set the gun down on the tile floor.

"Good. Now slowly turn around to face me and then kick the gun in the other direction."

As Tarik raised his head and prepared to turn, he whispered to Jass, "Stay behind me."

"Right," she whispered in return. "When I say drop, you drop."

*What?* No. That wasn't what he'd meant at all. But it was too late for further debate.

"Come on," Eltsin demanded. "Stop the whispering and do what I say. It would be a shame to have to shoot you in the back, but I will."

Grinding his teeth and drilling a look at her that clearly shouted "no way," Tarik forced himself to turn and kick the weapon out of range.

Jass stepped up so close behind him that he could feel her breath on the back of his neck.

*"Trust me,"* she murmured.

# Chapter 14

*Trust.* For days he'd been wanting her to trust him. Now he was faced with the reverse situation. But could he give her that much in return—without reservations?

"No. No." Eltsin waved his gun. "That's not the way I want you. Move out from behind him, Celile. You begin walking toward the dining room alone while I finish with Zohdi in here."

Ah. The Russian idiot actually thought he might kill off one covert agent and still have a chance at sex with the other? Tarik would've laughed in his face had the barrel of Eltsin's weapon not been pointed at the middle of his forehead.

"She's not going anywhere, Eltsin. You want her, you have to go through me."

"I will if I must. But I thought you might like a little information first. To satisfy your curiosity?"

Tarik could feel Jass rustling behind him, but she

stood her ground and didn't move out in the open. *Good girl.*

"You don't have anything I want." Tarik folded his arms over his chest.

"Oh? Don't pretend you know what was being exchanged here tonight. Nuclear detonators? Child's play. You haven't the first idea of how our revolutionary new technology for nuclear delivery will change the world."

Nuclear delivery systems? Tarik unfolded his arms. Now he knew he needed to find a way of capturing this ass alive. For information.

"Ah. I see that has sparked your interest. Are you willing to do as I say? You've got less than a minute to decide."

"I'll do what you want, Eltsin." Jass called out in a clear voice, but she didn't move a muscle. "Just don't shoot him. Or you get nothing from me."

Eltsin's eyebrows shot up. "What's happened to your heavy accent, Celile?" Then the Russian smiled as he narrowed his eyes with a look that Tarik never wanted to see again.

This wasn't good. "I have another question, Eltsin." Anything to capture the man's attention. "Don't you…"

"Sorry, time's up." Eltsin raised his gun hand.

*"Drop!"*

Tarik ducked and all hell exploded at once. Weapons fired. The smell of gunpowder assaulted his nose, and the too-close discharge of a weapon rang loudly in his eardrums, deafening him. He felt the sting in his upper arm and knew he'd been hit.

Cradling his painful right arm, Tarik fought to see

through the clearing smoke. He couldn't hear anything. Couldn't see anything.

What the hell happened to Jass?

Cursing under her breath, Jass pulled her fingers away from the silent pulse point on Eltsin's neck. Dead cold. Damn bastard wouldn't take no for an answer. She'd known how much Tarik wanted to take him alive. But she couldn't let the Russian kill her partner simply to get at the truth, could she?

"Jass!" Tarik's panicky voice reached out and tugged at her heart.

She stuffed her weapon inside the waistband of her skirt and sought him out through the lingering gun smoke. In two steps she was kneeling beside him and searching for signs of where he'd been hit.

There was some blood, but not much. Thank God.

"Where were you hit?" Her voice sounded a lot shakier than she felt.

"You're okay?" Tarik's own voice was hoarse as he struggled to sit. "Can't hear a thing yet. Where's Eltsin?"

Jass noticed Tarik favoring his right arm. Oh Lord, he'd taken a bullet. Sympathetic pain squeezed at her heart. She helped him sit up and then tried to inspect his wound.

He batted her hands away. "It's fine. A scratch is all. Bullet only grazed me. What happened to Eltsin?"

She leaned in closer and spoke in his left ear. "He's dead. Sorry. I tried to aim for his gun arm, but he was moving too fast."

Tarik looked at her quizzically. "You took the time to aim? How good a shot are you?"

Beaming at him, she sat back on her heels. "Not bad."

She heard him groan as he tried to stand. "We need to stop the bleeding and get you to a doctor." Taking his left elbow, she assisted him to his feet.

Pulling his arm out of her grip, he scowled at her, spun around and went into the pantry, returning with a kitchen towel. "Can you find something to cut this into strips and fashion a bandage?"

She took the towel from his hand and, using her teeth, started a small tear in the end. "This do?" she asked while neatly ripping the material lengthwise with her two hands.

"A sharpshooter and a medic? Nice." He took a length of the makeshift bandage but shook his head after the first attempt. "A little help here?"

Sighing, she took back one end of the material and lent him a hand as he wound it around his upper arm.

"Looks like the bleeding's already stopped." Her breathing was finally evening out. "But it still might need suturing. And someone should definitely sterilize the surrounding area."

"Nonsense. I said it was fine. We have to get out of here before any of Eltsin's buddies come looking for their boss."

He was right about that. "Agreed. Any ideas how?"

"Can you drive? I could do it, but one-handed may become problematic if anyone's chasing us."

"Sure I can drive." She bit back a smart retort. "But where are we going to find a car?"

Tarik took her by the elbow this time and twisted her around, heading for the pantry again and the same way out as they'd come in. "Shakir left one of Eltsin's cars standing by for us. That way we'll also have easy access to the gate codes. Come on, your chariot awaits, Madame."

* * *

"What are you looking for?" Jass kept one hand on the steering wheel as she flipped on the overhead light.

They'd left Eltsin's house an hour ago and were now making the turns right below Corcovado mountain. With its huge arms outstretched over the city and its lights blazing brightly in the darkness of the forest surrounding the mountain, the 125-foot statue of Jesus at the top of Corcovado seemed to be offering its blessing to any who needed help. Jass would be happy to receive all the help she could get.

Tarik was rooting around in her backpack with his good arm. "Turn out the light," he demanded softly. "We'll be driving into the city lights soon enough. Besides, I can find your communicator by feel alone."

"Try the outside pocket." She turned off the interior lights and checked her rearview mirror for maybe the hundredth time since they'd left Eltsin's mansion. The road behind them was empty and dark.

"Are you hoping to reach Ed?" She had a few words for her handler herself.

"Or the local station chief."

"Hit the star button at the bottom. It's a direct line."

A few moments later, Tarik swore lightly under his breath. "No answer. Where is everyone?"

"Why don't you try reaching your brother?"

"I've been hesitating to contact Shakir. He might still be in a car along with the Taj. I don't want to break his cover."

"I think you'd better try him anyway. I don't like being out of touch when things have just gone to hell. We need advice and assistance."

Tarik clicked his comm and held his breath.

His brother's smooth, deep voice answered nearly right away. "Are you okay?"

"Fine. We're in the car you provided and headed down the mountain into Rio. Eltsin's dead. Where are the Taj agents?"

"They're about to board a flight to Miami. I'm putting on a disguise so I can board the plane with them. I've been afraid to get too close for fear they would recognize me as a Kadir. I had one of the local men drive them into Rio."

"Miami? Why there?" Tarik asked.

"I was hoping Eltsin could tell us that. Did you get any information out of the Russian before you killed him?"

Tarik wasn't about to tell his brother that he hadn't been the one to shoot their prime information source. "All I know is Eltsin said he'd sold the Taj some kind of new high-tech weapon-delivery system. He didn't give us a chance to ask anything else."

Shakir groaned. "Hell. I have to leave. I can't lose the Taj. And there's not another commercial flight to Miami for twelve hours. But I've arranged for you and Jass to take a U.S. military transport leaving Brazil right before noon. Bosque, the CIA station chief, will be waiting for you at your hotel room. He'll have instructions and passes."

Shakir didn't linger long enough to say anything else. He cut off and was gone.

Tarik relayed what his brother had told him. Jass didn't make a comment, but, through the dim dashboard lights, he watched her bite her lip.

"You're thinking the same thing I am?" He didn't like voicing his suspicions aloud, but had no choice. "That our traitor might be Bosque and we'll be walking into a trap at the hotel?"

"I've considered the possibility. But I want to gather my equipment from the hotel room. And how else are we going to get the passes we'll need for transport to Miami?"

Tarik sat quietly for a few moments, mulling over the possibilities. Finally he said, "We have no choice. But I have a plan."

"Oh, no. Not another plan. Lord help us."

As plans went, this one was somewhat better than the last brilliant idea Tarik had come up with. Jass straightened her borrowed maid's uniform and shoved the laundry cart in front of her down the hotel hall-way.

"You need to go on a diet," she whispered, loudly enough for Tarik to hear. "This cart must weight a ton."

"Shussh," came the reply from deep under the dirty sheets and towels in the cart.

The hallways were silent at this hour. Six o'clock was too early for most hotel services and their luxury guests. But this was still a good disguise as far as Jass was concerned. As they drew closer to their room, she felt for her weapon under the cleaning supplies sitting on the cart's shelf.

After pulling the cart to a halt in front of their room, she immediately realized the door was ajar. "Trouble. The door's open."

Tarik stuck his head above the edge of the cart. "Wait," he whispered as he jumped out. "You go right. I'll take the left."

"What about your wounded arm?"

He frowned, then switched his weapon to his left hand and made her trade places. "On my mark."

Using the barrel of his gun, he pushed open the door as each of them waited with weapons at the ready on either side. But nothing happened.

Tarik held up his hand for her to keep her position and then he eased across the threshold. "I hear something."

Both of them slipped through the door and listened. Someone was groaning.

Jass clung to the wall as she carefully entered the main sitting room. There on the floor she saw Bosque, holding his bleeding head and moaning.

She stashed her weapon and went to him while Tarik checked the bathroom, bedroom and closet. "What happened, Bosque?"

"Ambush. I wasn't expecting it. Came out of nowhere." He groaned again.

Blood was everywhere. The place was in shambles. But Jass didn't smell any residual gun smoke. Obviously no one had fired bullets in this hotel room recently. Bosque's injuries had no doubt been inflicted with a heavy object and probably weren't life threatening. Tarik strode out of the bathroom carrying a towel, then held it to Bosque's forehead to sop up the blood.

"The place is clear," Tarik told them. "Whoever it was is gone. Call the desk and get a doctor up here."

She headed toward the desk phone, wondering what had been stolen from their room and who had taken it. She and Tarik hadn't left anything of real value in the room when they went to Eltsin's mansion. They'd taken all their high-tech toys and weapons with them. Except for her special CIA-issue laptop. Jass hadn't wanted to take the chance of Eltsin finding it. She'd locked it in the hotel safe as she'd packed.

After summoning a doctor and the hotel manager, Jass went straight to the safe. That door stood ajar exactly like the other one.

"They took my laptop," she called out.

When she came out of the closet, Tarik had Bosque sitting up in a chair. He was holding a wet towel to his forehead and the bleeding was down to a trickle.

Bosque gripped Tarik's arm. "Your papers and military passes are in my coat pocket. Take them and get out of here before anyone shows up and the questions start. I'll be okay."

Jass signaled for Tarik to grab the folder out of Bosque's coat. "Are you sure you didn't see anyone?"

Bosque moaned. "They came up from behind me."

"Have you heard anything from Ed Langdon, Jass's handler?" Tarik had the papers in hand and seemed ready to charge out the door.

"Yes, I'm kind of worried about Ed." Jass didn't like not being able to reach the man she'd grown to care about over the years. "I haven't been able to reach him for hours."

"I haven't heard from him since yesterday morning." Bosque lifted his head. "But I'll take care of notifying him and the Task Force. Now beat it. All your instructions are in with your passes. Go."

Tarik grabbed her hand and dragged her toward the door. "Thanks, man. Take care of yourself."

Bosque weakly waved them away and went back to holding the towel to his forehead. Jass didn't like the idea of leaving him here. What if the bad guys came back?

"Tarik, are you sure we should…"

"Let's go. He'll be fine. He's armed. I felt his undrawn weapon still in its holster when I pulled the passes from his coat."

"Still…"

"He's the CIA station chief. A big boy. And we can't miss our transport."

Tarik was right. But Jass's mind was whirling. Who had taken her laptop and left Bosque bleeding on the floor?

The ride on the air transport turned into one long and tedious affair for Tarik. Everything and everyone around him annoyed him beyond belief. Jass wouldn't let him rest until a medic cleaned and checked his wound. And when he'd tried to talk to her about who the traitor could be, she'd refused to discuss it, saying she needed time to think. Then instead of thinking, she'd passed out across two seats and slept for six hours straight.

Tarik knew what he thought. But he understood why she didn't want to consider—much less accept—the possibility. It seemed there could only be one person who had the means to accomplish everything that had happened. But if that were true, it would mean extremely bad news for Jass.

Still, they had to talk about it eventually.

Shakir met them at the airbase near Miami with a car. Jass had changed out of most of the Celile disguise on the plane, and she was back to looking like the woman he wanted to know a lot better. But she'd been too quiet. He knew the storm clouds in her heart were building to a terrible tempest. But if she wouldn't talk to him about it, how could he help her through it?

"Renting us motel rooms was tough at this time of

year in Miami," his brother told them as he drove them off the airbase. "I wanted us all together so we can use our rooms as a temporary headquarters, but uh…well, here's the thing, you two have to share a room. Or, Tarik, you can bunk down on my floor. Your choice."

"No choice there. We're good sharing a room. We've been getting by that way. And we probably won't be here that long anyway." Tarik took a quick glance at Jass, who sat silently in the backseat. She said nothing. He guessed she had no complaints about the arrangements.

Shakir cleared his throat. "Okay, then. But we've lost the Taj, bugger it. Only temporarily, mind you. No need to sweat, they won't leave the area without us finding out. In the meantime, the men we left in Brazil finally managed to get a little information out of that henchman of Eltsin's we've been grilling." He actually smiled.

"Have you heard from the Task Force or from my handler?" Jass hadn't put together more than a few words since they'd left Brazil, and Tarik was happy to see her finally taking an interest again.

But he wished she'd asked anything else.

"Not a peep from your handler. But the Task Force has been a big help here in the States." Shakir drove the speed limit as the Miami suburbs with their Spanish-style houses and their ubiquitous palm trees rolled by the windows. "They've paved the way for us and are assisting in whatever ways we need them. And there're more men available at your say-so. I think you two have finally convinced them the Taj are, in fact, international bad guys."

"What other intel did you get from Eltsin's man?" Tarik needed to know where the biggest danger lay.

"It appears that the nuclear delivery system you

heard about is state of the art. Small and innocuous, it supposedly fits inside an ordinary bottle or jar and will detonate with the usual cell-phone call signal." Shakir exhaled sharply. "But unlike the usual system, this device's explosion has a horrendous capacity because it's assisted by a new kind of E-technology."

"Electro-magnetic pulse? How does that work?"

Shakir chuckled. "Beats me. But our resident genius, Karim, says this new technology is the stuff of nightmares—like Armageddon. A handheld device, remotely detonated, that can take out half a city the size of Miami? Chilling."

"But why Miami?"

"Yeah," Jass chimed in. "There don't seem to be any military or political targets here that are big enough or would cause enough of a show for high-profile terrorists like the Taj who're trying to make a splash."

"Good point." Shakir shot her a respectful glance in the rearview mirror. "We asked the man in Brazil that same question. He claims he doesn't know where they plan on using the device, but the Taj didn't receive their new toy while they were in Rio. They paid for it there and expect to pick it up here in Miami."

"Where?" Both Tarik and Jass asked the same question at the same time.

"It's supposedly coming in via ship container. According to Eltsin's man, the Taj agents plan on picking it up and personally taking it to its final destination. But the informant didn't know anything more concerning the actual pickup." Shakir furrowed his brow. "The biggest problem we face is there're two possible ports in the general Miami area where ship containers arrive daily."

"So that's it? That's all we know?" Frustration coursed

through Tarik's whole body. How could they come this close and not finish the job?

"I might be of some help." Jass's quiet voice from the backseat brought a glimmer of hope.

Tarik turned as far as the seat belt would let him go. "What do you know?"

She halfheartedly shrugged one shoulder, but then spoke in a strong voice. "I tagged the elder of the two Taj agents while we were at dinner last night." She looked almost apologetic. "But we need the locating beacon software that goes with the GPS chip to find him. And that software was on the laptop that was stolen. If we can locate my handler or contact the local CIA office to borrow their software, we should be able to find that Taj agent by his chip."

"Consider it done," Shakir interjected. "I'm sure the Task Force will help. Good work."

Shakir dropped them and the car at the motel room and told them to get cleaned up and grab some much needed rest while he contacted the Task Force. Tarik didn't need sleep. What he needed was a long, serious discussion with Jass.

Their motel wasn't much. A two-story, cheap-looking affair with outside entry, it was near the Miami airport in a warehouse district. But when they went into their room, it was clean and neat with two double beds and a small but efficient kitchenette.

"Jass," he began when the outside door was locked behind them and they were by themselves.

"I don't want to talk about it." She grabbed the backpack and headed toward the bathroom. "I need a shower in the worst way first."

"Jass…"

"Alone, Tarik. This time I shower alone. Talk will come later." She slammed the door and disappeared.

She'd looked hurt. Without any words spoken between them, he knew her world was falling apart.

By the time she reappeared, he was already out of the cammos he'd changed into on the airplane courtesy of the U.S. Army and was ready to grab his own shower. He stood there like a fool with a blanket wrapped around his waist and watched her blow dry her hair in the big mirror over the tiny desk. She hadn't changed to her own clothes yet but wore only a towel to cover the parts of her body that he remembered well.

All that golden skin seemed pale and fragile in the low lighting of their room. In fact, Jass suddenly seemed fragile in a general way, though he knew that was nonsense. She'd taken out Eltsin without much remorse. She was a tough, professional covert agent of the United States government and nobody's fool.

But he knew she was hurting. And feeling all alone.

Hell. He was feeling pretty damned lonely himself.

He wanted to help her. He wanted for them to be closer. He wanted…

Without warning, he snapped. All the fear for her and the anger and the love—*Love? Yeah, love, damn it.* The realization of how he truly felt surged into his mind and drove desire along his nerve endings.

She stirred something in him that was uncontrollable. Unstoppable. It was white hot and beyond explanation.

Never blinking while he ripped the dryer out of the wall plug and dragged her into his arms, she came willingly. He lasered his mouth over those delectable lips and kissed her long and hard.

When at last he came up for air, his breathing was ragged, and he was relieved to find her in the same condition. But one kiss wasn't enough. Not nearly enough to relieve the tension holding him hostage.

There could never be enough of her.

# Chapter 15

Breathing hard, Jass knotted her hands in Tarik's hair. "I wish we had the time…."

His eyes were dark and so full of desire it left her breathless. "We may not get another time."

The unspoken understanding between them was real enough to be a solid thing. Not a barrier but more of a magnetic pull, drawing them closer when both of them knew it should not happen. Stupid or not, this was their time. Later may never come.

She saw the desire written clearly in his eyes when he made the choice for both of them. Spewing out a curse to whatever gods threw obstacles into the paths of lovers, Tarik backed her up against the wall, pitched her towel in a corner and filled his hands with her aching breasts.

Pleasure, sharp and jolting, blossomed as he lowered his head and took one of her nipples into his mouth.

Pulling back to tease her with his tongue, Tarik murmured, "We still need to talk."

"Yeah." The tingles were already skipping along her spine and heading south. "I got that."

She frantically dragged his head lower and tried to keep him right where she needed him the most. "First this."

He nipped her gently and she keened his name. What he did made her forget everything. Made her crazy with lust. Made her stupid.

The next thing she knew he was already inside her, driving into her. She gripped his shoulders, dug her fingernails into his skin to urge him on. He helped her hook a leg around his hips, then grabbed her bottom with a firm hand, lifting and going deeper.

"Oh, yeah." She was out of breath and didn't care.

She didn't care about anything but letting him know the true depth of her feelings without using words. She took in all his fear for her along with his arousal. At the same time he seemed to lose all control and slammed them both off the map into oblivion.

Here was fire and passion. Here was a place she could belong. Here was her temporary refuge from cold, looming reality. Too soon, stars exploded behind her eyelids as they both reached that high, safe place as one entity.

A thousand heartbeats passed between them as they clung to each other, sharing air and a lifetime of wanting.

Slowly, he released her to slide to the floor. "Steady?" he asked when she wobbled on her feet.

"I may never be steady again." She laughed, and when he laughed too, she knew her heart was lost to him for good.

* * *

Jass was delicious, all fresh from her shower yet sweat-dampened from making love. He felt drunk on her sweetness.

Still swimming in testosterone and half-crazed physical demands, Tarik managed one thought loud and clear. *This is love.* This is the way love is supposed to be.

He adored the way she'd called his name in the heat of passion. He adored her tiny gasps and the way she swallowed his desperate groans. He adored her quick mind and stark bravery. He plain adored her.

She started to turn away, but he swung her back and pressed his face to her neck. He would give her anything. Everything. His loyalty. His fortune. Anything he'd ever valued.

Moreover, he would even give her the scary things with no names—those reflections of the scared and lonely child he'd once been. The nightmares of being left alone that he'd kept hidden throughout the years. He would give her his life—and his whole future.

*I love you, my little secret agent.*

Jass held her hand to her pounding heart and chuckled deep in her chest. "As much as I hate to break this off, I have to dress. There's work to do." She backed up a step, stared up at him wide-eyed and smiling, and then headed to the bathroom.

Tarik took a deep breath and watched her walk away, knowing what had to come next.

As soon as she closed the bathroom door between them, he slipped into his clothes and called his brother on their family's satellite phone. "Where are you, Shakir?"

"We're about twenty miles north of the motel at one of

the two shipyards. Our brother Darin has been working on the problem from his office. He had the idea that the container we're looking for would be shipped into a place where they could store containers." He cleared his throat. "And it seems only one of the two shipyards in the Miami area actually stores containers instead of shipping them back out directly. We're on our way there."

"Good thought. But I need your help on another matter. I have to find Ed Langdon, Jass's handler. I think he's the traitor and he's most definitely a missing link in the puzzle. We need to pick him up before he causes any more trouble."

"Why don't you have Jass contact him?"

"She tried while we were still in Brazil and no-go." And now she wouldn't even discuss the problem.

"Tell her to keep trying. Meanwhile, I'll carefully inquire about him to the Task Force. Maybe they can help locate his current whereabouts."

Tarik thanked his brother and hung up just as Jass reappeared out of the bathroom. She looked so beautiful in her casual jeans and tank top that she took his mind away from the problems at hand.

Looking over at him, she absently put her hand to her hair and blinked. "What is it? Is my hair sticking straight up or something?"

He stood there shaking his head, over and over, without being able to utter a word. There was something still nagging at him. Something he'd forgotten while in his lust-filled haze. And it was something important.

The way he felt about her was simply astonishing. Never before in his entire lifetime had he needed anyone the way he needed Jass. All he wanted to do, all he could think about, was cocooning her in the warmth of his embrace and finding a way for the two of them to disappear off everyone's radar screens.

A silent beat came and went.

*Oh, hell.* That was it!

He schooled his voice and tone, trying not to frighten her. "Are you still tagged with a GPS chip?" he asked as casually as possible.

She shrugged. "Sure. I'm surprised you didn't…uh… feel it a little while ago. It's implanted under my left breast, right inside the crease."

"You need to remove that chip. Now." Okay, that was a little over the top. But he was fighting panic.

Jass laughed and ran her fingers through her hair. "You're nuts. The mission isn't over. I'll have it taken out when we're finished."

He swallowed hard and tried another tack. "Have you called your handler since we've landed in the States?"

She looked a slightly embarrassed. "Yeah. Actually I've tried a couple of times with no luck. But I'm sure Ed will turn up pretty soon. At least, I hope Eltsin or the Taj didn't find him and hurt him. He should be okay, don't you think?"

"Jass…"

"No, don't say it. I don't want to talk about that." She wouldn't listen, but quickly turned and headed toward the motel-room door. "Have you heard from your brother? Let's go get something to eat unless you think Shakir needs us right away. I'm starving."

She threw open the door and bright sunshine spilled into the room, temporarily blinding him. When Tarik could focus again, he saw his worst nightmare standing at the threshold of the door.

"Ed!" Jass sounded pleased.

Obviously she didn't see the weapon in her handler's

hand—or the younger of the Taj agents standing right beside him.

"Back in the room, Jass." Ed lifted the gun's barrel an inch and pointed it at Tarik. "Don't try anything, Kadir, or she'll be the first to go."

Jass took a step back, far enough that the two men could enter the room and close the door behind them. "What on earth is going on, Ed? Talk to me."

She still seemed oblivious to the weapon in Ed's hand. Tarik began to worry she was trying so hard to believe in her handler that she might get herself killed.

Reaching out, Tarik took her by the elbow, dragging her back to his side. "Ed's here for a reason. Let's hear him out."

"Sure," she said without looking at Tarik. She stood mutely, facing Ed and the weapon in his hand.

"Oh? He asks and now you listen? You wouldn't listen when I begged you to." Ed spit out the words with disgust. "I tried and tried to convince you to leave Kadir and abandon the mission. But you thought you knew better.

"Damn it, Jass," he went on, as a pained look appeared on his face. "Why'd you stop listening to me after all these years? Why with him?"

"I don't understand what you're saying." For the first time since Tarik had known Jass, her voice sounded weak.

"Yes, you do." Ed scowled. "You understand fine. You don't want to believe your own instincts. You've been playing that same game for years. Looking the other way when the things I did or said didn't add up. Time to grow up, Jass."

"Years? But…"

Tarik wanted to reach out to her. His every sense told him she needed him more than ever right now.

"Don't even think about it, Kadir." Ed pointed his gun directly at Jass's chest. "Give me one more chance to talk to her or watch her die before you."

Tarik would've loved to put his hands around Ed's neck and squeeze the traitorous life right out of him. But he knew Jass would have to hear the man out, as hard as it would be on her. He would give anything to protect the woman he loved from the coming pain, but this was one time when she had to be strong—alone.

The young Taj agent turned to Ed and spoke with a heavy accent. "Why are we waiting? You said you meant to kill them."

Ed waved the man off. "Give it a few more minutes first. There's time."

"Wait." Jass raised her chin and stared at Ed. "You're telling me you have always been—what? A traitor to your country? I don't believe it. You were my father's best friend. His partner. He died in your arms."

Ed chuckled. "Don't tell me you still believe the sappy story I made up? Jass, you have to be smarter than that. I thought you were as intelligent as your old man."

Jass's body went ramrod straight. She fisted her hands at her sides.

"Oh please," Ed said with a sigh. "You're saying you didn't know your father was selling secrets to the Russians? Or that he and I were more than covert agent partners? And here all this time I figured you were trying to learn the ropes from me. That you and I would be the same sort of business partners one day."

Jass took a tiny, nearly unnoticeable, step to the left, covering Tarik's position with her own body. He wanted to scream at her to stop it. To get behind him and let him be the protector. But he didn't dare call attention to what she was doing or make any sudden moves.

But he did manage to secretly slide his arm around behind his waist, fingering the weapon in his belt. He was set. All he needed was a small diversion.

"Tell me what really happened when my father died."

"Ah, come on, Jass. You don't want to hash this out right now. Just tell me you don't give a damn about Kadir and let's get out of here. There's a large fortune behind the deal. I'm willing to split it with you."

The Taj agent looked confused. Tarik imagined the man felt betrayed but couldn't be totally positive he understood because of the language difficulties.

"Okay, yes. But tell me about my father first."

The handler sighed. "You don't want to hear it. Not truthfully." Then the dirty double agent seemed to come to some private conclusion. "Oh, all right. Your father, my old partner Denny, suddenly decided he'd had enough. After years of our working deals together."

Ed waved his hand in the air. "Your old man said his change of heart had something to do with you. What a load of bull. But whatever it was that came over him, he wanted out. Pompous ass said he would go to our CIA superiors and rat on our Russian contacts." He shrugged carelessly. "Well, I couldn't let him do that, could I?"

Jass drew a breath and whispered, "So you killed him."

Ed caught her words and scowled. "Of course, I killed him. The bastard was going to turn me in."

Something in Ed's manner changed. He tensed as though ready to fire. Tarik palmed his weapon and balanced his stance in preparation.

"I'm sorry to do this, Jass. Really. But you've left me no choice."

"Ed...no..."

Instead of firing at Jass or trying to get Tarik first, Ed swung his body to the left and shot the stunned Taj agent directly through the forehead at point-blank range.

"This is the best plan," Ed murmured as the body went down. "A big shoot-out will work to my benefit. All of you will have died trying to kill the others."

Tarik could see the handler's arm muscles tightening again and realized what came next.

"Duck!" All Tarik could do was react—and pray.

Jass went down like a stone while he pumped three silenced rounds into the surprised double agent, who had turned to fire at Jass but never got off the first shot.

With no loud gun blasts, the sickening sounds of bullets hitting flesh competed for attention with the sight of blood spatter as Ed crumpled to the floor. Tarik waited for any further movement, but none came.

"Tarik!" The smoke hadn't even cleared when Jass jumped up and spun around. "Oh my god, are you hit?"

Tarik opened his arms and she fell into them, clinging to him as tears sprouted on her cheeks.

"I'm not hit and it's all over, love," he murmured soothingly. "I'm fine. And you're going to be okay."

He knew her real wounds were hidden and went deep. That it might take years for her to get over what she'd had to face. Her whole life had been a sham. How was anyone supposed to put that aside and go on?

But he would be there for her—however long it took.

Letting her sob into his shoulder, Tarik threw a glance

at the handler and the Taj agent laying still in growing pools of blood. They were both gone for good.

It didn't take too long for Jass's tears to subside, but she didn't move out of his embrace. Tarik figured she would be going into shock at any moment and needed professional attention.

"Let me call Shakir," he whispered. "Get him over here to deal with the bodies so I can take you to the hospital."

"I don't need a hospital. I wasn't hit. But I need to finish this mission." She reared back and threw a quick look over her shoulder at the two dead men on the floor. "How're we going to find that delivery device now?"

Tarik sighed and let loose of his hold on the too-tough covert agent. "You need to stop now, Jass. Let me and my family handle things from here. Go home. I'll find you and let you know how things turn out. I want you to take enough time to get your head together."

Jass frowned and stepped away. "My head is okay." She folded her arms protectively around her middle. "Maybe this revelation was a bit of a shock, but not completely out of the blue. Despite what you and Ed must've thought of me, I'm not totally stupid. I wouldn't discuss it because I wanted to talk things over with Ed first.

"The sight of his weapon changed everything," she admitted. "I decided to play along for info."

Tarik didn't know what to say to her, or what to do *for* her. She needed help, but while she was in covert-agent mode, he would never get her to accept it.

When he didn't say anything for a long time, she said, "I was serious. Time is short. A maid could stumble in here at any moment. Do you have any thoughts on how to find the delivery system now?"

"There's still that chip you planted on the elder Taj agent. Shakir is working on getting the CIA software that we need."

Jass stepped out of his immediate space, leaving him feeling more alone than ever.

"Ed may have killed the other Taj agent, too." She pointed down at the dead body closest to her feet. "Judging by the expression on this young Taj's face, it wouldn't surprise me if the kid thought he and Ed were a team, double-crossing his boss. But he trusted the wrong man, poor kid. Triple crosses didn't seem to be out of the question for good old Ed."

Tarik looked down at the Taj agent, too and noticed something he hadn't seen before. Bending on one knee, he pushed the kid's loose long-sleeved shirt up past his elbow, allowing him to study what appeared to be a new tattoo on the boy's forearm.

"What are you looking at?" Jass bent to study the image, too. "The tattoo? What about it?"

The picture was of a dagger. Not an unusual decoration for the Taj Zabbar—when it came to pictures or images. But body decorating was not something the Taj accepted.

"It's new." Tarik touched the outline. "Done within the last twelve hours."

"You mean this kid must've stopped here in Miami long enough to get a tattoo? That is odd." She peered closer, studying the decoration. "Do you see this? Look, along the knife blade. Is that some kind of writing or hieroglyphics?"

Tarik bent his head lower. "They're numbers, written in the Taj Zabbar language."

"What does it mean?"

He sat back on his heels and thought about why a

young Taj agent would take the time to do something like getting a tattoo when that was so abhorrent to his culture. There was only one reason Tarik could think of—money.

"What if this set of numbers corresponds to the marking on the container holding the delivery device?" he muttered almost to himself.

"Now that's a clever thought." Jass straightened up and folded her arms over her chest. "Shipping containers all look alike with the only difference being their number designation. I like it. Can we find someone to translate those numbers into something we can understand?"

"No problem." Tarik stood, went to the desk and retrieved paper and a pen.

"Oh? Who do you have in mind?"

He came back and starting copying down the numbers. "You're looking at him."

Adrenaline overload let-down. Jass was familiar with the symptoms, but the shock-like feeling was still a pain in the butt. She brushed past the shakes as they threatened to send her to the floor and produce serious quantities of tears. Going through the motions on autopilot, she grabbed her backpack and left the room with Tarik on their way to the port and one of the shipping container storage areas.

After the motel-room door closed behind them and the sight of all that blood and gore disappeared, she gulped down another breath and fought the onslaught of nausea. *Damn it.* She refused to be this weak.

Just because a few moments ago she'd learned that her father had been a double agent—and her beloved friend Ed had killed him—was no reason to collapse when there was still a job to be done. Jass prided herself on being calm in the midst of chaos. No allowances for personal dramas.

She took a stab at being flip. "I'm sure glad your shooting arm was tended by that medic on the plane. You can thank me later for nagging you about it. Good shot, by the way."

"Good ducking," Tarik answered as he opened the car door and let the buildup of hot air escape before climbing in to turn on the A/C.

Their partnership was almost at an end. He would soon go off to fight more of his family's battles. And she would be stuck in endless rounds of post-shooting debriefs.

Just as well. She wasn't sure she could handle dealing with her newfound feelings for Tarik at the same time as she was dealing with life-changing knowledge about the people whom she'd thought loved her.

*Greed.* It had all been about greed. Her own father had sold out his country for money.

Heartbreak and pain. Too much of both were threatening to consume her. She wasn't ready to face either one.

For now she shoveled all her baggage, questions and misery into a corner of her mind to deal with another time.

Tarik set the GPS and drove the car out of the motel's parking lot.

"Do we know where we're going?"

He shot her a quelling glance and pulled his SAT phone out of his pocket. "I'm calling Shakir to send someone to take care of everything here. And to give him a head's up on this container number. Maybe he can narrow down the possibilities."

"Good idea. There's probably hundreds of containers in the storage yard."

It turned out there were more like thousands of containers in ten different yards. Every minute of the day containers were being off loaded from ships and sent to storage. Then those containers were eventually loaded onto semi-tractor-trailers for shipment by truck throughout the U.S.

Shakir met them at one of the yards. "We're most fortunate to have a genius in our family."

"Cousin Karim? What'd he find out?"

"He was able to hack into the shipyard computers and track the container by its number. It should be somewhere in this yard."

Jass scanned a glance over the many containers. Then she noticed a nearly quarter-mile-long line of trucks waiting to be checked out of the yard with their shipping containers now securely attached to their tractors like any other load.

She turned to Tarik and Shakir. "Are we sure that container hasn't already been loaded onto one of those trucks?"

Tarik looked over her head at the line of semis. "You take left. I'll take right."

"I'll stop the trucks at the gate," his brother called out as all of them scattered in different directions.

Jass pulled her weapon from her backpack and took off down the line, checking numbers as she ran. About ten containers later, she was huffing and stopped to take a breath.

When she looked up into the cab of the next truck, she spotted a driver with his ball cap pulled low on his forehead. But Jass couldn't miss those black, beady eyes. The elder Taj agent!

He looked up then too and their eyes met, held. Then he disappeared. Jass dashed around the front of the truck and found him climbing down out of the cab.

"Hold it." She held her weapon with both hands, training it on his substantial gut. "It's over."

Instead of raising his arms in surrender, the elder Taj turned and ran.

Jass roared, all the frustration and anger rising to the surface, and leaped on his back, slamming him to the hot asphalt. Air escaped his lungs as she rammed her knee into his back and pressed the barrel of her gun to the back of his neck.

"Don't give me a reason to pull the trigger." Shaking badly by the time he groaned out his acceptance, she tried to release her finger, but her hand was frozen on the gun.

"You're done, my love." Tarik appeared, standing over her and easing the weapon from her hand. "Let go, Jass. The mission is finished. Let me take over from here."

Her hand opened for him, only for him, and sudden uncontrollable tears blinded her to everything else.

# Chapter 16

"I want to see her." Tarik scowled at his brother. "I don't understand why the powers-that-be insisted on separating us." It had been nearly six hours since they'd captured the Taj elder and recovered the nuclear delivery device, and he hadn't caught sight of Jass in the last five.

Nearly sunset by now, tourists on the beaches would be ordering cocktails or having beers with their friends. But the Kadirs, the Task Force and the local CIA were more or less imprisoned at the Broward County Sheriff's office, waiting for General Wainwright to arrive and take charge of the situation.

The CIA had spent the whole day taking Jass's statement in one of the interrogation rooms. Tarik hadn't liked it. Hadn't liked the chalky look of her skin or the sunken appearance of her eyes when they'd ridden in the back of the sheriff's cruiser over here. He'd wanted her to see a doctor. Maybe even a whole staff of psychologists.

Instead, Jass had agreed to be sequestered to tell her old superiors at the CIA what little she knew of her handler's secret activities. Without Ed alive to grill, the CIA and the Department of Defense would have to piece together the real story of treason from old files and Jass's memories.

"I understand they're moving her to D.C. in a little while." Shakir stood quietly with his hands folded behind his back. "Our job's done here, brother. We located the delivery device and now the DOD, the State Department and the entire Executive Branch will have to accept that the Taj Zabbar are dealing in international terror."

"They should've listened a year ago when we tried to warn them." Tarik's patience was wearing thin, but he didn't want to tick off his own brother. "Do we know whether the Taj elder has told them anything yet?"

"Are you serious? Someone from the Pentagon showed up this morning at the container yard near Port Everglades and whisked that elder Taj agent away as an enemy combatant. He's long gone.

"But our brother Darin's people have retrieved interesting tidbits from the internet," Shakir continued with a smug smile. "According to the Net, the Taj agents were supposed to drive that truck with the delivery system all the way to Washington D.C. They'd plotted to detonate the nuclear device either beside the Capitol or the Pentagon. Planned on making a big splash. And force the U.S. imperialist machine to sit up and take notice."

Tarik was amazed. "After all this secrecy, the Taj themselves planned to publicize their terrorist dealings to the world?"

"In a big way."

Tarik began to pace the tiny conference room where they'd been waiting for hours. "Do we know how they managed to get Ed Langdon in on the deal?"

"Big payoffs, would be my bet. That Russian in Brazil, Eltsin, used to be connected to the Russian mafia. He'd probably worked with Langdon years ago when he was a double agent."

"Langdon was a real piece of work. He planned on killing his partners along with Jass and then telling the Task Force they'd killed each other."

"Scumbag," his brother retorted.

"I want to see Jass," Tarik said between gritted teeth. "Before she leaves. What do I have to do to convince—?"

"Sorry, Kadir." General Wainwright appeared at the door. "She's flying to D.C. within the hour. The Task Force will be going through a major overhaul over the next few months. The idea that two of our own were double agents and one of them endangered an entire mission has shaken everyone."

The general came all the way into the room and closed the door behind him. "I don't suppose I could talk you into coming back as a consultant to help us sort through the intel?"

"No, sir. I'm sure my family still needs me. I doubt the Taj Zabbar are going to be any happier with the Kadir family now that their grandiose terror plot has been ruined."

The general nodded. "Only *temporarily* ruined, would be my guess. I understand. But if you can find a way to consult for both of us, the Kadirs and the U.S. government, the offer remains open."

"I appreciate that, sir."

"In the meantime," the general went on. "The President has asked to see you and your brother. I think he wants to thank you for being on our side."

"Yes, sir. Now?" Tarik asked.

"Tomorrow morning. We'll be taking a military flight back to Andrews at 8 a.m. However, I'm sorry you won't be able to enjoy any of the south Florida activities this evening, gentlemen. The President has granted you diplomatic immunity, but there's still a lot of questions we will be answering for the sheriff and Homeland Security tonight."

Tarik wasn't going to leave it at that. "Yes, sir. But…I need to see Jass before she leaves. Can you arrange it?"

"She hasn't been asking to see you, son. I'm sorry…"

"A couple of moments is all I need. It's a matter of life and death."

It was. His life. He would die if he didn't get a chance to talk to her before she disappeared into her world of secret agents.

The general actually smiled. "All right. It wouldn't be my fault if we just happened to be leaving the office to grab a bite of dinner at the same time as they were leaving for the airport, would it?" He checked his watch. "I'll speak to the sheriff about sending a deputy with us for security. Be in the parking lot in ten minutes."

Tarik nearly saluted the general as he smartly spun around and left.

Rubbing suddenly sweaty palms against his thighs, Tarik turned to his big brother. "What can I say to her in only a few minutes in a public parking lot?"

Shakir shrugged. "Say what you feel. I've found that's the only thing that works well with the woman you love."

* * *

Jass would give up a day of her life for a shower. In fact, she would gladly give up *this* day. It had so far been the absolute worst.

Except, of course, for the few minutes she'd spent alone with Tarik this morning in their motel room. That was something she would never give away. The memories were going to have to hold her for the rest of her life.

"Wait here," her CIA companion and guard told her as they entered the late-afternoon heat of the open parking lot. "I'll bring the SUV around."

As the young man sprinted off, she stood, tapping her toe against the searing asphalt and thinking about Tarik. She hadn't said goodbye. But then that was probably for the best.

What they'd done—what they'd been to each other on this mission—it was special. But it was over. She couldn't afford to look back.

Closing her eyes, she let the dull ache of never seeing him again wash over her. More pain.

She had enough pain on her plate already. That's why years ago, when her father went away and left her with a mother who'd never loved anyone but herself, Jass had erected those walls around her emotions. To keep the pain and loneliness at bay. Tarik had climbed those walls and she wished to hell that she'd kept him out. Letting Tarik stay in her world for any longer now would only open her up to more heartbreak than she thought she could withstand.

"Jass! Wait up."

Turning to the familiar voice, she bit down on her lip to keep from crying out his name. Oh Lord, the man was sinfully gorgeous.

A single tear threatened to leak from the corner of her eye but she willed it back. "I'm…leaving, Tarik. There's no time to—" She bit her tongue. "Well, to say goodbye."

He put his hands on her upper arms, holding her firmly but gently. "Are you okay?" He looked at her as though she were the most precious jewel in a crown full of expensive diamonds.

"I will be." She stood straighter and eased out of his grip. "General Wainwright has arranged for me to spend a little time in psych eval at Walter Reed, starting tonight. It'll be like a nice short vacation before the real work of reorganizing the Task Force begins."

"Good. That's good. They'll help you." Tarik reached out a hand. But when she stepped away, he dropped it back to his side.

"Jass, I want to see you again. There're things we…" He looked around at the busy parking lot. "We need to talk. I'm flying to D.C. in the morning to see the President. But if you'll be in the hospital for a few days, I'll wait."

She began shaking her head. Unable to say what needed to be said. Unable to cut him out of her life forever when that was exactly her best course of action.

"Don't do this." His voice tensed, strained. "You know we're not done, damn it. Not by a long shot."

A big, black SUV pulled up alongside her, the driver leaving its motor rumbling in neutral. Relieved to have an escape route, she opened the passenger door.

"This is for the best, Tarik. We come from different places. There's nothing I can add to your life. Forget me. Forget us. Go save your family and the world."

Tears were threatening to spill over. But she refused.

She turned her back on the only man left on earth who mattered to her at all and climbed into the SUV.

"Jass…" Tarik stood there with his hands fisted at his sides and the saddest expression on his face.

She would never forget the way he was looking at her. Not in a million years.

"Goodbye, Tarik. Take good care of yourself."

Slamming the door, Jass held tightly to the handle because otherwise she might fly off into oblivion. She held on and kept swallowing hard as the SUV pulled out of the lot.

Running away. Yes, it was true. She was scared and running as fast as she could from a relationship that was bound to cause her more pain than her battered heart would ever be able to withstand.

Four weeks. Tarik's need to see Jass, to be with her, grew ever more insistent as the days dragged on.

He stood, staring out the window of his hotel room suite at the sun setting over the Potomac. Cherry blossoms blew in the spring breezes, and at times the city looked so romantic it made his heart ache with loneliness.

But he wasn't alone. Various members of his family had arrived in D.C. over the weeks, hoping to convince him to give up his quest and come back with them.

No chance.

This was crazy. How could the one person he'd fallen for hard be the one person who refused to even talk to him?

It must be some kind of perverted justice. Retribution for a life spent playing games and hiding behind hundreds of different faces.

But Tarik rejected what everyone else thought was

his fate. Jass had sent him a message the other day explaining that they had nothing left to say to each other. He didn't agree. He had a lot left to say. And wanted a lifetime to say it.

"Are you sure you don't want to go out to dinner with us, Tarik?" Rylie, one of his new sisters-in-laws, appeared in the doorway of the suite's second bedroom.

She and Darin were here in Washington ostensibly to take a second honeymoon. Tarik knew the real reason why they'd come. The same reason the rest of his family had shown up at various times over the last month.

"No. But, thanks."

"You can't sit around forever and mourn a relationship that didn't get off the ground." Rylie came closer and spoke softly. "I know it's hard for you. You've never been turned down before. But sometimes no just means no. That's when you need to accept things the way they are and go on with your life."

He exhaled sharply but said nothing.

"Come back to the Mediterranean with us." She laid a gentle hand on his arm. "Your family still needs you, bubba. We love you and want you with us."

Swallowing down the threatening tears, Tarik forced a smile at his sister-in-law and her Texas twang. "Yeah, the Task Force says they need me, too. But I can't work. I can't do anything yet. I have to talk to her, Rylie. There has to be a way."

But neither the Task Force nor the CIA would give him Jass's phone number or address. He'd sent message after message. Knowing full well nothing would work as well as it would if he could take her in his arms and tell her in person.

"There could be a way." Darin came out of the

bedroom already dressed in his expensive designer suit. "Ambush might be a little extreme, but I trust she wouldn't call the cops on you if you simply showed up at her apartment."

Rylie didn't look happy with her husband, but she stepped back and folded her arms over her chest, staying silent for the moment.

"I can't locate her address or, believe me, I would try."

Darin waved his arm in the air as he shot his cuffs. "Nonsense. Call Karim. If anyone can find her, he can."

"Darin!" Rylie scowled at her husband. "Don't tell your brother to do something like that. The CIA would be furious with Tarik if he had Karim hack into their system. Not to mention how unhappy Jasmine O'Reilly will be if he simply shows up at her place."

Darin shrugged. "It's his life, sweetheart. Let him try."

Tired and cranky, Jass climbed into her sweats and opened all the windows in her apartment to let the brisk nighttime breeze cool off her overheated brow. Another day from hell was finally behind her.

All she wanted was to do now was turn the TV on to some thoughtless channel and vegetate on the couch while she contemplated her future. She refused to spend any more time with the psychologists. Enough was enough.

The one she'd seen today actually had the nerve to tell her she would have to go through all the stages of grief in order to heal. The same as if a loved one had died. The fool doctor said learning about Ed had been a kind of death of innocence and she needed to grieve.

Bull. What she needed was a lot less new-age crap.

The fact was, she'd turned in her resignation from the Task Force to General Wainwright last week and was now free to do as she pleased. And what would please her was to be left alone to think.

The general had said, "But we need you on our side."

Not anymore they didn't. Every man in the Task Force knew the story of Ed's traitorous dealings. How could she live with that on the job? How could she explain that she'd never known?

The CIA had pieced together enough facts to learn that her father was not the traitor Ed had claimed he'd been. The news was a relief of sorts. But in Jass's mind the new information simply made her father seem incredibly dense for not recognizing what his partner had been up to.

Of course, she hadn't seen Ed for what he really was over the last ten years either. And that was something she would have to someday settle in her own mind. But talking to a bunch of shrinks had not been helping.

The only one of them who'd made a lick of sense had said she should consider this an opportunity to begin again. To start a brand new life.

How right he was. She'd already quit her job—she had enough in savings that she didn't need to go to work again anytime soon. She would take the time to rethink her life. Maybe she would even go back and get her law degree the way her dad always wanted.

One thing was for sure—she would be moving out of this apartment. As of tomorrow. It reminded her too much of the past. Jass even wanted to move out of D.C., but she wasn't sure where to go.

And yes, she knew that meant she was running away

again. So what? No amount of distance would erase the real problem—her memories of Tarik. He was always there, in her mind, talking to her. Consoling her. Being her friend when everyone else around her only wanted something or saw her as a job.

Changing what she did for a living and where she slept at night was not going to change how she felt about Tarik one iota. And she'd finally come to the conclusion she didn't want it to change. Thoughts and dreams of Tarik would keep her company throughout the years.

She'd given up on the idea of ever trying love again with anyone else. Where would she find someone with the same blinding smile? Or with Tarik's way of being in tune with her thoughts? Or with those same soft, mushy gazes whenever he looked in her direction?

She hadn't received a message from him in the last couple of days. Good for him. She hoped he'd given up and left the area. He deserved a new start, too.

She couldn't live with herself if she'd caused him any real hurt. Surely these messages she'd been receiving from him all stemmed from a wounded pride. He'd overcome that soon enough.

He was a special person. She didn't think she'd ever met anyone as strong and determined as Tarik Kadir.

Or as warm and loving. Or as sexy and erotic.

Giving herself permission to have yet another crying jag, she rolled over on the couch and buried her face in the pillow. *Have a good life, my love.*

God, he must be seriously in love to take his life in his hands this way.

Tarik was so nervous that his whole body shook as he lowered himself to the apartment ledge under an endless star-filled sky. But it wasn't the idea of dangling in midair again that made him shaky. It was knowing he would only get one chance with Jass.

When his feet finally hit solid surface, he balanced precariously on the narrow ledge and unbuckled his harness. He was more wired from nerves than from the flying device. Which only went to show how important Jass was to him.

He'd been afraid to try knocking on her door. Too easy for her to lock him out and send him away. And then he'd caught a break and discovered her windows were open.

No fire escape and no balcony. But hell, he couldn't let that stop him.

Inching along the ledge, Tarik held his breath and refused to consider the dark abyss below. He tried to think of all the things he wanted to say, but his mind went blank as he set one foot inside her window.

"Hold it." Jass's voice was loud and strong through the darkness. "Come on inside but watch your step. This .38 has a hair trigger."

Yeah, he would bet it did. "It's me, Jass. Put your weapon down."

She stepped aside and flicked on a table lamp but held the gun on him as he climbed inside. "What on earth do you think you're doing, Kadir?"

Dressed in winter running sweats and heavy socks, she wasn't wearing a speck of makeup. That amazing head full of chestnut hair was standing straight up in spikes. And those exotic hazel eyes had darkened to the deepest green and were wary as hell.

Yes indeed, her protective walls were still high and tight. He'd have a devil of a war coming in order to break them down.

"How are you doing, Jass?"

"Fine. Why are you here? You should've gone back to your family by now." She was still holding the gun, but the barrel had dipped to point at his feet and she'd released her finger from the trigger.

"I need a little of your time."

"And that means you come in through my window in the middle of the night? You're lucky I didn't shoot you in the ass and ask questions later."

"Hey, and thanks for that. Grand gesture on your part considering not many bad guys could fly into your window five stories up."

The corners of her lips tipped up at that remark and she dropped her weapon to her side. "All right. Come in and sit down. Tell me whatever it is and then go away."

He didn't want to leave this woman. Not ever again. *Man up, bubba,* as Rylie would say. Time to face love down.

"Look." He sunk into a side chair and hoped she would sit on the couch beside him. "There's something I didn't say the last time we were together. That was a mistake. I…"

"The only thing I want to hear from you is that you're leaving and starting a new life. Do what's best for everyone, Tarik." She averted her gaze, refusing to meet his eyes.

He'd expected a war. Still, her words hit him like a nuclear warhead.

Standing again, he tried to keep the whine out of his voice. "You don't even want to hear me out? I thought… we cared about each other. Is that how you treat people you care about?"

She shot him a quick glance, then stared at the floor. But in that instant he'd seen longing. Regret. Hope.

He was at her side in a click. He put her gun on the

table but then stayed his hands, kept them from drawing her close. "I know you're afraid. But…"

"I'm not afraid of anything."

Oh, his sweet love. "Right. I get it. You're not afraid of anything but me. And of the possibilities of love."

"There is no such thing as love." She backed up and sat on the couch with her hands clutched in her lap.

"Not true, Jass. I know because I'm in love with you."

He heard her soft whimper and it threw him back to a time when she'd closed her eyes and climaxed around him. A vivid image of the two of them soaring was not what he needed to stay strong right now.

"You don't know what you're saying," she finally managed in a tight voice. "It was just the job. We had to be lovers and…uh…things got carried away. You'll get over it."

Tarik thought he'd better sit before he fell over. She was a tough one to crack. She'd been hurt too much in her life. He plopped down beside her and took her in his arms.

She began to protest, but he folded her into his chest. "Shussh, my love. I'm not going to get over loving you anytime soon. I figure it might take a thousand years or so. Is that enough time to convince you?"

"Don't talk crazy." Her words were almost interrupted by a sob, but she held on. "It was a job. We were partners."

"Oh? So you've slept with your partners on other jobs?"

"Of course not." She reared back with tears in her eyes.

"Then I meant something to you." He held her tight

and let his gaze tell her how he felt. "We belong together, Jass. People who love each other should be together."

"Oh, you should see your face," she said in a rough voice. "At the love clearly shining in your eyes. No one has ever looked at me that way before."

Finally able to breathe again, he relaxed his shoulders as she pressed kisses over his eyelids and along his forehead, signaling the war was over. Soon, though, he couldn't stand sitting still and relaxation flew out the open window. He plundered her mouth slowly. Deeply.

"This is a first for me," she told him through breathless tears. "No one has ever loved me the way you do."

"Stick with me, sweetheart. Our life is going to be filled with lots of love and lots of firsts."

"I love you, too, Tarik." She smiled up at him and sniffed back more tears.

"Good thing. It's always good to love the man you're going to marry."

She laughed as he kissed her again. This time without the urgency. But with the intensity of a man making a lifetime promise. A lifetime he suddenly knew would definitely be worth all the trouble.

# Epilogue

"Come walk on the beach with me."

Jasmine O'Reilly Kadir looked up from the table to find her husband of one week standing over her with his hand outstretched. Moonlight shined on his face as the soft sounds of the tempting Mediterranean washing ashore sent romantic music to her ears. That same mischievous look was back in Tarik's eyes. She'd always known that look would cause her big trouble.

"Not fair, Tarik." Shakir's wife, Nikki, who was sitting next to her at the table, gave her brother-in-law a pout. "You didn't give us a chance to meet your bride before you two married. And not even giving us enough time to come to your wedding was just plain wrong. We're only now getting to know her. Sit down and have a drink with us."

Shakir stood up from the table. "Time for that later,

Nik. Let the lovebirds have their honeymoon in peace. For now, come walk on the beach with me."

Nikki looked flustered, but she rose beside her husband. "Will the kids be okay for...?"

"The kids are fine. Come on." The two of them wandered off down the beach.

Still seated at the table, Rylie laughed and sipped her drink. "Well, I want to hear what y'all have planned for your future, Tarik. Are you staying here with us and working for the Kadirs? Or will you be going back to the U.S. and working for the Task Force?"

Jass answered first as she reached up and took her husband's hand. "Both. The Task Force needs Tarik's expertise to put them back on the right track. And I've told Darin I would be happy to help train covert agents for the Kadirs since it looks like the Taj Zabbar aren't about to give up their vendetta against the family anytime soon."

"Yes, and we're grateful, sister." Darin walked up to the table from out of the darkness and stood behind his wife. "Especially cousin Karim. He wants to be your first pupil."

Darin glanced down at Rylie and put his hand on her shoulder. "Come walk on the beach with me, wife. There's a beautiful moon."

He didn't have to ask Rylie twice.

Tarik gently pulled Jass to her feet as Darin and Rylie went off in the other direction. A wicked thrill rushed through her. She could scarcely believe how lucky she was. That this wonderful man loved her was still a shock. But a good shock.

"I'm not that crazy about the sand," she said as she laid her hands against his chest and looked up into his eyes.

"Thank God." Tarik slid his arm around her shoulders and turned them around to head in the direction of their apartment. "Let's go home."

Sighing, Jass let her husband's love wash over her like the music of the sea. They had all the time in the world to walk on beaches and talk about their pasts. The rest of their lives. She would never tire of being with him.

As Tarik said, "I may stop loving you some day—oh, in about a thousand years or so."

\* \* \* \* \*